UNVEIL

ELODIE HART

This book is for everyone who's had to teach themselves sex positivity because it was never modelled for them.

I see you.

CONTENT ADVISORY

SHORT VERSION: They both fuck other people on the page.

In front of each other.

LONGER VERSION: This book doesn't have the religious trauma or bereavement themes of the first two books in this series, but it was intense to write because Anton is a lot, sexually speaking. And he demands a lot.

Unveil is set in a sex club, and you'll find the following on the page:

Group activities, spit-roasting, voyeurism, exhibitionism, prostitution, domination and submission, bondage, toys.

While they both have sex with other people before they are a couple, once they actually get together there are no OW / OM dramas.

Unveil has a monogamous HEA.

1

GEN

I have a problem with faking orgasms.

Let me rephrase, because that's unclear. You could take it to mean I object to the principle of faking orgasms, and you'd be right.

I run a sex club, for Christ's sake. The entire point of its existence is to ensure real orgasms on tap.

Or you could also take it to mean I have a problem, and the problem is that I have to fake orgasms.

You'd be right on that count, too.

Maybe I'm being a typical female and making myself the problem, when, in actual fact, the problem is *them*.

The guys I date.

The guys I fuck.

I have an admirable dating life out there in the world and a red-hot sex life behind Alchemy's closed doors. Or, more accurately, the closed doors of its Playroom.

The *problem* is, those worlds don't converge.

I have indeed had orgasms on tap last week and every week. Take, for example, that hot Turkish guy last Friday night who tied me up and fucked me in one of Alchemy's private rooms like he was being sent off to serve a life sentence. But when a guy looks—and acts—like he's just walked off the set of *365 Days*, it behoves you to give him a wide berth when it comes to actual dating.

And when, time after time, attractive, successful bankers and entrepreneurs and hedge fund managers and tech moguls ask you out for dinner, and are full of intelligence and wit and charm, and there's a cerebral spark of sorts, and the conversation is stimulating, and the evening flies by?

Well, *then* it behoves you to take things back to your bedroom where you end up faking it out of politeness and a desire to draw a line under the evening and get them the fuck out of your flat. Because, while most of them are in possession of a decent-sized cock and know where to put it, they are vanilla *as fuck*.

And no matter how hot they are, or how much they work out, or how genuine the intellectual spark between us is, I'm not going to go up in flames at some unimaginative missionary, no matter how hard they give it to me.

Of course, I never say anything, except for *oh, yes* and *oh my God, that's—right there, yeah*, and whatever else I can muster up. The poor guys don't have a clue that I need more. Because, outside of the debauched confines of Alchemy and in my actual, real life where I'm searching for an actual, real life partner, I don't speak up. I don't complain. And I don't ask for what I need. I mean, what's the point?

Alchemy's ruined me, obviously. That much is true. Sleeping with a nice, sensible guy after being fucked by the animals at the club is like trying to sate yourself with a cosy mystery after reading the most disgusting dark romance you can get your hands on.

In a word...

Underwhelming.

It is entirely possible, after all, that the problem is me, in a myriad of ways I'd rather not explore too deeply.

Things could be worse.

As I mentioned, I have the sex life and I have the glittering dating life.

Just not together.

But, quite frankly, 'could be worse' is not good enough for me.

I SETTLE myself on the smoke-grey velvet sofa in Alchemy's main reception room, which is a beautiful space at the front of the enormous stuccoed Georgian building that houses the club. The room is airy, its plain white walls allowing its fabulous features to sing: the panelling, the original Adam fireplace, and the spectacular cornicing on its high ceilings. The furniture is pared back and expensive, the only touch of frivolity the vulva sculpture crafted from pale pink onyx that glows ethereally when lit from within.

It's Monday morning, and I feel suitably refreshed. There were no fake or real orgasms happening last night. Not for me, anyway. Queen Charlotte and King George III had plenty on my TV screen, and they were wonderful.

The five of us meet each morning to catch each other up. I co-founded this place with three of my best friends from uni—Rafe, Zach and Cal—and, while the Alchemy team has grown to encompass a host of hospitality and security staff, we still form the core management team.

Put it this way: the four of us, as well as our social media manager, Maddy, are the only ones who actually show our faces at the club before 5pm.

Rafe's our CEO. Alchemy was his brainchild, and he

used the hell out of it until a stunning young virgin, his neighbour, Belle, signed herself up to our Unfurl programme to take ownership of her sexuality and got well and truly Rafe-d. Or maybe he got Belle-d. Either way, he only makes use of Alchemy's facilities with his girlfriend these days.

Zach's the Finance Director, and, up until about five months ago, had zero interest in anything that went on at the club. As long as the cash flows were healthy, he gave it a wide berth. He's had a beyond shitty time of it, losing his wife to cancer and having to navigate the perils of single-parenting while he and his daughters suffer a deluge of grief.

In a plot twist I didn't see coming, however, he started fucking Belle's friend Maddy soon after she started working here to manage our social media. What we all assumed was a much-needed physical outlet for him turned into far more, and they're now blissfully loved-up. She formally moved in with him and the girls a month or two ago.

I'm very fond of Maddy. She's vivacious and open-hearted, and she owns her sexuality in a way it warms my heart to see in a young woman. And, while she and our very own amazing but repressed Zach couldn't be more polar opposites in every way, somehow she has been precisely what he needed. She's brought colour and light and love back into his and the girls' lives, and for that we're endlessly grateful.

In fact, Zaddy, as we call them to annoy them, serves as a wonderful reminder that I like to think I'm wise but that I actually have no fucking clue about life or the human race, because I never, ever saw that one coming. Even though they're perfect together. They're sitting next to each other across from me, and while they're not touching, the love is palpable. The connection. Their bodies are leaning in towards each other like they simply cannot help themselves.

All you need to know about Cal is that he's a total man whore, a rock-solid guy and a great friend. Unlike me, he's given up all attempts at dating and spends most of his evenings either at Alchemy or at the gym. He's a major extrovert whose role as Chief Marketing Officer is a thin facade for him to spend his days organising parties and special events for the club.

As for me, I'm the COO of Alchemy and responsible for new memberships. It's a role I love. I crave inflicting order upon chaos. Give me a clipboard, and I'm happy as a pig in shit. If Rafe's the big picture one, and Zach's the data nerd, and Cal's the party guy, then I'm the systems person.

In the sex club industry, nothing can be left to chance. It's all very well having a big idea to create a beautiful, inspiring, *safe* space where people can fuck each other's brains out, but creating that environment doesn't happen by accident. It requires endless policies and procedures and security and troubleshooting and hygiene and vetting.

The vetting part is why I oversee the process of approving new members. You can have all the safeguarding and explicit consent policies and NDAs in the world, but if you allow a load of dickheads into that space, you're nothing. Safety and respect come first.

End of story.

And when the membership fees are as hefty as ours, weeding out entitled dickheads who want to join can be a full-time job.

Cal is innocuously singing *The Teddybears' Picnic* as he takes his seat next to me. His voice is decent, but the knowing sideways grin he's giving me makes me want to slap him.

'If you go down to the woods today, you're sure of a big surprise,' he sings. *'If you go down to the woods today, you'd better go in disguise...'*

'Got something you'd like to say?' I enquire. My tone is icy, my eyebrow arched. The combination has been known to fell men on many an occasion.

'Today's the day, isn't it?' he asks, disappointingly unchastened.

'What day?'

I know bloody well what he's getting at, but I'm damned if I'm going to give him an inch.

He grins at me. I know for a fact that grin has melted plenty a pair of panties off, but it has no effect on me whatsoever. I lived with the guy at uni, for fuck's sake. I've had the deep misfortune of seeing him unconscious in a pool of his own vomit more than once. He may be the debonair man about town now, but he'll always be a gormless, if lovable, rugby-playing twat in my eyes.

'Today you're meeting the Big Bad Wolff,' he says, articulating the last three words in a way that's decidedly creepy.

'So what the fuck are you singing *The Teddybear's* fucking *Picnic* for?' Rafe asks him before I can ask the same thing. 'The surprise is the fucking teddybears. There's no wolf. Wrong song, mate.'

Zach throws his head back and laughs the kind of deep belly laugh that we heard far too rarely from him up until he got together with Maddy. The sound of it warms my heart and makes me laugh.

'It's the *Lil' Red Riding Hood* song you want,' Rafe continues. 'You know...'

He launches into a sketchy rendition of some song I've never heard of. Maddy starts giggling.

'Fuck's sake,' I mutter under my breath. 'Is it too much to

ask that you all grow up a little so we can actually begin this meeting? And please, for the love of God, try to hold it together if you happen to see Mr Wolff in here later. We're all *supposed* to be representing the Alchemy brand.'

I glare at them all. I refuse to let my amusement show through, because, as usual, I have to play school marm with these three. Maddy's fourteen years younger than the rest of us, but I swear, she and I are the only adults in the room.

'Got it.' Cal clears his throat. 'So I can't say'—he bats his eyelashes and adopts a breathy, Marilyn Monroe-esque falsetto—'*what time is it, Mr Wolff*, if I see him?'

My glare intensifies as I attempt to make laser beams shoot out of my eyes and burn his obnoxious good looks to the ground. Everyone else in the room falls about laughing.

Zach reaches for Maddy's hand as he fixes his alarmingly blue eyes on Cal. 'And you definitely shouldn't say, *my, my, Grandmother dear. What big teeth you have.*' His falsetto is even more porno than Cal's.

'*All the better to eat you with!*' Rafe and Cal roar in unison before cracking up with laughter. Their schoolboy humour is so infectious that my mouth begins to twitch right as I roll my eyes.

I'm laughing at them, not with them.

Just to be clear.

'I detest and despise you all,' I say calmly, smoothing my hands over the pleasing cover of my Smythson notebook. 'Anton Wolff is an impressive businessman who's far more successful than any of you twats. And let me remind you he's a prospective member here. So, for fuck's sake, show him some respect if you see him.'

'Didn't he apply a few months ago?' Rafe asks, brushing an imaginary speck of fluff off his excellent trousers. Not only is the guy objectively and seriously attractive, but he's always perfectly turned out. 'I seem to remember you getting your knickers in a twist about it then.'

'How ridiculous your memory is,' I huff. 'I don't get anything in a twist over *any* prospective members.'

Lie. I was seriously flustered when Mr Wolff's application first came in for reasons I'd rather not examine too closely.

Cal sniggers.

'And yes,' I clarify in response to his original question, 'he applied in the Autumn but his assistant put it on hold for some reason. She got in touch last week to set the wheels in motion again. I'm assuming he was wintering somewhere hot.'

This time, it's only a partial lie. My TikTok For You Page tells me that billionaire tycoon Anton Wolff has indeed been enjoying the pleasures of the Caribbean this winter, but he's also had a voluptuous and very beautiful Colombian TV star on his arm for most of that time. My FYP may or may not have informed me about a month ago that the two had parted ways.

Fucking TikTok. You look up someone once to perform a little professional due diligence, and its algorithm won't let you move on. It has the memory of an elephant and the unwelcome stickiness of gum stuck to the sole of your shoe.

'Well, don't take any shit from him,' Rafe says, which I'm pretty sure is exactly what he said when Wolff's application first came in. 'He's subject to the same requirements as everyone else—make that clear.'

'I'm sure Gen's got this,' Maddy says with a flick of her glossy brown hair. The woman is gorgeous, and her legs look insane in those nude heels. She's a sweetheart *and* a knockout, and I couldn't be more ecstatic for her and Zach.

'*Thank you*, Mads,' I say pointedly, giving my three so-called friends another glare for good measure.

'Anyway,' Maddy says, 'he's sexy as *fuck*. I mean, seriously. The guy is ridiculous. You've got to let him in, Gen.'

'Hey.' Zach grips her bare thigh, looking outraged. I grin. That wiped the smirk off his face.

She pats his hand. 'For the singletons, babes. I only have eyes for one guy these days, but I'm invested in having hotties around for my fellow females to have fun with.'

I suppress a shudder that's definitely not revulsion. Quite the opposite. Because the thought of *the* Anton Wolff getting down and dirty in our club is one I cannot allow myself to compute.

2

ANTON

I sleep easy at night.

Every move I make. Every deal I broker. Every pound or dollar or euro I risk. Every human being I fuck over, literally or figuratively, comes at a cost.

It's my job to assess those costs. To understand them. To make peace with them.

Especially the hidden ones.

Because it's the hidden costs that can really cut you off at the knees, particularly if you don't anticipate them.

That rarely happens to me, because people who misunderstand or deny hidden costs are amateurs, and I am no amateur.

Everything comes at a price, and everyone has a price.

And if the prize is worth the price, then I have no regrets. Because regret and resistance and rumination and recrimination are a fucking waste of time and head space.

To put it crudely, if the end justifies the means and the risks by my calculations, then I'll go ahead and roll the dice. Because an educated gamble is very different from an uneducated one.

I educate myself on every single step I take, which allows me to increase my risk appetite far more than the guys who can't be fucked to do their homework.

And ninety-nine times out of a hundred, I come out on top.

Of course, the moves I make aren't just an outcome of my intellect, but of my values.

And, of course, my values can mis-align with the values of others. With those who may suffer from naivety or piety or self-judgement or the moral high ground or a misapprehension as to how the arenas of power and money and sex really operate, or any other fucking thing that causes them to rail against outcomes when they go my way rather than their way.

When they become collateral damage along the way.

And I don't give a flying fuck.

I told you.

No regrets.

I don't regret or resist who I am. What I am. What I do. How I like to fuck. Second-guessing and overthinking are for the weak.

And I didn't get where I am today by being weak.

MY PRIMARY PHILOSOPHY for operating at this level is as follows.

Scale is everything.

Opportunity is infinite.

My capacity is finite.

My success has come from applying my greatest skills to the most worthwhile opportunities. Simple. Gay Hendricks put this eloquently in his wonderful book, *The Big Leap*. I devote my time and energy to operating solely in my genius zone, which includes, but is not limited to, judgement, farsightedness and nerves of fucking steel.

Everything else is a commodity.

Everything else can be outsourced.

Hear that? That's important.

I am only interested in spending my time making money and enjoying life. End of story. All the rest is secondary.

Which is why I'm starting my morning as I start every weekday morning, meeting with my Chief of Staff, Max, and my Executive Assistant, Athena. Everything we discuss points to our single agenda item: ensure my calendar is structured to reflect the best possible use of my time.

My corner office above the intersection of Berkeley Square and Bruton Street is light-filled and opulent. None of this minimalist bullshit for me. Its walls and panels are painted a deep, warm grey, its carpet is white and opulent, and a few favourites from my art collection adorn the walls —all oils save for a delightful little Degas sketch that my second wife gave me.

She may not have lasted the distance, but that sketch is one of my favourite things in an existence where *things* are all too commoditised.

The three of us sit on a sofa and two low armchairs in a corner of the room as Athena runs through today's line up with the precision I expect from her. I have internal sit-downs and Zooms until ten-thirty, when I leave for my meeting with Alchemy.

I frown, my mind uncharacteristically failing to home in on exactly what *Alchemy* is.

'The sex club,' Max says. His tone, as always, is dismissive. Arrogant.

'Of course it is,' I say, instantly sitting up a little

straighter. Max notices and sniggers. 'Do I really need to do it in person?'

'They were most insistent,' Athena says. 'All members must be vetted face-to-face. Otherwise it's a no-go.'

'So they can make sure you're not totally hideous in real life,' Max drawls.

'Totally depraved, more like,' I observe.

'I'm pretty sure *depraved* is a pre-requisite for getting in,' he says. 'But, you know, don't go baring all your teeth at them just yet. They need to know you're just the right side of a monster.'

Athena's pretty little mouth twists in amusement. She's nothing if not circumspect, but I'm sure she has her own view of quite how monstrous I can be.

'What do I need to know?' I ask no one in particular.

'It's the most discreet place we've found,' Max assures me, 'and the classiest. Their NDAs are ironclad. We couldn't find anything on them. It's owned by four long-term friends —three men and a woman. It's our kind of client list. Loaded. Well-connected. Word is the female members are smoking. And the kink is good. You know, regular stuff. If you want to dress up in a nappy and breastfeed, it might not be the place for you.'

I arch an unamused eyebrow. 'I think we both know that's not my kink.'

'The interview seems more of a formality,' Athena says. 'Yes, it's a way of making sure you're the right fit for the club, but it's also a forum for them to understand what you're into, so they can accommodate you as fully as possible.'

I allow myself a small smirk. I'm not sure if she intended that last *double entendre*—you never quite know with that one—but I sincerely hope this Alchemy place can *fully accommodate* me.

'Who am I meeting?'

She doesn't consult her iPad. 'Genevieve Carew, sir. She's co-founder and COO, and she onboards new members.'

I nod. 'Very good. What's after lunch?'

Athena fills me in on the rest of the day's schedule while Max chimes in with information on the prep work he and his team have done for each meeting.

'Will there be anything else, Mr Wolff?' she asks as she closes her laptop. The question is innocuous, as is her facial expression, but something in her tone gives me pause.

I consider.

In two-and-a-half-hours, I need to stroll around the corner and interview for membership at a sex club. I need to discuss my proclivities in a calm and rational manner while not getting hard.

If the hallmark of a good EA is anticipating one's needs, then Athena is the very best.

'Sure, why not. Get on your knees. Max, give me that P&L and get out.'

Athena immediately rises and comes to stand in front of me before sinking elegantly to her knees.

'Aww,' Max whines. 'I was up till midnight preparing this bullshit for you. The least you can do is let me join in the fun.'

I look from his irritatingly handsome, patrician face to Athena's beautiful, upturned one. She's such a good girl. So compliant. She looks particularly lovely today, in a pale blue wrap dress that showcases her spectacular tits, her long auburn hair falling around her shoulders in soft waves.

Wrap dresses are her uniform, for reasons I don't need to spell out to you.

As I expect, she nods, her cheeks blooming prettily with the faintest blush. 'That's okay with me, sir.'

I sigh. 'Fine. You can help get her off.'

'Nice,' Max says on an exhale. He lifts the glass coffee table and moves it out of the way so he can get behind Athena.

I let my head fall back on the sofa and lazily survey the scene ahead of me. Yeah, I'm a monster who likes to blur lines. But I'm also a man who understands the importance of enjoying the finer things in life while valuing efficiency, and this little rendezvous ticks both boxes.

Athena kneels between my open legs and busies herself with my belt and my flies. Max, in turn, is crouched behind her. There's a predatory look in his blue eyes as he reaches between her legs. I can tell by the sharp intake of breath she makes as she unzips me that he hasn't wasted any time in putting his hands where she needs them.

She tugs my shirt tails up and eases my boxer briefs down over my already-hard dick. I cross my hands behind my head and interlace my fingers as she dips her pretty head and the tip of her warm, wet tongue hits my crown.

This is the fucking life.

The view of the two of them is pretty fucking good, but I let my eyes drift closed for a minute. Fuck, there is no simpler pleasure in life than the sensations of a woman's mouth on one's dick. Especially when that woman is as skilled and sexy as Athena.

She's a relatively new EA from an agency I co-founded a few years ago through a web of holding companies and shell companies so complex that it's practically impossible to connect me with it.

Seraph.

That's the name we opted for, and at times like this it feels very fucking apt, because Athena is a real angel.

I'm not alone amongst men of my status in prizing both efficiency and sex highly.

My employees are first-rate.

So are my women.

Seraph operates in a niche that's as lucrative as it is small. It provides world-class executive assistants to the most powerful men in London. Each assistant comes with an MBA from a top business school, and each has also been trained in delivering world-class pleasures of the flesh to the men they serve.

See?

Niche.

They are very well paid, and very good at what they do, and, most importantly, very much *into* what they do.

I set Seraph up between wives two and three, but had no use for their services while I was in my last marriage or with Melissa, my most recent girlfriend.

When I'm in a relationship, I'm faithful.

When I'm not, I'm an animal.

Cutting ties with Melissa coincided with my hiring Athena. I'd had five months of vanilla sex with a stunningly beautiful woman, and I was champing at the bit to unleash myself. This Alchemy place will form the final piece of the puzzle that is adequately sating my appetites, hopefully, but between the debauched nights I enjoy with strangers, Athena looks after my days very well indeed.

She has an MBA from London Business School and a mouth that begs to be defiled.

I open my eyes and glance down at Athena's glossy head bobbing up and down on my cock. She's draped one arm over my thigh for balance as the other works my shaft just the way I like it—a firm grip, but no large movements at this point. She knows I want to make it last.

The reason she's using me for balance is that she's got that gorgeous, plump arse of hers in the air for Max. He's shoved the thin jersey of her dress up to her waist so I can see a flesh-coloured thong and two perfect globes of pale skin. Max ranges above her—he's standing up on his knees—and his face contorts in satisfaction as his wrist twists. He's tall enough to reach her tit without bending forward, and he's doing something right, judging by the strangled whimpers she's making around my dick.

'Tell me what you're doing to her,' I say, the idle tone of my voice belying my intense interest. I sit forward slightly so I can scoop her silky locks up in both hands before transferring them to my left and wrapping them around my fist.

They were both right, as usual.

This is an excellent start to my day.

'The old bowling ball position,' he drawls, making eye contact with me. 'Two fingers in her cunt, a thumb up her arse, and she is fucking loving it.'

Jesus fuck. It's my dick she's got her lips wrapped around, but I'm jealous. Though I suspect the grass is greener from where Max is, too. He must be dying to get his dick wet.

I nod my approval. 'Nice. She wet?'

'Soaking. Listen.' He pulls his hand out of her, then pushes back in fiercely, and I'm treated to the exquisite combination of her lips clamping down around my dick and the clear sound of her inner wetness sucking Max's fingers in.

That's it.

'Fuck. I need a feel. Athena.' I tug on her hair to pull her face up, and she looks up at me all glassy-eyed and swollen-mouthed. She really is delicious. 'Straddle me, sweetheart. Max, help her and get rid of the dress.'

He stands and hoists her up under the arms. I close my thighs so she can straddle me and still have enough room to keep her pussy raised off my lap.

Enough room to play with her.

Athena plants each knee on the sofa and straddles me, gazing down at me. She's already in a state of mild dishevelment, but she keeps a hairbrush and makeup in my private bathroom for precisely this kind of situation. Then Max is standing behind her, reaching over so he can untie the sash at her waist and tug her dress open.

I smile with appreciation as her incredible tits come into view in a white lace bra. Her nipples are so hard they're practically ripping through the lace. I reach up and pinch them both as Max pulls the dress off her arms, and she gasps loudly. My gaze trails down over the soft, pale curves of her belly to the little nude thong that looks quite ill-equipped to withstand my and Max's dastardly intentions.

Poor little thong.

Poor little girl.

She's less than half my age, and she's only been with me for four weeks, but she's a quick learner.

On both sides of the job.

I look back up at her. My dick is rock hard. Angry. Her saliva has cooled and dried on my flesh. But I can hang on, because it's time for some fun.

I pinch harder. 'What do you need, sweetheart?' I ask.

I don't need a mirror to know my smile has turned positively wolfish.

3

ANTON

'I want to make you come,' she manages, her big hazel eyes fluttering shut as I roll and tweak her nipples.

'I didn't ask what you *want*. I asked what you *need*.'

I'm vaguely aware that this is escalating into something far more time-consuming than a quick, perfunctory blowjob, but I'll happily eschew efficiency in favour of pleasure.

'I need you to let me come,' she moans. She goes to lower herself onto my cock, but Max's hands are back under her arms, holding her up on her knees.

'*You*, plural?' I ask, knowing full well what the answer will be. I release her nipples and place my hands on her bare thighs.

She hesitates. 'Yes,' she admits, and I fucking love that. I love that she's still a little shy about voicing her needs, that being here at the mercy of the two of us has her feeling a little bashful. A little vulnerable.

As well it should.

I love that shame and desire are roiling through that soft

belly of hers right now, because it'll make it all the sweeter when we eventually let her come.

'Course you do,' I croon. 'Max, take her tits. Athena, sweetheart, you spread those little legs for us, alright? We need to get you ready to take our cocks.'

Her moan is answer enough, but her fevered, whispered *please* is the sweetest gift, because there is nothing I love more than hearing women beg.

Max threads his arms further forward so he can hold her up by his forearms while palming and cupping and playing with her tits through the lace. The sight of him massaging them, squishing them together, rolling his fingers over those pretty nipples, is magnificent, and I know he's putting on a show for me as much as he's getting her wound up.

Precum leaks from my angry, neglected crown as I trail my fingertips up her thigh and slide them under the scrap of lace.

Max was right. She is fucking soaking, and so warm.

'Jesus Christ,' I grit out. I shove the lace to one side and let my fingers explore her slickness. I circle her clit and she moans. I ram three fingers inside her tight, wet cunt and she cries out before pushing down on them.

'Good girl,' I tell her. 'So good. All your holes are for us, understand?'

'God, yes,' she cries.

'Max,' I say.

He doesn't need me to expound. We've played with enough women together in the past. He releases one of her full breasts and spits on his finger. I know the second he breaches that tight little hole of hers because she gasps, and her internal muscles clamp harder around my fingers.

'One,' I say, sliding out. I know Max is doing the same, because this is a well-trodden path for us. We both push back in at the same time that I reward her swollen clit with a firm rub from my thumb, and she bucks, sagging against his remaining arm.

'Hold yourself up like a good girl, darling,' I warn her, ' or we stop. Got it?'

'Sorry, sir,' she gasps.

'Two.' We withdraw and thrust in again, finger-fucking both her holes in tandem as I fondle her clit and Max pinches her nipple.

She really is a lucky, lucky girl.

'Oh, God,' she says. Her thighs are shaking with the effort of holding herself up and holding her orgasm off.

'Fuck my dick with your fist,' I growl, and she immediately takes me in her hand. Fuck me, that feels amazing. She runs a thumb through my pre-cum, smoothing it over my crown. I'm going to need to blow, and soon.

'Three.'

'I think she's close,' Max remarks.

'Course she is,' I say. 'She's taking both our fingers like a champ. Okay, sweetheart, get down and suck my cock.' Because I'm thoroughly enjoying this little threesome and I'm feeling charitable, I add, 'Max, fuck her while I come in her mouth.'

'Seriously?' he asks as he hauls Athena off me and back onto the carpet.

I nod. 'If it's okay with Athena.'

'Yes please,' she says immediately, and I smirk, because there's no bashfulness now. She's so fucking desperate to be impaled on our cocks at both ends that she has no problem voicing her needs.

Just the way I like my women. Desperate and vocal.

I settle back on the sofa and open my legs. Athena scoots between them on all fours. Her mascara is smudged, her tits hang, heavy and luscious and barely tethered by her bra, and her pale arse sways as Max sheathes himself in a condom from the box on the coffee table.

It really is very nice of me to let him play. But it'll be even nicer when Athena chokes on my dick through her orgasm. In fact...

'Move back,' I order. She shuffles backwards and I drop to my knees on the carpet in front of her, pushing my trousers and boxers down so my cock and balls are right in her face. Max gives me an approving smirk before settling himself between her parted legs.

'I'm going to fuck your mouth, okay?' I ask.

She looks up at me, and the raw hunger on her face nearly undoes me.

'Yes please, Mr Wolff, sir,' she says.

'Good girl.' I gather her hair up again, wrapping it around one fist like I did a moment ago, but tighter this time. With the other hand I fist my dick at the root, as she's going to need both hands when Max starts railing the living daylights out of her.

Her beautiful mouth closes around me once again, enveloping my dick in its wet, velvety warmth. I groan at the sheer pleasure of it as I watch Max feed his own big cock into her cunt, his hands white-knuckling her hips. He bottoms out in her, and she jolts forward so my dick hits the back of her throat.

Fuck.

I grip her hair and hold her there, both of us balls deep in her. She gags a little but doesn't pull back, and the two of us exchange a triumphant glance over her naked back.

'What a good girl,' Max mutters, smoothing a praising hand over her arse. 'She takes cock so well.'

And then he starts to move.

I'm not into guys, really, but I have a keen appreciation for the dynamic that is two successful men, fully dressed, bringing a highly intelligent and well-educated, almost-naked woman to her literal knees with frantic need and feeding her our cocks.

It's a power dynamic I will never fail to get off on.

I respect women.

I adore women.

I steadfastly believe they are our equals in some ways and our superiors in most.

But I love nothing more than indulging in a little scorching hot, consensual abasement of the female party, because shame is one of the most powerful aphrodisiacs I've ever seen.

Athena's credentials are impeccable. Her CV is immaculate. And while you could say she's servicing both of us, in reality, we're servicing her just as much. Filling her chock-full of the cock she so desperately craves. I can tell Max's admirably punishing thrusts into her pussy have her close to blowing, thanks to the delirious, breathless way she's sucking and licking and gargling on every inch of my cock as I force-feed it to her and Max simultaneously rails her.

God, I'm close. I am so fucking close as she struggles to take me in and Max's latex-sheathed cock rams into her over and over. And then he reaches around and presumably finds her clit, because she lets out a garbled scream around my cock and closes her mouth more tightly around me, sucking harder.

She wants it. She wants it from both of us, and we're going to give it to her. I raise a questioning eyebrow at Max and he nods.

Yep. Everyone's about to blow their loads.

'Coming. *Fuck*,' I warn her as I grip her makeshift ponytail even more tightly and hold her against me, emptying myself into her. It feels like I just keep on coming as she gasps and sucks and attempts to swallow around me.

'Good girl,' Max tells her. 'You got the boss to blow, so now we can all come.'

I hold her firmly in place by her hair. I have no intention of letting her get away from my cock just yet. Max rams home, effort etched onto his face, his hand still wrapped around her front. And then she's moaning and sobbing out choked cries as she shudders uncontrollably through what looks to be an epic orgasm at Max's hands.

Next time I'm taking the other end.

He follows her over the edge, and I watch avidly as he convulses against her. I'm far more interested in how he's making her feel than how he feels right now.

He stills inside her before pulling out and clambering to his feet, looking dazed. I release her hair and allow her to suck me clean before she sits back on her knees. She looks utterly spent and well-fucked. Her mascara is everywhere. God knows how many tears she spilt as I gagged her with my dick. She places her hands on her thighs, the perfect picture of submission.

She's not a sub—I definitely do not have time in my life for a full-time sub—but she's beautifully subservient in both a sexual and professional manner, and it pleases me enormously.

I tip up her chin before I get to my feet.

'You did very well, Athena. You took our cocks beautifully. Didn't she, Max?'

'You're a fucking angel,' Max tells her. 'Jesus Christ, that was hot.'

'How do you feel?' I ask her.

She sighs. Her eyes are still glassy. 'God. I feel absolutely amazing.'

I nod my approval. 'Good. Now, go bring me a wet flannel and then Max will help you get dressed and you can fix your makeup. Then I want that P&L Max ran printed out by week as well as month before the nine o'clock.'

4

GEN

Watching Anton Wolff—billionaire tycoon, philanthropist, celebrity and veritable ecosystem—walk into a room is reminiscent of listening to Carly Simon sing *You're So Vain*.

Except I don't think it's vanity that gives him his walking-onto-a-yacht swagger so much as unshakable confidence. And I suspect with that confidence comes the sense of entitlement that he not only belongs in any room but can dominate it, too.

It's always odd meeting someone in the flesh when you're familiar with them from the media. Sometimes it's even surreal. But in this moment, my overwhelming perception as he walks towards me is that Anton Wolff is *more*.

More of everything than he is on screen.

Taller.

Broader-shouldered.

More heavily built, with a toned bulk I wouldn't expect from a guy who's apparently fifty-two years old.

More tanned.

More lustrous and floppy and dark of hair.

Better looking, though his features are stronger, craggier, in the flesh.

And generally more imposing.

More... *more*.

Jesus Christ. Now is not a good time for my basic articulatory skills to leave the building. Pull it together, woman, for fuck's sake.

He's clean-shaven and dressed in that standard wealthy-businessman uniform of impeccably cut charcoal-grey suit and white shirt.

Top two shirt buttons open.

No tie.

It fucking works.

I'm five-eleven in heels, but he must be pushing six-foot-four. He'd be lanky if it wasn't for those immensely broad shoulders. I wouldn't be surprised if he was a rower or a swimmer in his day.

Bloody hell, his tailor is good.

I realise I'm smoothing my hands over my Chanel-tweed-covered hips and cease instantly, holding out a decisive hand for him to shake.

'Mr Wolff,' I say in the trademark tone of understated authority I pride myself on. 'I'm Genevieve Carew. Welcome to Alchemy.'

He stops in front of me, and I have to tilt my head up to meet the discomfiting gaze of his deep brown eyes. His hand is big and warm, his grip strong.

'Genevieve,' he says. 'Call me Anton.'

I nod briskly to cover the inappropriately girly thrill that runs through me at my name on his lips. 'Anton it is.'

'That's better,' he says, and he full on *grins*.

To use the only pathetic cliché that comes to mind in this inopportune moment of brain-fail, it's like the clouds part and the sun emerges. His smile is astonishing. His features are strong, craggy, even, and indisputably masculine. But when he grins, two delightful dimples flash before getting swallowed up in a deep pair of laughter lines.

It's boyish and mischievous and sparkling.

It's quite something.

Also, he has excellent teeth. I'm pleased to note his incisors look very much human.

The guys will be disappointed.

'Coffee?' I ask, extricating my hands and taking a step backwards to put a little space between us, because he's a *lot*, and he smells really great too, in an understated, herbal way.

'Espresso, please,' he says easily, but I don't miss the fleeting once-over he gives my figure.

Enjoy the view, pal.

It's all you'll get.

'Have a seat,' I say.

I head to the Nespresso machine. I tend to make the coffees for prospective members myself, because I don't want our receptionist interrupting what are sensitive conversations. But, really, I'm grateful to have something to occupy myself with, because for some reason the Big Bad Wolff has me nervous, and I have no idea why.

It's probably just because the guys have been winding me up all morning.

Fucking Cal.

'Busy morning?' I enquire in an inelegant attempt at small talk. I glance over at him to find his gaze planted squarely on my arse, a discovery that gives me more pleasure than it should.

'You could say that,' he says with a smile that can only be described as smug.

Whatever.

'How did you hear about us?' I ask as his espresso pours. I certainly don't need one of those. I'm jittery enough already.

'My former EA found you a few months ago. But I ended up in a relationship, so I shelved it.'

I make a polite *mm-hmm* sound that suggests this is new information for me.

'We're always happy to consider applications by couples,' I say noncommittally.

Digging much, Gen?

His coffee's ready. I pick it up and take it over to where he's settled himself on the big corner sofa. Setting it on the coffee table in front of him, I take a seat adjacent to him but not too close and cross my legs.

He appears to be choosing his words. 'My most recent ex was a lovely woman, but this kind of thing wasn't her bag.'

'Of course,' I say.

'It can be hard to find someone who ticks every box,' he continues. He twists his mouth and gestures around the room. 'Especially *this* box. You know?'

Better than you realise, mate.

His tone, his demeanour, and his gaze are all confiding. This is why guys like him are so successful, right? They draw you in, make you feel like you have their confidence and they have yours. They make you feel like the only person in the room.

He's good.

I mean, he's also very much correct. His subtext is precisely what I've been bemoaning in my own life recently.

But again. He's good.

So I'll be circumspect.

'I understand,' I say. If he's looking for me to confide in

him in return, he'll be disappointed. 'That's why we set up Alchemy. It's a safe place where like-minded adults can tick whatever boxes they like.'

I am an emancipated woman who runs a sex club, for fuck's sake. So I'm unsure as to why all this talk of *boxes* with Anton Wolff is making me sweat.

'Sounds intriguing.' There's that grin again. Oh my Lord.

Cal may have been onto something.

He's definitely a wolf.

5

GEN

I push on. 'Well, thank you for completing the initial NDA,' I say. 'That covers us for this meeting. Should we extend a membership to you, there'll be a full NDA to protect all parties.'

'I'll get my lawyers to go through it and suggest changes,' he says.

Hasty there, cowboy.

No one's offered you membership yet.

I smile tightly. 'I assure you, we don't make any exceptions to our policies.'

'I'm not angling for an exception, or any exemptions,' he says. 'I want to make sure I'm fully protected.'

'By all means, feel free to have your lawyers look over anything,' I tell him. Our NDAs are iron clad. His lawyers won't need to worry about their precious client having any of his naughty shenanigans leaked. 'I have a questionnaire to walk you through, unless you'd rather go through it in your own time, and then I can take you through to have a look at the club if that suits? It might be easier to talk through our offering in situ.'

He settles back on the sofa, hitches up his trouser leg at the thigh, crosses one ankle over the opposite knee, picks up his espresso cup, and holds it to his mouth.

'Shoot,' he says. He takes a sip, and my eyes linger on the slight pout that sensual mouth makes as he does so. I reach hastily for my iPad. We have different questionnaires depending on the profile of the individual seeking admission to the club. Those interested in our Unfurl programme, for example, tend to be less experienced, and we usually suggest they work through the questionnaire in the privacy of their own home.

I'll never forget the boner Rafe got when he read through his now-girlfriend, Belle's, questionnaire. I thought the poor guy's dick was going to break off. It was priceless.

Anyway, for those like the enigmatic Mr Wolff, we don't need to tread so lightly. A three-minute stint alone in a room with him tells me he's not a shy little lamb.

A lethal predator, more like.

'Do you have a preferred term to describe your sexuality?' I ask.

'I like women,' he says. *'Plural.'*

The way he emphasises the last word gives me actual chills.

'Do you play with other men at all?'

'Sure.' He takes a sip of his espresso as I wait. 'But only when we're all fucking the same woman. Or women.'

'So you don't partake in sexual acts by or on others who identify as male.'

'Never say never,' he says. 'But generally, no.'

'How would you describe your primary objectives for joining Alchemy?'

He takes another sip before setting the little cup and saucer down on the table in front of him. Then he leans forwards, spreads his legs and rests his elbows on his thighs as he surveys me. He strokes his chin with the fingertips of one hand, considering the question.

There's something about this man's presence that has my nervous system very confused. Being the focus of his attention feels alarming and thrilling in equal measure. He is a force to be reckoned with—it's impossible not to notice. I'm deeply disappointed with myself for being unable to come up with a more cerebral way to describe his aura than the crass but wholly accurate concept of Big Dick Energy.

The guy has it in spades. He could be ugly as sin, and he'd still exude an undeniable magnetism.

Unfortunately, he's far from ugly.

'Discretion,' he says finally, his gaze roaming around the room. 'Variety. Convenience. I'm a busy man. I like the idea of every sort of fucking being served up to me on a platter. Open-mindedness. Relative anonymity, I suppose. And... challenges.'

He looks directly at me as he throws out that last word.

'You've come to the right place,' I say lamely, breaking eye contact on the pretext of making a note on the iPad. 'You'll find variety and open-mindedness and acceptance here at Alchemy, but I also hope you'll feel as though our members share commonalities, like integrity. Most of our members are, like you, hugely successful. Many of them share your priorities.'

He nods, his face impassive.

'You'll see the facilities shortly. Our main recreational area is The Playroom. The bar is a clothes-on space. We have twelve fully-kitted-out bedrooms, six on this level and six downstairs. Also downstairs is The Vault, a space for our more adventurous members to play. But the main Playroom has a stage and a few St Andrew's crosses. We're big on themed nights and party events. Slave Night, foam orgies, that type of thing.

'We also have a concierge who can arrange bespoke scenarios on and offsite for you. Nothing is too much trouble. We have a couple of female members with kidnapping kinks—one finds herself the victim of elaborate 'kidnappings' on an almost weekly basis, thanks to our concierge. And my colleague had a full-size confessional that he salvaged from a church reconstructed in one of the rooms downstairs—religious kink is very popular with our members.'

There's that wolfish grin again. 'I can relate.'

A sudden vision assails me. Anton Wolff, dark and predatory in priestly garb. A man of God unleashed. Fucking and fucking and fucking the repression out of his system.

On me.

Holy fuck. I blame Rafe for the priest thing. He and Belle have done far too much of that here.

I clear my throat. 'Would you like to share any preferences or fetishes you may have with me at this point?'

I swear it's getting hot in here. He steeples his fingers together as he surveys me.

'Control.'

'Mm-hmm.' I pretend to write it down in a valiant attempt at escaping from his assessing gaze.

'Abasement. Of willing participants, naturally.'

My palms are starting to sweat. The stylus feels slippery in my hand.

'Those are the big ones. Everything else stems from those. Everything I do, every toy I use, every person I choose to fuck, or to edge into fucking oblivion. It all comes down to those two things. Being in control and having women submit to me completely. Having them be so desperate for that orgasm they'll let me do anything. They'll let anyone watch. They'll let me and my friends do whatever we like to them because the *only thing they can think about* is how badly they need to come.

'I will never, ever tire of that dynamic and I'll take it every which way I can. *That's* what I want from this place, because in every actual fucking relationship I have, it seems to be off the table.'

I'm staring at him, but I can't help it. Those eyes of his are locked on me, so dark they're almost black. I watch his unfairly perfect mouth enunciate words that make me half-sick with need.

Control.

Abasement.

Submit.

Need.

Orgasm.

One thing is horribly, painfully, unfairly clear to me.

This guy is the real deal. He may think he's showing me his dark side. In fact, the way he said those things felt like he was trying to shock me.

Or more terrifyingly, *test* me.

The worst bit is that some part of me wants to pass his test. To please him. And as I shove that part of myself deep down inside my carefully curated, polished, circumspect facade, I silently admit that if a woman *did* want the kinds of depraved things he's articulating, then she could do no better than to allow Anton Wolff to deliver them.

I bet he's a true master of his dark arts.

I bet he'd be fucking relentless until he'd got me right where he wanted me.

The stylus slips from my hand.

6

ANTON

She is quite simply lovely.

Lovely.

And she doesn't fool me for a second. She may think her immaculate Hitchcock-heroine act is convincing. She certainly looks the part. She's Grace Kelly with flesh on her bones. Betty Draper's blonde, patrician beauty with Joan's incredible tits and arse.

Jesus Christ, what man could withstand that combination?

I see what she's got going on here. She's playing the whole in-control Domme role. The sexy schoolmarm. That iPad may as well be a clipboard. I bet she runs this place like a Swiss watch. It's almost sweet, and it might be convincing to someone less perceptive.

But I didn't get where I am by being unable to read people, and, from where I'm standing, Genevieve Carew is as readable as a fucking three-year-old's picture book.

I saw the look on that beautiful face when I outlined my particular set of appetites.

I saw what it did to her.

Yes, I may have been unnecessarily salacious, but I was looking for a reaction.

And boy did I get one.

Her huge baby-blues went wide. Her pupils dilated faster than you could say *on your knees*, and an extremely pretty flush bloomed on her cheeks.

Not to mention, she dropped the fucking pen.

I should feel sorry for her. I should feel bad for making her hot and bothered, but instead I'm thrilled.

I told her I was looking for challenges.

I suspect I've just found my first one. Something tells me she won't easily succumb to the inevitable.

I'd be hugely disappointed if she did.

She throws me a few more questions, but I can tell she's still rattled. She's a cool customer, and she runs a sex club, for God's sake, so I assume she's used to running these interviews. Used to discussing all manner of sordid secrets.

Therefore, I can only conclude that it's me who's getting her all hot and bothered.

Just how I like it.

'Would you like to see the club?' she asks somewhat abruptly, laying the iPad down on the coffee table.

'If you've got everything you need from me then yes. Very much.'

She nods and stands. I get to my feet too and gesture for her to lead the way.

The back view is quite as spectacular as the front. This woman has the old-world curves of a Hollywood bombshell, and she certainly knows how to dress to show them off. She's in a sleek, form-fitting pencil skirt that nips in at the waist and stretches over her fantastic arse, and whose rear slit hints at a tantalising sliver of thigh. Nude stockings. High heels and fucking amazing legs.

Her platinum-blonde hair is perfectly coiffed in some kind of up-do, and the silk shirt she's wearing is palest lavender and sleeveless, showcasing toned arms. The pussy-bow tie at the front gives off a sexy-secretary vibe that I can —surprise, surprise—definitely get on board with.

Everything she's wearing, down to the starched white cotton camellia brooch that's unmistakably Chanel, screams class. It's almost as if she's terrified anyone might deem her unseemly.

Come to think of it, the camellia feels apt. It's pure. Flaw-less. Intricate. Highly structured. No room for improvisa-tion. For mess. None of those big, blowsy petals other flowers go for.

It's perfect.

Just like her.

And yet this immaculate, golden goddess runs a *sex club*. Fascinating. I find myself intrigued by her as I watch her arse sway in front of me, thanks to those four-inch heels she's wearing.

I follow her out of the room and down the wide entrance hallway where I came in. Its walls are lined with chrome sconces, its floor a highly polished black-and-white chequer. This building has good bones. It's a wonderful example of a classic Georgian villa—I wouldn't be surprised if Adam himself designed it.

'This is how the guests enter in the evening,' Genevieve says. 'And this is our main bar.' She stops in front of a pair of double doors and opens them with a flourish.

The room I step into is large. Light-filled. Impressive, even when empty. There are French doors at one end with a leafy garden in view, and heavy oak doors at the other. The main feature is the long, pale pink onyx bar dotted with heavy chrome bar stools, their leather seats an eye-popping emerald green.

It's a beautiful space. Chic and tasteful. The type of bar I'd expect to find at the Connaught or the Berkeley or at a swanky members' club like Annabel's, not at a sex club. I'm sure that pink bar looks stunning in the evening when it's backlit. The room smells heavily of what I recognise as Diptyque *Baies* candles, and sure enough, I spot their iconic matte black votives everywhere. It's a scent that, unfortunately, instantly evokes Marie-Claire, Wife Number Two, who had *Baies* burning all over the house.

I look forward to overwriting those memories with new ones.

Memories that involve sex and only sex.

'We wanted to capture an exclusive feel,' Genevieve explains, gesturing around the room. 'We didn't want it to appear too overtly sexual. Members can bring guests this far, and many of them use it as their club, even when they're not planning on going next door.'

Next door is The Playroom, and I swear the air thickens when she opens the heavy doors and ushers me inside.

Yes. This is more like it.

Even if it's far more... girly than any sex club I've been in before.

I'm used to black and red. Whips and chains. This is prettier. It's a vast white room whose lightness is tangible even in the absence of any natural light save for that filtering through the open doors. The huge windows are firmly shuttered.

There's a bar on one side, a stage on the other, and the space in between the two is cleverly punctuated by huge white pillars from which hang billowing white curtains. I prowl around the room as I take it in, Genevieve following me.

'I assume it's more bacchanalian at night,' I mutter.

'Definitely,' she says. 'Though not the drunken part—we have a two-drink limit per member to protect everyone. But the orgy part, yes.'

It does feel like some Ancient Grecian temple where the young and the beautiful can indulge in utter debauchery, and I like it. It's not sordid like some clubs I've been to—it's upmarket and unapologetic. The sheer number of white leather sofas and daybeds and ottomans leave no room for doubt as to the purpose of the room, but it feels... elevated.

I'm confident the kind of sex I can have in here will be elevated, too.

Even the three St Andrew's crosses in a row are stylish, crafted from smooth, blonde wood with tan leather cuffs that look like they could have been crafted by Hermès' own artisans. But the sight that sends an anticipatory tug to my groin is the sight of a waist-high, chesterfield-style ottoman with cuffs chained along the top.

Because cuffing a woman and bending her over that thing could work very well.

Come to think of it, Genevieve Carew's arse would look particularly fine bared like that.

Which prompts my next question.

7

ANTON

'**D**o you partake of these facilities?' I ask her in as even a tone as I can manage, my eyes still trained on the equipment in front of them.

She's quiet behind me for a moment. 'I don't think that's relevant to this discussion,' she says finally.

'It's a simple question. You're pitching me your club, and I'm wondering if you stand behind its offering.'

'Of course I stand behind it.' She takes a step forward so she's next to me, and I glance over at her. Her face is an impassive mask.

'So you do partake.'

This time, it's not a question.

'Not all business owners have to use their products. Our FD, Zach, was married when we founded this place.'

'That's not an answer.'

'It's not something I feel the need to discuss with prospective members.'

I turn to face her, so I can give her my full attention. Those blue eyes of hers look up at me with studied aloofness.

'There are only two reasons, as far as I can see, that you wouldn't allow yourself to enjoy the charms of this place. One, you're in a monogamous relationship.' I swallow the distaste that particular relationship state holds for me currently. 'Two, it's not your bag. But you're not a silent partner. You're the first face new members see. You just asked me about my fetishes, for Christ's sake. So there's no way you're as prim and proper as you look.'

Her mouth twists as she studies me. I can tell she's unimpressed by my doggedness, but tough shit. I stand by it being a fair question, and I'm used to pushing until people give me answers.

She spins on her heels. 'I do *partake,* if you must know. It's simply not relevant to you. Let me show you the bedrooms.'

As she click-clacks away from me, I sweep my eyes over that arse again. I wonder what she's like when she's here at night. She's so buttoned up. Does she go for it? Scream her head off on those crosses? Or is she discreet, zeroing in on the person or people who can give her what she wants and tugging them off to a quiet room?

'Why is it not relevant?' I insist. I pull on the handle of the heavy door she's stopped in front of and hold it open so she can walk through it. 'We're both adults. We're both going to be here in the evenings, assuming you extend me a membership. Doesn't it follow that we might fraternise?'

She heads down the corridor and opens a door. 'Here's one of the private rooms. You can book these in advance, otherwise it's first come, first served.'

I put my hands in my pockets and raise a quizzical eyebrow at her as I saunter past her into the room. It's opulent. Intimate.

Midnight-blue painted walls.

Enormous bed made up with a black sheet and black scatter pillows.

No cover.

Leather headboard.

Cuffs on chains suspended from the ceiling and from either side of the headboard.

More attached to the floor at the end of the bed.

An open doorway reveals a bathroom. There's a large lacquered cabinet against one wall and a few bowls of condoms and lube. Silk gowns hang from a peg on the wall, but otherwise it looks fairly innocuous.

Cuffs aside, of course.

Still, it's atmospheric, and it's obviously set up for a single purpose, so it's impossible not to feel the tension ratchet up when in here alone with this woman.

'I asked you a question, which you ignored. Again.' I turn to her, jangling my keys in my pocket. 'And don't try to fob me off about you not fraternising with clients, because everyone in this club is a client of yours, so if you do "partake", as you've admitted, then by default you're fucking your clients. We're all consenting adults, so what's the problem?'

I take a step closer to her, and she backs up so she's practically up against the wall.

'The *problem* is that who I do or don't fuck is none of your business, whether or not we frequent the same club,' she says. Her tone is icily professional, but her face is defiant, and it really makes me want to put her over my knee.

'So I wouldn't make the shortlist?' I push. 'Why? Because I genuinely can't work it out. Unless you're not attracted to me, of course, but that's bullshit, because you've been eye-fucking me for the past twenty minutes.'

She opens her mouth in what looks like outrage, but I

keep going. 'So the only other reasons I can think of are that you don't share my kinks, or you're scared. And it's not the former, because I saw how your entire body reacted when I told you what I like doing to women, so it must be the latter. Am I right?'

A glance downwards tells me that, beneath her demure Miss Moneypenny blouse and discreet bra, her nipples have hardened.

Interesting.

Once again, she's far less opaque than she'd like to think.

'Don't be ridiculous,' she huffs. 'Of course I'm not scared. But I choose who I fuck, and I don't want to fuck you, nor do I have to explain myself to you.'

'Course you don't,' I lie smoothly, because she does, and she will. 'But I'm bewildered as to why you'd deny yourself an experience you so clearly want, just to piss me off. Surely Alchemy is all about exploring new horizons? Pushing your boundaries? Or do you deny yourself even when you're here? Do you stay like your little camellia,'—I nod at her brooch—'all buttoned-up and perfect and tasteful? I doubt it very much.'

'My sex life is none of your business.' She pushes off the wall and comes to stand next to me. 'What I do here is none of your business. Neither is who I do it with.'

I stick out my lower lip in faux defeat. 'It's just a shame. Because you're precisely the kind of woman I hoped to find here, Genevieve. And I know how good I can make it for you. I'd fuck you over that ottoman thing out there, so everyone could see how fucking beautiful you are when you let go. Or, if you're feeling shy, we could come in here. Alone, or with whoever else you want. Depends on how many cocks you can take in one night.

'But make no mistake about it. If I got you on this bed I

would be fucking relentless until I'd made you fall apart over and fucking *over.*'

She's staring at me, and boy is she magnificent. Her face is flushed with disbelief and arousal, her tits are heaving as she tries to catch her breath, and she keeps licking her lips, a fact I'm sure she's unaware of.

She pulls herself up to her full height and holds out her hand, which I take with amusement. '*Mr Wolff.* Alchemy is pleased to extend an offer of membership to you. We'll email you over the signing documents and full NDA. But.' She squeezes tight around my hand. 'This will be the last time you get to touch me. You will not get to lay a hand, or any other body part, on me, no matter how often our visits here may coincide. Got it?'

I allow myself a full grin, because she is fucking spectacular. 'You may think that, Genevieve,' I say. 'But I don't like your chances. Because I want you. And I'm used to getting what I want.'

8

GEN

'Arrogant *twat*,' I huff to myself in the hallway's mirrored wall after I've ushered him out and watched him saunter into the back seat of a sleek black car waiting outside.

I cannot believe the hubris of that man.

I feel odd. A little breathless. He's rattled me, and I resent it.

It was all that chat. That predatory stance of his. Being alone in a bedroom with him was bad enough without him saying *those things* and ranging that big body of his over me like that.

'So?' Maddy asks with a saucy wink as I march back into the office towards the rear of the building. The reception room where I hosted Anton Wolff and the area where our desks are would originally have been an enormous double drawing room. The two rooms are still interconnected thanks to huge double doors that I made sure remained firmly shut throughout my meeting just now.

I sigh and make a beeline for the Nespresso machine

before redirecting to my desk. I'm all over the place, which is frankly ridiculous. 'He is a piece of fucking work.'

'Yay.' She shimmies her shoulders in pleasure. 'Tell us more.'

Rather than take a seat, I plonk my backside on the desk and survey the others. We sit in a horseshoe arrangement that allows for informal chatter when we're all around. It's a full house today, which is unusual, given Cal's always out and about and Rafe and Zach also run a kind of hedge fund with some of their mates.

'Is he in?' Rafe asks, surveying me over his mug.

'He is,' I admit.

Maddy squeals, and Zach shoots mock daggers at her.

'Did he give you any shit?' Rafe continues.

'Nothing I couldn't handle. He's entitled and persistent, which is always an irritating fucking combination, but I have no reason to believe he'd cause problems in the club. I suspect he tries it on with everyone.'

'So he tried it on with you?'

I cross my arms over my chest. 'Yes. I'm sure he was just being opportunistic. Look, he's fine. He's as expected. Charming, persuasive, smug as fuck and clearly entirely too used to people rolling over for him.'

I regret the final few words as soon as they leave my mouth.

'Are you going to roll over for him?' Cal asks with his trademark cheeky grin.

I shoot him a look I hope adequately communicates how deeply beneath me it would be to rationalise that question with a response.

'We've got bigger problems,' Rafe says brusquely. 'Ciara snuck into Rapture last night and said the place was on fire.'

My shoulders slump. That is a big problem.

Rapture is a new sex club that opened up around the corner from us last month in a prime Mayfair position. Whereas we're discreet, classy, it's showy and tacky.

But make no mistake, it's going after our clientele.

We've already had so many members, mostly male, pulling us aside or texting us images of the hot-pink invitations from Rapture that have landed on their doormats. Some are amused, others outraged or indifferent.

But some are interested.

Some are checking it out.

And a handful of people have even given notice on their Alchemy membership.

Rafe managed to get one of our hosts, Ciara, smuggled in last night. God knows how.

'What else did she say?' I demand now.

'Sounds gimmicky,' he says. 'While they're ramping up their membership, they've forked out for a lot of hosts. I mean, a lot. Ciara said most of the actual members there seemed to be men, which fits with what we knew anecdotally.'

'So they're going after the guys and throwing women at them,' I muse. 'Sounds more like a brothel than a sex club.'

'I suspect they're blurring that line,' Cal chips in. 'She said there were a lot of dancers, too. They have to make the place look busy. Overall, they're going for a very gaudy, Golden Age vibe, as far as I can tell. But it's sticking for some people.'

'I'm all for people having places they can let loose,' Rafe says. 'You know that. And we've made our name on discretion, which a lot of our members value. But these guys are going large.'

'Who the fuck is funding them?' I wonder aloud.

'It's a group of guys from various hedge funds,' Rafe says.

He reels off the names of several major funds based between here and Berkeley Square.

'Shit. So they're proper insiders,' I say.

'Yeah. And they have an insane network. Obviously, all their brokers from the City will go to them to curry favour. It's a total fucking shit-show.'

Jesus.

First Anton Wolff and now this.

I push myself off the desk.

I need a camomile tea to soothe my frazzled nerves.

9

GEN

A s I stride into the kitchenette as fast as my pencil skirt will allow, Maddy catches me up, sliding the door shut behind us and Zach's black lab, Norm, who's followed her in. He's as obsessed with her as Zach is.

'You okay?'

I grimace. 'I'm fine. I just let him get to me, that's all.'

'Did he upset you?'

'God, no.' I grab the kettle and pop the lid open so I can fill it from the tap. 'Want one?'

'Yeah, but builder's.' She takes two bone china mugs down from the cupboard and opens the tea caddies, pulling out an English breakfast teabag for her and a camomile one for me.

She knows me well. I drink coffee or camomile. Nothing in between.

It's odd how quickly Maddy and I have got close. We're not particularly alike. She's far younger than me, but I greatly respect her liberated approach to sex, and I think for that reason she's a good influence.

You'd think someone who co-founded a sex club and

'partakes' of its delights, to quote Anton Fuckface Wolff, would be emancipated as heck, but nope. My willingness to have sex with strangers belies the hangups that still plague me.

I actually see far more of myself in Rafe's girlfriend, Belle, who's Maddy's polar opposite. I may not have suffered the intense religious trauma that Belle has, but I've cultivated the same good-girl persona she has, with all the guilt and lack of agency over one's own mind and body that she's struggled with. And, while my father isn't the religious nut hers is, thank God, they're both patriarchal pricks who only value their daughters when we're playing ball.

That's why hanging out with Maddy is good for both of us. Besides, she's the sweetest, sunniest girl and she brings the light. The fun. She's a force for good, and the way she's bringing Zach and his daughters back to life is nothing short of miraculous to witness.

With the guys, I play the tough cookie. I give as good as I get. That's been our dynamic since our uni days. They treat me as one of them, even if, underneath all the banter and teasing, they'd die to protect me. Still, I tend to put up walls with them.

I tried to do the same with Maddy in the early days, but she was having none of it. She sort of gets under your skin and crawls past your defenses, and you just have to accept it and give in.

She's a bit like a puppy in that respect.

So when she asks me, 'What's the problem, then?' I have a feeling she already knows the answer.

'Ugh.' I put the kettle back on its stand and flick the power switch. 'I didn't like how he made me feel.'

'Uncomfortable?'

'Yep.'

'In a bad way?' she presses.

I fix her with a loaded look. 'In a *far too good* way.'

She presses her lips together and opens her eyes wide and squeezes her hands into fists like she's about to explode, and then, sure enough, a squeal escapes her.

'I knew it! I fucking knew it! Tell me, tell me.'

'Don't breathe a word of this to the boys,' I say. 'They'll be unbearable. Besides, I have no intention of acting on any of it.'

'Oh, bollocks to that.' She bends to pet Norm, who has his nose buried in her crotch as usual. 'Why wouldn't you go for it with him? He's sexy as fuck.'

'Because he's dangerous,' I tell her. 'He's not the kind of guy you fuck and recover from.'

I stand there and watch the kettle, and I squeeze my thighs together as I recall how heady it felt to be the object of Anton Wolff's attention.

Of his desire.

Make no mistake about it. If I got you on this bed I would be fucking relentless until I'd made you fall apart over and fucking over.

Over and over.

Jeeee-sus.

She makes a disappointed face. 'Really? You wouldn't be tempted to just... dabble? Have some hot sex with the hot billionaire? Did he have Big Dick Energy?'

'He had *very* Big Dick Energy,' I say, and she lets out a happy sigh.

'I knew it. Honestly, babes, I can see you guys being hot together. I know I always say this, but you need a proper grownup. You need someone with, you know, real gravitas. Like a proper power player.' She points a pink-painted fingernail at me. 'That's what he is. A power player. He's a real man.'

'You're not wrong. Norm, sweetie, move it.' I edge him out of the way before turning and pouring boiling water into our mugs.

'Is he kinky?' she asks. 'What did he say his kinks are?'

'NDA,' I remind her. I look up to find her screwing up her pretty little nose like a kid who's been told *no*.

'But I work here.'

'Yeah, but only the leadership team gets to see the applications.'

'Can't you tell me anything?'

I consider. 'I can't tell you the contents of his question-naire, but I don't see any reason why I can't tell you the inap-propriate things he said to me downstairs.' It's a shame I can't tell Mads the things Anton Wolff enjoys doing to women. She'd fucking love hearing them.

'Tell me *now*,' she insists.

'Well,' I say, dragging out the word like I'm trying to recall what he said, exactly. As if it's not emblazoned on my pussy's brain already. 'He asked me if I use the club. He went on and on about it, so I told him yes but that it was irrele-vant to him. And then, when I was showing him one of the rooms, he basically told me he knew I wanted it and suggested I'd been eye-fucking him throughout our interview.'

Maddy presses her lips together like she's enjoying this far too much. 'And?'

I attempt a nonchalant shrug. 'And then he told me he'd fuck me any which way but that if he got me into bed he'd be, you know, totally relentless.' I finish with a disapproving shake of my head, but Maddy's jaw is hanging open.

'Relentless? Oh my God. I'm actually turned on on your behalf.'

'Don't be. It's not going to happen.'

'But Gen.' She lowers her voice. 'It would be so fucking good. You know it would be. Jesus Christ, he'd be amazing!'

I roll my shoulders backwards in the hope that a straighter physical backbone will allow me to grow a mental one. 'Not helpful,' I say stiffly. 'Because it's not going to happen.'

She tut-tuts as she adds milk to her tea, but before she can say anything, there's a soft knock before the door slides open. It's Zach, gazing at her with hearts in his eyes.

'Sorry to disturb. I thought I'd grab you while you're in the kitchen.'

He's speaking only to Maddy, obviously. I grin at him, because seeing my friend this happy never fails to move me.

'She's all yours,' I tell him. 'Later,' I mouth at Maddy, who pouts at me before turning the full beam of her smile on her boyfriend.

As I leave the kitchen, nudging Norm out in front of me, Zach already has her bundled up in his arms.

10

ANTON

There's no sign of Genevieve Carew's platinum locks or tantalising arse when I finally get around to visiting Alchemy.

My shiny membership card arrived by courier a couple of days after I signed the final paperwork. To say I've been looking forward to road-testing the newest and most potentially hedonistic of my various playgrounds is an understatement, but work trips to Monaco and Sophia Antipolis over the past three or four weeks have prevented me from heading over there.

Until tonight.

I stay late in the office, shower in the palatial bathroom off my office and head straight over to Alchemy, clad in a brand-new version of my standard uniform: black trousers and a white shirt. Fortuitously, my Milan-based tailor hopped over to Monaco to measure me up for some new threads while I was down there.

The patrons may be obliged to behave themselves in the bar area, but the atmosphere is far headier than when I visited in broad daylight. It still has the vibe of an exclusive hotel bar, but there's an edge now. The women are dressed to the nines, exposing plenty of flesh, and the guys scream finance.

I've frequented far more hardcore kink clubs than this, where the clothing is more bondage-heavy. Tonight's attire is more playful, more luxuriously slutty than outright fetishist, and I like it.

The more expensive-looking the woman, the more enjoyable it is unravelling her.

And there are plenty of expensive-looking women here.

I'm nursing a scotch by the glowing pink bar and evaluating my many options when a guy approaches. He's dark haired and wearing a not dissimilar ensemble to mine. The honey blonde in the microscopic gold dress hanging off his arm is far younger than him, and a little skinny for my usual tastes, but so breathtakingly beautiful I'd be glad to make an exception. My initial take is that the calibre of women here is sky fucking high.

The guy holds out his hand.

'Mr Wolff? Rafe Charlton. I'm the CEO here.'

We shake, and I tell him to call me Anton. I suspect he doesn't suffer fools, which I like, but he's far friendlier than certain other people on his management team.

Probably because I'm not trying to get in his pants.

'This is my girlfriend, Belle,' he says, sliding an arm around her waist. The gesture reads as proprietary, its subtext clear.

I don't share.

I grin.

'How do you do, Belle,' I say in my most charming tone, and I'm rewarded with a blinding smile. She really is exquisite.

'Am I right in thinking it's your first visit?' Rafe enquires, tucking her into his side. She's golden and feline, and the easy sensuality of their embrace serves as an unwelcome reminder that committed relationships have their advantages.

'Yep,' I say, my eyes scanning the room. Over Rafe's shoulder, someone opens the double doors to The Playroom, and the fleeting glimpse I'm afforded of its dim mysteries has my appetite ratcheting up. I'll savour the anticipation over my scotch and then I'll dive right in.

'Genevieve here tonight?' I enquire casually.

Rafe frowns. 'Not sure, actually. I haven't seen her.'

'She's not,' Belle offers. 'She has a date.'

A *date*.

Is that so?

My displeasure must show on my face, because Rafe steps smoothly in.

'I wondered, Anton, if I could introduce a couple of friendly faces to show you the ropes once you head next door? I thought our hosts could make you feel at home.'

'Yeah,' I drawl. 'Good idea.'

If Ms Carew's not here then there's no reason not to sample as many of this club's delights as I can.

'Excellent,' he says. He looks off to the side and jerks his head in a *come hither* motion. There are two young women standing off to the side. They're both on the curvier side, both stunning, and both in identical, figure-hugging white dresses. One has pale skin and tumbling auburn curls, the other has dark skin, long black hair, and spectacular tits.

My interest is immediately piqued.

'Meet Jess and Alexia,' Rafe says. 'Your wish is their command. All our female hosts wear the same thing so you can spot them easily inside. Our male hosts are in black polo shirts and black trousers. Switch it up as much as you like.'

I glance at him. This delicious little minx may have tamed him, but I recognise something of myself in him.

I'd put money on him having been as predatory as they come before he set his sights on the ultimate prize.

I turn my attention back to Jess and Alexia. Their names are already imprinted on my brain. You don't get where I am without having a strong game when it comes to names and faces.

Without perfecting that gift for making everyone, male or female, CEO or servant, feel like the only person in the room.

'Good evening, ladies,' I say, enjoying the smiles they give me in return. I let my eyes rove over them, my gaze leisurely.

I tip the rest of my scotch back and plant the heavy crystal tumbler on the bar.

'Show me,' I tell them, nodding in the direction of the double doors as I slide an arm around the soft skin of their shoulders.

Anticipation is overrated.

11

GEN

I can't conceivably stay away from the club much longer.

It's my fucking club, for fuck's sake. I refuse to be deterred by the possibility of running into some random member. It is, quite frankly, ridiculous.

Besides, I need an orgasm at the hands of someone else. I'm burning up for it. That date last week with a commodities trader didn't extend beyond a quick dinner at Zuma. In my haste to wrap things up, I even turned down their caramel chocolate fondant, which is unheard of. I almost considered faking a goodbye and ducking back into the restaurant for dessert, but decided against it.

Somebody else has been eating a whole lot of dessert, by the sounds of it. My spies—okay, Belle and Maddy—tell me the Big Bad Wolff has a thing for eating pussy. He's been going down left, right and centre, bestowing *petites morts* among Alchemy's clientele with admirable largesse.

Rapacious is how Belle described his behaviour to me the other day when she popped into the office after work and

Rafe was otherwise engaged. It's an uncomfortably vivid description, and one that's stuck in my head.

Maddy, who spotted him earlier this week and got a brief view of him in action, as it were, before Zach dragged her off to a room and presumably fucked her senseless, told me she could sense his magnetism from across the room.

'He's got that kind of power you can't miss,' she said. 'You know? Like you just want to put yourself in his hands and let him do whatever he wants with you because you know it'll be so fucking good.'

I grimaced, because that was distinctly unhelpful.

'The hosts and clients are lining up for him,' she continued gleefully. 'Like, literally. There were a few of them bent over the Banquette for him the other night.'

The Banquette was more of a conveniently waist-high ottoman, but the nickname had stuck because the double entendre of *bonk-ette* was too good not to use.

Evil girl. If she was trying to goad me, it worked.

Which is why I find myself at Alchemy tonight, enjoying a coupe of champagne with the team at one of the low tables dotted around the outer area of the bar.

'You look so fucking hot, babes,' Maddy tells me, patting my knee.

I know I look good. I'm in a new dress that I treated myself to in the Harrods Superbrands section on Saturday, when I was attempting to get my kicks from shopping instead of orgasms. It's an Alexander McQueen number that's a feat of engineering.

Thin straps. Black lace over an opaque nude silk slip. Corsetry that has my tits on a platter and makes my figure look more hourglass than I may ever have achieved. I've been working out more lately, toning up, and I can feel the difference. My hair's swept up in an artfully messy chignon, and my heels are high and patent.

I'm perfectly put together, and I'm ready to be undone by someone skilful and appropriately appreciative.

'Thank you, darling,' I say, patting her hand. She's my biggest cheerleader, and she's a sweetie.

'We should have a threesome with Gen,' she tells Zach. 'Look how bloody gorgeous she is.'

The others hoot with laughter, and Zach rolls his eyes. I'm pretty sure he lives in a constant state of adoration, amusement and total bewilderment when it comes to Maddy.

'Do I need to put you over my knee and explain monogamy again?' he asks with a glint in his eye.

'Um, pretty much, yes,' she says, fluttering her eyelashes at him.

'Thanks but no thanks,' I tell her. 'She's all yours, Zach.'

I don't really do women. And, while I may have got naked and messed around with both Rafe and Cal on one particularly crazy evening in the early days of the club, it's something I drew a line under right after.

Those three guys are my best mates. Fucking them is of no interest to me.

Maddy's eyes widen and she squeezes my knee.

'What?' I ask.

'Behind you,' she hisses, her eyes darting to my face and over my shoulder again in a way that's anything but discreet. 'One decidedly vulpine billionaire.'

Oh, buggery shit.

I despise the roll of excitement that hits me right along-side the irritation at the knowledge that Anton Wolff is in the house.

The Big Bad Wolff has come out to play.

That's the thing about Alchemy. It's so in your face. There's no pussyfooting around and wondering if someone you spot in the bar area may be available. Interested in taking things further. If they're here, they're here for sex. Which is usually a good thing, but which can, at times, be an exceptionally bad thing.

Not that it's of any interest to me. I don't care if he's here, or who he puts his hands on, as long as it's not me. I raise my coupe to my lips and take a sip of perfect effervescence.

A second later, predictable as clockwork, I hear my own name. It sounds like a command, and that plain pisses me off. I dislike the fact that my entire body tenses at the sound, but I make sure to arrange my features into my preferred impassive mask before I crane my head around and up.

'Mr Wolff.' I shoot him my most obviously fake, tight smile. 'How delightful.'

'We've talked about this,' he says, a smile playing on his lips.

My smile tightens. 'Anton,' I concede.

'Better,' he says. He's indecently attractive in a pristine white shirt and black trousers, the cut of both of which is impeccable. From my position on a low stool, his size is even more apparent. The sheer force of his physical presence is such that he seems to loom over me when he is, in fact, standing a respectable distance away.

This is a man who knows how to take up space and embraces that advantage.

I could learn a thing or two from him.

He has a tumbler of whisky in his hand, and the flash of his cufflink as he tilts the glass in an unspoken toast makes me wonder what he does when he's getting ready to eat a woman.

Does he take the cufflinks off?

Roll those pristine white sleeves up?

Flex forearms that I just know are strong? Muscular? Perfectly tanned and hairy?

'Can I beg a minute of your time?' he asks.

I sigh inwardly. 'Of course,' I say, and I stand, conscious that all my so-called friends are watching this little exchange avidly.

Disloyal dicks.

As I round my low stool to face him, his gaze sweeps appreciatively down my body.

'Are you still sticking with your no-touching-each-other rule?' he asks in a low, intimate voice.

'I am,' I say, my voice a little less confident than I'd like. But it seems he gets the message, because he nods and rakes a hand through his thick, dark hair.

'Understood. It's a shame, though. You look perfectly lovely tonight.'

His brown eyes search my face for a reaction as he says it. I straighten my shoulders, determined to hold firm in the wake of an unexpectedly old-fashioned compliment. Coming from the guy who wondered aloud how many cocks I could take in one night last time I saw him, it's disarming.

I'm sure disarming people is one of the many weapons he has in his arsenal.

'Thank you,' I manage. 'Is that all you wanted to ask me?'

'I—no. I had a membership question. I'd like to recommend two of my friends for membership. Well, my chief of staff and one of my lawyers.'

He pauses.

I wait.

'I was wondering if you could fast-track them,' he says flatly.

'Absolutely not,' I say with a polite smile. 'But they're welcome to apply, just like everyone else. Anything else I can help you with?'

He twists his mouth with what looks like rueful amusement. 'Not unless you'd like to accompany me next door.'

'I'm sure there's no shortage of women who'd be delighted to accompany you next door,' I tell him, my polite, phony smile still plastered on my face. I want it to look phony. I want him to know this is one battle he's not going to win.

I just hope I can stay resolute and win the war, because, to quote his words, he, too, looks perfectly lovely tonight.

And I have a horrible feeling this could be a lengthy war of attrition.

We stand there, inches from each other, my face tilted up to his, and I think he's going to take no for an answer and bid me good evening. His expression is serious. Thoughtful.

But the next words out of his mouth shock me.

'Come and watch me, then.'

12

ANTON

'E*xcuse* me?' she asks.

I wasn't lying. She does look perfectly lovely. That body in that corseted dress is every fantasy I've ever had brought to life. Her pale blonde hair is loosely pinned back, leaving some tendrils framing her face. Her makeup is Old Hollywood—red lip, cat's eye—and she resembles an icon of the silver screen.

Lovely.

What's not lovely, but is instead seriously fucking frustrating, is her insistence on denying this charge between us. I may be an arsehole in many ways, but I don't make a habit of harassing women who genuinely aren't interested.

However, women who betray, with every lick of their lips and ravenous stare, the depths of their interest are fair fucking game.

It's ridiculous, and tedious, but if I'm a conqueror in the world of business, I'm a fucking Viking when it comes to getting what I want from the opposite sex.

And what I want is Genevieve Carew, naked and writhing and begging me for her orgasm.

I repeat my challenge. 'Come and watch me. You seem worried about trusting me, for some reason. I have no idea why, because if you trust me not to violate the codes of your club then surely you trust me not to violate your own codes, except in all the ways you need. So come and see me in action, as it were. Decide for yourself. And if you don't like what you see, for some unfathomable reason, then I'll leave you alone.'

She purses her lips, then shakes her head and takes a healthy swig of her champagne. 'You're fucking deranged.'

Hearing her swear is her first overt concession that I'm getting under her skin. And *that* is a shot of tequila to my bloodstream.

'Nope. I have excellent judgement in all things. I know you don't like me, for some reason. Probably because I make you feel intimidated. But you do desire me, just like I desire you. So let me de-risk the whole process for you. It's a generous offer. You get to see exactly what I have to offer while someone else road-tests me for you.' I lean in and grin down at her. 'And if you don't like what you see, fine. No harm done. But if you do... I'll give you the keys.'

I'm half expecting, at this point, to feel the full force of her remaining champagne splashing over my face. Stinging my eyes. But she doesn't throw it at me.

Instead she narrows those feline eyes and surveys me thoughtfully.

I stand there and afford her the same treatment. It's no hardship to match her stare.

'You just want to show off,' she says finally.

I grin. 'Exactly. What's the problem? Some lucky woman will get the full treatment.' I drop the grin and lower my mouth as close to her ear as I dare. 'But the performance will just be for you, Genevieve,' I whisper.

When I pull back, her blue eyes are fire.

'Fine,' she whispers through gritted teeth. 'I'll come take a look, see if your actions can live up to those words. Because you have a *lot* of words. But if I get bored watching, I'm out of there.'

'Sounds fair,' I say confidently. I can't believe she's going for it. She's deluding herself that she'll be anything less than transfixed.

'Two more things,' she says, holding up a red-tipped finger. 'You can't fuck any of the staff tonight. That's awkward for me and for them. And I'm not stepping foot in a private room with you. You can do whatever you need to do out in the open.'

'Done,' I say. 'Now, come on.'

I'm giving her half an hour before she's fucking begging for it.

13

GEN

I am officially unhinged.

I've agreed to watch a man fuck another woman in front of me, which is not that odd in itself, given we're in Alchemy.

What's odd is that I've had a physical reaction to this man that, much as it pains me to admit it, beats any curiosity or hunger I've felt for anyone in quite some time.

And what's downright disturbing is that he's propositioned me time and time again, and I've turned him down again and again because I'm too fucking scared of how he'd make me feel if I handed my body over to him, and now I have to watch some other woman take pleasure that should be mine and give him pleasure that should be mine to give.

I am so fucked up it's not funny.

I didn't miss the flash of surprise on his face when I conceded, before he covered it up with that trademark smirk.

He's such an arrogant twat. That I have a golden, wondrous opportunity to wipe that smirk off his face is my only consolation. Getting him off my back once and for all is the only silver lining.

Pretending to be unmoved as he fucks some lucky bitch right in front of me will require harnessing all the poker-face skills I've honed over the years, but it'll be worth the effort.

Worth the pain.

I'll zone him out and pretend I'm watching cricket or some other boring-as-fuck sport.

That's what I tell myself as I turn to the others. Anton's already moved away towards the doors to The Playroom. 'I'm going to put him in his place,' I tell them, jerking a thumb over my shoulder.

Belle's eyes are wide. Maddy looks positively thrilled, and I can tell she's jumped to a very incorrect conclusion as to what *put him in his place* means.

I shake my head. 'Not like that,' I mouth.

'You going to be okay?' Cal asks with a frown. The guys will always be over-protective of me, and I can tell they're not sold on Anton Wolff given the less-than-glowing character references I've given them.

'I'll be fine,' I promise him, and with that I spin around. Anton's waiting a little way away, hands in his pockets, his ram-rod straight posture radiating confidence.

Power.

With a single sentence, I could revoke my stupid rule and allow him to drag me beneath the surface of this ridiculous mask I wear.

But I know I'll stay silent.

'Make sure whoever you pick is okay with being watched,' I tell him as I nod to the burly doorman to let us through.

'Obviously,' he says.

I follow him through the doorway into the dim, pulsing space.

He cuts through the crowd like a starving panther, single-minded as he eschews less worthy prey in favour of the ultimate prize. I swallow as I weave between our members.

Alchemy is in full swing.

The pillars are softly up-lit in white and pink, the drapes billowing softly between them. One of my favourite burlesque dancers is performing tonight: Zeina. She's doing an elaborate fan dance while balanced on stage on the top of a plinth in nothing but a black thong and nipple tassels. She's mesmerising, but Anton ignores her as he stalks past several women pleasuring a ripped guy on one of the crosses with feathers and their mouths.

I imagine he's like this in business. Focused. Attuned only to his own thirst and the win that can slake it. And I choose to believe that his attention is as much on this woman behind him as it is on the woman he'll select to claim tonight. I choose to believe that my presence, our little arrangement, will add a frisson that his conquest alone could never provide.

He pauses.

Considers.

Moves in for the kill.

She's sexy rather than beautiful. Platinum blonde, like me. Fuller-figured, like me. I wonder if that's deliberate on his part. I wonder if Anton has a type, or if he wants me to see myself in the woman he's chosen so I can more readily imagine it's me in his hands.

As if I'd need help imagining that.

But, unlike me, this woman hasn't constrained her curves. Hasn't used thousands of pounds' worth of craftsmanship to wrangle them into submission to achieve the ultimate hourglass shape.

Instead, she's in a red silk slip dress that falls to her ankles and showcases her assets plainly. The straps are tiny. The neckline is draped low and reveals her tits swinging loosely beneath. Her puckered nipples. The soft curves of her belly. Her hips. Her thighs.

She looks ripe for plunder, and I can tell at a glance that however similar our physical types, our personalities are polar opposites. I shift slightly to the left, which puts them both in perfect profile. I have an unobstructed view of the two of them.

Anton plants a palm against the pillar behind her, effectively caging her in. He bends his head to whisper in her ear, and my pussy clenches on instinct at the undeniable dominance of his position. His desire for authority is consistent, it seems. I watch as her face tilts up to his and her body melts into the pillar.

He's got her already.

He hasn't touched her yet. He's talking softly. Grinning. Charming her before he moves in for the kill.

The man is a smiling assassin. He speaks to her again and her face turns in my direction. She gives me a smile that's bordering on smug, and I instantly want to slap her, but I can't blame her.

She should be smug as fuck.

I cross my arms.

She says something to him, and he lowers his head further so he can hear her. I can't see her face any longer, but I certainly see his fingertips trailing across the silk draped over her hip, wrinkling the fabric. It's a leisurely, assessing movement, and her body reacts instantly, arching against his.

He pushes off the pillar, straightening and flicking both her spaghetti straps off her shoulders so the flimsy fabric tumbles straight down and her breasts are bared. I draw in a breath at the uncompromising sight before me, because shit just got real. Anton's staring at her heavy breasts with a naked intensity that is far more stirring than anything I've imagined, and I have the distinctly unpleasant feeling that he's moved on from our game.

I bet he's already forgotten I'm here.

Her dress is pooled around her waist. She's let her head fall back against the pillar, her hands hanging at her sides. He slides his hands up the sides of her body before he cups her breasts. Fuck, he looks gorgeous. He's so fucking huge, standing there in his impeccable clothes as he openly pets a half-naked woman. Especially because she's seriously petite. He must have almost a foot on her.

He strums his thumbs over her nipples, and she opens her mouth in pleasure. I can't hear her moan over the heavy, sensual beat of the music and the carnal sounds of everyone else around us, but I don't need to.

I'd fucking moan if Anton Wolff did that to me. I'd be helpless to hold it in, no matter how desperate I was not to give him the satisfaction.

And then he gets to his knees in front of her.

14

GEN

'm not sure what I was expecting Anton to do for this little performance. He told me he likes dominating women, after all. I suppose I was expecting him to force her to her knees and fuck her mouth, but it looks to me more like he's about to worship her.

He's so tall that even on his knees he's pretty much level with her tits. He holds her in place against the pillar with a strong grip on her waist as he kisses his way up her stomach.

Fuuuuck.

Seeing Anton's sensual mouth on a woman's bare skin does serious things to me. Some guy comes up behind me and presses himself against me, sliding an arm around my waist. I'm getting more and more turned on by the second here, and the guy smells great, but, as much as I need his semi-hardness pressed up against my arse right now, there's no way in hell I'm letting someone get me off while I watch Anton.

That would tell him everything he needs to know: that watching him devour another woman is getting me hopelessly aroused.

I slap the guy's arm, and he gets the hint and moves away.

I wouldn't say I'm usually voyeuristic. I don't particularly get off on watching people having sex. It pains me to admit this is Anton-specific, because what I do get off on is watching the man whose mouth and hands I've imagined on myself using them on another woman.

Spelling out for me what I'm missing.

And I know he's only just getting started.

He continues to move that mouth up her body, over her skin, teasing one taut nipple with lascivious strokes of his tongue before latching on and sucking. *Hard.* I can tell by the way his jaw works. His cheek hollows out. And that lucky bitch bucks against him. His eyes drift closed as he switches between her nipples, alternating between laving and sucking. She's wriggling so much in pleasure that he's having to hold her in place with his hands. Her palms stroke down the pillar behind her as she seeks relief, her blonde head flailing from side to side, red lips open.

Her lipstick is still perfect, and that's when I realise he hasn't kissed her.

It's a tiny victory, but I'll take it.

Then he's pulling away, turning her roughly and edging backwards on his knees before pulling her hips away from the pillar. I think he says something, because she shuffles further back and bends over, laying her hands and forehead against the pillar. Her breasts hang free and heavy.

Anton leaves her like that for a second, releasing her hips, and when one hand goes to the opposite wrist, I realise what he's doing.

He's going to roll his fucking sleeves up before he gets stuck in.

Just as I fantasised.

The woman's big, shapely, crimson-silk-clad arse is waving in his face, but as he removes a cufflink and rolls one sleeve up, he turns his head and looks straight at me.

I blink.

He smirks and mouths two words.

Watch this.

He makes fast work of the other sleeve, sticks his cufflinks in his pocket with ease, and then he's tearing her dress down over her hips so it pools in a scarlet puddle at her feet, and she's naked except for her heels.

With a big hand on each of her arse cheeks, he parts them and licks her once, slowly, front to back. He keeps his face far enough from her pussy to afford me a clear and unwelcome shot of what he's doing. His tongue seems indecently large and long, his lick decadent and greedy.

Fuck me.

I'm dripping with arousal now. My nipples are rock fucking hard and chafing against the built-in bodice of my dress, my thighs rubbing together.

He sits back on his heels, makes a point of sticking three fingers in the air, and rams them inside her, crooking them. She jumps like she's about to shoot off the face of the earth. His watch glints in the dim light, and those fucking forearms are everything I hoped for—huge and hairy and tanned and taut.

But they're not the worst part of it. His long fingers disappearing into her cunt aren't the worst part of it, either.

Nope. The absolute worst part is the look on his face as he slowly and deeply and deliberately finger-fucks her. Because the thin veneer of respectability has been wiped clean away, leaving the animal he really is. His face is tense with want, his jaw clenched, and if he turned to face me I wouldn't be surprised to see his mouth twisted into an actual snarl, because the boys were right.

He is a fucking wolf.

And right now, she's his sexy Red Riding Hood, once crimson-clad and now naked for him, and I'm nowhere in this scenario.

I'm nothing.

Then he's leaning in again and tilting his head so he can get around his fingers to her pussy, where I can tell by the way his jaw's working that he's really fucking letting her have it.

Fuck my actual life.

Because watching Anton Wolff on his knees, devouring some woman's pussy, is the hottest, most carnal thing I have *ever* seen.

The rhythmic slide of his jaw.

The faint shadow of stubble that I'm sure feels seriously great for her.

The fact that his nose and mouth are buried in her completely, but I can still just about make out the dark fan of his eyelashes against one cheek as he works her.

She starts to come. I'm actually impressed she's lasted this long. I wouldn't have lasted thirty seconds in her place. Anton doubles down, licking and finger-fucking her, forearm muscles flexing, watch face glinting. Then he's getting to his feet behind her and looking around for a condom. He finds one on a poser table right beside him—condoms are everywhere in this place—and unbuckles his belt.

It's the moment I've been dreading.

He pushes down his trousers and his black boxer briefs just enough to free his cock, which springs up from between his shirt tails.

It is fucking gigantic.

Oh my Christ.

I have to physically restrain myself from clapping a hand over my mouth.

Then he fists it.

And he turns his head and looks straight at me.

15

ANTON

I'm used to being watched, but usually the thrill comes from knowing that the woman I'm fucking is beyond caring about our audience. That I'm putting her through her paces so thoroughly that all she can do is submit and enjoy the ride. That her inhibitions fall away, forgotten in a blaze of need.

The connection is between me and her.

The audience merely adds an edge.

In this moment, though, the connection is not between me and the attractive woman who's just come all over my tongue. She is, alas, a willing set of holes. She's the vessel into which I'm pouring my arousal and frustration, but the *connection* is between me and Genevieve.

As is this game of chicken we're playing.

I haven't allowed myself more than a couple of brief glances her way. I'm assuming the only reason she's agreed to this little charade is to prove a point. My fleeting looks in her direction tell me she's putting on a good show of disinterest.

But not good enough.

She has no idea who she's up against, bless her.

Because *I don't lose.*

I've been sexually active for almost four decades. I'm a fucking pro. Literally. And I have the upper hand here by a mile, because *I get to come, and she doesn't.* I can throw myself into this, I can gloat, I can blow my load, and I can fuck this woman into oblivion right before Genevieve's eyes while she stands there and battles to feign indifference.

With the game this rigged, I'm amazed she was reckless enough to step up to the table.

My cock is rock fucking hard, but it's the knowledge that Genevieve is watching my performance that has the pre-cum leaking liberally from its tip.

Because that's what it is.

A performance.

I've presented enough pitches in my career where the stakes are high. Where a ten-figure win is singularly dependent on my ability to execute.

To perform.

To impress.

But I've never pitched like this. I've never wanted to impress anyone as much as I want to persuade this beguiling, enigmatic, beautiful woman that I am not a man to turn down. That I'm worth taking a chance on.

I can't resist a glance at her as I fist my angry cock. I'm close to blowing, but, as in all things, I'll exercise self-control and hold off on my orgasm till I've delivered the performance of a lifetime inside this sexy, squirming little blonde.

Genevieve's still standing in the same position. Arms folded over her glorious tits, feet so close together I'd put money on the fact that she's clenching her thighs under that lace. Her face is still the same impassive mask, but her eyes give her away. They flash from my face down to my cock, and they widen. Her glossy pink lips part involuntarily, and I know I'm not alone in imagining them wrapped around my cock right now as she licks the moisture away.

I'm tempted to turn this girl around and get her on her knees and make her suck me off in front of Genevieve, but frankly, I'm too close to last, and I need her to see me fuck someone. I need her to witness my *pièce de résistance*.

I give her a smirk before dragging my eyes away from the emotions warring beneath the surface of her lovely face and focusing on tearing the condom wrapper. Rolling it carefully over my hard dick. Once it's on, I bend over the blonde so I can whisper in her ear.

I may like to abase women, in the sexual sense of the term, but I would *never* confuse that with disrespect. I fucking adore women, and I also adore making them feel amazing.

I'm going to make sure this one has the time of her life while she helps me out with this little favour.

'You tasted fucking delicious,' I say in the vicinity of her ear, loud enough for her to hear above the music. She's been waiting patiently like a good girl as I eye-fucked Genevieve, but now she wriggles that gorgeous, soft arse against me, and my dick twitches in appreciation.

'We're getting an audience,' I tell her. It's true. A few more people have gathered around us. One guy has his dick out, and another couple are touching each other as they watch us. 'We're going to give them a show. You just push back against me as hard as you can once we get going, okay? I'm going to make you explode.'

'God, yes,' she moans, and I smile in satisfaction.

'Good girl.'

As I slowly straighten up, I reach underneath her and cup her tits. Fuck, they're fantastic. Full and lush, hanging heavily. I strum her nipples, and she wriggles against me again.

Point taken.

I stand, and grab my latex-covered dick, and position the flared, angry crown right at her entrance. She really does have a lovely pussy—bare and pink and, thanks to my hand-iwork, wet as fuck. I may be big, but I don't think I'll need lube for her.

I push my crown in, gripping one hip hard to hold her in place. Fuck, that feels fantastic. She's tight, and I'm fucking desperate. Even with the barrier between us, her heat envelops me as her muscles accommodate me, clenching around my tip.

Jesus. I make a show of roaming my free hand, which is the one nearest to Genevieve, over the woman's flank, massaging her arse as I feed the rest of my length into her, inch by inch.

I'm sweating with effort, trying not to ram home too quickly so she has time to adjust to me. I bottom out, and her entire body stiffens for a moment before she pushes back against me with a luxurious shimmy of her hips, and I'm gone.

'Okay?' I say, leaning forward slightly. Her breathy *yes* is a green light where I'm concerned, and I let her have it, grip-ping her hips tightly and holding her up, because her upper body must be getting tired. I pull almost all the way out and drive back in with a powerful thrust of my hips.

Fuck. *Yes.*

God, this is everything. I may get a kick from the myriad of skills I use and abuse in the business world, from completing deals and calling stocks and manipulating people into doing what I want, but nothing, and I mean *nothing*, beats the feeling of having a hot pussy squeeze my dick with the finesse of a silk glove.

I force myself to make my movements as slow, as deep, as intentional as I can, not just to drive the woman I'm fucking crazy but because I have an audience.

And I want Genevieve to see everything. I want her to have the opportunity to appreciate the sight of my thick, hard cock disappearing into the soft, welcoming pussy of a woman *who is not her*.

I want her to regret every choice she's made since I walked into that meeting room, including the one where she allowed me through The Playroom's doors to plague her, and *especially* the one where she turned me down.

I want her wishing, with every last vestige of strength she has, that she could trade places with this woman. That she could be naked and at my mercy while I give her what she needs.

I want her so filled with longing and resentment that she caves.

That she begs me to put her out of her misery.

The ache is building in my balls as I power into the woman in front of me. The sweat is prickling on my forehead. And I can't resist a glance.

It takes Genevieve a second to meet my eyes, because hers are fixed squarely on my cock and that mask of hers has well and truly fallen. Desire is etched on every fucking feature of her beautiful face. Triumph surges through my veins as I drive forward, still watching her.

I'm close to blowing.

So. Fucking. Close.

But the triumph is short-lived as an uglier emotion comes over her.

It could be contempt, but I'm pretty sure it's hatred.

It's so damning that my instinct is to freeze, but I'm too far gone. My biological urges have taken over. I couldn't stop myself from coming now if I tried. Even if I pulled out.

As I shoot my load into the condom protecting this stranger from me, Genevieve shoots me one last filthy look and walks away.

16

GEN

I can't I can't I can't.

I can't stand there a minute longer and watch Anton Wolff's monstrous dick pump in and out of another woman while he holds the most intense eye contact with *me*.

I can't take the need on his face, the intensity, as he gets closer and closer. His thrusts don't falter. They're flawless. Smooth and rhythmic and unwavering. But I can see in his expression, in the dark eyes that are usually calculating and are growing more wild, that he's close to losing control, and that's the thing I really cannot handle.

Because it's too cruel.

I want to be the one that makes him feel that way. The one he unleashes all that glorious pent-up frustration on. And I *hate* that he's making me feel this way.

I mean, what the actual fuck? He's got me standing here, a lonely observer, as he does whatever the fuck he wants to her. I've gone from wondering what it would be like to have Anton Wolff let loose to *seeing* it with my own eyes, in such vivid detail I can never un-see it. And I'll be damned if I'm going to stay and watch him finish the job.

He knew exactly what this would do to me, and I'm a total fucking idiot for allowing him to reel me in, to hold me captive while he has the time of his life.

I don't fucking think so.

I do the only thing I have any power to do under the circumstances, which is also the thing I know will piss him off more than anything else.

I shoot him my best look of utter contempt, and I turn on my heel and walk away.

I need release.

Badly.

My first instinct is to lock myself in an empty room with a vibrator and get myself off as quickly and vigorously as possible, but that's plain depressing. Right now, I require the brutal comfort of a hard fuck.

I need a man's dick inside me, and I need him to be as desperate for it as Anton was. I don't wonder for a second if all that raging desire on his part came from a desire to fuck that woman into oblivion—he made it pretty clear at the end that I played a major part in it—but whatever twisted commutation the two of us were performing in his mind, it did the trick.

The guy was an angry bull, and I need precisely that.

I push through the crowd, through the throng of people dancing and naked bodies, to the bar.

'Vodka. Neat,' I tell Doug, the barman, holding out my hand. He grins and stamps it to show I've had my second drink before pushing a shot glass in my direction. I knock the clear liquid back to take the edge off any remaining inhibitions. Arousal is muddying my thoughts right now, but I still struggle to let loose, and I certainly don't share Rafe and Cal's total lack of qualms about fucking in this public space.

While I'm highly selective when it comes to the men I'm with, my tastes have changed somewhat since opening Alchemy. I'm no longer drawn to looks alone. Rather, it's a guy's vibe that draws me in.

Take Anton, for example. He's classically good-looking. Gorgeous, even. But that's not what makes me wish his head was between my legs in the darkest hours of the night. It's his demeanour. His attitude of power. Control. It's that dratted Big Dick Energy again. I swear to God, BDE will get me on my knees far faster than any amount of model good looks. I'm far more interested when a guy radiates the kind of confident competence that lets you know you're guaranteed a good time.

Speaking of which.

I cast my gaze around the people nearest to me and clock a guy at the other end of the bar. He's around my own age—mid-thirties. I've seen him in here before, but we haven't interacted since his interview, and I can't actually remember his name.

Right now, that's probably a good thing.

He's Mediterranean-or-further-east-looking, his hair slicked back into what's either a man bun or short ponytail —I can't see—and there's something in his arrogant expression and cruel mouth that tells me he'll give it to me good.

Our eyes lock. I put down my empty shot glass and lean an elbow on the bar, letting my body curve as my hip juts out. Sure enough, his eyes travel from my face to my tits, all the way down and back up again. I raise my eyebrows in silent challenge, and he takes it, coming towards me.

He's tall and rangy and wearing all black, his shirt open enough to reveal olive skin and just the right amount of chest hair. His beard is black and perfectly trimmed. I'd be absolutely amazed if he wasn't in finance. I can tell a hedge fund guy a mile off.

He keeps on coming until we're almost toe to toe, then bends his mouth to my ear. 'What do you need?' he asks in a broken accent. Lebanese, maybe? Turkish? I seem to be on a roll with Turks. 'Can I taste you?'

I shake my head against his face. 'No.' There's no time for that. 'I need to be fucked. Hard. Think you can do that?'

He pulls up and grins at me. He's definitely hot, and he looks dirty as fuck. He's not Anton Wolff, but two out of three ain't bad. 'Come with me, beautiful,' he says, and puts his hand out.

Okay, so his chat's not great, but frankly, his mouth's not the body part I'm interested in.

There's a section on this side of the room that's even darker than the rest of the space. Heavier drapes provide a screen. It's not totally private, but it's far less in your face. When he leads me in, there are what looks like three bodies entangled in the far corner, but I'm way past giving a shit.

All I can think about is being filled up like Anton filled that woman up.

'So you want it rough,' he says. It's not a question. The smile has gone, and a frisson of nervous excitement shudders through me.

'Yes.'

'Dress off.'

I turn and present him with my back. He makes quick work of the zip, sliding it all the way open so he can push the dress down over my hips.

'Fuck me,' he says, his voice strangled, and I can tell my lingerie has hit home. Black lace bra. Matching suspender belt that rises to my waist and gives me definition. No knickers.

Easy access.

'On the sofa,' he says. 'Hands and knees.' He prods me in the back, and I sashay over to the nearest huge sofa, positioning myself lengthways on it like he asked. I wiggle my bare arse as he gets on behind me, kicking my legs further apart with his knee.

'Condom,' I say.

'Sure, baby.' I can't hear much above the music in here, but the shuffling behind me tells me he's getting his dick out and wrapping it up. He runs his knuckles right between my cheeks. Grazing over my wetness from back to front. Assessing. A couple of fingers ram inside me, hard, and the intrusion reminds me of Anton finger-fucking that woman in front of me.

I close my eyes.

In my mind, Anton's entering the alcove and spotting us. He shoves this guy out of the way and takes over, his long fingers probing, scissoring inside me. Demanding everything from me and sparing me nothing.

God, that's good. This is what I need. I need someone who knows what they're doing to take all this useless fucking turmoil I'm in and channel it. Harness it. Mould it into something beautiful, something I can use to turn myself inside out in exactly the way I need.

The guy's fingers continue to stretch me as his thumb finds my clit. He rubs it hard, and I moan. Anton would kill for this, I know he would, and the thought sends desire coursing, hot and heavy, through my veins.

For all the misery and humiliation he put me through just now, I have something he wants and can't have, and that is a glorious kernel of knowledge. Yeah, he got his rocks off, but I was the one who turned him down. He wants to touch me, and instead some random is fingering me and playing with my swollen clit and getting ready to fuck me.

He leans over me and mutters something. I hear the word *wet* and I nod. Come on, mister. Knock yourself out. It's pretty obvious I'm ready.

Then the blunt latex-covered tip of his dick is lining up at my entrance. He massages my arse cheek and then slaps it before smoothing his hand over it again. I wriggle with pleasure against him, and he pushes in.

Oof.

He's *big*.

That's a bonus.

He shoves all the way in, hard, and the intrusion knocks the breath out of my lungs. Oh my *God* that's good.

I exhaust myself on a daily basis with endless rumination and second-guessing and over-thinking. And I have solutions. Wine. Epsom salt baths. Nineties thrillers. But there's nothing that can quiet my mind like being rammed full of the rigid length of a man's cock.

It's the most sublime sensation I can ever conceive of. It obliterates all thought, all insecurity, all inhibition. It's my favourite kind of takeover.

I dig my hands into the pleather of the sofa, which doesn't offer me much purchase, and brace myself as hard as I can against his thrusts. He's not holding back. I wanted rough, I'm getting rough.

He reaches one hand underneath and squeezes my breast through the lace of my bra, his fingers rubbing harshly at my nipple. The friction is perfect, and I tell him so by arching my back and pushing against him on his next thrust. I'm not interested in drawing this out; I want this quick and dirty for both of us.

In and out he drives. In and out. He's big and he's good and he's kind of savage, which is truly excellent.

This isn't how it would be with Anton, though. I mean, it would undoubtedly get like this at the end, but he'd start slow. Totally in control. He'd punish me for making him wait. I know he would, sadistic fucker that he is. But I also know that finally getting inside my body would be too much for him. That even *the* Anton Wolff is only human.

I saw that on his face a few minutes ago. He may not have been inside me, but the ravaged look on his face was that of a man about to go under. About to be subsumed by his needs.

The thought of it has me burning up. As this guy pumps me, dragging his sizeable dick up and down against the nerve endings of my internal walls, the fantasy of Anton struggling to contain himself, to fight this, to quash the demons of lust that I know consume him as much as they consume me, engulfs me.

It's not my temporary fuck-buddy's ragged breaths and grunts I hear behind me, but Anton's. And as the heat ignites into flame across my body and a stranger hits the part of me that detonates my entire nervous system into beautiful nothingness, it's Anton's anguished face I see behind my eyelids.

17

GEN

I'm sitting at my desk, processing new membership applications and barely being able to read them because I'm so preoccupied by the events of last night. I may have got myself a good seeing-to, but the only image in my head is that of Anton, his eyes fixed on mine, dark and desperate as he rammed home inside somebody else.

Over and over.

Sometimes your life choices really do come back to bite you in the arse.

When the boys pitched the concept of Alchemy to me, I was sceptical, to say the least. The commercial side of me was hooked, but the uptight, good girl, sex-is-something-for-behind-closed-doors side was actually quite shocked.

Horrified, even.

It was Cal who got to me in the end.

'As long as we've known you, you've complained about men not having a clue in bed,' he pointed out. 'And I'm sure that's true for some guys, but let's not bullshit each other. We all know you're a lot kinkier than you let on, so for fuck's sake, here's your chance to do something about it.'

He sold me on the concept of a beautiful, exclusive space where I could come and be me. The real me. Not the me I'd always been at such pains to project.

Not the former head girl.

Or the netball captain.

Or the JP Morgan associate who got promoted to VP a year ahead of all her peers.

The me who had an itch no guy could ever scratch.

And look at me now. My itch has become, figuratively speaking, a full-body rash, and there's only one person who I want to scratch it.

Fuck my life.

It's only when the doorbell rings and Maddy returns from answering it that I snap out of my stupor. She's standing in front of my desk, holding an immaculate bouquet of camellias out to me.

They're stunning. I didn't even know you could get camellia bouquets. I guess you can if you're Chanel, which is what these seem to be, given the black square logo-ed carrier bag they've come in. Does Chanel normally do flowers?

The bag is small and neat, perfectly sized for the bouquet, which features only the most flawless white camellias and a few of their shiny, dark green leaves.

Maddy holds out a white envelope bearing the double C logo and my name.

'Who delivered these?' I ask her.

She shrugs. 'Courier.'

I break open the black wax seal and pull out the card. It reads:

I wish it had been you last night.

And if you think this is me playing games,
I can assure you I'm doing precisely the opposite.
A.
PS these flowers remind me of you

Fuck fuck fuck.

18

GEN

'How's tricks?' I ask my baby sister. Darcy is twelve years younger than me, and possibly an even bigger disappointment to my parents than I am. While I was overachieving at prep school, my mum suffered miscarriage after miscarriage. Her successful pregnancy came long after she and Dad had given up hope, and when Darcy arrived, she needed to do nothing to earn their love.

She was adored for exactly who she was. And quite rightly. She was, and is, the most perfect, adorable and good-natured person on the planet. Unhappily for my parents, she rejected their babying from an early age, acting out and demanding autonomy on every front.

I should have paid more attention. I could have learnt from the master. It took me far longer to demand my own autonomy rather than trying to please everybody else.

The way my sister and I have turned out is fascinating to me. It's no major surprise that I finally broke and decided to be my own woman. It's more surprising that Darcy, who'd never had to lift a finger to get attention or adoration, reacted so strongly and was so intent on not giving an inch from a young age. I suspect she found my parents' love stifling.

In any case, whereas I'm straddling the uneasy divide between respectability and being my authentic self, Darcy has no such qualms. She's currently in Brisbane, where she's working in a bar far dodgier than Alchemy as a dancer.

'Tricks are very lucrative,' she says through my computer screen with a wink.

I bet they are. She's fucking gorgeous. Whereas I keep my curves in check through a strict workout regimen, she has the toned physique of a dancer without compromising the arse and tits men love.

'They'd be more lucrative at Alchemy,' I tell her with a wink.

'Winter here is better than summer there,' she retorts, and I know she has a point.

'What time is your shift?' I ask.

She stretches languorously. She's catlike in her movements. She's the most physically unselfconscious person I've ever met. 'I need to leave in half an hour.'

Working in a bar suits my sister. She's a night owl. I, less so. I sip my camomile tea and consider how well she looks. How glowy. I need to get my arse on a Mediterranean sun lounger before the summer is over. Maybe I'll see if any of my girlfriends are keen, though an alarming number of them are loved up now.

'Thought so,' I say. 'You're looking particularly slutty.'

'And you look like an uptight pain in the arse.'

We screw up our faces affectionately at each other. God, I miss her.

'You still shagging that surfer?'

She smiles her signature catlike smile. We've been told

we have identical smiles, but I doubt I look as sexy as she does when she does it.

'Yep,' she says dreamily. 'Ryan. Hot as fuck. Bit basic, but he loves going down on me, so I'm not complaining. You're getting plenty of action, I assume, you dirty bitch?'

I laugh, though it's not fucking funny, because the King of Pussy is eating everyone but me. And it's all my fault. I wouldn't confide in anyone about this humiliation, but Darcy is Darcy. She's my sister, and the least judgemental person on the planet, so I take a deep breath.

'You sounded so Aussie when you said that. And I have a little conundrum, actually. Between us.'

She grins and wiggles her eyebrows. 'Do tell.'

'A guy's joined the club,' I say. 'Very wealthy, very high profile. He's pursued me from the get-go. I mean, right from his initial interview. But he's an arrogant shit, so I told him I'd never let him lay a finger on me.'

I sigh.

Darcy grins. 'You're such a self-sabotaging twat. Let me guess—now you're gagging for his cock?' She swigs at her Red Bull. I don't know how she drinks that stuff, but she has a long night ahead of her, I suppose.

'Nicely put,' I say, though I would most definitely be gagging *on* his cock if I got out of my own way. 'But it's worse, actually. He kind of challenged me to, um, watch him the other night in the club. So I did.'

I have the gratification of watching my sister choke on her Red Bull. Serves her right. When she's recovered, she splutters, 'Are you actually insane?'

'It's very probable,' I tell her. 'And if I wasn't insane before I saw his donkey dick and watched his jaw move when he ate her out, I definitely am now.'

'So do it,' she says, waving a hand. 'Your problem has always been that you overthink everything. Just fuck him.'

'I definitely *under*-thought letting him give me a full porno audition,' I tell her, 'and that didn't work so well for me. But he sent me this beautiful bouquet of camellias yesterday with a note saying he wished it had been me the night before, so...'

I trail off at the look on my sister's face. Her jaw is practically on the floor. 'Oh my God,' she says. 'That's so *sexy*. So what the hell is your problem?'

'My problem is I feel like a conquest. He's like a dog with a bone. He's not used to women turning him down—that's for sure—so he's determined to fuck me just to prove a point. That's my take, anyway.'

She frowns. 'Could be. Or he could be genuinely interested.'

'I don't think so,' I say drily. 'He can have anyone he wants, and I'm not sure I'd ever recover if he fucked me and dumped me.'

She makes a sympathetic moue with her mouth. 'What kind of a celebrity is he, anyway? Is he, like, an actor or something?'

'No, nothing like that,' I say. 'He's a very successful entrepreneur—he's well known in business circles. But because he's drop-dead gorgeous, and he's a billionaire, he has a *lot* of groupies.'

She slams her can down on the table. 'Oh, for fuck's sake,' she says with a sigh. 'You've just ruined it all. You can't get together with him. Well, you can fuck him, but you can't be a thing.'

'Why not?' I ask, amused.

'Because can you even imagine Mum and Dad if you bagged a billionaire? They'd be fucking unbearable. The fact that you're a dirty, sex-club-owning ho would be swept under the carpet and all would be forgiven.'

'God, yeah,' I say. 'They'd be far too happy.'

'How are they, anyway?' she asks in a quiet voice.

I shrug. 'The same. Haven't seen Dad in a while. I had lunch with Mum a couple of weeks ago when she was up here and it was all relentlessly shallow and upbeat, and so fucking pointless. You know, so-and-so's daughter from the golf club is engaged to an obstetrician. That kind of bullshit. She didn't ask me about work once.'

She groans. 'Ugh. I'm never coming home. I couldn't bear it.'

'Come and see me,' I say softly. 'I miss you so much. And Maddy wants to meet you. I've told her all about you.'

My baby sister is dancing in a bar on the other side of the world, and I can't help but wish she was home so I can keep an eye on her.

19

ANTON

'I have Genevieve Carew on the line for you.'

One of my PAs, Rix, sticks her head through my office door. Unlike my EA, my PAs only do actual office work. Like her, they're very good at what they do.

I smirk to myself as I nod at Rix. 'I'll take it.'

Well, well, well.

The flowers I sent Genevieve last week were met with a stony silence, but I had a feeling my latest move might prompt a response. Not that I did it to rile her.

I did it because when I see an opportunity, I always act.

Winding her up was merely a beautiful bonus.

I accept the call on speaker. 'Wolff.'

Her voice comes through, crisp and melodic and pissed off.

'What the fuck do you think you're playing at?'

I grin widely. Christ, that woman needs a good seeing to, and the sooner she accepts it, the better for everyone.

'Good morning to you too, Genevieve,' I say smoothly, settling back in my armchair for a little light verbal sparring, which is always my favourite form of foreplay.

'Why did your henchman email Rafe to call a meeting?'

'That's the point of the meeting,' I explain as if she's a small child. 'To lay it all out for you.'

'We're not for sale, if that's what you're thinking. So there's no point in sniffing around.'

'I'm not trying to buy you, *Genevieve.*' Ah, the imprecision of the English language. Usually cause for rue, but the ambiguity of the word *you* in this instance allows for some entertaining subtext.

'What do you want, then?'

'I have a proposition for your management team. Very little risk to you guys and a lot of upside.'

'It sounds sketchy.'

'It's not.'

'Why did you email him?' she demands. 'I'm your contact.'

Ahh, the little lamb is jealous. So sweet. 'Firstly, I didn't email him. My chief of staff, Max, did. And while your possessiveness is truly touching, Max emailed Rafe because he's the CEO, unless I'm mistaken?'

Silence, though I swear I hear a huff of annoyance. My favourite ice queen is far worse at concealing her reactions than she gives herself credit for.

'Get over yourself. And Rafe doesn't take meetings unless he knows the agenda up front,' she says. 'None of us do. It's a waste of time.'

'I'm hardly some random. I am, objectively speaking, the highest-profile serial entrepreneur in this country. Come on, Genevieve. People would kill for a minute of my time. And here you are, blowing me off because you're pissed off about the other night. Don't let whatever unfounded ill feelings you have for me get in the way of business. I'm excellent at what I do. And I have a *business* proposal for your team that could kick Alchemy up a gear. Several gears. So do I get a meeting or not? Because most business owners would kill to get into bed with me.'

God, I am king of subtext today. I let that image linger between us for a moment.

'Fine,' she grits out.

I nearly say *good girl*, but stop myself just in time. 'Excellent. I'll get my assistants to set something up. Now, what are you wearing?'

'Stop being a creepy old man. What the hell is wrong with you?'

I snigger. I can't help it. She's quite ridiculous. There's nothing old about me or my stamina, and she damn well knows it. 'Just tell me.'

'Dior.'

'I didn't ask *who* you were wearing, I asked *what.*'

'That's all you're getting. Now please go away and stop wasting my time. Don't you have an empire to run or something?'

She's right. I shouldn't have taken the call. I shouldn't even be bothering myself with this spark of an idea. Max could kick-start it easily and allocate a VP to run with it, but I can't help myself.

First, it gets me closer to her.

Second, no matter how many decades I spend in business, this is the part that still gives me the biggest kick. My more mature businesses, like Wolff Media and Wolff Property Holdings and Wolff Chemicals, with their complex structures and stable cash flows and nice, dependable dividends bore the utter fuck out of me. Trying to implement any change in those beasts is like turning the Titanic.

It's the kernels that get to me, that make me feel like a boy again.

This isn't even a kernel, in the grand scheme of things. It's more of a pet project. Something to amuse me while I run my other businesses at arm's length. Something to light that fire in my belly—the fire that grows tougher to ignite the more my success, my entrenchment in British industry, grows.

But I won't admit any of that to Genevieve. Not yet, not when she gives me so little back.

'You called me, remember,' I say, my tone colder now. 'I took the call as a courtesy.'

'Whatever,' she says, her tone clipped. 'Goodbye, Anton.'

'I meant what I said on that card,' I tell her, and I end the call before she can respond.

20

ANTON

I'm back in the room at Alchemy where Genevieve first interviewed me. Only this time we're not alone. There's no big board table here—I suppose it would be odd if a sex club had a boardroom.

Instead, we're on the huge modular sofa where I sat last time. Its three sides more than accommodate us—that is me, Max, my good friend and Wolff Enterprises' Senior Counsel, David, Genevieve, and four of her colleagues. Rafe, who I met at Alchemy on my first night, and three others. I'm introduced to them as her co-founders Zach, the FD, and Callum, who runs their events, as well as a startlingly beautiful younger brunette called Maddy who's apparently their social media manager and is sitting in on the meeting to 'get experience.'

I'm not sure that's strictly necessary, but she's so easy on the eye that I'll happily allow her presence. I don't miss anything, though, and I've already seen Zach stroke her bare arm when he thought no one was looking, as well as a fair amount of mutual eye-fucking, so I suspect there's more to that relationship than a purely professional one. Fair play to him—she's a stunner, if a little on the slim side for my liking.

The immaculate blonde in the curve-skimming sleeve-less dress is far more my style. She's fucking magnificent, and she even deigned to break her no-touching policy long enough to give me a brisk, schoolmarmish handshake when I came in that did nothing to dent my interest level.

I'm glad she has some professional courtesy, at least.

She's currently sitting on the opposite side of the sofa and trying her best not to look at me.

That's fine. It's her prerogative. She can ignore me all she wants, but it won't undo the fact that she stood there last week and watched me eat and then fuck another woman while her gorgeous face told me far too much about how aroused that made her.

David's presence today is probably no more necessary than Maddy's, but I've wheeled him out to show the Alchemy team I'm serious about this. Besides, I'd be amazed if Genevieve didn't try to find a million ways to kibosh this project before it even began, so having a lawyer here to out-argue her will be both helpful and gratifying.

'Thanks for making time to see us,' I say to kick things off. It's not faux humility. Everyone has time constraints, and they seem to be a small team. From everything I've seen at Alchemy so far, they run a shipshape operation.

'It's our pleasure,' Rafe says.

'I'll get to the point.' I lean forward, elbows resting on my spread knees and fingers steepled. 'We're interested in licensing the Alchemy brand and taking it to the South of France this summer for a pop-up club during peak season. We'd do all the work, but we'd use your name and your brand attributes, your network, and, of course, your membership vetting policy. Think of it as a low-risk way for you to size up the market in Europe. Deliver proof of concept.'

Callum's entire face breaks into a grin, and I know he's already mentally there, fucking any amount of hot European chicks.

My kind of guy.

Rafe and Zach's faces are impassive. Maddy's eyes widen, but she clamps her lips together like she's trying to stay quiet.

Genevieve lays her pen on top of her notebook and watches me steadily through her clear blue eyes.

I sit back and spread my hands wide. 'Thoughts?' I won't give any more away until I've heard their knee-jerk reaction.

Rafe speaks first. 'Time frame?'

'First weekend in July to the end of August.'

'That's seriously tight,' Gen says. 'What's the rush? Why not plan it properly and try for next year?'

'Because then we've wasted a year,' I tell her. I lean forward again. 'In my experience, it's best to act fast, pilot these things fast, and fail fast if you're going to fail. I have no idea what expansion plans you guys have, but if you wait till next summer you've wasted a year.

'If this goes well, you have a minimum viable product, as it were, by the end of the summer that means you could take it wherever you want next year—Ibiza, Mykonos, The Hamptons. Anywhere. I'm offering you the perfect opportunity for a dry run at no financial risk.'

'There's a lot of reputational risk, though,' Genevieve says. 'If we try to rush this through and it goes wrong. Especially on the application side. All we need is one incident and our brand takes a massive hit.'

'You're one hundred percent correct,' Max cuts in smoothly. 'That's by far the most important thing to get right. The rest of it—licences, staff, venue—we can execute on easily. But this experiment lives and dies on Alchemy's brand. Which is why we'd propose a couple of things. First, you guys oversee the membership selection process, or at least commit time to training up staff at our end who can handle them appropriately.

'And second, we'd start with your own black book. Anton tells me the clientele here feels very European heavy. Am I right?'

'You are,' Genevieve says.

He flashes her a winsome grin. Sleazy twat. He knows exactly what my dynamic with her is, and he's attempting to charm the pants off her anyway. 'I hope to find out for myself someday soon. David and I applied this week.'

Gen smiles, cat-like, and I can already tell he's in.

Motherfucker.

'The most effective way to duplicate the culture you've built here is to offer your members automatic access to the French club if they're willing to pay an add-on fee,' he says. 'Or you could reduce the fee. I'm sure things quieten down around here over the summer, right?'

'It's dead,' Callum says. 'Especially in August. And yeah, a lot of our members are from Southern Europe. I suspect a tonne of them end up on the Côte d'Azur.'

I take over again. 'So make them founding members, if you like. It keeps the culture intact, they get their friends to sign up—it helps with word of mouth and with reputational risk. And you guys get a financial boost during the quieter months. What do you think?'

21

ANTON

Zach, who's been nodding and processing, speaks up. 'It's a decent hedge. I'm surprised we haven't thought about doing it before.'

'Cal and I have thrown it about,' Rafe tells him. 'We didn't think you'd go for it.'

'We'd put up the money,' I point out. 'There's no need for you to find room in your budget. You take a flat licensing fee or a revenue split.'

'Revenue split,' Zach and Rafe say at the same time, and I grin. Not only is this proving far easier than I expected, but these are my kind of people. There's no way they'd leave potential upside on the table.

Neither would I.

'Are you thinking St Tropez?' Callum asks. I give him my full attention. He's a good-looking guy—I can appreciate that. He has *party boy* written all over him, too. I reckon he's the most hedonistic of the lot of them.

'Cannes,' I tell him. 'St Tropez's tempting, but the infrastructure in Cannes is a lot better, and it's easier for Monaco. We'd have our pick of venues. We could go for a classic club concept, like Jimmy'z, or we could stick with the aesthetic you've got here but transfer it to a Belle Epoque villa. Alchemy, but with half the action outside.'

I know we're onto a winner. We have a proven brand and formula prime for transference to one of the sexiest, most exclusive party destinations in the Med.

It'll be a fucking money-printing machine, and this little pilot is merely the beginning. Because I may not be angling to buy these guys outright, but acquiring the rights to any future overseas operations could fit nicely into the Wolff Property Holdings portfolio.

'Look, it's an interesting idea,' Rafe says. He holds up a hand like he's trying to slow things down. 'But Gen's the COO. She's the execution expert. You make a strong case, but at the end of the day, she's the one who'd have to do the bulk of the work at our end to make it happen.'

So she's *Gen* to these guys.

Hmm.

I love the name Genevieve.

It's feminine and elegant and timeless.

Just like her.

But now I have a new goal.

To get on *Gen* terms with Genevieve Carew.

She is, predictably enough, shaking her head. 'I don't know.'

'Talk to me,' I order. My voice is sharper, my tone more commanding, than I mean it to be, but she responds instantly, even if that response takes the form of her straightening up and glaring at me.

'It's one of those ideas that looks great on paper but would be a total nightmare to execute in the space of two months,' she says, twirling her pen between her fingers. She breaks eye contact to look down at her notebook. 'The reason Alchemy works well is that we've taken our time to make every detail perfect. Rushing this through could be an unmitigated disaster. You don't mess around with stuff like this.'

I don't want to patronise her, but it's clear this club is a passion project for the four of them, and they've done a great job. But this is the big leagues, and I'm not sure they understand what's possible.

'When you have deep coffers, like we do,' I explain carefully, 'we can make a lot of the problems go away through sheer force of manpower. Two months sounds like a short amount of time, but we can put as many people on it as we need, and we can hire the best people on the ground. My team has launched fully fledged companies in the past in less time. David?'

David shifts forward beside me and brandishes a folder. He's quieter than Max is, an eagle-eyed observer. 'This isn't a contract, but we've drawn up a list of the issues we'd foresee both parties wanting to include in any legal agreement.

'Anton's right. Two months is a generous amount of time where we come from. There would be a time commitment required from you and your team to transfer knowledge so our guys can execute. The attached is extremely comprehensive, but we'd consider any additions your lawyers would want to make to the final contract.

'If you see fit to transfer any salaried staff to the pop-up for the summer months, we can adjust the revenue share agreement accordingly to reflect staff costs at your end. All we ask is that you turn any paperwork around as quickly as possible, because clearly time is of the essence. I've got a big legal team—we can draft all the terms for expediency and your lawyers can make edits. But we'd need contracts finalised and signed within a week so we can crack on.'

'Would you take our advice on events?' Callum asks.

'Let me make this clear,' I tell him. 'This is your brain-child. You're the experts—you know what works. We're the executors. You control the details. We make them happen, down to every last, I dunno, cocktail napkin. Every condom. Got it?'

I've deliberately planted the word *condom* to remind them what's at stake here. We're talking about taking the best orgy in London to the home of the Med's most beautiful people. It'll be fucking amazing. And if Genevieve continues to freeze me out, I'll up sticks to my pad in Antibes for the summer and fuck every European in sight.

'I still think St Tropez would be amazing,' Callum says with a sigh. 'Like Nikki Beach, but with people fucking everywhere.'

'If you don't think people fuck everywhere at Nikki Beach, you haven't been paying close attention,' Genevieve says drily. 'Besides, I far prefer the idea of a mansion. No one wants sand in their vagina, Cal.'

That raises a laugh around the room.

And as for me? Genevieve just said two dirty words and openly praised one of my suggestions.

I'll take that as a win.

22

GEN

There's a moment of silence as Rafe shows Anton, Max and David out. By unspoken agreement, we're waiting for him before we discuss this bombshell.

I glance down and tap my pen against the fat list of legal considerations David left with us. He's certainly thorough. There are things here it wouldn't have occurred to me to include, and the suggested waiver for staff and members alike is frankly terrifying at first glance.

They're an impressive team, no doubt about it. I'm not sure why such big guns are bothering with something as small as a little Alchemy pop-up. It's below their pay grade, surely.

Especially Anton.

He came here for you, a little voice says in my head. Even though he didn't do or say anything inappropriate. Even though he didn't flirt with me in the slightest. Something tells me he wouldn't bother himself with a project this minor if he didn't have an ulterior motive.

That same instinct tells me he's playing a long game.

How does that saying go?

Long term greedy.

Damn it, he's hot when he's in tycoon mode. Nothing impresses me more than intelligence and competence, and he has both in spades. He's earned the gravitas that oozes from every pore. He's achieved his experience the hard way, and we can learn from that.

We're all highly qualified professionals, but Alchemy is still very small scale. Yes, the guys have made a small fortune from their hedge fund, Cerulean, in which I'm a happy investor, but this is a chance to play with the big boys.

It's far harder to turn that down than to reject a mere opportunity to boost the coffers over the summer.

I liked David and Max, too. David seems very serious, Max very charming. They're both strikingly attractive. David's simply beautiful—tall and Black with a closely shaved head, eyes so dark you can't see his pupils, and possibly the best posture I've seen on a man.

Max is hot in that quintessentially English way where he's utterly charming but quite obviously filthy as fuck just below the surface. He should be too pretty, with his Matt Bomer-esque looks and perfectly coiffed fair hair, but there's something predatory in those thoroughbred features that gives him an edge.

At face value, they look like the perfect Alchemy members. I scribble down a note to take a look at their applications later. It would definitely help on the execution front if they have hands-on experience, to use an unfortunate turn of phrase. And I suspect the female members would thank me for letting these two into the mix.

Rafe strolls back in, hands in his pockets. 'Well?' he says.

I take a breath. 'It's fraught with potential disasters, but this is a lot more than just a pop-up. He's basically offering to flex our business model for us and see how much opportunity it has for expansion.'

Rafe nods. 'Agreed.' He sits.

'It's hard to argue with such an attractive offer,' Zach says. 'The financial downside is completely ring-fenced. As Gen says, the reputational and execution issues are by far the biggest concerns.'

'I'm always up for trying these things,' Cal says, 'but come on. Our members have suggested this multiple times. We've tossed it around too, but the timing's never right 'cause it's a lot of work. We know our limits. Let's test this baby out while someone else is offering to do all the hard work and pay us for the privilege. It'd be crazy not to.'

'I agree with Cal,' Rafe says, 'but it comes down to you, Gen. You'll be doing most of the heavy lifting at the beginning, though I'm sure Cal will be *very* hands on if we take the party out to Cannes.'

He grins, and it's infectious, because this is a bloody dream of an opportunity, and I don't think any of us needs a push to spend some time down on the Côte d'Azur this summer.

'I'm up for it,' I say more blithely than I feel. I try to push my misgivings deep down into my belly. 'Yeah, it'll be a lot of work, but it's a gift-horse, right?'

'Fucking *yes*,' Cal says dramatically, letting his head fall heavily back against the sofa and punching the air.

Maddy laughs. 'Ten quid on Cal having booked his Cannes Airbnb before the day is up.'

'On it,' he says, grabbing his phone and pretending to get to his feet.

The guys peel off shortly after we allow ourselves a brief but exuberant conversation around how Alchemy Cannes will look. Or perhaps it should be *Alchimie*. Either way, our business brains are engaged and our imaginations activated.

Maddy hangs back. We've made a collective decision to give her more exposure to the leadership side. She's smart and hungry and commercial, and Zach won't leave it long before making her an official part of the family, I'm sure.

She was quiet in the meeting, observing and taking notes. But now she jumps up and down and grabs my arm. 'Holy fuck!' she yells. 'I'm *dying*.'

'Course you are,' I say. My mouth twitches. 'Excited for the TikTok opportunities, are you?'

'Exactly.' She grins. 'And for my chances of persuading Zach to spend August in France. Heaven. This is going to be *amazing* for the club, I can feel it.'

'It'll be brilliant,' I agree. 'It really is a gift.'

She steers me further away from the open double doors leading to the office space. 'Okay. Anton Wolff is so fucking hot that I nearly *screamed*. Old, but hot.'

'You've seen him before, in the club,' I point out.

'I know, but watching him run a meeting made him even sexier. What a total daddy. And he looked at you the whole. Fucking. Time.'

'He did not,' I protest, though I'll admit I caught him staring at me several times during the meeting. The looks weren't predatory, nor were they amused or sleazy. Those I could have handled. They were more... serious. Hungry. Wistful, even.

The kinds of looks that get right under the surface and squeeze your heart. And other body parts.

The man moves me. It's undeniable. His mere presence has me hot and bothered. And on days like today, when he's not fucking people in front of me or generally behaving like a dick with no brain attached, he's really bloody impressive.

Maddy's right. He's the real deal. He's a power player. A proper grown up who feeds my competence kink—and every other kink—like nobody's business.

'He really did,' Maddy says now. 'Honestly, the whole time. I was literally *swooning*. All three of them were hot, Gen, but he is a beautiful man, and he's clearly interested. Would you not give him a chance? Do you really think he's that dodgy?'

'I don't think he's dodgy,' I say, which is not exactly the truth, but I cannot allow myself to judge people based on their sexual appetites. Not when I run a sex club. 'I just don't think—I think he'd hurt me. He's too much. I mean, who could let a man like that close and not get torn apart?'

She makes a sad face, visibly deflating. 'I get it. He's pretty special. But maybe you'll get to spend some time with him in France—you might see a different side to him?'

Her hopeful suggestion sends a shiver down my spine, because it reminds me of Anton's parting words.

That, if we do go ahead with this deal, as COO of Alchemy, I'm the best person to go venue-hunting with him in Cannes.

Now *that* would be a disaster waiting to happen.

23

GEN

I t's a testament to the efficiency and hard work of the legal teams on both sides of the deal that we manage to pull the whole thing off by David's deadline. A week after our initial meeting with Anton and his colleagues, I find myself travelling to his offices to sign the final contract.

It's been a speedy induction into the world of Anton Wolff.

When you have his money and energy and network, *no* is not a word you need to hear. Nothing is impossible. Everyone comes around, and everything gets done just as you want it, when you want it.

No wonder he's been so bad at hearing the word *no* from me.

No wonder he doesn't respond well to being kept waiting for anything.

A Google search told me the offices I'm visiting today a few streets away from us in Mayfair are the headquarters for Wolff Holdings, the umbrella corporation for Anton's myriad business interests. Dotted around London and the rest of the world are countless more offices representing the various sectors in which he operates.

Simply trying to absorb an online diagram of his holding structures made me feel dizzy. With this many moving parts to juggle, his presence at last week's meeting felt even more suspect. There's no way Anton Wolff could have justified taking an hour out of his day to sit in on an exploratory meeting about a little pop-up.

He was either there for me, or he was there because he has a vested interest in setting up a second channel for sex on tap over the summer.

I'm not sure which makes me feel more uncomfortable.

Anyway, I'm armoured up in a fitted black Dolce and Gabbana shift dress, my highest black heels, and beautiful black lace underwear from Fleur du Mal. I feel elegant and competent. Empowered. I have no idea if I'll even see the Big Bad Wolff today, but I always like to be mentally ready, and channeling my inner goddess is always a good way to prepare for going head to head with the patriarchy.

Besides, there's never an excuse for a bad lingerie game.

Ever.

The headquarters are certainly imposing. They're in a dashing old-school office building, and they have a timeless quality about them. I was expecting soulless steel and glass, but instead the vibe is that of an old bank. Opulent. Exclusive. Slightly intimidating.

I'm representing Alchemy alone today. Our lawyers have been through the final version of the contract and given me the green light to sign it in person. I'm met in the lobby of the fifth floor by a stunning young woman who resembles a Titian painting and introduces herself as 'Athena, Mr Wolff's Executive Assistant'.

What a shocker that Anton Wolff hires attractive staff

members. Max and that lawyer, David, were both easy on the eye the other day, too.

Speak of the devils. They're both sitting on a low, plump sofa when I enter the room. They stand at the sight of me, but my eyes go straight to the man himself. He's reclining in a big leather chair behind a huge desk, backlit against a wall of windows. His stance radiates power and success, as does this whole setup. I'm sure it's designed for this exact effect, but that doesn't stop it from working.

It's working for me very well indeed.

He pushes to his feet with a smile more appreciative than any he granted me last week. He's got a self-satisfied vibe, too. And why shouldn't he? He's baited me into his lair, and I'm about to get into bed with him, professionally speaking. He's in his usual uniform and, as usual, the crisp white shirt, open at the neck, looks seriously great on him. Is he more tanned than last week? It seems that way.

'Genevieve,' he says. 'It's good of you to come.' He rounds the desk, a hand extended, and I shake. It would be incredibly rude not to, and I managed it last week, after all. Besides, the sky won't fall because I shake the guy's hand.

My no-touching policy doesn't need to affect my basic professional demeanour.

Anton's grip is warm and strong, and for some reason, I feel engulfed by it. His deep brown eyes hold mine as we shake, and I have to force myself to hold eye contact. Even fucking eye contact with this guy is a *lot*. My initial impression from that first interview, that everything about Anton Wolff is *more than* in the flesh, reasserts itself.

'You remember Max and David,' he says, and I shake their hands, glad of the reprieve from having Anton's eyes boring into my very soul.

Despite the bright light of a sunny May afternoon, the

room feels wonderfully intimate. It's the warmth of the deep grey paintwork. The richness of colour from the stunning oils punctuating it. They're diverse, but cohesive. And is that a Degas on the wall?

I take a seat on the long sofa between David and Max. Athena pours everyone sparkling water before perching on the edge of one of the armchairs. We make a little small talk, we all sign several copies of the contract with a flourish, and Anton calls for champagne.

What the hell? It's six o'clock. The Big Bad Wolff is at his most charming, the presence of the others has assuaged my nerves somewhat, and Max is so drily hilarious as he riles Anton and good-naturedly teases Athena that I begin to relax. On my other side, David's energy is quieter. More gentlemanly. He has a protector vibe, and it gives me reassurance, too.

I have the oddest feeling, as we make quick work of the first bottle of vintage Krug and Anton himself opens another with dramatic flair, that he's cast some sort of spell on me. It's as if I'm a fairytale heroine and he's the charismatic but morally grey antihero, coaxing me into forgetting the real world exists. Into believing that all that matters is being here, in his enchanted kingdom.

He's charmed me into a false sense of security.

Everyone's loosening up. *I'm* loosening up. Anton's charming, and witty, and disarmingly frank, as we begin a low-level gossip session about the state of most of our Members of Parliament and leaders of industry.

He knows everyone, it seems. He has a story about most of them, and he divulges his inside scoops in the most delicious way. If I've previously suspected him of wielding disarmament as a weapon, I'm sure of it now.

And yet I'm going along with it, riding high on a tide of

intellectual stimulation and delicious champagne and feel-good hormones. The bubble is real, and intact, and a delightful place to be.

It stays intact until Anton leans forward in his seat, legs wide and hands steepled and body language open.

Until he says the following.

'I think it's time to have some fun, don't you?'

Until he looks straight at me as he says it.

24

GEN

I return his look with a glare. 'Meaning?'

'Meaning you should audition the guys here for their Alchemy membership.'

I don't like the change in his voice. It's got deeper, more menacing all of a sudden, its timbre low and intimate and sexy and fucking *dangerous*.

'You know we don't hold auditions. We hold interviews.' My tone is dismissive, but my nervous system is ratcheting right up. I cross my legs defensively, like that's going to save me from him.

'And I'm sure they'll nail them,' he says suavely. 'After all, everyone's getting on famously today, wouldn't you say? But I owe you one, and the least I can do is make my team available for your enjoyment.'

God, he's rude. I glare at him, because this is so far from appropriate in an office environment that it's not funny. 'You don't owe me anything,' I say through gritted teeth, though I'm all too aware of what he's alluding to.

That night at Alchemy.

His face relaxes into a broad grin, and it throws me. 'I'm

being disingenuous, obviously. I suspect you already know I'm a self-centred beast at heart. This isn't about you. It's about me. You've seen me come—or you would have, if you hadn't walked away so rudely the other night.

'You've seen me lose control and fuck someone like a beast, so you have the upper hand.' He lowers his voice. Chooses his words. 'Now it's my turn. I want to see you lose control, Genevieve. You know it's all I think about. Watching you come undone in the messiest, most glorious way. I won't rest until I get you so worked up you're fucking shameless.'

Holy fucking hell.

I am in way over my head here.

I squeeze my thighs together, telling myself it's a sort of emergency chastity belt, but I don't like the way he's making me feel. I don't like the thud-thud of my heart as he pins me with those devil eyes, and I definitely don't like the throbbing pulse between my legs as he talks utter filth in front of these total strangers.

'You're quite ridiculous,' I manage with a huff. 'This is extremely inappropriate.'

He shrugs, unbothered. 'These guys are fine.'

I drag my eyes from him and dare to glance to my left. I'm so mortified that Anton would disrespect me and his team enough to let the conversation turn to sex, and public sex at that.

It's excruciating.

But when I look at David's kind, beautiful face, it's neither surprised nor outraged. Instead, it's watchful. Expectant.

A glance to my right is even more unmooring. Max flashes me a grin that's less appreciative than downright lascivious.

'We're *very* fine with this,' he drawls, crossing one

shapely ankle over the opposite knee. He rests an elbow on the back of the sofa, his hand hanging between us.

Even Athena is unmoved. She's still perched on the edge of her chair, pen in hand, face politely blank with no trace of discomfort as she watches me, and suddenly I understand everything.

She's not just his EA.

And I'm not just here to sign a contract.

I've been ambushed.

25

GEN

Jesus Christ.

I stand like the sofa's on fire.

'I'm out,' I tell him. My body's in a mad panic, a whirlwind of emotions and danger cues wreaking havoc with its ability to function. I bend to pick up my handbag—no way can I forget my prized black Birkin—and make for the door, but Anton's too quick for me. He's up and out of his seat, bolting in the same direction.

I half expect him to block my exit, but he merely puts a hand on the door handle and opens it for me. He ushers me through and follows me out, shutting it behind us and taking a step forward, his huge bulk looming over me.

'You can leave right now, Genevieve,' he says in a voice that's barely above a whisper, although we're alone in the spectacular marble-floored lobby. 'Of course you can. I'd never want you to feel uncomfortable, except in that very particular way I know you need, because it's written in every perfect hair on your head.'

I stare up at him, speechless.

'I will always respect your boundaries.' He raises his

free hand as if to stroke it down my bare arm before letting it drop to his side. 'You've told me I can't touch you, and I won't. But we're far more similar creatures than you'd like to admit. We both get off on the same thing, and those guys are so up for it it's indecent. So let me give you this.'

I can't believe we're even having this conversation. Yeah, I've had group sex before at Alchemy, because it's my safe place. It's the only place in the world I've ever been able to discard my perfect, immaculate, over-achieving, good-girl persona and unveil what lies beneath. *Revel in it.* Wallow in the filth like an animal. Allow those dark urges to take over my mind and consume my body.

This isn't Alchemy.

That fact should make the decision to leave an easy one, but, strangely, it's making it harder.

As is Anton's face, which, for once, looks wiped of any smugness or cynicism or machinations. It looks totally sincere, and that's far more powerful than any of his usual tricks.

'Please, Gen,' he says, and I watch his mouth enunciate my nickname. A nickname he hasn't earned the right to use, but which sounds so gloriously intimate, so confiding, on his beautiful lips. His eyes are almost all pupil, and they're burning right into me. 'Let me give us what we both need so badly.'

I close my eyes, because I can't make sense of my thoughts when I'm looking at him. 'What are you proposing I do, exactly?'

'Nothing,' he says quickly. 'You don't need to do anything. Just submit. Let us... take over. I'll orchestrate it all.'

Orchestrate. Jesus. Like he's the godlike puppet master

and I'm his pliant little puppet. There is no doubt in my mind he can pull every string I have.

There's never been any doubt on that front.

'You put yourself in our hands,' he says, 'and we'll do the rest. It's been a hectic week, I know. Just let us fucking wipe your mind clean. I promise you I already know what you need better than you do. I can make sure they give it to you.'

God, yes.

How can he be speaking my language so beautifully? How can he know that it's his competence, his ability to dominate every situation he's in, that attracts me to him more than anything else? It's almost as if he's a trained hypnotist.

Nothing would surprise me when it comes to Anton Wolff.

I open my eyes and jerk my head towards the door. 'What about Athena? Are you making her do this?'

'Certainly not. Athena's a professional, in every sense of the word. She takes her duties very seriously, and serving me gives her enormous fulfilment—and pleasure. You'll see. I'm happy to explain our arrangement to you another time.'

'Is she your sub?'

He laughs. 'Do I look like I have the time and energy to devote to dealing with a sub? Fuck, no.'

'Can you kick her out?'

'I can put a blindfold on her, if you want,' he says, 'But she stays. I'm not as strong as you. I can't watch them with you and just stand there.' He pauses. 'If you won't touch me, she will.'

My heart breaks a little, right there. It's partly the knowledge that, once a-fucking-gain, another woman will get to be with him in a way that I'm denying myself for God knows what fucked-up reason. But it's also his words.

If you won't touch me, she will.

He makes it sounds vulnerable, somehow. Almost human. Which, coming from the Big Bad Wolff, is no mean feat.

Like this weird, fucked-up dynamic is hurting him too.

And it's that little gesture from him that's my undoing.

I let my bag drop to the floor, and the dull *thunk* of defeat has him smiling a smile of genuine surprise and delight.

It's beautiful.

Of course it is.

His teeth are white and even, and those gorgeous dimples flash before the double laughter lines swallow them up.

'You won't regret this,' he tells me. 'This is for you as much as for me. I told you when I sent the flowers, I'm not playing games with you. I have a pretty good idea of what this beautiful body is capable of'—his dark eyes rake down my front—'but I want, very much, to see it with my own eyes. And if you won't let me be the one to unravel you, then at least put me out of my misery and let me watch.'

My hand goes to the door handle.

'You'd better not make me regret this,' I tell him, and I open the door.

Inside the room, I lean heavily back against the wall, weary with the weight of trying to out-manoeuvre the master while my body prickles with anticipation. Anton steps in beside me, not taking his eyes off me as he says, 'Athena. Prepare the room, please.'

His voice is still low.

It's the voice of a man who knows he doesn't have to raise it to get what he wants.

And still we eye each other up.

Athena rises and moves about gracefully. Quickly. She's done this before. I tear my gaze from Anton and watch her. She's so placid, so submissive. Anton has clear dom tendencies—he made that clear in his interview—but I wonder if this is what he actually wants in a woman. Does he like them sweet and pliable, or does he prefer a challenge?

A click of a remote and the charcoal grey blinds lower over the windows, blocking out the evening sun and casting a pall of intimacy over the room. Some music that sounds a bit like a sexed-up version of Gregorian chanting starts up. And lights that weren't needed when the blinds were up appear as dim dots along the skirting boards.

Day to night.

Business to sin.

Just like that.

The atmosphere in the room which has, until now, been easy, celebratory, darkens. It's not menacing so much as heavy with promise, and I give myself tacit permission to embrace it.

To allow the sensual beat of the music to seep into my bloodstream.

To give myself up to these strangers.

To take from Anton what he's willing to give by proxy and to inflict on him the very thing he inflicted on me—the agony of watching the person who's got under one's skin get off. The agony of standing by, helpless and frustrated and eaten up with longing.

Above all, I allow myself to do the very thing I promised I would not.

Yield to him.

Because he may not be planning to lay a finger on me, but he'll sure as hell be pulling all the strings tonight.

26

ANTON

As Athena puts the champagne glasses on a tray and the other two move the glass-topped coffee table over to the wall, I take a step towards Genevieve. I'll never admit this to her, but I'm gobsmacked that she didn't run for the hills just then.

The flawless, dignified woman before me can't turn down the chance to have a couple of guys crawling all over her, and I fucking love that about her, despite the jealousy I feel.

This is wholly out of character for me. Usually, I take what I want and I make sure never to leave the spoils for anyone else to enjoy.

That goes for both business and women.

But Genevieve has turned me down, something that frankly does not happen, so I have to pivot.

I have to take what I can get.

Even if that means letting David and Max put their greasy paws all over her.

That's how desperate I am to undo her.

I'm not blind; I've observed her reaction to them in our

meeting at Alchemy and this evening. She's attracted to them *and* she feels far less threatened by them than she does by me. So if this—in my view unnecessary—work-around is the only way I'm going to see her naked and screaming anytime soon, so be it.

Besides.

It may be their hands on her, but make no mistake about it.

It will be my instruction, my twisted desires and the sound of my fucking voice in her ear that will have her begging for mercy.

I lean forward. She's still plastered against the door frame. 'It could have been just the two of us,' I murmur. 'But instead there'll be five of us in the room. Greedy, greedy girl.'

Before she can answer, I walk away from her to attend to Athena. First, Athena's the only person who's doing this because she's being paid to be here, so I owe it to her to check in with her. I never want the Seraph MO to be synonymous with the remotest coercion.

Second, I need to brief Athena so that the presence of another woman doesn't make Genevieve more self-conscious while we put her through her paces.

Third, while Athena has one duty to fulfil—sucking me off when the ache in my balls gets too much—I'm all too aware that my paying her attention will make Genevieve jealous.

I'm counting on it.

Yes, I'm a monster. But I have never, not for one second, doubted her reasons for steering clear of me. They have nothing to do with attraction and everything to do with self-preservation.

My job this evening is to tip those scales in favour of the

former, and, given my hands are metaphorically tied here, I'll employ every dirty trick I can to aid me.

Glasses cleared, Athena stands patiently by my desk, awaiting instruction. I reach into a drawer and pull out a sleep mask I use on her occasionally, bending to tug it gently over her pretty curls and cover her eyes. Then I steer her to my desk chair and sit her down on it, swivelling it to face the wall of windows for good measure.

She can stay there till I need her. I know from experience that the anticipation, the torture of being able to hear but not see anything, will have her soaked. I'll make sure to show my appreciation. Her reward will be all the sweeter for having waited.

Athena calms me down, both because she's a sure thing and because she's so even-tempered. Not like this badass I've developed an unfortunate fascination for.

But it's precisely Genevieve's badassery, and her insistence on holding me at arm's length, that makes me determined to dig beneath her surface.

David and Max have guided her into the space between the sitting area and the boardroom table and are hovering by her, flirting gently in David's case and more overtly in Max's place. But they're putting a smile on that beautiful face, so I don't care.

I meant what I said about having fun.

I address her first. 'Would you like a blindfold like Athena? I have a spare.'

She raises an eyebrow as she grants me a withering look. 'Do I look stupid?'

I swallow a smirk. I wouldn't abuse her trust by touching her while she was blindfolded, but clearly I have work to do on persuading her of that.

'Have it your way.' I turn to the guys. 'I bet she looks

beautiful with her hair down,' I muse idly, hands in my pockets.

David reaches behind her. She has her hair twisted elegantly up in one of those big plastic clips. He gently opens it, and her platinum locks tumble down. She shakes her head from side to side. Her hair is wavy from the up-do, but it falls to just above her shoulders, making her look instantly softer.

I lick my lips. 'I was right.'

Genevieve is doing a stellar job already. I know she's apprehensive, but at the same time, she's growing quieter. More serene. She's changing before my eyes. It's as if she's exhausted from putting on a front, from holding off, and the relief is making her more pliant.

It's as if she's already mentally given herself over to this. Put her wellbeing in my hands, because she knows, deep down, I'll do right by her. She knows she can relax and let me take charge.

Will I ever.

I cast my eyes down her. She's watching me, but she's not *watchful*. More curious. Her body is, quite frankly, banging. It'll be fucking indecent when we get her clothes off.

'Let's take a look at her,' I say. 'I want to see what she's got under there. Don't you?'

I'm already struggling to keep my voice even, but I know it's the commanding, controlled pitch of it that she responds to. Just as I know instinctively that talking about her to the guys in the third person, as if she's an anonymous plaything who's here purely for us to fiddle and fuck and pet and pleasure, will give her a kick she'll both resent and revel in.

'Fuck, yes,' Max says, edging David out of the way so he can step behind her. He's more naturally dominant than

David—the latter is honestly more of an extra set of hands attached to a hot body that women seem to respond to.

He'll also cherish Genevieve, worship her like I want her to be worshipped. He was quite vocal about her charms on the short walk back from Alchemy the other day. I suspect he might be a little smitten.

Good.

Between the two of them, they'll worship her and abase her and give her everything I'd give her if I had her to myself.

Max pushes her hair out of the way on one side and buries his face in the crook of her neck, inhaling deeply. 'Mmph,' he mumbles. 'Smells amazing.'

'Wait till you get to press your nose to her pussy,' I say. 'Imagine how fucking good she'll smell down there. I bet it reeks of her arousal already.'

Genevieve jolts, and I lock eyes with her, watching in extreme gratification as her lips part.

I know I'm correct.

She's already excited, and I can tell my words have taken her aback in the best way. I'm not sure what she was expecting from this, but I fully intend my filthy, pornographic commentary to work her up even more than Max and David's skills.

After all, we all know who's in charge here.

'She'll taste so fucking sweet,' Max groans into her hair as he unzips her. The sound of metal teeth grating against each other is, as always, pregnant with promise.

I push down a wave of jealousy that these two twats will get to taste her before me.

Long game.
Remember?

David stands in front of her, preparing to relieve her of her dress and partially blocking my view.

'Move,' I order.

He steps aside. Max's hands go to the neckline.

'Okay. Slowly,' I tell him. I only get to unwrap Genevieve for the first time once.

I'm determined to make it count.

He slides her dress down from behind her. The fabric skims over her shoulders, down her arms, black bra straps with a pretty lace scallop coming into view.

Fuck me.

Her tits.

They're fucking amazing. Plump and perky and perfect, encased in black lace through which her nipples can't hide their taut arousal.

I could get lost in that cleavage.

Bury my face in it.

My cock.

'Beautiful,' I breathe, my smile triumphant, because getting this far with her is no mean feat. My cock swells at the mere thought of fighting its way into that snug space. I'd keep her bra on so her tits stayed exactly like that, sheathing me as tightly as possible.

'Touch her nipples,' I tell David, moving slightly to the side to maintain my view. 'Just a bit. Don't give her too much —not yet.'

I want her begging us to let her get off.

27

GEN

I can't drag my gaze away from Anton as he takes me in. His face may be admirably impassive, but his eyes are burning at what they see, and the strained way he says *beautiful* about my breasts hints that he may be struggling more than he'll ever admit to maintain this facade of control.

Max has my zip undone so my dress bundles around my waist. A few more inches and he'll be able to slide it over my hips and expose my body in just its lingerie. His mouth returns to my neck, my shoulders, his lips and nose skating over my skin as his fingers tease the exposed base of my spine. It's delicious, but I need far more.

As soon as Anton gives the order, David cups my breasts through my bra, his thumbs going to strum my nipples softly through the lace. It feels so good I gasp, my eyes shooting to David's face. The intensity in his dark eyes tells me his gentle touch is less about being respectful and more about torturing me.

At my gasp, his tongue peeks out through his lips and he

grants me a rougher touch, one that uses the lace to chafe at my aching nipples. Oh, God. I arch my back, a tiny sound escaping me.

'Fucking yes,' David groans, and I wonder if I've underestimated him. He seems quiet. Gentle. But he's partaking in this scene, isn't he?

Anton laughs. 'She likes that,' he tells David. 'Back off.'

He does as he's told, and Max slides my zip the rest of the way open, tugging my dress over my hips until it pools around my ankles. David stoops to help me step out of it, affording Anton a clear view of me.

I have a man kneeling at my feet.

Another right behind me, one hand sliding over my bare hip as the other traces its fingers oh-so-lightly along the back of my thong where it disappears between my cheeks.

And a third, the one whose attention, whose approval, makes me light up in ways I despise and adore in equal measure, staring at me like he'd love to shove his henchmen out of the way and pillage me right here.

How did I *ever* think this was a bad idea?

Alchemy has saved me in so many ways, but being in Anton Wolff's office while his men put their hands on me and he tries not to salivate is another level. The unfamiliar corporate setting gives it a raw, dangerous edge that's jacking up my heart rate with every passing minute.

Anton's intent on undoing me, and I have no doubt he will. That's what I'm here for. At least, that's why I've stayed. But I'll be damned if I don't take him down with me.

There's nothing better than reducing a man who likes to be in control to a desperate, ravenous animal who'll fuck any hole he can find to slake his need.

I put a hand on my hip and lick my lips. My body's curvy as hell, yes, but I'm in great shape and I'm fucking proud of these curves. My lingerie is beautiful. These heels make my legs look endless. And hopefully my up-do's made my hair soft and wavy.

I don't need to imagine the picture I make.

I can see it reflected in Anton Wolff's eyes.

So yeah, I'm ready to submit. I want these guys to do their worst.

His eyes drag up my body. Up my legs. Over my thong. My stomach. My breasts. To my face, where my smile spurs him into action.

'Touch her,' he commands. 'But don't take off her underwear quite yet.'

I widen my stance a little, both to stabilise myself in these heels and in the hope that someone will touch my pussy, which is warm and damp and needy. In response, Anton does the same, planting his feet further apart and crossing his arms over his chest.

He looks like he's inspecting a prize pony or racing car, and I fucking love it.

'Your eyes don't leave mine,' he tells me through gritted teeth. 'Got it? They stay on *me*.'

I nod. I'm playing nicely, but it's all part of the game to me. The more I submit, the more I yield to his power and to the power David and Max have over my body, the more exquisite my reward will be.

David stays on his knees having disposed of my dress. He plants his warm hands on my thighs and strokes up, around, and back down to my knees. His touch is sure, and I want his hands higher. He doesn't give me that, but he does bend his closely-shaven head to my pelvic bone and inhale hard.

'Jesus,' he rasps. 'You were right. She smells fucking amazing. She's so turned on.'

'You can touch her over her thong,' Anton says, and David dutifully skims a large hand up my thigh, tracing the lightest line over the fabric of my thong, back to front. It feels so tantalising against my sensitised flesh that I jolt. Jesus—staying standing in heels might be more difficult than I thought if they're going to touch me like this.

In an instant, Max is pressing right up behind me, hard muscle and crisp cotton hitting my back as his undeniable erection pushes against my bottom. He bands a strong arm around my waist, holding me to him, as his other hand threads through my arm and caresses my breasts.

Mmm. I lean my head back against him, my eyelids flickering shut in pleasure as he takes his hand on a meandering tour.

'Eyes on me,' Anton says tersely, and I jerk my head upright. My guess is the guy's FOMO is ratcheting right up. I flick my gaze to his crotch, and yep. His trouser FOMO indicator looks pretty fucking hard to me.

'Pinch her nipples,' he tells Max. 'Hard. I want her feeling like she needs to come just from that. David, hold off.'

And just like that, Max ramps up and David, agonisingly, holds off.

The cliché about billionaires being control freaks is definitely true of Anton Wolff. And I love it. I love everything about this scenario.

His bossiness.

His distance.

His scrutiny.

His command of the situation.

His knowledge of my desires—how to fan them, and, I'm sure, how to use them to torment me.

If I'm the instrument, he's most definitely the maestro,

conducting this exploration, this celebration, of my body. And there's no doubt this composition is one of his own creation.

He may not be the one touching me, but as I keep my eyes locked on him, he's the only one who matters.

28

___

ANTON

She's magnificent.

Many men with similar proclivities to mine seek out women who are subservient from the outset. That's their prerogative, but where's the fun in it? Yes, there's a comfort, a familiarity, in engaging intimately with women like Athena. You know exactly what you're going to get.

But give me a Genevieve over an Athena any day of the week. It's far more erotic, far more thrilling, to set your sights on a strong, glorious powerhouse of a woman who's your intellectual equal. The worthiest of adversaries.

Because when a woman like that submits to you, it means something.

It means she's doing it for herself as much for you.

My eyes stay locked with hers as she stands there in beautiful, classy lingerie that'll be on my office floor in a moment, and I know that to be true.

She's submitting beautifully. Taking every instruction I issue to Max and David like a champ. But I'd be kidding myself if I believed for a moment that's anything other than triumph in her eyes.

Because every acquiescence is a choice. She's serving herself, just as we're serving her. No one is deluded here.

Still, I'm determined to stay in control for as long as it takes.

Max plays with her tits for a little longer, and then I give David the go-ahead to slide his fingers up and down over the thin strip of lace covering her pussy. Her beautiful face grows more expressive with every stroke, but her eyes stay on me.

As they do, as she gives herself over more and more to the sensation, our connection grows.

I can feel it.

It's quite extraordinary, actually. I've removed myself physically from this scene at her request, but it's as if she and I are the only people in the room. My colleagues' breaths are growing more ragged, but I zone them out quite easily.

Because everything falls away when I'm looking at her.

'Take it all off,' I rasp in a voice that definitely doesn't reek of control. She closes her eyes for a moment, probably in relief, but they open again, clear and blue, fixed on me as I take in the sight I've waited patiently to see.

Her tits. Holy fuck, her tits. They're fucking perfect. So perky. Shapely. Tits a man could get lost in. What I wouldn't give to get her on a bed right now and bury my face in them. Her nipples are pink and so hard they look ready to snap off.

Then David slides her thong down, and a neat, light brown strip of hair comes into view.

Of course her pussy is immaculately groomed.

Just like the rest of her.

She's stunning and perfect, from the swell of her tits to the dip of her waist and the curve of her hips. It's clear she works out. Her arms and thighs are toned, her stomach gently rounded with a hint of definition.

She's a goddess.

'Just beautiful,' David tells her.

'Very fucking sexy,' Max growls as he slides his hands up her waist to cup her bare tits. He weighs them, bouncing them a little. They sit luscious and heavy in his palms.

Best view I've ever, ever seen.

David bends to untangle her thong from her heels as she steps out of it, and I hit my limit, because she's naked save for her heels, and she's *right in front of me*, and if I can't touch, I can definitely use my other senses.

'Get her on the table,' I demand. *'Now.'*

I want to fucking look.

She smiles her Mona Lisa smile at me and turns.

Jesus fucking Christ.

Her *fucking* arse.

I suck oxygen in through my nose, because I want to bend her over that table *right* now, and kneel behind her, and drag my nose and mouth and tongue through every crevice of her cunt while I spread those sumptuous cheeks and massage the fuck out of them.

I want every one of her holes, and I *will* have them.

Long term greedy.

She looks over her shoulder at me as she saunters to the table. And I love it. I fucking love that she's so confident, so sure of the effect she's having on me.

And rightly so.

She knows how she looks.

She's a sight for sore eyes.

'On her back,' I tell Max.

Fuck, I haven't asked her for a safe word. I'm losing my grip on this situation.

'I need a safe word, Genevieve,' I tell her brusquely as she plants that bare arse elegantly on the polished walnut of my meeting table. It sits ten people comfortably, and I'll never be able to look at it in the same way again.

She arches an elegant eyebrow at me and props her hands behind her, which serves to thrust her phenomenal tits out. I both love and hate how poised she is, because I won't consider my job well done until I've ignited her and melted every last bit of her *sang-froid*.

'Let's go with camellia,' she says in that cool, sensual voice. Her eyes slide to my dick and back to my face.

I edge closer.

'You heard the lady,' I tell the guys. 'Now get her on her back.'

She lowers down, elbows first, David cradling her platinum head tenderly as it lowers down to the table. He really is very caring. Max has a hand under each knee, holding her legs off the floor, which is perfect, because I want that pussy right on the edge of the table.

I'll let him go to town on her pussy with his mouth, I decide. Then David can get her on her knees and choke her with his cock before Max bends her over the table and fucks her.

Orgasms all round.

For everyone but me.

I'll grab Athena when I can't physically hold off any longer, but for now I want to stay in control.

Undistracted.

I want to wring every last drop of pleasure out of this sumptuous visual repast.

She looks so perfect lying there. Like every man's ultimate bombshell fantasy, her voluptuous body spread out for us to enjoy.

To feast on.

To profane.

She's quite perfect, but still. There's an image in my head, and it's been stuck there since that first moment I walked into Alchemy's office and her cool beauty assaulted me.

The image is of what she'll look like *after*.

After two or more orgasms. After being licked and bitten and sucked and fucked. After choking down Max's huge cock. I need her hair mussed and her mascara smudged and that pretty coral pink lipstick smeared and her body relaxed, sated. *Marked.* And I want every last drop of pleasure and satisfaction reflected on her face.

That's what I need.

And I know she won't disappoint me.

29

GEN

The moment my back hits the cool, smooth surface of the table, I experience another surge in my anticipation levels.

There's nothing like this.

No feeling in the world that matches it.

My heart rate may be up, but my mind is still and clear.

I'm naked except for my heels, laid out on a table for three fully clad men to enjoy. To worship and debase and command. To wring from my body everything it has. And I know one of them will push me to my limits and orchestrate every touch the other two give me.

And it will be beautiful.

I've had this feeling about Anton since I first met him. Not just a strong reaction to his physical attributes, but a reaction to his *energy*. No one I've met or dated or fucked has ever had quite such a strong sense of feral desire concealed beneath cold ruthlessness.

And no matter my distrust of him or my dislike of my reaction to him, I can't deny there's no one in whose capable hands I'd rather put my body.

Metaphorically speaking.

I turn my head to the side and watch as he takes me in. His eyes are dark and hungry. He hasn't commented on what he sees, probably to maintain his dominance, but he doesn't need to.

There's not an iota of doubt in my mind as to the effect my naked body and submissive pose is having on him.

He prowls around to the end of the table, to where Max is holding my legs up.

'Wider,' he barks, and Max obliges, pushing my legs apart so I'm completely open to him. It's warm in the room, but the air still feels cool against my exposed pussy.

He can see everything.

The thought inflames me.

The energy of our dynamic rolls through me.

I, of course, hold all the power. I can stop this with a single word. But it's far more fun for everyone in the room to pretend I'm powerless here. That Anton holds all the cards.

The inconvenient truth is that he does, because I'm completely in his thrall.

In my peripheral vision Anton bends and leans over Max to examine me just as David begins to play with my nipples. He rolls and pulls and pinches, and it feels fucking amazing.

'Open her up for me,' Anton tells Max, who slides a couple of fingers to my sensitised folds, parting them.

Anton's anguished exhale tells me everything I need to know about whether the sight of me has pleased him.

I arch my back into David and Max's touch, but, really, it's the heady knowledge that Anton is right there, inspecting every inch of my most intimate areas, that has the desire rolling over me in waves. My entire pussy feels hot. Needy. Max's clinical touch isn't where I want it, but it's enough to have my flesh begging for more.

'So fucking sexy, having her wide open for us like this,' Anton hisses. 'Look at her clit. It's so pretty. How does she feel?'

Max continues to hold me open with one hand as he runs another finger over my swollen clit and down through my centre until it's at my entrance. I suck in a breath at the trail of bliss.

'Soaked,' he tells Anton. 'And soft. Perfect. She's so ready for my cock.'

'Not so fast,' Anton warns, and I realise the sadistic arse-hole probably has a grand master plan. 'Keep her held wide open like this so she feels everything. You'll be tongue fucking her in a second—'

Yes.

'—but she doesn't get anything unless she begs. Genevieve?' he asks sharply, and I jolt.

'Yes?' I ask. David pauses his ministrations on my breasts. Max is still holding me open, but Anton rounds the table so he's standing opposite David and looks down at me with those dark, heated eyes that drift over my naked body, settling on my face. He rakes his hair off his forehead.

'You remember how I told you I like my women, don't you?'

'Yes.'

'How do I like them?'

I may be spreadeagled for him, but I muster up every ounce of dignity I possess when I answer him.

'Debased and begging, I believe.' I manage a smirk as I finish, and amusement flashes across his face in response.

'Good girl. And do you know why that is?'

'Because you're a narcissistic, power-hungry arsehole

who needs to demean women to stave off your own insecurities?' I guess.

Max laughs from somewhere between my legs.

Anton rewards me with a full-on grin that's devilishly sexy. 'Fuck, I knew I liked you. Nice try, gorgeous. I may be all of the above but I actually adore women. And when I see a woman like you, who's successful and beautiful and uptight as fuck, I know I'm the man to help you unwind. But I can only do that when you let go'—he leans in closer and enunciates—'and embrace your shame. It's only when you give into being dirty and shameless and wanton, and name your desires, and ask for what you need, that you can feel fully liberated. Am I right?'

I lie there and glare at him, because that is way too close to fucking home.

His voice softens. 'And that's what I get off on. Seeing you give into the darkest parts of you, and let them out, and go through the fucking roof with pleasure.'

He gives me one more lingering look and turns abruptly away. I'm thinking he may actually be human when I hear his voice turn cold. Authoritative.

'Now's the part where she begs.'

30

GEN

There must be some gesture from him that I don't see, because David begins to touch my breasts again with firm, assured strokes, and Max's tongue hits my clit, and holy *fuck* it feels good. I let out a whimper despite myself, my back arching off the table once again, and Max hums his appreciation against my flesh.

'She likes that,' Anton observes. 'How does she taste?'

'Spectacular,' Max mutters. 'Fuck.'

'Fingers,' Anton orders, and two fingers are thrust inside me. It's the best kind of invasion. God knows, I need the fullness.

Anton's crouched down too far for me to really see him, but I don't think he'll pull any stunts as far as touching me goes. He's far more likely to use Max and David to torture me.

He's speaking to Max in a low voice, talking him through his moves. I catch snippets of his directives.

Not too hard... Keep her open, though... Fuck, her clit looks good against your tongue... Suck a bit. Yes. Like that.

Max sucks hard on my clit and I practically come then

and there, so it's no surprise when Anton tells him to cut it out. I focus on David looming over me. He's ditched the tie he was wearing for our meeting; his shirt is unbuttoned at the collar, and he's rolled his sleeves up.

There's hunger written starkly on his face, but he shoots me a sweet, conspiratorial smile. He's way too nice for this, but the way he's pinching my little pink nipples between his fingers is really fucking hot.

Anton murmurs something else to Max, and suddenly his fingers thrust roughly inside me at the same time as his tongue hits my clit, hard.

'Oh my God,' I moan, because it's perfect. It's fucking perfect, and I need more. I need David's hands, and Max's fingers and tongue, and preferably someone's thick cock inside me. I need everything—I need them to keep working me like this and I swear I'll give Anton Wolff everything he wants, because my post-orgasmic body will be plastered to the ceiling.

It stops.

Fuck.

'No more until she asks for it,' Anton says smoothly, and David stops too, like the obedient henchman he is.

I grit my teeth. 'More, please. I need it.'

This time, all I get is a leisurely swipe of Max's tongue from my clit, all the way back. There's nowhere near enough pressure, and they know it.

I lie there for a moment, trying to catch my breath, to ease my racing heart, to ignore the desperate pulsing in my pussy. Because I know what Anton's trying to do. He wants my pussy's hunger to override, to obliterate every last shred of decency and decorum and manners.

He wants me unleashed and begging, and he's not far off getting it.

I know no more touch will be forthcoming. That the ball is in my court. And I also know from experience that Anton's right.

If I can throw off my inhibitions and reach into that place where the shame and the darkness and the need live, if I can grab them and pull them to the surface, then my reward will be all the sweeter.

And I don't just mean the reward these guys see fit to bestow upon me. I mean the reward from my nervous system when I show it that the only thing lying on the other side of fear, of inhibition, is unthinkable pleasure.

I've come this far.

I've allowed three suited men to strip me and lay me down naked on a table. To experiment with my body.

In for a penny, in for a pound.

You could hear a pin drop. Max circles my entrance experimentally with a finger, his touch too light to do anything but provoke.

'*Fuuuck*,' I groan. 'Please.'

'You can do better than that,' Anton tells me.

I entertain a brief but thrilling fantasy of tugging my left leg out of Max's hold and kicking Anton hard in that aquiline nose of his, but I want to come too much.

'Please let me come,' I beg. 'I need to so badly.'

'Tell us why this turns you on so much.' His voice is quiet, controlled, but there's also a note of hunger that I can't deny. A note that tells me I'm not the only vulnerable party here. Everyone is turned on. The magic in this room is affecting everyone.

We're all in this together, and it is fan-fucking-tastic.

'Because this is my fantasy,' I manage. I turn my head so I can see him a little better through downcast eyes. 'Being naked with all of you. Being your plaything. The idea that you can do whatever you want to me.'

'Good,' Anton barks. 'More.'

Max rewards me with a light lick of my pussy.

I take a brave breath. 'It makes me, I don't know, melt inside. It gets me so aroused, seeing you inspect my body and treat me like a set of willing holes and probe me and examine me. I know I'm safe, but I feel so exposed, and *God*, I just want you to go to town on me.'

Silence.

'Go to town on you how?' It's Anton again. 'You need to say it.'

I sigh. 'In every way. You've got me here on this fucking table, for Christ's sake. Just fucking *touch* me. Manhandle me. Get rough—I can take it. I want you to lick me and fuck me and fill me up and get me on my knees and make me choke on your cocks. Just please, unleash yourselves on me, for fuck's sake.'

I let my eyes flutter closed, because I'm wound up and turned on and wiped out and I just need to fucking come already. When I open them, Anton's looming over me, staring at me with what looks like awe and approval and all the other good things.

'See?' he says on an exhale. 'Told you you had it in you. I fucking knew it, first time I saw you. Knew if I got you naked and spread out for us you'd be gagging for it. *That's* what I'm talking about.' He shakes his head, like he's actually surprised he got me to this place.

He looks beautiful and savage. His eyes are black, bottomless pools, and I'm in such an advanced state of arousal that if he climbed on the table and put me out of my misery himself, I honestly wouldn't object.

Who am I kidding?

I'd *love* it.

'You little beauty,' he says. He reaches out a hand before stopping himself, pulling it back abruptly. 'You heard her,' he tells the others. 'Give her what she needs.'

I expect him to go back to his position at the business end of the proceedings, but he doesn't. He straightens up and stays where he is, and I twist my head to one side where I keep it by unspoken agreement.

And as David stands across from him and gets to work on my nipples while Max begins his glorious onslaught with his tongue and fingers, we hold eye contact.

I know he needs this. I can't believe how hard it must be for a man like Anton to stand aside and let his subordinates have all the fun. But I know he needs to see me fall apart. It's my gift to him, my way of showing that his concessions are strengthening my trust in him.

I need it, too.

I've been brave and vulnerable and shameless and wanton, and forcing myself to gaze into the dominant, merciless face of this man as his orchestrations unravel me is my final step on this journey of abandoning every part of me that keeps me suppressed.

It's how I show him that I've allowed him to unveil the real me.

It doesn't take long. My climax begins to spiral out of control as soon as the others lay their hands on me. It courses through me as Max laves my pussy and fucks me with his fingers. As David bends his head and takes one nipple between his teeth, flicking his tongue relentlessly over it as his hand mimics the movement on my other nipple.

'Oh God,' I gasp. I'm shuddering. 'Oh God. So good.'

Anton watches my face.

'Harder. Harder—fuck. Jesus.' I writhe. I arch into their touch. I shove my pussy against Max's mouth and hand. My body is on fire, my only conscious thought is my need to get off as violently as possible.

Anton watches my face.

I come. Hard. So hard, as the guys work every erogenous zone and hit me with an orgasm so hard it's less a wave than a wall, practically knocking me out as white-hot pleasure radiates from my pussy outwards, coursing through my bloodstream and setting my nerve endings on fire, so I'm conscious of little else except his eyes on me and this brick wall of sensation.

I'm gasping, and crying out, and full-on convulsing on the table as my nails scrape against its smooth surface and my greedy body takes every single morsel of pleasure they're willing to give me.

And still, Anton watches my face.

31

ANTON

The experience of looking into Genevieve's huge blue eyes as she comes apart on my fucking conference table is religious.

Transcendent.

I'm not exaggerating. It's up there with watching my four children coming into the world. With seeing the sun set behind the long grasses of the Kruger.

It's up there with coming myself.

That I'm not the one touching her, not the one whose hands or mouth or dick is making contact with her body, is almost immaterial.

Almost.

She wouldn't let me touch her, but she gave me this, and I stand there and observe in wonder as she comes down, licking her lips and catching her breath, tits heaving as she does so.

Rib cage rising.

Falling.

She's lovely.

I'm conscious of David drawing his hands over her tits

and down her stomach, as if signalling the end of a massage. Still, she and I regard each other in silence.

It's me who looks away first, breaking the spell. My zip is in danger of leaving its teeth embedded in my cock, and I'm not finished with her yet. I need to amend my plans, though, because I can't hold off much longer.

'You were fucking amazing,' Max tells her, trailing kisses down her thighs. 'You came so hard for us.'

'Yeah,' David adds. 'You're so beautiful.'

Genevieve stretches, cat-like, on the table and makes a throaty, satisfied sound that goes straight to my dick.

So that's how she is after coming. Relaxed and pliant. Imagine how she'll look after she's been fucked at both ends.

'Looks like she owes you both one hell of an orgasm,' I remark idly. 'Why don't you get her on the floor, chaps? You can both use her at the same time. Max, you fuck her.'

Together, they get her off the table, Max's hands going around her waist while David gets her vertical. She's barely on her hands and knees on my thick white carpet before Max is kneeling behind her, unbuckling his belt and shoving his trousers and boxers down his thighs.

'Cushions,' I say, because it doesn't take a genius to work out that she'll need to be elevated to reach David's cock comfortably. He grabs a couple from the sofa and there's some faffing as they reposition her. I take advantage of the brief lull in proceedings to grab Athena.

'You've been so patient,' I tell her softly, because it's true. I can tell by the way she's been white-knuckling her thighs that the sounds of my instructions and Genevieve's orgasm have aroused her no end. 'Now you get to suck my cock, and if you take it all nicely you can make yourself come.'

I lead her by the hand over to the expanse of carpet

where Genevieve is now on her hands and knees on two cushions.

Jesus fucking Christ.

The sight of her is quite extraordinary. I want to cast her in bronze. No—marble. Marble for her smooth, pale skin and perfect curves. Behind her, Max is rolling a condom over his dick, which looks as hard and painful as mine feels, and in front, David's shoving down his trousers and black boxer briefs. He's also on his knees. I watch as his cock tumbles heavily out, practically slapping her in the face.

But most of all, I watch her. I stand far enough away from them that Athena can get to her knees in front of me, but close enough to take in every last ounce of Genevieve's great beauty in this provocative stance. She's perfect in profile, tits swaying heavily below her, back arched and flawless arse in the air, shooting me a look that manages to be coquettish and smug and hungry as she awaits Max's cock.

Smug because she knows the effect she's having on me.

And she knows I can't go near her.

I'll show her.

Envy segues through me, sharp and bitter, and I grab Athena's arm, indicating she should get down. Even blind-folded, she sinks gracefully to her knees and fumbles with my belt. I help her, impatience making me clumsy and the sheer extremity of my erection hindering my ability to lose my boxer briefs.

'What are you waiting for?' I bark at all four of them, because surely everyone else in this fucking room is gagging for the next phase just as much as I am?

At my signal, they begin to move in sync, a sensual feast.

Just for me.

David cups Genevieve's jaw and feeds his pretty fucking

sizeable cock past her beautiful lips. As if by magic, Athena fists me at the root and swipes her little pink tongue oh-so-slowly over the precum leaking from my poor, swollen crown. The sensation is so fucking welcome that I suck in a sharp, noisy breath through my teeth.

It feels un-fucking-believable.

On instinct, I slide my hands through Athena's silky curls, gripping her head so I can control her pace. Her depth. So I can ram my cock to the back of her throat when I reach the point where her lips and tongue simply aren't enough.

When I need to really fuck her mouth.

But it looks like David, my gentle giant, is starting slowly, too. Even kneeling, he looms over Genevieve, his head thrown back with pleasure, his powerful body braced. I hope he lets her have it—I'll make sure of it—but as Genevieve sucks and teases and laps at him, Athena does the same to me, and it makes it so much easier to imagine I'm in David's place right now. To imagine it's Genevieve Carew's smart little mouth welcoming my cock.

As Athena wraps her lips around me, making a seal, Max tests the readiness of Genevieve's pussy with a couple of probing fingers. She's undoubtedly soaking, and, sure enough, he goes for it, fisting his cock and feeding it straight in.

I can't see her pussy from here. Only the glorious dip of her arched spine and the swell of her arse that together bring to mind the shape of a violin. But I can most definitely see the way she jolts when Max sticks his cock inside her, the way the action forces her forward onto David's dick.

The two guys exchange a triumphant look over her head. I've been there plenty of times, mainly with Max and Athena, but fuck knows I'd be high-fiving right now if that was me sheathed in the tight, wet heat of her pussy or her mouth.

Scratch that. If she let me touch her, there'd be no one else in the room with us.

End of story.

Just look at her.

The glacial, normally impassive blonde who only lets others see what she chooses to disclose, unwrapped for us. For me. Impaled at both ends, a glorious, bare, Rubenesque nude writhing and slithering between two fully dressed men.

This is what I imagined as soon as I laid eyes on her.

This is the version of her I needed.

She wriggles that fucking arse a little more as she accommodates Max. He puts his hands on her cheeks and massages as he bottoms out in her, and she releases a little whimper that is a hundred times better for sounding strangled around David's cock.

I want that.

Need more of it.

Max pulls slowly out without releasing his grip on Genevieve's hips before ramming back in, and it's like a twisted, stunning game of dominos as she bucks and gasps again and jolts straight towards David's balls.

This is some particular form of torture, where one beautiful woman is getting me off but the other, the one I actually want, is currently being spit-roasted by my friends, my *subordinates*, right in front of me.

It's all getting mixed up in my head. The ministrations of Athena's warm mouth and slippery tongue against the engorged, tortured flesh of my crown, the decisive squeeze of her grip around my shaft, Max's huffs and thrusts, Genevieve's strangled, garbled noises, and David's low, masculine groans of appreciation as she fucks his cock all by herself.

The whole glorious, messy circus has my own pleasure spiralling through the fucking roof. I dig my fingers into Athena's scalp, her jaw, as I drag her head backwards and then pull her harder towards me. She makes a surprised choking sound, and I'm rewarded with the unbeatable sensation of that soft, spongy flesh at the back of her throat rubbing against my cock.

Fucking hell.

She drags her fingernails down my thighs, and I know from experience that's her way of saying she's fucking loving this. She and I have our rhythm. Our system. Our cues. Her safe word is *Sorbonne*, and if she can't use it because I've got my cock rammed too far down her mouth, she slaps my right thigh hard and I stop immediately.

This flailing and clawing and strangled moaning isn't a red light, but a green one.

'Fuck, *yes*,' I rasp, and, to my extreme gratification, Genevieve attempts to crane her head in my direction. The woman has a huge dick filling her up at each end and it's *me* she wants eyes on.

That I'm not the only one of us with FOMO makes something swell inside me.

'Go on,' I bark as I wrap a tangle of Athena's curls around my fist. 'Fuck her harder. *Both* of you.'

32

ANTON

David responds by easing his length out of Genevieve's mouth and looking down at her. 'Is that okay with you?' he asks.

Jesus Christ. I roll my eyes, but a second later I'm grateful he's asked when she gives her response.

'God, *yes,*' she says, looking up at him, her voice hoarse and raspy and so fucking needy that I'm this close to dragging her away from the two of them and giving her a good pounding over that table, just like she needs. *'Please.'*

'That sounds to me like she needs a damn good fucking,' I hiss, thrusting hard into Athena's willing, gasping mouth. Fuck, yes. I'm so turned on I can barely speak. Can barely string a sentence together. All I know in this moment is blind need. I'm an animal rutting himself into relief and release. Into the light. 'Come the fuck *on.*'

I throw my head back and will myself to hold on longer. Just a little longer. Because this is heaven and hell, and it's simply too good. 'How does she feel, Max?' I ask, because he's far filthier than David.

'So. Fucking. Good.' Max punctuates each word with a hard

drive of his hips. He's really giving it to her now. His thrusts are speeding up, and Genevieve is having to claw her fingers into the carpet to keep her position. I observe through my haze of need that she's stopped jolting forward as much. Rather, she's meeting Max thrust for thrust like that greedy cunt of hers needs every last fucking millimetre of dick it can get.

I fucking love that.

'David,' I tell him, drawing on whatever vestiges of blood flow that remain beyond my cock to form a sentence, 'fuck her mouth harder.'

He grips her head and gives in. Gives in to my instructions, into the animalistic need that, unlike Max and me, he tries to keep at bay.

And he fucks her mouth.

This is the beautiful part.

This is the fucking symphony, where it all comes together. Where *we* all come together. Where everyone is so lost, so blinded by a fog of white-hot desire that they exist simply as a slave to their own need.

'You can touch yourself,' I manage to tell Athena, because the way she's sucking and licking and pumping my dick while scratching my skin and grabbing at my bum and rubbing her tits against my thighs tells me she's this close to blowing, too.

She makes a strangled sound of thanks and removes a hand from my balls. It disappears between our bodies, and over her shoulder her arse gyrates as she works her own sweet pussy. My balls miss her touch, but she's sucking harder as she gets herself off, so I'll let her have this.

Besides, it keeps her happy while I observe the magnificent crescendo of this little scene I've created.

David comes first. I'm amazed he's lasted this long. I'm

amazed *I've* lasted this long. He climaxes with a roar, holding Genevieve's head in place as he fills her mouth with his cum. He pulls out so she can swallow, then he's sinking down so his bum rests on his heels. He kisses the top of her head and his hands snake around her sides so he can play with her tits.

That's my boy.

She moans and arches her back harder and I watch through hooded, heavy eyes as he works her tits with squeezes of her flesh and pinches of her nipples. I can't see her face—David's bloody shoulder's in the way—but she's writhing wantonly, her moans no longer gagged by his cock but ringing clear.

'Move so I can see her face,' I bark at David.

He shifts, and she turns her head and looks straight at me.

Fucking *yes.*

Her mascara is all smudged. Her lips are puffy and just fucked and so fucking sexy. Her hair's a mess. But best of all is the imminent orgasm written all over her face as Max drills into her. As she takes his cock.

And that sends me over the edge. Seeing her face. Watching the two of them work her, watching Max pump the fuck away against her pussy. He's holding nothing back. No one is.

'Fuck,' I spit out, holding Athena's head in an iron grip. 'Jesus fuuuck.' And I'm over the edge, thrilling, searing heat racing down my spine and through my balls and along my dick, unthinkable pleasure coursing through my body as I go rigid and empty myself into Athena's mouth.

She takes it all and swallows like the good girl she is, the circles she's making with her hips telling me she's close. But still, she cleans me up and licks me dry even as she's still working her pussy furiously.

I glance behind me. The sofa's just there. Sliding my still semi-hard dick out of her mouth, I tug my boxer briefs and trousers back up. Then I grip her arms and haul her to her feet, banding one arm tightly around her so she doesn't get light-headed and fall over. She's still blindfolded, bless her.

I get a hand between us and yank her wrap dress open and her knickers down before perching on the back of the sofa. It's the perfect height for me to shove a wool-clad leg between her thighs.

'Put your arms around me,' I tell her, 'and rub that little bare pussy on my leg until you come.'

She moans and sinks her head into the crook of my neck, her arms going around me. I band my arm back around her and hold her in place as she grinds against me. I can feel her damp heat through my Italian wool.

'That's it,' I croon. 'I know how much you like to come, you dirty little thing. Rub your clit against me as hard as you can. I want to hear you.'

'Oh God,' she gasps against my neck as she squirms and rides my thigh. Her breath is hot, her body warm and pliant and gorgeous, and her mewls gratifyingly needy.

And the whole time, as I hold her and let her grind against me, my eyes are locked on the woman who won't let herself need me. The woman who's on my office carpet as Max rails the living daylights out of her. The guy knows how to fuck, and it fucking disgusts me to see him wind her higher and higher.

But I'm a beggar, and beggars can't be choosers.

Speaking of which...

'Make her beg,' I say stonily to Max, my voice far more authoritative now I've taken the edge off my frustration with

Athena's world-class blowjob. Not that that will slake my thirst for long. I'm definitely bending her over the conference table when I've kicked everyone else out.

Max leans forward, the cotton of his shirt brushing over Genevieve's skin. He drags a hand through her hair and over the indents of her spinal column.

'Tell me how badly you need my cock,' he says through gritted teeth. He's a man on the brink.

I know that feeling.

He straightens up. His shirt tails hide most of his cock, but I can tell he's slid almost all the way out of her.

'Tell me.'

'Please,' she says, 'fuck me, Max.' Her voice has taken on a lazy, dreamlike quality, as if she's already sinking into subspace. I know her mind is clear. I know it has one focus, and one only.

The beautiful orgasm shimmering on the horizon.

Her reward for being brave. For being strong. For choosing herself, and her right to pleasure, over whatever forces in her life have conspired to make her choose her perfect, ice queen persona.

It will be *so* well deserved.

She may be begging Max, but her eyes are fixed on me. On the blindfolded woman grinding against me, using my leg to chase her own base pleasure. On my arm around her waist. She's *my* fucking ice queen, and she knows it.

I hope she also knows that, with a single word, this could have been her.

I hope she's fantasising that it's me fucking her senseless right now.

I hope it's fucking killing her the way it's killing me.

Max pulls out slowly and halts again. 'Tell me what you need,' he says, and it's the perfect thing to say. Because this isn't about humiliating her for the sake of it. It's about showing her the prize and keeping it just out of reach until she finds the courage to use her words.

Until she finds her words to be the magnificent, shameless little beauty we all know she can be.

She makes a sound that's half sigh, half moan. 'I need you dragging that dick of yours out of my pussy like that and then stuffing me full of it again,' she says. There's such a contrast between her clipped, Mary Poppins accent, and the filthy things she's saying, and the raw sex in her tone.

'*Yes,*' Max says, and he thrusts against her so savagely that she cries out as her head butts into the cradle of David's huge chest. 'More.'

'I need you to fill me up.'

'Why?'

'Because I love cock. And I love having both your hands on me.'

'Yes. More. You can do it.'

He pulls out and slams back in hard, and David kneads her glorious, heavy tits.

She cries out, then says in a strangled voice, 'It's the only way I feel alive. It's so fucking dirty... I—I can't live without it. I need it all.'

Her eyes are fluttering, and she's trying to catch her breath, and in this moment she is filthy perfection.

'Yes you do, sweetheart,' I tell her. 'You *are* so fucking dirty, and you're so fucking gorgeous like this. Max, fuck her into oblivion.'

I'm getting hard again. I slide a hand between my and Athena's bodies and slip a finger under her pussy, rubbing her wet, swollen clit so fucking hard that she comes instantly with a loud gasp and convulses against me, shuddering through her own beautiful orgasm.

As she does, Max throws his head back and rams his hips forward and really lets Genevieve have it.

She scrambles down to her elbows and braces with an arm on either side of David's legs. Her entire body is arched for Max, taking everything it can, her hands squeezing into fists, her facial features contorting with anguished pleasure as he releases a volley of savage thrusts.

And then she's coming, crying out with a voice so raw and pure and greedy as she drinks me in with her eyes, and I'm stock still, frozen with desire and awe. It's not my cock that's giving her this pleasure, but I have the distinct sense that she's giving this spectacular orgasm to me.

Max is still going, feeding her hunger, driving her further and further over the abyss into fucking oblivion, and her climax draws impossibly out before she squeezes her eyes shut and mouths a single, strangled word at me.

Anton.

Not *Max.*

Anton.

I've endured a lot tonight. I've known great pleasure and awe, but a man of my temperament does not usually share.

With anyone.

This is what I needed—to see all the bullshit and manners and intellect and culture wiped away until all that remains is this stunning woman in the throes of passion, unlocked and unveiled and fucking unleashed.

Nothing we've done here this evening has reduced her. It's elevated her to the queen I knew she was.

Because, as she lies there after Max has come, with her head resting on David's thigh and her sated face turned to me, she has never looked so majestic.

33

GEN

This apartment is my haven.

It's for me and me alone.

And, while it's not girly by any stretch, its energy is feminine. Serene.

My professional life is demanding. My personal life can be... intense.

Exhibit A: this evening's spontaneous orgy.

I work hard for my money, and I play hard, and it's critical that I have a safe space to retreat from the professional and social and sexual onslaughts I inflict upon myself.

I'm extra grateful for it tonight as I stand robed in my all-white bathroom, body showered and hair washed. God knows, I need to decompress. I should be exhausted, and my body certainly is, but my brain hasn't got the memo. I'm wired to the hilt, crawling out of my skin. All that stimulation has my adrenal system over-functioning.

The face that looks back at me in the mirror is objectively wrecked but somehow glowing. I suppose orgasms really are the best facial. I fixed my just-fucked hair and smudged eye makeup in the little bathroom off Anton's office and reapplied my lipstick, but I'm far from the usual groomed version of myself that I present to the world.

I put on my towelling beauty headband and get to work, pumping a generous dollop of my favourite gel-to-oil cleanser onto my palm and spreading it over my skin. Working it in. That sensation as the gel turns to oil is my favourite, and my skin deserves every second of TLC tonight.

The aftermath of tonight's sex-fest was... interesting. We're big on aftercare at Alchemy. Maddy recently led a huge social media campaign around educating our members on its role and its importance. That said, in the main Playroom there tends to be more of a fuck-and-leave approach. Aftercare is more prevalent in our private rooms.

This evening had aftercare *and* after-celebrating. Anton helped Athena back on with her thong and, it seemed, whispered what was most likely the filthiest form of praise to her before she took herself off to the bathroom and then slipped out of the room.

David and Max, meanwhile, were all about helping me get dressed, given all they had to do was stuff their dicks back in their boxers and haul their trousers up. They got me on my feet and held me between them as they slid my thong up, hooked my bra, and zipped up my dress. Max slipped a hand up said dress as he put my shoes back on as if I was Cinderella while David held me steady, a worshipful expression on his face.

If I had to guess, I'd say he doesn't indulge in this kind of thing much. He's less overtly dirty than Max and Anton are, though it's safe to say he enjoyed himself this evening.

Max was in his element as he got me dressed, laughing and making dirty jokes and ribbing Anton.

And the Big Bad Wolff?

He zipped himself back up and stood there, watching every second of the fun I was having with the other guys.

Because it was fun.

It wasn't awkward or excruciating, like it could have been. I was seriously chilled after two orgasms, riding high on feel-good hormones and on the heady experience of being the only person Anton Wolff had eyes for.

As Max flirted and kissed up my back before zipping my dress closed, Anton watched me still.

His expression was impassive, but his eyes were burning.

I can feel them burning into me even now.

I apply my serums and moisturiser and pad through to my apartment's spacious reception area. This is my favourite room on this planet. High ceilings, original plasterwork and an Art Deco-style drum chandelier are all the features it needs. The floorboards are polished originals, the walls and furniture are off white, and double doors lead through to my white kitchen. One whole wall is lined with well-thumbed paperbacks, and my enormous coffee table holds an orchid and an edit of my coffee-table books.

Dior.

Chanel.

Oscar de la Renta.

Cartier.

Capri.

All the classics from Assouline.

There's a *chaise longue* in front of the huge windows, cream upholstery with an iconic beige Hermès blanket strewn across it. It's my favourite place to sit and read, or daydream.

Which is what I do as soon as I've put a chicken dish my part-time chef cooked in the oven to reheat and poured myself a glass of beautifully chilled Chenin Blanc.

I sit down on that *chaise longue* and I put my feet up and let my head fall back against the headrest. My apartment smells deliciously of Diptyque candles—*Feu de Bois*, to differentiate from the *Baies* candles we have peppered around Alchemy to mask the scent of sex. I've got some soothing classical piano music on. I'm surrounded by the womb-like serenity of my apartment, and still I feel jolted.

The group sex didn't make me uneasy. I made a decision long ago to refuse to feel any guilt or self-loathing over what is a harmless and healthy and highly gratifying activity between consenting adults.

Six years of being sexually active without achieving a single orgasm at the hands of anyone other than myself focused the mind. It tipped me over the edge when Rafe proposed the concept of Alchemy to us. And it focuses the mind on nights like this, when the come-down could be hard and the temptation to ruminate could be too great.

I pause, take a sip of wine, and check in with myself.

Nope.

No guilt.

No self-recrimination.

No slut-shaming.

No judgement.

Science tells us that orgasms are seriously fucking good for female health. They deliver oxytocin, they increase blood flow to the brain, they aid sleep, they help our *skin*, for fuck's sake, they strengthen our pelvic floor, and they're absolutely brilliant for our immune systems.

There's a reason they call her *Mother* Nature.

So, nope. There are no problems here. Once I've had a chance to wind down gently, I'll go to bed and get a great night's sleep, and it's all thanks to Anton Wolff.

As I recline in the glory of a summer sunset, I grudgingly admit to myself that Anton's parting words to me at the door may be in part responsible for my buoyant mood.

He stood in the doorway, one palm up on the doorframe in a particularly alpha pose, and said the following.

Not *you were magnificent.*

But *you are magnificent.*

34

GEN

The office is the same as it is most days. Norm is snoring at Zach's feet. Maddy's teasing Cal about the women he fucked last night. Rafe's not here—he's at his hedge fund, Cerulean, today for a quarterly strategy meeting.

And I'm attempting to put basic plans in place for the French pop-up.

It's not happening, though, because my pussy is still tender from the royal fucking Max gave me, and my soul is still tender from the utter mind fuck that was coming and coming while my eyes were locked on Anton Fucking Wolff's twin dark pools of sin.

It was like having an eye-gasm and an orgasm simultaneously. Worse, because he got into my brain and under my skin, and the filthiness, the depravity of having him watch while his friends fucked me and he got his assistant off ratcheted the whole episode from hot to unspeakable.

Unforgettable.

My mobile ringing interrupts my useless attempts at organisation. It's a number I don't recognise. I put my earbuds in, giving some serious side-eye to the fresh, flaw-less bouquet of camellias that arrived first thing and is now taunting me from my desk. The note read, naturally, *You are magnificent.*

As if I needed reminding of the words that are tattooed on my brain.

'This is Genevieve.'

'Good morning, Ms Carew. This is Rix calling from Anton Wolff's office,' says a voice that's upbeat and cultured in equal measure.

The sound of his name thrums somewhere deep in my belly, and my first thought is *I wonder if he fucks her, too?* The image of that beautiful woman wrapped around Anton, shuddering through her orgasm while he watched with raw, unflinching intensity as I bucked and cried out through my own will be forever seared onto my brain.

What will *not* be seared onto my brain is the name I mouthed as I came for the second time, because that moment never happened and will never be discussed.

'What can I do for you, Rix?' I ask now, hoping that Anton hasn't made her call to schedule another pounding for my pussy at the hands of his admittedly gorgeous hench-man, because right now I just want to be left alone with my memories and my Ibuprofen.

'Mr Wolff would be grateful if you'd accompany him and some members of our Wolff Hospitality division on a two-day trip to Cannes next week,' she says.

I bet he would.

She prattles on. She sounds like she should lay off the coffee. 'The aim is to scope out possible venues for your pop-up and be on site to make initial decisions around theme, decor, staffing and promotional activity. Are you available Wednesday to Friday next week?'

I frown. 'Could we not do it in a single night?'

'Mr Wolff would be grateful if you could spare him two nights. He proposes flying out Wednesday afternoon and back Friday afternoon.' She pauses. 'He asked me to pass on that he's happy to host you over the weekend if you'd like to prolong your trip.'

'That won't be necessary,' I say quickly. A weekend in the South of France with the Big Bad Wolff is up there with the worst ideas ever. 'Let me check my calendar.'

I have a networking lunch and a couple of interviews scheduled with prospective members next week, but nothing that can't be moved. I huff. I resent having to jump when Anton calls, but I also appreciate that this pop-up is operating on a ridiculously tight set-up schedule, and I know I'm the right person to oversee this stage from Alchemy's perspective.

At some point in the next few weeks, we'll get Cal over there to work his magic, but as the COO I should be there to ensure that every tiny detail reflects the Alchemy brand.

And nothing is more important than the venue.

Besides, I love Cannes. I love the glamour, the weather, the energy. I adore the endless rosé and blue skies and the people-watching over seared tuna.

'That should be fine,' I say, making a concerted effort to make my voice sound friendly, because it's not this woman's fault she works for a vagina-wrecking-from-ten-paces sexual monster. 'Who else is going from your end?' I squeeze my eyes shut as I await my answer. *Don't say Athena. Or Max. Or David.*

'His Chief of Staff, Max, who I believe you've met, and...'

She reels off three or four other names I'm not familiar with and I exhale. One of out three ain't bad. Besides, Max may be a dodgy fucker but he does have the ability to put me at ease with his unique blend of humour and flirtatious swagger.

I'm definitely keeping my hotel room door locked and bolted, though.

'Can you let me have the flight and hotel details and I'll have my assistant book it all up?' I ask.

'Mr Wolff has insisted on arranging the accommodation,' she says in a sing-song, 'and you will all be travelling on his jet from Biggin Hill at two o'clock on Wednesday if that is convenient?'

I sigh. Great. Now I have to endure a ride in Anton Wolff's Big Dick jet while trying not to think about how many organs I'd be willing to sell in exchange for membership of the Mile High Club with him.

'I can make that work, yes,' I tell Rix.

We cover off a few more logistical details and I'm preparing to wind up the call when she says, 'Mr Wolff would like a quick word.'

'That's not—' I begin.

That's not... *necessary*.

Advisable.

'Genevieve.' His voice comes down the line, saying my name in his trademark tone.

Clipped.

Deep.

Commanding.

Just how he said it last night, when he was instructing his guys how to fuck me.

Just how he said it when he was ordering me to beg.

I despise that I'm not strong enough to withstand the Pavlovian response I have to it.

I sigh. 'Anton. What can I do for you?'

A pause. 'I wanted to check in.'

I'm not giving this guy an inch. He got what he wanted, didn't he? Well, he didn't get to fuck me, but he got the next best thing, which was me in a puddle on the floor. I go for disingenuous. 'About France?'

'No, not about France. About yesterday evening. I just wanted to make sure you were okay.'

'I'm absolutely fine, thank you.'

'Glad to hear it.' He pauses again. He seems less sure of himself than usual. 'So... will I see you at the club this week?'

'Unlikely.' My tone is businesslike. 'I'll be working late most of the week, trying to pull things together from my end for Cannes.'

'Got it,' he says. 'I'll see you on the plane, then. Let Rix know if you need any assistance from our end.'

He sounds cool. Dismissive. Maybe I've hurt his ego. Or maybe he's already moving on, thinking about his next fuck. Or deal. I'm sure he enjoys closing deals and women equally.

'Anton,' I say before he rings off. 'Don't try any funny business with our hotels, okay?'

'I can't imagine what you mean,' he drawls. Cheeky fucker.

'No interconnecting rooms, or creepy open-plan suites, alright? I want my privacy. This is a work trip.'

'I promise you, Genevieve, I won't try any funny business with hotel rooms,' he says. 'That good enough for you?'

It'll have to be, I suppose.

When we finish the call, I put my head in my hands.

I'm going to need some serious Maddy time to get through this.

35

GEN

'And he just *looked* at you? The whole time you were coming?' Belle asks.

'Both times. And he wasn't just looking at me, he was also making his EA blow him and then letting her hump his leg, and calling out instructions to the other guys and generally being a revoltingly dominant, sexy, multi-tasking motherfucker.'

I grimace and take a generous slug of rosé from a glass filled with wine and large ice cubes. The French call it *une piscine*—a swimming pool. I suppose it doesn't hurt to get in the mood for the South of France.

'Jesus Christ.' Maddy crosses her legs and squeezes her thighs together. 'That's the hottest thing I've ever heard. Like, even hotter than him actually fucking you. It's so repressed.'

They're an excellent audience; I'll give them that. They look positively titillated. I knew they wouldn't judge me. On the contrary, I knew they'd go crazy, in a good way, for what went down last night.

Pun intended.

'Believe me, no one in that room was repressed,' I say drily.

'I know, but him holding back on touching you like you asked but then eye-fucking you and pulling all the strings.' She shifts on her bar stool. 'I'd say that's very fucking hot.'

Sadly, I have to agree with her. I've never done anything quite like that—never had a guy call the shots like that when he's not the person I'm actually fucking.

And I've definitely never had the kind of sexual and emotional and physical intensity with a bystander of a sexual act like that.

The whole thing was a total headfuck. Twenty-four hours later, I'm still reeling.

Maddy, Belle and I are in the Red Room at the Connaught Hotel, a bar that's far less *Fifty Shades* than its name suggests. We're treating ourselves to a drink, a catch up, and some decadent bar snacks before we go across the road to Matches Fashion's gorgeous townhouse for an emergency pre-Cannes personal shopping appointment, at Maddy's insistence.

She also insisted on bringing Belle along, so I don't end up with a selection that's too slutty (her words). Belle has a very different body shape than me—she's incredibly slender —but our taste in clothes is probably more similar than mine and Maddy's.

They also perfectly represent the two sides of my character. When I first interviewed Belle for our Unfurl programme, I saw myself in her. She was far less sexually experienced than I was at her age, but I recognised in her circumspect, guilt-ridden attitude to sex the same demons I'd grappled with. I'm happy to say we're both far more liberated these days. And, although she's in a monogamous and sickeningly happy relationship with Rafe, I see enough of them at the club to know they're in no way boring.

Maddy, on the other hand, is totally shameless, and I mean that as a massive compliment to her. It's not something I see that much in women, even among our clients. In my experience, it's difficult for women to be shame-free about their sexuality in a way that's not complicated or darkened by any experiences they may have had. And Maddy, to her full credit, is.

Let's just say Zach is a lucky guy.

In some ways, Maddy's my hero. Even at the tender age of twenty-three—*fuck*, these two are young—she represents the ideal. The gold standard for which I consciously strive. That's why events like last night are turning points for me. They're my way of proving to myself that I can throw off all those layers of shame and etiquette and social conditioning and pursue my fantasies, no matter how far-fetched.

And fucking Anton Wolff's colleagues on the floor of his office while he art-directed was pretty far-fetched.

I'm munching on some outrageously good truffled *aranchini* when Maddy puts her glass down. 'So I have a question for you, and you're not going to like it, so don't go all scary on me, okay?'

'I'm not scary,' I protest when I've swallowed.

They both snort. 'Please,' Maddy says. 'You're fucking terrifying. Like, if Elsa from *Frozen* was a headmistress.'

I smirk. I rather like that analogy, actually. I'm glad the froideur I cultivate works. 'And your point is?' I ask haughtily.

'Right. I hate to say it, but Anton seems pretty perfect for you,' she says with a flick of her hair. She wiggles her eyebrows at me. 'So, honestly, I don't know what you're playing at.'

I frown. 'That's ridiculous. The man's a bloody nightmare.'

They exchange a pointed glance. 'We don't know him, really, but it sounds like he's behaved pretty well so far,' Belle says gently.

'*Well?* He ambushed me into being spit-roasted in his office, for Christ's sake!' I say, lowering my voice, because this is really not the stuff polite chit-chat is made of.

Maddy's mouth twists in amusement. 'Poor little Gen, corrupted by the Big Bad Wolff. Sounds to me like you got pretty stuck in.'

I glare at her and take a large swig from my *piscine*.

'Seriously, though,' she continues. 'I mean, he may have played a bit fast and loose with your rules, but he didn't technically break them, did he? You've told him not to touch you, and he hasn't.'

'He just *watched* you. A *lot*,' Belle chimes in unhelpfully, a gleeful grin on her far-too-pretty face.

'He's good with boundaries,' Maddy sing-songs. She's boundary-obsessed, and I don't like how valid her points are.

'Oh Jesus,' I groan with an eye-roll. 'Please don't give me your boundary spiel again.'

'It's important,' she says. She picks her glass up and drinks before waggling a finger at me. 'And, you know, it sounds like every single thing he's done has been to get your attention. And I think that's very sweet.'

I don't think anyone in their right mind could call Anton Wolff *sweet*,' I say through gritted teeth.

'I think he's really hot, though,' Belle says.

'Like, seriously fucking hot,' Maddy agrees. 'He's a total daddy. That's the other thing.' She turns to me, finger now jabbing the air. 'You're always complaining that guys are

either total animals who are completely socially unacceptable, or they're lovely, decent, smart guys who are totally
fucking boring in bed.

'I hate to tell you, babes, but he's the real deal. He's, like,
a proper grownup. That's exactly what you need.'

'Ooh, yeah,' Belle coos, and I'm reminded why I
shouldn't hang out with women this young.

'Right?' Maddy asks. 'He's a billionaire, which is hot for
a million reasons, but mainly for competence kink reasons,
which I know you have in spades, my dearest, beautiful Gen.
The guy's a fucking legend, and he wants *you*. He couldn't
make it clearer. He's successful, he's gorgeous, he's a sexual
predator but in a *totally* amazing way, and he wants to blow
your mind.' She sits back and crosses her legs prettily. 'So
for the love of God, woman, tell me what the fuck your
problem is.'

36

GEN

Maddy's words are still rankling when we leave the Connaught. There's nothing in life more irritating than not being able to find a flaw in other people's logic. Especially when it opposes yours. In my head, Anton Wolff is a dangerous man whose dangerous looks and dangerous appetites could totally derail me and the carefully honed equilibrium of my life.

So her and Belle's insistence on painting him as this worthy, honorable, eligible suitor pisses me off, frankly.

Matches' personal shopping services are located in a beautiful redbrick townhouse on Carlos Place, right across from the Connaught. The room we're in has thick white carpet and sage-green walls. A large brass free-standing clothes rail hangs empty, waiting to be hung with goodies.

My personal shopper, Amandine, has excellent taste and knows me and my style well. I don't buy everything from Matches, of course—they don't carry Chanel, or several of my other favourite labels—but together Amandine and I have created a timeless, elegant capsule wardrobe that showcases my figure and sees me through most of my professional and social engagements.

I have a feeling that's about to be blown out of the water.

'The stuff you put her in is stunning,' Maddy's telling Amandine now, 'but she's off to Cannes, and we think she needs to loosen up a bit.'

'Structure works best for my figure,' I warn Maddy, trying not to lose my shit too early. 'Amandine knows that. Tailoring is my friend.'

'We can do some hidden tailoring, maybe,' Amandine muses, looking me up and down. 'It won't be too hot yet, so you can stick to structured if you prefer.'

'Excellent,' I say at the same time Belle says, 'Maddy's right. You should go loose and flowing and sexy.'

An image of myself in Grecian-style drapery, flowing sensually in the breeze, makes me want to giggle.

'Loose and flowing and sexy is for women like you guys, who have hollow legs and unfairly good figures,' I retort.

'Nope,' Belle says. 'Uptight is not a good look in the South of France, Gen. Maddy's right. You need to loosen up. Would you wear a bikini?'

'Absolutely not,' I say in horror.

She turns to Amandine. 'We're going to need some great one-pieces, then. Sculptural. You know. Maybe some one-shouldered ones, a bit of cutout waist action, maybe a belted one.'

Amandine nods. 'Completely agree. And some gorgeous cover-ups to match.'

'Yep.' Belle nods. 'Do you know where you're staying yet?'

I shake my head. 'Not a clue. I imagine somewhere in the middle of town. The Carlton? The Martinez?'

'I think we should try some more flowy numbers for

evening, too,' Belle muses. 'Can you bring out some Zimmerman and some Chloe? What else should she consider?'

Amandine surveys me once again, tapping her chin. 'Farm Rio?' she suggests.

Maddy and Belle both *oooh* in unison. What the actual fuck?

'What is Farm Rio?' I demand.

'Brazilian brand. Highly patterned. Very fun and fabulous,' Amandine says.

I narrow my eyes. 'That doesn't sound like me at all.'

'Well it needs to sound like you,' Maddy tells me. 'We need *all* the prints, because you are going to be fun *and* fabulous next week if it kills me.'

Fifteen minutes later I'm standing in my knickers and surrounded by a haze of colours I haven't worn in years. My palate is usually monochrome, neutrals and blush tones. Two of the dresses on the rail are actually orange, for fuck's sake.

I try on a glorious Lanvin which is a little too formal for what I imagine we'll be doing next week, which is hitting up some bars and clubs. Next up is a Farm Rio maxi-dress in lightweight cotton with a flounced skirt whose fullness is beautifully balanced by a plunging V necklace and subtle cutouts on the waist. The print is large-scale royal blue and green on an off-white background.

It's like nothing I'd ever choose for myself, but I truly love it. I look like a totally different version of myself.

'It's amazing!' Belle says, clapping her hands together excitedly. 'You have to get it! God, you have gorgeous skin.'

'Only one problem,' I say, tucking my hands under my armpits like a chicken and tugging at the armholes of the sleeveless dress as I survey myself in the mirror with narrowed, critical eyes. 'I can't wear a bra with it.'

The concept of going braless is horrifying. I know my body, and it appreciates having some serious architecture underpinning its clothes.

'With tits like that, you don't need anything,' Maddy says. 'The Big Bad Wolff will go wild for it. Let it all hang out, that's what I say.'

'Why does it feel like that's more of a life philosophy than a boob philosophy for you?' I grumble.

But I know I'll take the dress.

37

ANTON

I know Genevieve told me she wouldn't be frequenting the club before our trip, but I'm still disappointed and vaguely pissed off not to see her at the Alchemy bar tonight. I eye up The Playroom's double doors before jerking my head in the other direction.

She may be working from home, having slipped into something comfortable and curled up with her laptop, but it's worth checking to see if she's still here, isn't it?

I drain the second of my two permitted shots and head out of the bar, back down the hallway towards the main entrance. The doormen's shadows are visible through the frosted glass of the front door, and the glamorous young brunette who greeted me when I came in is still at her post here in the hallway.

'Is Genevieve still in there?' I ask, jerking a thumb towards the closed door to the front meeting room where she's hosted me on previous occasions.

She hesitates. 'Oh. Um...'

I shoot her a confident smile. 'We're business associates.'

Or near enough. 'If you'd like to check that she's happy to see me before I barge in, by all means, go ahead.'

Her face brightens. 'Of course, Mr Wolff. Just give me a second, please.'

She opens the door and slips through, and I hear murmurs before she re-emerges. 'Please go on in,' she says with a smile I'd usually find seductive, but which now leaves me cold.

I cut through the empty front room, smiling at the pink onyx vulva sculpture which is lit and glowing from within in the dusk. I know from my meetings here that the Alchemy teams' desks are on the other side of the double doors.

Sure enough, I spot Genevieve before I'm even through them. She's lit just by the setting sun and her computer screen, and she looks perfectly lovely, as always.

She doesn't get up.

'Hello,' she says tiredly and, I think, warily.

'Hi,' I return. I indicate the edge of her desk. 'Can I perch for a minute?'

'Of course.' She pushes her chair back to give us a bit more space. 'Want some wine?'

I glance down. She's got a glass of something white and chilled while she works. 'Why not?'

'Give me a sec.' She pushes herself up and heads towards the back of the room as I enjoy the view of her shapely arse. Her dress is just tight enough to graze every curve. Nobody nails that mix of class and feminine sensuality like Genevieve. She exudes them both. Her arse looks fucking amazing, though I prefer it bare.

Arched.

And her dress has a zip running from neck to hem. Tut tut. What a naughty girl.

She disappears into what I assume is a kitchen and

returns a moment later with a glass for me. I take it and raise it. 'Cheers.'

'Cheers.' We clink.

'You weren't lying about working late.'

'No.' She gives a little laugh and scratches her forehead with her thumb. She looks shattered. 'As luck would have it, our Operations Manager is away this week, so I'm having to set up all the workflows in our system myself.'

'That doesn't sound particularly glamorous or fun,' I say.

'It's definitely neither. But it has to be done. I'm the details person—the guys take the piss out of me for it. I've been sleeping really badly, imagining all the things that could possibly go wrong with the pop-up.'

I've also been sleeping really badly, imagining having you cuffed to my bed while I fuck your pretty cunt, I think, but I opt not to share that information.

'I feel bad,' I say instead. 'This is our project. You're just supposed to sit back and take the money.'

That earns me a laugh. 'Yeah, no. That was never going to happen. But if we build systems and workflows for this pop-up, then we have everything in place to project manage any others we might do. The key is to streamline everything so we can roll it out easily.'

'Like a franchise model,' I suggest, and she nods.

'Exactly. The problem is, it's all in here'—she taps her temple—'and it needs to be in *there*. I wish I could stick a USB in my brain and download it all, but it needs to be done manually. This time.'

'This time,' I echo. 'Well, I promise you I'll show you a good time in Cannes. I promise we'll have some fun.'

She gives me some serious side-eye. 'Last time you proposed we have fun, look what happened.'

I take a sip of my wine before I reply. 'You can't say that wasn't fun.'

She purses her lips. 'It was.' She makes it sound like I'm forcing a confession under duress. 'So, you've made me a few promises now. I hope you can keep them.'

'Have I?' I say, amused.

'Yes.' She counts on a perfectly manicured hand. 'That we have fun—the non-sexual kind, and that you don't try any funny business with hotel rooms.'

'Ahh.' I stretch out my legs and cross my ankles, thoroughly enjoying myself. 'I can promise to deliver on both of those.'

'If you say so.' She looks thoroughly unconvinced.

'I do.'

She'll be fucking furious when she finds out the accommodation plan.

But it definitely doesn't involve a hotel.

I can't wait.

We regard each other for a moment. She really is a classic beauty. Her bone structure is extraordinary. High cheekbones and huge eyes and a way of holding herself that brings to mind stars of the silver screen. She's immaculately made up, as always, and I allow myself to recall those heady images of her, smudged and tousled and just-fucked and so extraordinarily shameless.

'I should let you get back to it,' I say reluctantly, because she's clearly shattered, and I don't want to keep her here any longer than she needs to be.

She hesitates. 'Are you going back inside?' she asks. Her tone is casual, but something tells me that's deliberate.

Or maybe that's just wishful thinking on my part.

'Nah,' I say. Any allure The Playroom held for me earlier has vanished. I take a good slug of my wine. 'This is my third drink, and I don't want to flout your rules. They're there for a reason.'

She gives me a small smile. 'I think you'd be fine.'

'Nevertheless,' I say. 'I'd better go.'

We stare at each other. The air is thick around us, and no fucking wonder. Jesus, I've only met this woman a handful of times, and yet the experiences we've shared together already—fucking hell. It's impossible not to feel the weight of all that desire, and tension, and memory.

I make a split-second decision. I genuinely came in here with no agenda beyond seeing her, but I'd like to clear the air before France.

I'd like to do more than clear the air—I'd like to clear up any misapprehension on her part, too.

'I just want to say.' I clear my throat and fix those blue eyes with mine. 'You seem to have a certain impression of me, which I may or may not deserve. But know this. If you ever grant me permission to touch you, that will be it for me.'

Her eyes widen, shapely eyebrows arching in a silent question.

I forge ahead. 'I mean to say, once I touched you, I wouldn't touch anyone else. No one. I know how to play, sure. But when I'm with someone I'm genuinely interested in, that's it. Not out of obligation, but because that's the way I want it. Do you understand?'

I leave the rest unsaid.

I'm genuinely interested in you.

She stares at me, lips parted. I seem to have taken the wind out of her sails. I know she doesn't trust me as far as she can throw me, but I've respected her boundaries so far, in every way, and I think I've earned the right to speak my mind.

Finally, she nods. 'Yes—um—understood. Thank you.'

'Alright then.' I put down my half-finished drink and stand. 'Thanks for the wine. I'll see you at the airfield in a couple of days.'

I turn to go, but she's out of her chair before I can leave.

'Wait.' She puts a light hand on my shoulder and, leaning in, presses a kiss to my cheek. Her scent envelops me in a heady, musky haze. 'Goodnight, Anton.'

38

GEN

I'm having one of those experiences where my emotions are all over the place and I'm overthinking every single thing and I can't decide if I'm in heaven or hell.

Case in point: this insane jet of his. It's fucking enormous and more luxurious than my apartment, with huge cream leather armchairs whose headrests are monogrammed with a bronze-coloured embroidered *W*. Max told me with a wink as we waited in the terminal that there was also a "private stateroom" at the rear.

I want to hate it. Part of me feels like all this is the human equivalent of Anton fanning his peacock feathers in a display of wealth and power and superiority and opulence, all of which I despise myself for finding attractive. But I'd be a miserable bitch if I allowed that to be my reaction.

Because, if I take all this at face value, it's seriously generous of him to fly us all out to France like this, as well as being practical and time-efficient. Besides, it's not like he commissioned this jet for me. It's clearly a corporate jet, albeit one that Anton has first dibs on. And making it all about me is icky and immature.

Still, I can't help but feel like it's a mating ritual of sorts. Neither can I help but feel wrongfooted by it. Because I can't compete with this sort of thing, and it pisses me off that he gets to showcase his revolting wealth so openly and that I'm a sitting duck who has to suck it up.

I know.

I'm an ungrateful, ungracious bitch.

I feel a bit like Catherine in *The Thomas Crown Affair*, when she wakes up in Crown's house the next morning after having angry hate sex on every marble surface of his palatial home. She's all *you live very well* and *I hate being a foregone conclusion*, and he's gracious with a dash of smugness. But I always feel her intense sheepishness in that scene. Her vulnerability.

Because, damn it, she let her guard down and she let him ravage her in a way they can never go back from, and she's squarely on his turf.

And he's hot as sin and rich as Croesus, and he most definitely has the upper hand there. And even though he's been wonderfully hospitable and utterly charming, she feels laid bare.

That's how I feel.

I comfort myself with the knowledge that I haven't actually fucked Anton as I accept a glass of vintage Krug from a very poised, very attractive, very blonde flight attendant. I have some dignity left, at least.

The trappings may be borderline overwhelming—the plane, the impeccable interior, the monogramming, the Krug, the hot female staff—but the man himself is the biggest problem of all.

He has, predictably enough, taken the seat opposite me,

and here, in his natural habitat, he looks even more gorgeous than usual. He's in a white linen shirt, its sleeves rolled up, and light beige chinos. Brown suede loafers. No socks. Very Euro. Head resting against the seatback bearing his initial, hair a little tousled, skin tanned. Brown eyes watching me, taking me in as I in turn take in our surroundings.

When my glass is filled, he lifts his in salute, and it strikes me that his smile is slightly more unsure than his usual smug style.

The ninety-minute flight goes far too quickly, thanks to the free-flowing champagne, delicious canapés, and the conversation. There's no time for awkwardness and even less for ruminating about what's going on in the brain of the man sitting opposite me or, worse, what's going on in *my* brain that I'm refusing to give oxygen to. Anton's quieter than usual, but Max is on hilarious form. One of their events team members, Lara, is a loud redhead with a broad Essex accent and a relentless desire to rip the piss out of Max, to everyone else's amusement.

Before I know it, we've buckled up for landing at Nice. Below us is one of my favourite sights: the Mediterranean, azure and sparkling and spectacular and dotted with white boats, its coastline looking glamorous. Even from here, it's obvious it's the perfect playground for the rich and famous.

'Where are we staying?' I ask Anton. I've had such an enjoyable time on the flight that I haven't thought to ask until now.

He surveys me. 'Well,' he says after a pause,' these guys are staying in Cannes, and Max is going to visit his special friend in Mougins.'

'My special friend whose husband is away this week,' Max interjects with a cocky smirk, and I smile.

'How predictable,' I tell him before turning back to Anton, my smile wavering. 'And... you and me?' I ask hesitantly, because I can't quite bear to say *us*.

'You're staying at Anton's fat pad on Cap d'Antibes,' Max says before he can answer.

My jaw falls open. *'Excuse me?'* I manage.

'I have a house here,' Anton tells me, his dark eyes fixed on me. He shrugs. 'No need to bother with hotels.'

I know he's purposely used the word *hotels* to remind me of what I made him promise.

Buggery shit.

I've been fucking ambushed.

Again.

'I see,' I say through gritted teeth. I don't want to make a fuss in front of his colleagues, but Anton Wolff knows damn well that he's played dirty, and I'll make sure he knows how fucked off I am. 'That's really not necessary,' I continue. 'I'd rather book myself into the Carlton.'

'You really wouldn't,' Max says. 'I promise, Anton's place makes the Carlton look like a fucking airport Ibis. And it's a lot more, ahem, peaceful, too.' He coughs pointedly.

I glare at him and Anton in turn.

'I'd be honoured if you'd let me host you,' Anton murmurs quietly enough that the others can't hear. His face is impassive, but that dark gaze burns into me.

I roll my eyes. 'Fine,' I say ungraciously, before letting my head sink back against my plush leather seat.

Jesus Christ. What the fuck have I got myself into this time?

39

GEN

The punches keep on coming, and I keep rolling with them. The others take their leave at the airport. Apparently, Max will drop the rest of the team in Cannes before their driver continues inland with him to Mougins. Anton and I, however, are taking a helicopter to his house, even though Antibes is en route to Cannes. Sure, it's rush hour, but I wouldn't have minded sitting in traffic for a few minutes more.

It's all utterly ridiculous.

But as Anton leads me through the private terminal at Nice Airport towards the heliport for what will presumably be a five-minute journey in the air at most, I can't help the frisson of pleasure that ripples through me.

Because who am I kidding?

An impossibly tall, impossibly gorgeous man is accompanying me from his jet to his chopper which will, in turn, whisk us off to his presumably stunning villa in one of the most beautiful and exclusive enclaves in the Mediterranean.

He's bent some rules to get me to himself, and, irritating as that may be in theory, in practice it's actually pretty sexy.

If I'm to be hijacked, then I can think of far worse people and far worse places to suffer.

I notice he's not striding like he tends to do. He's walking more slowly than is surely natural for him so I can keep up as I click-clack over the gleaming white-tiled floor in my high wedges. I thought they'd be a more practical choice than heels, but the thick base makes them so vertiginous that I feel off balance.

Anton halts a couple of steps ahead and smiles at me. His hands are in his pockets, and he keeps them there, sticking out the elbow nearest to me.

'Take my arm,' he says, and I glare, then sigh and acquiesce. I tuck my hand into the crook of his arm, which he flattens back against his body, trapping my hand there between his bicep and his side. The heat of him pumps through his linen shirt, and I feel even more light-headed than when I was trying to stay upright by myself.

A man in a smart pilot's uniform passes us, swinging his carry-on bag, and shoots us a friendly nod. *'Bonjour Madame, Monsieur,'* he chirps.

'Bonjour,' we echo in sync, and that frisson grows, because I know we must look like a couple.

A well-heeled couple on their way to their chic French retreat.

Fuck my life.

'Please don't tell me you'll be flying this thing,' I mutter as we emerge onto the sweltering tarmac where our helicopter awaits.

He looks down at me and grins. 'Definitely not. Not my core competency.'

'Thank fuck,' I say. Not just because I'd fear for my life, but because such an act would be way too Christian Grey, and the assault on my competence kink would probably knock me out.

It's a relief to let go of his arm and to take my seat in the chopper and don my headphones. It's a four-seater, but we sit side-by-side, facing forward. We're right at the very edge of the airport, beyond the runways and almost level with the sea.

The Cap d'Antibes, or simply Cap d'Antibes, as most people call it, is a peninsula south-west of Nice, and going as the crow flies will take us straight across the water. Anton explains that if I sit on the left-hand side, I'll look out to sea, and from the right I'll see the coastline. He offers me the choice.

I take the right-hand seat.

'Whereabouts is your house?' I enquire through my headset as we rise up, my eyes trained on the view of the airport below us. 'Millionaires' Bay?'

There is a literal *Baie de Milliardaires* on the cape.

He laughs. 'Not quite. Those houses are mainly Russian-owned. No, mine's on this side, not far from *La Garoupe*. Do you know it?'

'I do.' *La Garoupe* is a charming beach featuring a low-key but fantastic beach club and restaurant. I arch my back and stretch out my shoulders as I peer down, willing myself to relax. If nothing else, this will be an idyllic place to base myself for a couple of days. I need to move past the insane tension between Anton and me and allow myself to enjoy what should be a delightful mini-break in an idyllic spot.

The stretch of coastline between Nice and Antibes isn't the most inspiring, but soon we're approaching the more heavily wooded jut of the cape which is underpopulated and home to verdant stretches and fuck-off estates.

From my lofty vantage point the sparkling body of water

laps gently against rocky outcrops while, further inland, my eye is drawn to white wedding-cake villas with bleached, pinky roof tiles and the immaculately landscaped and irrigated gardens of the super-rich. As always, my favourite part is spotting the perfect little turquoise-coloured postage stamps of each property's swimming pool.

We're losing height already at a pace that the contents of my stomach can just about handle. I'm not a massive fan of the safety profile of helicopters, but views like this are undoubtedly a privilege. There's a stretch of beach below, and I spy the iconic salmon pink render of Hôtel Imperial Garoupe. I risk a fleeting glance at Anton and find he's watching me. I smile tentatively, because this kind of intimacy with him, cocooned in this overpriced death trap with the noise of the blades intense despite the headphones, is odd, to say the least. Odd, but... nice. And, once again, that sensation of being the sole object of Anton Wolff's attention seeps through my veins and heats my bloodstream like the finest, smoothest single malt.

However pissed off I am that he tricked me into getting me to himself, I recognise what an honour it is that he's allowing me into his inner sanctum. There's no denying that, and as the thrumming blades allow gravity to pull us lower and lower, the prospect of being at his home grows more real and more heady. Excitement and nerves collide in my belly, and I put a hand on my stomach to calm myself.

And then we're down.

Holy shit, we're down. I'm Alice, or Dorothy, or *someone*. Because we've landed squarely on the white H emblazoned into the lushest lawn, and as we came down the last few metres I was treated to views of spectacular grounds and canopies of local pines as well as an elegant, cypress-lined driveway and a Belle Epoque villa so elegant, so pristinely white, and such a perfect example of its type that it almost hurts my heart.

The pilot opens the door for Anton, who jumps out and comes round my side to help me down. I smile at him. I can't help it—this place is stunning, and heady, and I can't not be affected. I've just stepped foot on his property and already I don't want to leave.

40

GEN

If the unmistakable smell of France hit me as I walked through the terminal at Nice Airport, the scent that hits me as I descend, slowly and carefully and clutching Anton's hand, from the helicopter, is pure crack. It's French pines and fragrant flowers and seaweed.

It's heaven.

This is heaven.

As Anton releases his grip on my hand and tucks it once more into the crook of his arm for the uneven, high-risk trip across the coarse, springy grass, a man makes his way across the lawn towards us. He's around Anton's age, wearing khaki shorts, a pristine white polo shirt with a *W* monogrammed onto the chest, and a wide grin. Another reminder that we're at an outpost of the venerable Wolff empire.

'Salut!' he calls, and when he reaches us, he and Anton greet each other not with a handshake, as I expect, but with an animated bro-hug followed by a kiss on both cheeks and a torrent of affectionate French on both sides.

Okay then.

Simmer down, I tell my vagina. *It's just a bit of French. Of course he speaks French. And German. And Italian. You know this from your online stalking. It's not a big deal.*

'This is my friend, Genevieve,' Anton says in English. 'Genevieve, this is Cédric, who runs things for me here.'

'Welcome, *Geneviève*,' Cédric says, taking my hand, his grin unwavering. He pronounces my name the French way —Gen-ev-i-*eve*—making the *eve* part a separate syllable and rendering it significantly more alluring.

'*Bonjour*, Cédric.' I shake his hand heartily. I'm not only grateful for the warm welcome but relieved to have this small clue that Anton runs an informal household here.

'*Vous avez passés un bon voyage?* You 'ad a good journey?' he asks Anton as we walk together towards the house. The view from ground level is even more spectacular. From what I can see it's a perfect square of white stucco that looks like it's repainted every week. Almost all the windows look to be French doors, with the upstairs rooms boasting balconies edged in slate-grey iron railings.

If I'm correct, the other side of the house must face onto the sea, but from some height. In front of us is an imposing front door under an elegant portico above which stands the largest balcony, but before that lies the driveway, inlaid with smooth grey pebbles that look amazing but present a hell of a problem for my wedges. I eye it warily.

'Very smooth, thanks,' Anton replies. He cocks his bent arm at me. 'Take it, Gen.'

I disregard the flash of heat that washes over my skin at the endearment and take his arm gladly. The scent of nature mingles with the scent of him as we walk towards the house.

We walk through the open front door. Holy fucking crap. I am so screwed.

It's stunning. Beyond stunning. It's like a perfect, bijou luxury hotel. Neutral but the furthest thing from bland. The neutrals work perfectly, in fact, because this house has such incredible bones that it needs merely the lightest touch to showcase them. The floor is polished limestone tiles, the walls are covered in mirrors and contemporary artwork, and in the centre of the hallway stands a round table with an artfully casual, and fucking enormous, arrangement of fresh flowers and greenery that's heavy on the olive and eucalyptus branches and smells divine.

But what steals the show is the view. Because the hallway runs the entire length of the house, and the far side of the space is completely open to the sea. I see blue sky and bluer sea fringed with more glorious pines.

'Oh wow,' I say. 'Anton, it's incredible.' I smile up at him, unable to help myself, and he returns the gesture with a warm, welcoming grin of his own. He's undoubtedly king of this castle, but I have a feeling he's a gracious ruler.

'I have an idea.' He gently extricates his arm from my grip. 'Why don't we take off our shoes and we can have a proper look around? The grass is very soft.'

I hum my appreciation, because clearly I need to lose these dangerous wedges far more than he needs to lose his loafers. It's thoughtful of him. Before I know it, he's squatting and looking up at me.

'May I?' he asks.

'Sure, thanks,' I say awkwardly. He undoes the tiny buckle on my strap before reaching for my hand so he can steady me as I step out of it and lower my foot a good five or six inches to the ground. Then he does the same on the other side, the soft brush of his knuckles against my ankle sending a flutter of goosebumps over the skin.

'Better?' he asks as he stands, my wedges in hand. 'Bloody hell, these weigh a tonne.'

'*Much* better,' I tell him. 'And yes, they'd make excellent door stops. Or weapons.'

'I'll bear that in mind.' He places them carefully by the front door, toeing off his loafers and sliding them next to my shoes. 'After you,' he says, gesturing towards the glorious vista ahead of us.

I'm already moving around the central table, drawn by the siren song of the Med right there beyond the grounds. 'Why the hell do you base yourself in London?' I breathe as I take in the vivid greens and blues.

He chuckles softly behind me. 'I ask myself that every fucking day.'

I get that. On the one hand, Anton is the ultimate alpha male, and that office where I so willingly submitted to him and his friends felt like the perfect reflection of his dominant, hungry personality. But here, as we pad barefoot across cool, smooth stone to take in the wonders of his home, he already seems softer. Less frenetic.

I suspect I do, too.

We cross the threshold and exit onto a gorgeous terrace that wraps around the back of the house. On one side sits a long wooden table under a leafy pergola that hangs heavy with bougainvillea and ivy. On the other is a large cluster of smart outdoor furniture around a coffee table.

And in front of us?

Lawns.

Trees.

Steps down to what looks like a spectacular pool.

And the sea.

'At least my kidnapper has good taste in hideouts,' I remark as I shoot him some serious side-eye. Luckily for him, his hostage is thawing, and far more quickly than she'll let on.

He grins. 'Glad you approve. Take a look down here.'

I pick my way across the terrace and down shallow stone steps to the pool level. We're high enough to have an incredible view of the sea, despite the line of trees that shields us from properties further down the hill.

The pool is bloody spectacular: a turquoise oblong with curved ends and a fan of shallow steps at one end. It's surrounded by sleek white paving and bookended with a seriously bling-looking summer kitchen and bar to the left and another gorgeous covered area to the right that looks like the perfect spot for a post-swim doze. If Slim Aarons were still around, he'd undoubtedly approve.

The dozen or so beds that line the near side of the pool area are, unsurprisingly, gorgeous too. They're a mix of heavyweight teak loungers with white mattresses, cushions and bolsters, all bearing the obligatory swirly *W* and a couple of huge white canopied daybeds.

My feelings for this guy may be a complicated, fucked-up mess, but I'm not one to withhold praise when it's due. He stands beside me, barefoot and hands in his pockets. His head is tilted back and his eyes half-closed as he immerses himself in his surroundings. If I'm thrilled to be here, I simply can't imagine how heady it must feel to call this home.

'It's absolutely stunning,' I tell him softly, and he shades his eyes with his hand, looking down at me and smiling.

'Glad you like it,' he says. 'I hope you make yourself at home while you're here.'

And then some.

'You can take care of the recce tomorrow, correct?' I say airily, waving a hand in the direction of the loungers. 'Because I'm not going anywhere.'

He chuckles, pleased. 'As you like it. I'll tell Max you got food poisoning.'

'Do you have a boat?' I ask, admiring the white yachts and sleek speedboats dotting the blue water in the distance.

'I do. It's round the other side of the cape, at Port Gallice.'

'Is it a gin palace?'

'Some less polite people might call it that,' he says. 'If you change your mind and decide to stay for the weekend, you can try it out for yourself.'

I start. There's something about the tone of his voice when he says it that gives me goosebumps. It's less challenging and more... hopeful. Tentative.

He must notice my reaction, because he continues quickly. 'But let's get you settled in before I start giving you the hard sell, shall we?'

'Sounds good,' I say.

I have a horrible feeling it wouldn't be a hard sell at all, I think.

'It's just you and me tonight,' he says with a sidelong glance at me as we turn towards the house. 'I hope that's okay. It seemed a shame to haul ourselves out again, having just arrived.'

I follow him reluctantly. I could stay out here forever, but I could also use a shower, and I definitely need a hat and shades if I'm to spend any more time in the sun.

'I agree. That's fine,' I tell him. We've been here five minutes, and already this place is working its magic on me. It's clear this entire situation is a massive set-up, but now that I'm here, I find I couldn't care less. I'm already in its thrall, and I already like the version of himself Anton is when he's here.

I hope I like the version of myself this place makes me, too.

'I'll give you a full tour later,' he says, 'but let me show you to your room first. Then drinks on the terrace in, say, an hour?'

He leads me up a magnificent central staircase to a first-floor landing, gesturing to the right, which is the front of the house. 'My room's down there,' he says, and yours is right at the other end.'

He winks at me.

He knows exactly what's going through my head.

Keep me away from the Big Bad Wolff.

My room, if you could call it that, is spectacular. It's an enormous space with a huge white bed dressed in traditional white Provençal linen on one side and an elegant cluster of sofa and armchairs on the other.

There's an open fireplace with a sculptural limestone mantle, a fuck-off chandelier hanging from the centre of the ceiling, and French doors which are open onto a small balcony, their white voile curtains blowing softly in the welcome breeze. If I have my bearings correct, I'm right above the house's main entrance. My suitcase and vanity bag already sit on their own ottoman at the end of the bed.

Anton launches into full-on butler mode. 'This is your balcony,' he says. 'It overlooks the front of the house, where we came in. There are external shutters, obviously. Cédric will close them for you tonight and he'll turn on the air con, too. The control is here if you want it sooner. That's the bathroom through there.' He gestures. 'If you'd like anything unpacked or pressed, hit zero on the phone there. There's a wardrobe here...'

He opens the door of the antique armoire that stands against one wall and peers inside before stepping back, seemingly satisfied. 'If you have any problems at all, call Céd. Or me. Otherwise...' He clears his throat, and I realise he's nervous. 'Otherwise I'll see you for sundowners at seven. Casual. No need to dress up on my account.'

I hold back a smile. 'Got it. And it's all absolutely perfect, thanks.'

'The shower is brand new. The other one was a bit—anyway, it should all be sorted now. But again, do shout if you have problems, or there's a hammam in the basement you're welcome to use.'

I shake my head. 'I'm sure it'll all be great. Honestly.'

'Okay, then. See you.' He gives me a brusque nod, takes one more look around the room, and backs out, closing the double doors.

When he's gone, I exhale deeply as I circle the room where I stand, taking in the high ceilings and the air and the light and the luxury. Wowzers. This is a head fuck of epic proportions. I've landed in paradise, with the most attractive, confusing, and frankly terrifying man I've ever met.

His home is delightful.

He's being delightful.

And I am in so far over my head I may never, ever extricate myself from this.

41

ANTON

*J*esus.

I stand under the spray in the wet room off my suite and let the torrent of water consume me.

I'm here, in my favourite place on earth. I've shared this home with two of my three wives and all four of my kids. I've entertained God knows how many dozens of friends and business associates over the decade or so I've been fortunate enough to own it. I've eaten and drunk and partied and skinny dipped and fucked and wept and slept and held tense, silent vigils here.

This house has held me at my lowest lows. It's been my monastery and my sanctuary, my very own Alchemy, and my children's playground.

And it has never hummed with magic, with potential, like it has this past twenty minutes since I helped Genevieve off the helicopter and over my threshold.

Fuck me.

She's handled this latest ambush far more graciously than I feared she might. I was pretty fucking nervous, actually. Not that I'd ever show her that. I was counting on *La*

Perle du Cap, my beautiful villa, doing most of the heavy lifting for me, and my faith was vindicated. She was clearly enchanted as soon as she laid eyes on it, but she had no idea how *enchanting* her enchantment was.

When she's armed up and ready to fight, she's the best, most intoxicating kind of challenge. But when she's soft and delighted and lets that armour slip, she's dangerous, because she's irresistible.

I'm so tempted to wrap my hand around my cock and take the edge off, but I deny myself.

Because the edge is what makes me *me*.

It makes me hungry, and determined, and relentless.

Ergo, it makes me far more likely to get what I want.

And I know what I want.

Instead, I wash my hair and body thoroughly under the cool spray and dress in white shorts and a navy linen shirt. I leave the top couple of buttons undone and roll the sleeves up, pausing before opening the top drawer next to my bed and sliding a single foil-wrapped condom into my shorts pocket.

Some stupid fuckers would say this kind of behaviour is tempting fate.

I wholeheartedly disagree.

I'm manifesting. I'm putting my desire for this evening out into the universe, and that's worked often enough for me in the past.

I rake a hand through my damp hair as I exit my suite and risk a glance at Genevieve's double doors.

Still firmly closed.

I hope she enjoys her brief reprieve in her room, because, if I have my way, it'll be the only time she spends in there.

I pad barefoot downstairs, revelling in the simple pleasure of being in my favourite of all my residences. Of cool stone underfoot and sea breezes wafting in. Of the scent of rosemary and garlic and thyme and lemon coming from the kitchen.

A quick detour in that very direction provides me with a verbose and noisy greeting from my chef, Jean-Jacques, a great hulk of a man who bestows a wet, delighted kiss on each of my cheeks, slaps me so hard on the back that he may have cracked a rib or two, and launches into a comprehensive description of the feast (his words) he's preparing for tonight.

I'm enormously fond of Jean-Jacques and hold him responsible for all my culinary expertise. When I holed up here after divorce number three, I spent days alone in the house with him and Céd, travelling up and down the coast and even inland to food markets, shopping for bounty that we'd take home and cook, approaching every step with reverence.

It was, quite simply, therapy.

Tonight, apparently, we're having just-caught *rouget* (red mullet) with baked aubergine, potato gratin, and a green salad. Jean-Jacques, however, is far more excited about the selection of canapés he's prepared. He's arranged a colour-fully resplendent selection of crudités on a wooden board with lashings of *poichichade*, a Provençal dip made of chick-peas which the locals seem intent on refusing to acknowl-edge as basically humous.

There's caviar, and enormous langoustines arranged just so around an earthenware bowl of lemony, dill-seasoned *crème fraîche,* and croustades aplenty, loaded with green olive tapenade and black olive tapenade and sundried tomato tapenade... you get the picture.

When in Provence...

I extricate myself and wander outside. It's still extremely warm, but the terrace is now in the shade, though the view from the west side will be spectacular as the sun sets in its blaze of glory over Juan Les Pins later this evening. The shadows of the cypresses are lengthening on the grass.

Céd is fiddling with his favourite thing in the house, my vintage brass bar cart. I almost feel bad that there are only two of us to serve tonight. The guy is a frustrated mixologist. He'd thrive at one of the great American Bars in London— the Savoy, perhaps. Or Duke's.

He makes me a long G&T and I saunter down to the far side of the pool. This is my favourite time of day. This and early morning. I enjoy a swim and a sunbathe as much as the next person, but the midday heat can be punishing here in the summer. It's pretty perfect at this time of year, though.

There's something about this place that instantly takes my nervous system down a few notches. London and work feel far away. Irrelevant. All that matters is the breeze on my face, and the grass pushing between my bare toes, and muted sound of *bon viveurs* carrying, probably up from Keller Plage.

Then comes Céd's voice, and the tinkle of a female laugh, and I spin around.

Here she is. She's standing on the terrace, a vision in some brightly coloured sundress that strikes me as lighter and less formal than the things she usually wears.

Quite right.

I start towards her.

42

ANTON

I approve of Genevieve's idea of *casual*, even if it's fucking dangerous.

Still-damp hair combed off her face.

A white sundress with big blue-green flowers all over it and a deep V at the front that provides a tantalising glimpse of the creases beneath her spectacular tits.

No bra.

Flat gold sandals.

Light makeup except for a slick of coral on her cheeks and lips, no jewellery, and skin that's positively glowing.

'You look beautiful,' I tell her, and she flushes.

'Casual enough for you?'

'Perfect.'

I linger as Céd mixes her an Aperol Spritz in a goldfish-bowl glass and gesture towards the terrace's seating area. 'Here? Or down by the pool?'

'Ooh, let's do the pool,' she says.

We settle on the long sofa in the pool's clematis-covered pergola. Genevieve raises her glass to me, and we clink. She's sitting upright, and I know I'll need to work harder to ensure my beautiful guest relaxes in the way she deserves. Not that I can blame her for being on her guard.

'How long have you had this place?' she asks, looking around her.

'Ten years, give or take.'

'Did you have to do a lot to it?'

'It was in pretty good shape, but we modernised the kitchen and extended the basement.'

'It's immaculate. And very peaceful.'

'It's neither of those things when my kids are around,' I tell her. 'Which they will be next month, when they break up.'

She settles back against the scatter cushions. 'You have four kids, right?'

'Yeah. Two from my first marriage and two from my second. Felix and Scarlett are both at uni, and my terrible twins, Amie and Annabel, are sixteen. They're doing their GCSEs at the moment, which has been painful for everybody.'

She laughs. 'Do you see much of them?'

'As much as I can, yeah. Most of them are in London— Felix is at LSE. Scarlett's at Harvard Law, but she's promised to come and hang with her old man for a few weeks this summer. I'm pretty sure the house is more of a draw than I am. She's already begun negotiations over how many friends she can bring with her and how often they can take the boat out.' I pretend to shudder. 'She'll make a great lawyer.'

Genevieve is smiling at me. 'She sounds like my kind of woman.'

'She'd like you, definitely.'

She pats the cushion next to her. 'I love the monograms. Very on-brand.'

I smirk. 'Are you taking the piss out of me?'

'They really are beautiful.' She smooths an elegant hand over the embroidered *W*. I wish it was my thigh she was caressing like that.

'Let's just say three divorces proved an expensive lesson in the perils of his 'n' her monogramming.' I take a sip of my G&T. 'I learnt my lesson a lot later than I should have.'

'Not to get married, or not to get smug, couply monograms?'

I grin. 'Monograms, definitely.'

Céd approaches with an enormous tray bearing Jean-Jacques' fantastic assortment of canapés, and we halt our conversation as he lays the platters out on the coffee table and provides Genevieve with a quick rundown of each one. When he's left us, I turn to find her assessing me through narrowed eyes.

'What?'

'Three ex-wives is... impressive,' she says.

'Not sure that's the word I'd use. And why does it feel like a pretty lame euphemism when you say it?'

'Because I'm trying to work out what it tells me about you,' she says, cocking her head to one side. She lifts her glass and drinks as she continues to observe me.

'Probably that I'm either a ruthless love 'em and leave 'em type or a hopeless romantic,' I say lightly. 'Or, obviously, that I'm impossible to live with. Which would you choose?'

'A few weeks ago, it would have been the first or last. Now, I'm not so sure.'

I can't help but be touched by her words as much as her confessional tone. If I've risen that much in her opinion, albeit off a low base, I must be doing something right.

'They're all wonderful women,' I say, 'and Carmen and Marie-Claire gave me the most beautiful children. I'll never regret it, and when I went into each marriage, for whatever it's worth, I did so with a heart full of faith and love. But there are some things you can't fake in a relationship. I've learnt that the hard way. Finally.'

I look over. She's watching me, her gaze softer than it was. I wonder if she's remembering what I told her in my interview about my brand of kink being off the table in my previous relationships.

Because I am.

'I'm sorry.'

'Don't be.' I reach for a langoustine and dip it liberally in its lemony dip. 'Like I said, I have no regrets. Langoustine?' I hold it out to her, and she takes it.

'Thanks. You certainly don't sound like you've been put off the institution for life, though, which is impressive after three attempts.'

'On the contrary. I'm an optimist. I choose to be that way. And yeah, I work hard, but I live hard too, and I believe love is a very important piece of living a full life.'

'And sex,' she reminds me.

I grin and raise my glass. 'Amen to that. And Amen to Alchemy.'

'But they don't coexist for you?' she asks. 'Great love and great sex?'

I frown. 'You make it sound like I believe I can't have great sex with someone I'm in love with. That's not the case at all. I just haven't found it yet in my relationships—I mean, not to the extent I'd like to have it. You've had a front-row seat to my tastes. They're not for everyone. But it's also painful having to constantly tamp down your desires because they make the person you're with feel uncomfortable. Or worse, because that person tries to make you feel like there's something wrong with you for wanting that.'

She nods vigorously, and points a finger at me. '*That*, right there.'

'You've had that too?' I ask her, and she sighs.

'I did not mean to come down for drinks and launch into a conversation about our kinks with *you*.'

'Come on.' I spread my arms wide. 'I'm partnering with your sex club, for fuck's sake. The jig is up. Not to mention, I've had a front-row seat to your kinks, too.'

She purses her lips, though I suspect she's less disapproving than she makes out, and then sighs again. 'Okay, fine. Yes. I remembered what you said in your interview because it resonated with me, alright? Less the shaming, but more that feeling of not being able to have it all. Of wondering if I ever would. You know, lovely dates with great guys, and then the sex is shit. Or just... boring.'

'Lucky you met me, then,' I say, grinning. 'I'm the whole package.'

'And so modest, too,' she grits out.

'You know what I mean. You and I are the same, Gen. Can I call you Gen?'

'Given you've seen me naked and I'm enjoying your wonderful hospitality, I can hardly say no, can I?'

'If I'm modest, you're gracious,' I tell her. 'But as I was saying, *Gen*. You and I are the same. Like it or not.'

'Is this a date?' she asks wearily. 'Did you bring me here to seduce me?'

I pause and consider my words carefully. 'I don't like the word *seduce*. It suggests manipulation, which doesn't sit well with me.'

'You've manipulated me before,' she argues. 'When I signed the contract in your office.'

I frown. 'I'd argue that was more opportunistic than manipulative. Yeah, I had an agenda. And I'd checked with the guys and with Athena that if the evening was to unfold the way I wanted, that they'd be okay with that. But I propositioned you, and you made your choice. You stayed.

'And yeah, you could argue I've manipulated your desires, maybe. Like in the club, when I fucked that woman in front of you. But you didn't give me much to work with. I had to play whatever hand I had to get some kind of reaction out of you.

'As for now? I brought you here in the hope that if we spent some time together, you'd come to understand that we do actually get on well, that we have a lot more in common than you're willing to accept, and that I have the utmost respect for you.' I stop. 'Yes, my intentions are purely dishonourable. Fucking filthy. But you hold all the power here. *All of it.*'

She stares at me, those blue eyes huge as she absorbs what I'm telling her.

'I won't give you a hard sell,' I tell her. 'You're my guest. I'd never want you to feel uncomfortable. And if that happens, I'll have Céd drive you straight over to the Carlton, no questions asked. I'd love this evening to be a date, but if it's just good food and wine and excellent conversation between two new friends in peaceful surroundings, then that's fine too. Okay?'

I raise my eyebrows at her, and she swallows, then nods. 'Okay. Thank you.'

'My pleasure.' I sit back and cross my ankle over my knee. 'And, over dinner, you're going to tell me how you and those friends of yours ended up running the best sex club I've ever been to.'

43

ANTON

When Gen's not worrying about me seducing her, she's excellent company, an assured conversationalist, fucking hilarious, and surprisingly slapstick.

For a woman who's perfected the implacable ice-queen demeanour for those unfortunate souls who don't know her well, she has one of the most expressive faces I've ever seen. It's almost elastic, and it's a great prop when she's telling a funny story, of which she has many to tell.

I suppose you don't run a sex club without racking up countless anecdotes, even if most of them are inappropriate for normal dinner conversation.

I sit back in my chair and survey her appreciatively as I nurse my drink. Our meal has been a roaring success, and I don't mean the food, no matter how fresh the mullet was. The wine and the conversation have flowed equally smoothly, and I'm experiencing the unrivalled pleasure of having Genevieve Carew's company all to myself.

'Kinkiest thing you've ever seen there?' I ask.

She considers. 'God. I don't know. There's a lot. Probably some of the live sex shows we've put on down in The Vault.'

I raise my eyebrows. *'We?'*

'Fuck off. Our staff. You know what I mean.'

'Kinkiest thing *you've* ever done,' I ask, my voice deeper. I hold my breath.

'Nosy, aren't you?'

'When it comes to you, yes,' I tell her. 'I'm still trying to figure you out. You're a conundrum to me.'

'Pot and kettle,' she retorts.

'Maybe, but it's true. You're one of the most intellectually impressive, refined, poised women I've ever met. I suspect you had your pick of industries. And you chose to run a sex club.'

She taps a fingernail against her glass. 'It interests me that you see that as a conflict.'

'Not a conflict,' I say. 'Absolutely not. I love it. But you can't deny it's unorthodox.'

'Alchemy was the boys' idea,' she says. 'But I was working in Operations for a bank, and I knew I could run that side of it for them and do a good job.'

I narrow my eyes, because that sounds disingenuous. 'And the sector was irrelevant.'

'No.' She meets my gaze. 'It wasn't. I loved the idea. It was a massive departure for me—not exactly JP Morgan. But what you see as a conflict is deliberate. I've chosen to present this front of decorum so I can be taken seriously. Women don't have enough seats at enough tables. I want to be there, at those tables. In those conversations. I have as much right to access and networking as any other senior person in any industry.'

I think I'm in love.

'I couldn't agree more. So that's why you look like you're ready to run the country most of the time?'

She smiles, catlike. 'Exactly.'

'I told you you and I were alike. The difference is, they let me in without me having to work at it.'

'Tell me about it,' she says, tipping her head back and taking a healthy swig of rosé.

She's so fucking radiant.

I want to return to this conversation. I want to hear her view on every single topic. I could talk to her for years and never get bored. I want to help, to open any doors people have been too fucking stupid to open for her. To sing her praises from the rooftops of the City until she gets everything she wants.

But more than that, I want to kiss her till she moans into my mouth. I want to lick along her collarbones and slide that dress off her shoulders and suck her tits right here. I want it so badly I can't breathe.

And as I gaze at her in the fading light, the citronella candles on the table flickering between us, I can't keep it in anymore.

'Gen,' I say, unable to keep the pain out of my voice.

She doesn't reply. She just sets down her glass and looks at me.

Really looks at me.

And I know I'm not imagining the mutual hunger.

'Please,' I tell her. '*Please*. Let me touch you. You're extraordinary. I want to show you how extraordinary you are.'

44

GEN

I can't do this anymore.

I can't sit here and pretend that wanting Anton isn't consuming every last drop of energy.

I can't keep punishing both of us when the attraction is utterly insane, and he's brought me here, to his stunning retreat, and he's been nothing but kind and sweet and attentive and respectful.

I can't say no to him when he's looking at me like *that*.

Like I alone have the power to put him out of his misery.

To quiet his demons through the simple act of letting him put his hands on me and slay me.

Above all, I can't say no to him when he begs. Because Anton Wolff doesn't beg.

So I don't say no.

I say yes.

He stares at me. I don't think he's processing that I've changed my tune.

I nod.

I lean forward.

I put my hand over his and squeeze.

'I said yes. Touch me.'

He rakes his dark eyes over my face. A slow grin spreads, triggering those dimples I love before his laughter lines swallow them up.

'Touch me, what?' His voice is low but no less demanding.

So this is how it's going to be? Unbelievable. His humility didn't last long. But I smile, because I fucking love it.

'Touch me, *please*, Anton,' I say.

His hand clenches under mine. I want it on me. 'Where?'

'Everywhere.'

He sucks in a sharp breath. 'About fucking time.'

'Yes,' I agree.

'Come here.' He slaps the wooden surface of the table with his free hand. Cédric cleared away the main course about half an hour ago, and all that remains on the table are our drinks and the remnants of a chocolate-dipped strawberry platter. Anton explicitly dismissed him for the night, but I still feel a little exposed. I look back towards the house.

'We won't be disturbed,' Anton says. 'I promise. *Come. Here.*'

The final two words bear the strain of a man pushed to, or past, his limits, and they send a thrill dancing over my skin. I've held him off and held him off, and now I have no doubt I'll be punished for that.

However strong my attraction is to him, however strong my *feelings* for him, there's no doubt in my mind he's a predator.

He's still the Big Bad Wolff, and he wants me, and I have a feeling he's about to rip me apart.

And fuck, I'm so ready to put myself in his hands.

I rise and round the corner of the table. Anton pushes

his chair back to make room and stands. I stop in front of him, the edge of the table hitting the tops of my thighs below the full skirts of my dress.

He slowly gets to his feet. My flats are long abandoned under the table somewhere, and I have to crane my neck to look up at him.

He's so close.

So still.

All I can hear is the hum of cicadas, and the breeze stirring the leaves in the trees, and the sounds of our breaths.

He wraps one warm hand around my neck.

The other goes around my waist, tugging me even closer.

'Fucking *finally*,' he grits out.

And he dips his face to mine.

The first touch of our lips is like being plugged in. It's such a fucking relief to have his mouth on me. To have his face pressed against mine.

He doesn't start slowly, or gently, or reverently. He's way past that—we both are. Rather, his kiss is decisive and hungry and searching. He claims my lips and almost instantly forces them open with his tongue, so I taste wine and feel his ravenous, demanding probes.

It's an angry kiss.

A *why the fuck did you make me wait* kiss.

A *look how fucking good it is between us, you idiot* kiss.

An *I can't believe you were trying to deny this* kiss.

One hand has my neck in an immovable grip. The other has slid south and is grabbing my arse through my dress as he holds me against his hard body. I'm in freefall, my tongue sliding against his as it devours my mouth, my hands everywhere as I attempt to take in all the details I've obsessed over for so long.

God, his hair is luscious, and the forearm I drag my

fingernails over is taut and toned, and the small of his back feels like somewhere my palm could live happily ever after. And as for his smell? It's fucking crack. I breathe him in and a low noise of pleasure escapes my throat.

In response, he nudges me backwards so my arse is planted on the table and steps between my legs, his hand in my hair now, fisting it and tugging my head back before he pulls away.

I open my eyes and gaze up at him in a fog of lust. There's triumph on his face, and stark desire, and I know him well enough to realise he's battling with his self-control. Because when a man's appetites for sex and for control are both this substantial, and he's on the precipice of getting what he wants, you bet there's going to be some internal conflict.

He stares down at me, breathing heavily as he decides what to do with me. He could bend me over this table and be balls-deep inside me in about ten seconds flat, or he could drag me up to his bed and torment me for hours.

Who the fuck knows with this guy?

And *that's* the fun.

Because, Lord knows, I'm fine with either option.

45

GEN

Control wins.

He releases me and sits heavily back in his chair, dragging it forward until I'm standing between his legs.

'God knows, I'm a greedy man, Gen,' he says, surveying me through hooded eyes. 'But I have never, ever wanted anything in this life as much as I want you.'

Desire curls through my belly, thick and heavy, as the man who consumes my thoughts directs those unimaginable words at me. As he looks me over. I may be the one standing, but now that I've given him the green light, he holds all the power.

And that could not be clearer right here, in this moment.

He reaches under my dress and runs a hand up the inside of my leg. Up my inner thigh. His fingertip grazes the silk of my thong lightly, and I suck in a sharp breath of need and anticipation through my teeth.

His eyes flicker closed in bliss, but he withdraws his hand straight away and smooths down the fabric of my dress.

'Pull the top down for me, sweetheart,' he says in a tone that caresses my skin like silk. 'Those fucking tits of yours have been haunting me.'

'At least you've seen them,' I tell him. 'I've seen nothing of you apart from your cock, which you seem to get out whenever I'm around.'

He throws his head back and laughs, his teeth a flash of white in the dim light, the sound of his mirth cutting through the cicadas.

'You'll do a lot more than see my cock tonight. I promise you.'

'Good,' I retort. The V at the back of my sundress is even more low-cut than the one at the front, so I have enough leeway to slip the dress off my shoulders and pull one arm out, and then the other. I shove the bodice down so the entire thing is bunched around my waist, baring my breasts to the night.

To Anton.

The laughter dies on his lips at the sight of them. 'Cup them for me,' he barks. 'I want them on a platter.'

I do as he asks, cupping a palm under each of my breasts and pushing them up so they're on display for him. My nipples are hard and pinched, and not only from the cooling air.

He's standing again. Sliding his hands over mine. Grazing his thumbs over my nipples, his dark eyes locked not on my breasts but on my face. He pinches, and I pant a little, because God have I wanted this man's hands on my body for so fucking long, and now he's touching me, and it's even more perfect, more heady, than I imagined.

His lips brush against mine, and then his mouth finds me properly and his tongue breaches my defenses again, demanding. Invading.

'Lean back,' he mutters into my mouth, and I abandon my boobs and plant my palms flat on the table behind me so I can do as he says.

And then he's trailing licks and kisses and nips along my jaw and down my neck and over the skin of my décolletage and then he finally, finally finds my breasts. He puts one hand between my shoulder-blades to help support me as he catches one needy nipple lightly between his teeth and flicks his tongue over it.

I throw my head back and moan.

'That's right,' he grits out against my skin before his tongue continues its exploration, flicks turning to long, decadent pulls of his lips while his tongue laves me. He pushes further between my legs, the crown of his dark, tousled head the only thing I can see clearly aside from the broadness of the shoulders below it.

He switches sides, stopping briefly to grab an ice cube from the half-melted selection in the ice bucket beside us. He pops it in his mouth, and the sharp shock of cold on my other nipple has me crying out. I arch into him and push my palms down harder on the table.

'Does that feel good?' he asks after a few minutes of switching sides and rolling my nipples around with his ice-cold tongue.

'It feels amazing,' I manage, my voice high and needy.

'Good.' He looks up at me. His eyes are black and expression is fucking feral. 'You need more, though, correct?' He strokes down my bare back while he grazes along my jaw with the knuckles of his other hand.

'Yes,' I tell him. 'Please,' I add.

He grins, and it's positively diabolical. 'Nice try, sweetheart, but you know me well enough by now to know that's not going to cut it. Is it?'

'Probably not.'

'Exactly.' He lowers his voice. 'What do you need?' His tone is coaxing. Confidence-inducing. I roll my eyes, even though I've always known how it would be between us.

Because he's just as familiar with my predilections as I am with his.

'I need to come,' I tell him. 'I need to come from your hands and your mouth on me, because I'm so fucking sick of waiting.'

He cocks his head and rummages under my dress again, his hand sliding up my thigh. I automatically spread my legs wider for him.

'And whose fault is that?' he wonders aloud.

I sigh. 'Mine.'

'I would have fucked you that first day in your office, Gen.'

'You and your team all seem convinced you have to fuck me to get your memberships,' I say lightly.

Wrong call.

'We are *not* going to discuss you being with anyone else, in any capacity, while we're doing this,' he snarls. 'Understand?' His fingers trail further up my inner thigh, far too softly and far too lightly. 'And you know damn well the reason I would have fucked you that first time is because I took one look at you in that dress, with that haughty, uptight expression on your face and knew you needed me to fuck it out of you. Don't you?'

In an instant, he's shoved my thong aside and driven two fingers inside me. It takes me by surprise, and it stings a bit, but it also feels like nothing else on earth, and I know when he finally fucks me I will lose my actual mind.

He closes his eyes for a moment and licks his lips like

he's trying to keep his shit together. Then he's looking at me as he twists his hand and crooks his fingers.

'Don't you, gorgeous?' he rasps.

'Yes,' I moan.

'Yes what?'

'Yes, I need you to fuck everything out of me.'

'Yes you do.' He pulls his fingers out pumps them back in slowly. I can feel how wet I am. 'Fuuuck,' he groans. 'All I've ever wanted to do is make you feel amazing. Turn you inside out. I'm going to do that tonight, but you're going to have to give me everything.' He presses his thumb to my clit and holds it there, and I nearly shoot off the table. 'Got it?'

'Yes,' I gabble. 'I'll give you everything.'

'Good girl.' He drags the pad of his thumb down over my clit. 'You see? It's all a lot easier when you don't fight me. Isn't it?'

'It—yeah.' Jesus Christ. Once again I have the distinct feeling that he's pulling some kind of hypnosis shit on me. The words he used in his office float hazily back to me.

Just let us fucking wipe your mind clean.

I promise you I already know what you need better than you do.

I know that to be true, and right now I *want* to surrender. I want to be putty in his hands. I want him to make everything that is not him, and his touch, and his cock, go away.

'Good.' He withdraws his hand and I'm instantly, cruelly bereft. 'I'm glad we understand each other. I promise I won't hurt you, and I promise to give you everything you want. Is your safe word still *camellia*?'

'What?' My brain is dulled. Slow. 'Um—yes. Why?' I figured we were going to have very hot, lust-crazed, and reasonably vanilla sex. Why would I need a safe word?

'Force of habit.' He smiles and leans forward, planting a slow, dreamy kiss on my lips before stepping back and holding out his hands to me. 'Now get up and come with me.'

46

ANTON

The goddess holding my hand as I lead her down the shallow steps to the pool level is already on her way to being my favourite version of her. She's beautifully *déshabillé,* that wonderful French term for being in a state of undress while also suggesting an element of dishevelment. In fact, I suspect the English word derives from the Gallic.

She's not looking as fucked and ravaged and blissfully sated, as *undone,* as she will be. But she's worked up already. Her state of excitement was evident when I slid my fingers into the soaking heat of her cunt.

She's finally allowing me to unravel her. She's putting herself in my hands, with all her insecurities and inhibitions, and she'll be fucking magnificent when I've finished with her.

'Where are we going?' she asks. Her untethered tits bounce beautifully as we traipse down the steps.

'Away from the house,' I tell her. 'I want you feeling safe enough to let it all go for me.'

'Thank you,' she says and squeezes my hand. I know

Céd and JJ are almost certainly off the property by now, but I could tell she felt exposed up there, and I need her able to fully relax.

I tug her to a stop in front of a canopied day bed. There's an almost-full moon tonight, illuminating the sea in the distance. The pool is lit from within, glowing turquoise, but otherwise it's darker down here than by the house.

'It's time for you to get naked for me,' I tell her.

'Are you going to get naked, too?' she asks.

'I will,' I promise. 'Just not immediately. Now strip.'

She reaches behind and tugs at a zip, pushing the fabric over her hips till it's pooled at her feet, her thong with it. She's naked and beautiful, her hair soft and unstyled and her fucking glorious body bare for me to get lost in. Fuck, her tits are spectacular. Everything is. And, unlike last time I saw it, it's all for me.

I step forward. 'So beautiful,' I tell her, sliding both hands around her waist and tugging her against me. 'Feel how hard I am?' I ask against her lips, swallowing up her *yes* with a deep kiss. I allow my hands to wander over her perfect skin, dropping to her arse and kneading it hard as I shove my erection against her.

It feels like I've wanted this woman forever, which is nonsense, of course. It's only been a few weeks. But the sense of relief, of triumph, of possibility, is no less.

I have her naked in my arms.

She's mine to do as I like with, for tonight at least.

A woman like Genevieve will have impossibly high standards for anything other than a quick fuck, but I intend to break her and put her back together so beautifully that she'll have no choice but to accept that we should be together.

I sample her mouth for a few more minutes and force

myself to focus on delighting in this milestone—on the softness of her tits pressed against my abdomen and the feeling of her arse cheeks in my hands—rather than trying to get my end away as quickly as possible.

That said: my poor, poor dick.

'Turn around,' I tell her. My voice is soft, but there's no doubt it's a command.

She knows it, and she likes it, because she gives me a lazy smile and turns around, the dip of her waist and the pale globes of her arse picked out by the moonlight.

'Perfect,' I tell her, both because she is, and because I want her eating out of the palm of my hand. I want her desperate for that next scrap of praise. For that next touch. That next reward.

The daybed is a little low for my purposes, so I grab a couple of bolsters and put them right at the edge of the mattress, at the base of the bed.

'Bend over,' I tell her firmly, and she lets out what I think is a happy sigh and folds herself over before my eyes.

I was going to do this over the dining table, but this is better, because she's bent far further over than she would be up there, her arms stretched out before her on the mattress and her arse held high by the bolsters.

I have plans for that arse.

Standing behind her, I get to my knees. There's enough light from the pool to enjoy the sight of the glistening flesh between her legs. She's so wound up already, but I plan to see how much more tightly I can wind this incredible woman.

I slide my fingertips up her legs, and she shivers. When I reach her arse, I stop and palm her cheeks, spreading my fingers and pushing them apart so I can see her more clearly.

'All I have wanted since I met you is to do this,' I murmur, my gaze dragging over her. My nose is inches from her wet centre, and the scent of her is fucking intoxicating. 'It's all I've been able to think about.'

She shivers. 'Me too.'

'I don't know why the fuck you were in denial for so long.' I rub my thumbs over her skin. I haven't yet gone near the parts of her body where she needs my touch.

'I wasn't in denial.'

I lean in and feather kisses all over one deliciously plump cheek. 'No? Why did you avoid me like the plague, then?' I have a pretty good idea of why, but I want to hear her say it.

I *need* to hear her say it.

Silence, then, 'Because you're you.'

'Meaning?' I turn to the other cheek and give it the same treatment.

She huffs in frustration. 'Anton. I need you to touch me properly.'

'And I need you to be honest with me. That's imperative, sweetheart. If you're honest, I'll reward you. If not...'

I pull away from her skin. Point made.

'I was scared,' she confesses in a small voice, and I instantly feel like a total shit, but I'm also thrilled, and I'm not sure why. In any case, that merits a reward. I do what I've been dying to do and stick my face between her legs. My nose nudges her slick entrance, and my tongue finds her swollen clit, and I lick.

Jesus fucking Christ.

She's nectar.

'Oh my God,' she groans. 'Fuck.'

I halt. 'Scared of fucking me? Scared you wouldn't be able to handle it?'

'No.' Her voice is wobbly. 'I mean, maybe a bit? I know it's going to be a lot.'

'This evening is about us both taking what we've needed for a while,' I tell her, sliding a single finger inside her and relishing the way her silky inner walls grip it. 'I'll go easy on you, because I'm too fucking turned on to try anything more structured.' I add another finger, and she tenses for a second, but she takes it beautifully. 'But that's not what you're scared of.'

'No.'

'So?' I twist my elbow so I can get better access and hold her folds open with my other hand. The sight of her, wet and quivering and needy and right fucking there, does such painful things to my cock that I'm in danger of coming in my shorts.

'I was scared I wouldn't survive it afterwards,' she says haltingly. 'That we'd... fuck, and you'd move straight onto the next conquest, and I'd be fucked. I told you, you're *you*.'

I still. 'Meaning?'

'Come on, Anton. Don't make me say it.'

'I need you to say it, sweetheart,' I tell her in the softest tone I've used on her all evening.

She groans. 'Ugh. Fine. But you'd better give me a fucking orgasm after this.'

I chuckle. 'One orgasm coming up. *Spill.*' I wish I could see her face, but maybe it's easier for her to confess like this. No matter. I'll make her repeat it all to me.

Over and over.

'I knew I'd be insanely attracted to you before I even met you,' she says. 'And then when you walked into that room, you took my breath away, and I knew I was in trouble.'

Jesus fuck.

I was right.

I really needed to hear her say the words.

I press a kiss to her clit. 'Go on,' I say, the words muffled.

'There was nothing you said or did in that interview that quashed my fears. Because you came across as a total animal.'

'And you liked that?' I ask, withdrawing my fingers and sliding them back inside her, slowly. Slowly. She's mesmerising.

'Well I liked it on a sexual level, obviously. More than liked it. But when I tell you every single alarm bell was ringing in my head, it's no exaggeration. God, that feels good.'

'So why did you let me orchestrate things in my office, then?' I ask. 'And why did you agree when I challenged you to watch me fuck that woman in the club?'

'I thought we weren't talking about other people,' she shoots back. I may have her bent over my daybed, but she's no pushover, and I fucking love it.

'We are for a second.'

She huffs, then pauses. Then she speaks, and her voice may be low, but it's clear. Unapologetic. 'Because I wanted whatever I could get of you. Even if it wasn't enough.'

47

ANTON

The emotion that engulfs me is a tidal wave, and it almost takes me out.

Everything I know about Gen tells me she doesn't do vulnerability well. That is to say, it's her kink in the bedroom, but she protects it behind layers of thick, high walls at all other times. I've certainly been on the receiving end of that defence mechanism when it comes to her.

I knew what her reluctance was. I knew it was an issue of trust and not a matter of interest. But I made her say it, and now I need her to know it's not something to worry about.

'I know,' I tell her now, pressing my forehead to her tail-bone as my fingers flex inside her. 'Me too. And you did so well to tell me. So fucking well. I promise you, you won't regret this. I won't hurt you. The only thing I want to do is make you feel amazing. But to do that, I need you to trust me. Do you trust me?'

'I trust you,' she tells me, her voice soft and open, and I nearly fall apart.

'*Good*,' I say, and I get to work. I'm still holding her open, which feels significant. Symbolic. She's yielding to me in every way. Physically. Emotionally.

I can work with this. I can turn her inside out and give her pleasure she's never dreamed of.

I know her initial mistrust was warranted. I am who I am. But I've teased her and pushed her and provoked her, and she's taken it all beautifully and given as good as she's got. In this moment I just need to fuck her.

Show her.

I shove my fingers back in and tongue her roughly. Fuck self-control. We both badly need to get off. She moans, and the sound goes straight to my cock. I've had the privilege of hearing the noises she makes when she's aroused, but it's a whole other ball game when it's my fingers in her cunt and my tongue on her clit.

This is my favourite thing to do to a woman aside from actually fucking her.

Having her allow me between her legs.

Bending her over and spreading her out.

Putting my mouth on her most intimate parts.

Smelling and tasting and sucking and swirling and licking.

It's decadent, and filthy, and so fucking base.

And doing it to Gen is blowing my mind. She's grinding that arse in my face, the greedy girl, desperate for more despite the fact that I'm giving her plenty.

I stop.

'Stay still,' I order, 'or I'll tie you up.'

'Jesus, Anton,' she moans. 'For fuck's *sake*.'

'I'm serious. Stop fucking wriggling. I'm holding you wide open. Stay still and focus on every single lick. You know it'll be better.'

She huffs again. I love it. Love how brazen she is here,

with her clothes abandoned on the ground and her arse in the air and her cunt on my face.

'Still,' I warn her one last time, and I lick her long and very slow, from her engorged clit to where her entrance stretches around my fingers.

Her anguished moan speaks to the purity of sensation she must be feeling now. 'Better,' I say, and I do it again. And again. She's holding still for me, her legs shaking with the effort. She's soaking, and I swipe at her clit with the back of my hand to get rid of some of her natural lube, because she'll be too wet to feel anything.

I want her to have friction.

And then I go for it. I pump my fingers, I find her clit with my tongue, and I flatten it, licking hard. Rough. Fast. I really let her have it, both because I want the tsunami that pulls her under to be like nothing she's ever felt, and because my self control has gone out the window. I want to go to town on her. Want to drown in the insane musk of her arousal.

She's deprived me for too long, and I want to fucking feast.

'*Now* you can grind against me, sweetheart,' I tell her before resuming my heavenly banquet.

And she does.

She writhes and she grinds and she pushes and she mewls like a fucking kitten as I deliver the assault she needs on the parts of her she's withheld from me till now.

God, the noises she's making are fucking unreal. *This* is the Gen I wanted—naked and shameless, all decorum abandoned. She's whimpering now, and it's fucking beautiful.

And when she comes, it's spectacular, with gasps and cries and shudders that echo in my dick. I give her everything I've got, and she's still shuddering when I get to my feet and grab the condom from my pocket before tugging down my shorts.

I'm planning on keeping her bent over, I really am, but the first time I come inside her I want to see her fucking face. I've watched it while other men have made her come.

And now it's my turn.

'Flip over and scoot up, sweetheart,' I tell her hoarsely as I roll the condom gingerly over my close-to-exploding dick. She does as I ask, tugging the bolsters out from under her and scooting up the daybed on her arse. The sight of her, naked and wild-haired, tits unleashed and legs spread for me, is headier than any drug.

I reach behind my neck and tug my polo shirt off by the collar, chucking it away from me. I'm as naked as her, now, wearing only a condom, and the gratification in her eyes as she takes me in is evident even in the dim light of the pool.

'Wider,' I order, and she spreads her legs even more. I crawl up her body and crouch above her, stuffing a throw pillow under her arse to tilt her pelvis.

There will be a time, in a few minutes, when I kiss every inch of her plush skin, but right now I need to sheath my dick so far inside her she'll never be the same again, and there is not enough blood in my brain for anything else.

She bites her lip and looks between us where I'm fisting my poor cock as I brace on one arm. 'I didn't expect you to fuck me missionary,' she says tartly.

I've just made her come apart on my tongue and she's still giving me shit, even as she catches her breath after her spectacular orgasm.

'Shut the fuck up and put your legs over my shoulders,' I say through clenched teeth. I catch the excitement that flashes across her face at my tone. My little Gen likes it rough, which is zero surprise and yet gratifying as fuck.

Her lips part as she languidly lifts one long leg and then the other. I lock them against my shoulders, and I take advantage of her silence to line my tip up with her entrance. I swipe it through her soaking arousal once for good measure and then I'm driving in a single thrust that's so powerful I jolt forward, and she jerks, gasping audibly.

Fuck me, I'm nearly in.

Jesus fucking Christ.

I'm almost fully inside her body, and we stare at each other for a second in mutual shell-shock, because this feels like being plugged into the mains. I steady myself, sliding my hands up the silky skin of her legs and encircling her ankles with my fingers before I pull out and drive back in until I've bottomed out inside her.

Fuck fuck fuck. I'm seeing stars. She's so tight and wet, her heat seeping through the latex and her interior muscles clenching around my cock as I shake my head at her in disbelief.

In warning.

I squeeze my eyes shut and will myself to open them as I start moving, because I don't want to miss a second of how she reacts to me fucking her.

She's beautiful like this. Radiant. Staggering. Her gorgeous tits have fallen slightly to the sides, and every time I pump my cock into her, they jiggle so pleasingly. I'll get her on top next, and they'll bounce like fuck knows what. I'll make her wank me off with them. I'll take her bent over something so I can weigh them in my hands and pull at those nipples as I drive home again and again.

'See?' I manage. *See how fucking miraculous it is between us? See how insane you've been to keep us from doing this every hour of every day?*

'Yeah.' She nods, those baby blues filled with emotion,

and I just can't. I lower myself onto my elbows, bending her almost in half at the hips, and brace right above her, dipping my head so I can tug on her bottom lip with my teeth and run my tongue over its plumpness as her legs drape over my shoulders. She's seriously flexible, and I'm seriously happy about that.

I'm finding a rhythm, and the drag, the pressure, is so fucking good I might die. I abandon her lip and fuck her mouth with my tongue instead. Her hands are all over me, pulling her nails up my back and clawing at my hair as she tugs my mouth even closer to hers before she reaches around with both arms and grabs onto my hips, willing me to go faster.

Harder.

Deeper.

And I oblige, because I will give this woman everything she desires if it's the last thing I do. She's moaning into my mouth and ramming her hips up to meet every stroke as if we can never be close enough. I fist her hair, pulling at it so she turns her head and I can access her neck. I lick. I bite. I suck. I want to consume every last fucking inch of her. I want to overwhelm her so much that every one of her senses is aware only of me.

Of us.

'God, harder, Anton,' she moans somewhere near my ear, and the sound of my name on her lips as she urges me on is a fucking prayer, and it almost sends me over the edge.

Instead, I release her hair and pull out of her, shuffling back so I can lower her legs and flip her over onto her belly with an arm around her waist.

'Head down. Cunt up,' I tell her in my most command-ing, *don't fuck with me* voice, and she groans like she's been waiting her whole life for me to tell her to do that. She scrambles onto her knees, but I keep my arm around her and hoist her up anyway, such is my rush to be back inside her. She's now on all fours, so I put a firm hand between her shoulder blades and shove her down, and then I'm grabbing my dick and wedging its fat, swollen tip back inside her.

Fuck me, that's better. I can really let her have it without worrying about snapping her in half.

48

GEN

My cheek is pressed against the cotton-covered mattress, and Anton's holding me down with a hand still between my shoulders, but I still scrabble to find some kind of grip with my hands because boy is he letting me have it.

Having him on top of me, bearing down on me with that glorious, finally-naked body ramming into me over and over while he eye-fucked me with those beautiful dark eyes was... I don't know. It was the kind of sexual experience you don't ever get over. The *how is this my life* feeling, like winning the lottery.

But having him say *head down, cunt up* in *that* tone before he pummels into me, over and over on his knees while I kneel here and try to survive it without getting fucked off the bed? That kind of behaviour has me spiralling, winding tighter and tighter as a second, deeper and achier and more dangerous orgasm builds and builds.

His dick is my single point of focus. I'm an addict. Even when he's bottoming out in me, my entire body is shouting for my next fix. My cells protest every time he pulls that glorious cock out, and they tremble every time he drives back in.

We're both so close. He's got my hips in such a tight grip that I know I'll have five matching bruises on each side in the morning. He didn't say much when he was fucking me face to face and kissing me, but now I'm aware of a string of filth coming from that gorgeous, sensual mouth of his, and I'm as thrilled by the words as I am by the fact that Anton Wolff is unleashed and about to blow his lid.

And I want it. I want it all—I want him to use me and fuck me and unleash every filthy fantasy on me.

I know at an elemental level that we're just getting started, that the things we achieve together will blow the fucking roof off.

But right now all I care about is allowing this next, second, heavier orgasm to rip through me. Obliterate me. All I care about is how Anton is making me feel in this moment.

Because it feels like nothing on earth. I'm groaning, I'm practically mooing, and I take and take as he pounds and pounds.

'I'm going to break you in fucking two,' he rasps hoarsely as he thrusts. 'Take it, you beautiful, greedy girl. Fuck me, this cunt is greedy. I'm going to make you so desperate for my cock that you'll do anything I want. If I tell you to bend over and spread 'em in public, you fucking will. You won't be able to think about anything else but having me inside you. The whole. Fucking. Time. I'll ruin you. And you'll fucking ruin *me*.'

His voice breaks on the last word.

I break, too.

My consciousness splinters into a million tiny pieces, and the self I was when I stepped off that helicopter a few hours ago soars through the clear night air above us, leaving an addict whose awareness of the world has narrowed to one single, stupendous human being.

Anton Wolff.

He fucks me through my orgasm, his taunts morphing into praise as I shatter around him. And then he goes wonderfully, improbably rigid behind me, inside me, letting out an animalistic sound that seems to shudder through where our bodies are joined.

His jerks cease.

And he eases me carefully down so I'm flat on my stomach, arms around my head, and we're cheek to cheek, his entire weight on top of me.

I understand that weighted blankets can provide comfort.

Safety cues.

But *this?*

Having Anton's hard, hot body bearing down on me, enveloping me completely? Pressing me into the mattress? Acting like some sort of blessed buffer between me and the outside world?

It's nirvana.

He's still inside me, still pulsing, and I squeeze my internal muscles around him. He gives a little laugh, his breath hot on my ear as his arms mirror mine so he can lay his palms on top of my hands and interlace his fingers with mine.

'Too heavy?' he mutters. He's still finding his breath, and the sensation of his lungs filling and emptying against my back while his heart beats above mine feels like the type of connection I've been searching my whole life for.

'No,' I whisper. 'Stay.'

He brushes his nose along my cheekbone and presses a kiss next to my ear. 'I need to get rid of the condom.'

'Fuck the condom.'

He sniggers, but then he's pulling out of me and lifting his weight off me, and it's totally shit.

'Nooo,' I protest, before I catch myself. Needy much, Gen?

'Give me a sec,' he insists. He gets off the bed and I roll onto my side, propping myself up on an elbow so I can watch him, drink in the sculptural curves of his muscles as he stands poolside and knots the condom.

Then he's leaping back onto the bed and tugging me in towards him as he throws a leg over mine. I collapse onto the mattress.

We're nose to nose.

'I meant it,' he whispers, rubbing his nose against mine. 'You're going to ruin me.'

I swallow. 'You're going to ruin me, too.'

We lie there and stare at each other. In this light, his eyes are dark, fathomless pools. I smooth a palm over his shoulder cap. 'I finally got you naked,' I say. *And you take my breath away.* I feel overly emotional. Tearful, almost. That is *not* cool.

'I finally got you to myself,' is his rejoinder. He rolls me onto my back, and I spread my legs so he can settle between them. 'And I'm not fucking letting you go.'

I don't say anything.

I don't trust myself.

But it seems I don't have to, because he smooths some errant strands of hair off my face and kisses me slowly. Deeply.

He breaks away. 'And now I'm going to get to know every inch of your magnificent body.'

49

GEN

It's the squawking of seagulls that wakes me, but when I open my eyes, it's Anton I see. He's lying on his side, propped up on one elbow and tousled head resting on his knuckles.

He's gazing down at me.

He's smiling.

I smile back through my cloud of sleep and shift self-consciously as I reach out and stroke a fingertip down one of the deep grooves that bracket his mouth and that I adore so much. He encircles my wrist with his fingers and turns his head so he can press a kiss to my palm.

Who the hell is this gorgeous teddy bear, and what have they done with the Big Bad Wolff, ruthless conqueror of both women and the corporate world?

The sheet shifts around me, and his eyes slide to my exposed boobs.

There he is.

'Good morning,' I say, amused.

'Good morning.' He drags his eyes back to my face and grins. 'How did you sleep?'

'Like only a person who had too many orgasms can sleep,' I say, yawning and sliding a foot over the satiny cotton of the sheet. Jesus, this bed is soft. It's bloody amazing.

'You can never have too many orgasms,' he tells me intently, like he's delivering the secret of the universe, and I laugh.

'Fair point.'

'On that note,' he says to my boobs, 'Get over here.'

Something pulses between my legs at the command in his tone. Waking up with him is unreal, and I drink in the sight of him in the morning light. For a guy in his early fifties, he's in amazing shape. I mean, I knew he would be. It was pretty obvious that under those fitted white shirts and perfectly cut trousers was a body to die for.

But he really is beautiful. His skin's a lot more bronzed than mine. I suspect he's been popping over here to work on his tan this spring. He's nicely toned rather than completely ripped, but his flat stomach and the breadth of his shoulders and curves of his biceps speak to a regular workout regime.

I take in the soft smattering of dark hair that flares across his chest and tapers down his stomach. He's gorgeous. Gorgeous. I can't really handle how attracted I am to him. And not just to his body or his crazily handsome face.

It's his energy that gets me hot. That Big Dick Energy that I pinpointed in our first meeting. This dominance of his. The certain knowledge that he's a force to be reckoned with.

It makes me squirm with need.

I get over there.

He tugs me straight into his arms and I bury my face against his chest, inhaling the deliciousness of his sleep-warmed skin. There is no better scent. There's no better feeling than being cradled in his huge body.

There's nowhere I can imagine being but right here with him.

His hand skims down my spine, his long, strong fingers brushing so softly they ignite my nerve-endings as they go. He shifts, looping a hairy leg over me, and a hard column of flesh slaps me squarely in my lower stomach area. His embrace may be affectionate, but his dick means business, and my body instantly forgets the orgasms he doled out poolside last night and demands more. I make a dreamy little noise of pleasure against his chest.

That hand of his wanders south and takes a huge, greedy handful of my arse. He squeezes and mutters into my hair, 'Okay, sweetheart. Time for you to earn your bed and board.'

I'm not sure why the offensive suggestion that he might actually make me work for my stay here has my stomach clenching with pleasure and my pussy fluttering, but it does. What I do know is that he's not serious. I mean, he's deadly serious, but it's part of a game. It's part of our dynamic. Of the buttons he knows I need him to press.

I give a little laugh of appreciation, and he rolls us so he's on his back and I'm on top of him. I'm half expecting him to push my head down towards his dick, so he catches me by surprise when he hauls me up his hard body instead.

'What are you doing?' I murmur as I raise myself up onto my hands. 'I thought you wanted me to suck your dick.'

He glances up at me and grins. 'No, I want you to ride my face. *Then* I want you to ride my cock.'

I've worked hard on being uninhibited in bed, but this is a lot. The room is flooded with sunlight—I don't suppose closing the shutters was high on our list of priorities when we tumbled into Anton's bed last night—and I could do with a shower. I probably taste like latex down there.

Sitting on his face in broad daylight feels confronting. Exposing. Which I suspect is precisely his reason for suggesting it.

As always, Anton Wolff won't be happy till he's stripped me of every last insecurity and I'm the most brazen version of myself.

He senses my hesitation, probably because my entire body's gone stiff. 'Come on,' he says with a dirty grin, jerking his head towards the strip of condoms he left on the bedside table last night after he fucked me in his bed. 'Put one on me. Then get up here.'

I stare down at him. His stubble's come in overnight, and I already know how filthy and raw it'll feel to grind my clit against it as he tongue-fucks me. There's something about Anton that's so refreshingly shameless. He knows what he wants, and he goes after it. No second-guessing himself. No weighing things up. He's like an animal in that respect, and it's probably something I should aspire to more.

So I lick my lips and I tear off a foil square, ripping it open and taking great pleasure in rolling it down his enormous, angry cock until it's fully sheathed. Then I work my way up his body on my knees till they're either side of his head.

'Fuck,' he says, as I straddle his face. 'Stay there a sec. Hold on to the headboard.'

So I hover above him and, instead of resisting it, I allow myself to revel in the vulnerability of my pussy being about six inches from his face as he lies there on his pillow and takes in every exposed part of me. He takes a finger and circles my entrance with just the tip, and I moan with pleasure, hanging my head and seeing the total focus in his dark eyes as he takes me in.

'This is what you get for holding me off for so long,' he tells me, his finger drawing lazy, teasing circles on my flesh. 'You made me wait, and now I'm going to enjoy you for as long as I fucking want. You acted like you were terrified of letting me anywhere near your cunt, and now I'm going to show you why you were right to be scared. Because this pretty little pink cunt is mine now, and I'm going to play with it whenever I want.'

I shudder with desire as his finger slides forward through my wetness and finds my clit. It gives it a little rub, and I jolt. Jesus, he's amped me up from nought to sixty already, and I know it's his words even more than his touch that are doing it.

I attracted the attention of this devastating wolf, and I let him lure me into his lair, and know he's going to use me and use me till he's sated his appetites on me, and he'll wreck me and ruin me, and I'll fucking love every second.

'Do it,' I hiss.

He withdraws his finger and, without warning, hooks a hand around each hip and yanks me down so I'm squarely on top of him. And the sight of those dark, feral eyes staring up at me as he delivers his first long, deadly lick is the single most threatening and erotic thing I've ever, ever seen.

And then he starts to eat me.

50

ANTON

I suck on her clit, and I drive my tongue deep inside her, and a groan escapes me, because this is the fucking life. The mesmerising blonde goddess who's hijacked my brain and taken my sanity for a ride is fucking my face, and she tastes like heaven.

And when I've finished feasting on her, my favourite ice queen will be a melting, writhing mess who's desperate for my cock.

I could sense her self-consciousness about doing this, but that has to stop, because I have no qualms about wanting this, and nor should she.

I'm not aiming for finesse in this moment. I'll tease her later. I'm aiming for total annihilation, for making every single erogenous zone in her beautiful body sing. So I pull out all the stops. I use my lips and my tongue to suck and lick and fuck. I swirl and I flick and I probe. And I know my moves are having the desired effect when she starts sinking down more heavily onto me.

Not just sinking.

Grinding.

She's working her hips as if she really is fucking me, rubbing that drenched pussy all over my chin so she can get as much friction as she can from my stubble.

Greedy girl.

She's taking what she wants, and I fucking *love* it.

My dick is a fucking telegraph pole, pointing straight up at my ceiling as I plunder her cunt with my mouth. As soon as she comes I'm going to ram her down on it so hard she'll see even more stars.

It's clear she isn't a flight risk right now, so I release my grip on her hips and work my hands up to find her tits. Fuck me, they are glorious. She's holding onto the headboard, and she's so far gone she's actually resting her forehead against it now as she stares down at me, blue eyes glazed and that normally impassive face showing every ounce of her arousal.

She's working those hips so hard that her tits are jiggling, hanging pendulously, nipples hard and swollen. I close my palms around them, and Holy Mother of God. Utter, utter perfection. She gasps loudly as I knead and squeeze and massage before I find her nipples and pinch them. Pull them. They're magnificent, and they're so sensitive, and she is extraordinary.

'*God*, Anton,' she whimpers, rubbing her forehead against the padded linen of my headboard, her hips grinding harder.

She's close. She's so close. Her thighs are trembling on either side of my face, and her cries are regular now, rhythmical, coming in time with her thrusts and my licks. I pinch her nipples hard. I lave as roughly as I can on her clit, and I growl with the fucking assault on my senses. She's soaking; she's fucking dripping, and her smell is so musky, so intoxicating that I could die like this.

I give her one particularly angry lick, and she breaks. She breaks as beautifully as I could ever have wished for, and I stare up at her and watch in wonder as she shudders and cries and jerks her way through what I know is a powerful orgasm.

Before I've even finished licking, she's pulling away and manoeuvring herself down my body. She straddles my hips and wraps her fingers tight around my aching cock, and then she's lowering down. Impaling herself on it with more speed and force than even I would have used, so desperate is she for me to fill her up.

There's no ice queen now. She's fucking ravishing like this. Her beautiful hair is mussed, her mask has gone, and in its place is raw desire. I've unveiled the carnal creature beneath the flawless surface, and I can't get enough.

I wipe my mouth with the back of my hand, because she is *all* over my face, and I cross my arms behind my head. Then I thrust up and into her. My cock is angry at having been made to wait so long, but the sensation of being engulfed in her heat, squeezed by her still-quivering inner muscles, is fucking perfection.

Besides, this is one hell of a show. Because she rides me even more aggressively than she rode my face, pulling herself up each time and slamming down until I bottom out in her, taking every single inch I have to give her, those magnificent tits bouncing as she does.

'Come here,' I say, and she leans forward. I wrap a hand tightly around the back of her neck and pull her forward so I can kiss her while I fuck her. So I can fill up two of her perfect holes.

So I can consume her as much as I want to consume her.

'Harder,' I grit into her mouth, and she fucks me harder. She milks and milks, and my astounding need for release builds and builds until I fucking explode, biting down on her lip as I rut into her and shoot load after load into that condom.

When she's stilled, her head collapsed and her breath warm, uneven, on my neck, I wrap my arms around her tightly as my cock pulses out its aftershocks inside her.

'Stay for the weekend,' I say, and I don't care that it sounds like a plea.

Because it is a fucking plea.

'Please, sweetheart, stay till Sunday.'

51

GEN

After fast, animalistic sex and a slow, civilised breakfast on his shady terrace, Anton has Cédric drive us into Cannes to meet up with the others. I could happily have stayed sequestered in his villa for the whole day, but I suppose we do have a business venture to get off the ground.

Besides, delicious as it is to have Anton to myself, I have to admit it's pretty spectacular to stroll down the town's iconic promenade, La Croissette, with his arm draped easily over my shoulder. We're turning heads, and I don't know if it's because of the size of my smile or the fact that I'm canoodling with one of Europe's most eligible billionaires that's doing it.

I don't care, actually. Just as I don't care about his eligibility or his bank balance. I'm content with being staggeringly grateful that we're giving each other a chance, because whatever doubts I had are being swept right away by his kindness, and his passion. By his seemingly endless appetite for me and, most terrifying of all, by how *easy* it feels with him.

Starting my day by riding his face like a shameless sex maniac was an effective icebreaker. I'll admit that much.

We grab lunch at The Carlton's chic beach club and then meet up with the other members of Anton's team as well as Lola, an attractive and highly efficient local events manager who's lined up several potential venues for us to view.

Max looks particularly pleased with himself today, even by his usual standards.

'How's your "friend"?' I ask him teasingly as I kiss him.

'Insatiable,' he answers with a smirk. He's impossible to dislike. He nods at Anton, who's frowning at something Lola's telling him in rapid French. 'So you two finally got it on,' he continues. 'Took you long enough to get on board.'

I attempt to dissemble. 'I don't know what you're talking about.'

He laughs. 'Give me a break. I saw his hand on your arse before you spotted us.'

I'm not sure why, but I blush. I can feel the heat crawling over my face. 'Fine. We're... I don't know. Together, kind of.'

He nods. 'I'm glad. Just don't mess him around, okay?'

That's the most ridiculous thing I've ever heard. 'I have no intention of it. Obviously.'

'Good. Because he's obsessed with you. I've never seen him like this before.'

The heat grows at his words, and I glance over at Anton. As if sensing the weight of my stare, and the unasked questions I have, he rakes that gorgeous mop of hair off his face and shoots me a smile so warm, so crinkly, so *open*, it floods my entire body with wellbeing.

He's obsessed with you.

Can it really be so?

How can I possibly be this lucky? He's shown me, last night and this morning, the level of his appreciation for my body, and I suppose he's also shown me by way of his high-handed gestures, not the least of which was tricking me into staying alone with him at his villa.

Boy, am I glad he pulled that stunt.

But any words he's said have been sexual. Words of desire and need. Commands. We haven't talked about feelings. To even consider bringing up feelings at this stage feels insane.

It's only been a single night.

But I have an entire weekend with him. A whole weekend of leisurely lounging and fucking and chatting and getting to know each other against one of the most stunning backdrops this part of the world has to offer.

Again, how can I possibly be so lucky?

Max notices me demurring. 'He's a really good guy,' he adds in a lower voice. 'Seriously, one of the best. Yeah, he can be ruthless, but only because he knows what he wants and he always goes after it.' He shoots me a sidelong look. 'Which I don't think is a bad thing.'

NEITHER OF THE first two places we look at are quite right. The first is the entire penthouse of a modern and extremely luxurious apartment building. It includes a roof terrace and boasts its own infinity pool with amazing views over the sea. But it's too small, and it's not discreet enough. I don't want a venue where our patrons have to share the lift with residents. Neither party would be impressed with that option.

The second is a Belle Epoque villa in Super Cannes. It's huge and has exactly the vibe I imagined when Anton first pitched this concept, but on closer inspection it's a little run-down. A little grubby. Not luxurious enough for our efforts, and a big renovation is out of the question for an imminent pop-up.

But the third place is fucking perfect. Anton and I grin at each other as soon as Lola sashays through the entrance. It's more suited to the Hollywood Hills than Cannes, a huge, low box that's white-walled with glass everywhere. The grounds are massive and secluded, with a stunning pool running the entire length of the house. It screams *party pad*. It's flash, it's glamorous, it's decadent, and it feels fresh and modern.

My mind's eye instantly conjures up throngs of beautiful people fucking on the white mattresses and day beds that we'd scatter all over the lawn, while those glass-fronted bedrooms I can see along one side could be the perfect choice for those who like to be seen.

Inside it's even better. There's an enormous open-plan reception area, all white, with a square pool at its centre and stupendous art providing energetic splashes of colour along its serene walls. I thought it was single-storey, but I was wrong. It's built on a slope, and a shallow cantilevered stair-case curves down to a lower floor that wasn't visible from the front of the house.

We count fourteen potential private rooms, as well as plenty of space for a floor show and a freestanding bar. This place is a blank canvas, and the sexy things we could do with lighting are endless.

'How is it even available for the summer?' I ask.

'The owner is moving to Melbourne for a year,' Lola informs us. 'It was a last-minute decision. So they will not require it until next spring.'

Lara, Anton's events manager, and Lola debate the owners' likely latitude in allowing us to customise the space. The upshot is: a lot. If we want to hang cuffs from the ceiling, we can do it. At the price they're asking, we'll make it worth their while to clean up our handiwork afterwards.

As they chat, Anton steers me off to one of the bedrooms on the main floor. It's small and minimalist and perfect, with a glorious view out to the pool area. This place is so cool that we may well attract people who wouldn't normally visit a sex club. People who are maybe less experienced in our field but open-minded enough to come to a stunning private party and see where the night takes them. Where they can experience true freedom.

True alchemy.

I step up to the French doors, and Anton presses himself right up against me, his hard body radiating heat through his clothes and mine. I allow my head to fall back as his proprietary hands roam over my stomach.

'I'm going to fuck you in here, up against this glass,' he says, bending his head so his voice is in my ear. 'In the dark, so you can watch everyone fucking outside as I take you, or with the lights on, your beautiful tits pressed against the glass so everyone can see how fucking stunning you are.'

His tone is carnal, and his vision is piercing. Arousing. I'm instantly assaulted by an understanding of just how it would be. My body naked, my nipples pressed up against the glass, writhing on Anton's cock like the most salacious peep show.

I turn my head and tilt it upwards.

'I'll let you do whatever you want with me,' I say into his mouth.

52

GEN

Maddy's been texting me all morning.

WELL??????????

Yes

yes what? u guys fucked???

And then some

omgggggggggggg

tell me EVERYTHING

u in the same hotel?

Actually, he kidnapped me. I'm staying with him at his place in Cap d'Antibes. And it's fucking incredible, Mads screaming crying DYINGGGGG

I roll my eyes. She literally texts like an eleven-year-old.

I was pretty much doing all 3 of those too

STOP. don't. Omg. he loooooooves u. told u

he does not love me. he wants my body.
And I'm fine with that

whatever tell me how it happened

I'll give you the full details when I get back,
but it was by his pool and it was very
fucking hot

SCREAMING

Poor Zach

he loves it. he wants to know if its the best
sex u've ever had

No he doesn't

ok I do

Undoubtedly. He's just so gorgeous. And
hot. And kind. And did I say hot?

swooooon. ur gonna marry him and live in
France

tempting but unlikely

seriously. and how dirty is he????????

I mean, excellently dirty but not totally depraved. But I think we're still at the 'getting it out of our systems' phase, you know?

watch out. the big bad wolf will pounce when you least expect it

I suspect she's not wrong.

53

ANTON

I take Gen to the Hotel du Cap-Eden-Roc for supper. She's never been here, which surprises me, and it's a rite of passage in this neck of the woods. So, although I'm dying to get her back to the villa and fuck her senseless, I get Rix to work her usual magic and procure a booking.

Besides, it's one of my favourite places, and I want to show Gen off.

We slip back home for a quick shower and change, and she locks her bedroom door so she can complete her *toilette* in the necessary timeframe without me slipping into the shower with her and derailing everything.

Smart girl.

Still, it's a move that only serves to feed the beast inside me. The beast that last night and this morning sated short term and riled long term.

Because now I know what it's like to be with her, there's no going back for me. What I've done with her, *to* her, so far is the tip of the iceberg.

I'm just getting started.

I walk her down the iconic wide promenade that separates the main hotel from the Eden-Roc section on the sea-front. She's wearing a white sundress with large white fabric daisies appliquéd all over it. It's chic and beautifully cut while also being sexy as fuck, particularly because she's not wearing a bra. Again.

This relaxed, holiday side of Gen is a lot of fun. Her usual immaculate but uptight Hitchcock heroine look may be my kryptonite, but I love seeing her let loose a little. And as she walks down to the shore with me, her hand clutching my bicep and her laugh cutting through the still evening air like a silver bell, I look down at her, and admire her, and I think *you are fucking perfect*.

Because she is.

We take our places in the Grill, at a wonderful table that the *maître d'*, Gabriel, has somehow procured for us at the last minute. For a second, I pity whichever poor sod got kicked off their reservation, but only for a second. Because I'm this guy's bread and butter.

I love it down here. It's more my cup of tea than the formal restaurants up in the hotel. Eden-Roc is built on a low rocky platform that cuts straight down to the sea. The Grill is nautical in theme, with a teak-and-iron balustrade that prevents diners falling into the water below and a cheerful blue and white theme.

You still have to be richer than God to eat here, but I'm happy to pay any price to enjoy the fresh lobster and ice-cold rosé while being as close as I can get to the Med. When Gabriel and I have finished our mutual back-slapping and he's left us to it, Gen surveys me. Her eyes are hidden by huge vintage-style shades, but her mouth twists in amusement.

'You have a very nice life, you know,' she remarks, taking

a sip of the sparkling water that's already found its way to us.

'Thank you.' I shake out my thick linen napkin and drape it in my lap.

'I'm serious. I don't know why, but I assumed you were a total workaholic. Are you just playing hooky for a few days?'

I lean forward, elbows on the table, and steeple my fingers. 'It always amuses me that people assume a linear relationship between one's level of success and one's work ethic.'

'Why?'

'Well, because if you have more and more success and you keep pushing harder and harder, that's just fucking stupid, in my opinion. It's been more like a bell curve for me. Why the hell would I want to keep on punishing myself when I have more money than I'll ever need? What's the point if I don't take my foot off the pedal and get to enjoy it all?'

'You're right,' she says. 'There is no point.' Under the table, she runs a bare foot over my ankle. 'I just hadn't seen that side of you, I suppose.'

I lower my shades and grin at her. 'You hadn't seen the hedonistic side of me? Seriously?'

She makes a face back. 'I figured out pretty early it was all work and sex for you. But this is neither.' She gestures at the buzzing restaurant around us. 'I mean, it's a Thursday, and you're in France, getting up to no good with me.'

'We saw two properties today,' I argue.

'Yeah, and you could have had Max or Lara do that easily.'

I sigh. 'I'll always find the flimsiest of excuses to come out here. And honestly, I've spent the past four or five years manoeuvring myself out of a job. I love the big picture stuff, but I don't want to be stuck in the weeds when I can be taking on passion projects and spending time with my kids— when they'll let me—and making love to beautiful women.'

That gets a laugh. 'Making love? Is that what you call it?'

'Banging their fucking brains out,' I amend.

Once the server has dispensed some rosé and olives, she asks, 'So the Alchemy pop up is a passion project for you?'

You're a passion project for me, I think. I clear my throat. 'It's a bit of fun. It's also a shameless way to get closer to you. But I honestly think the brand has tonnes of potential. Why on earth haven't you expanded before now?'

'A few reasons,' she says, swilling her rosé. 'Mainly that I don't think any of us were in a massive hurry for various reasons. Zach's wife died a couple of years ago, for one. That was a major shocker. We'd all been great friends with her, so he went into survival mode and, obviously, so did we.'

I grimace. 'Fuck. That's terrible. Did they have kids?'

'Two girls.' She looks down at her glass. 'And yeah. It was horrific. Pancreatic cancer—she was gone within a month of diagnosis. But he's dating Maddy now, our social media manager.'

I nod. I remember those two in our meeting. It was pretty obvious they were together.

'And there were other reasons, too. Zach and Rafe run a small kind-of hedge fund with some of their friends, and we're all invested in it. It makes us far more money than Alchemy. So no one's worried about paying the bills. We've been having fun with the club—it's far more than just a business to us.'

'I can believe it,' I say sternly, and she smiles seductively before her tone turns more businesslike. 'And it's not the kind of thing we want to rush. It's important to get every single detail right with a venture like that. That's why I'm scared shitless about this pop-up. It all feels so fast.'

I lean across the table and squeeze her hand. 'I promise you. We will throw whatever money we need to at it so no detail is overlooked.'

'Thank you,' she says, squeezing back. 'But I'm also excited, because it's an amazing chance to see if the brand travels well.'

'It will be hot as fuck,' I forecast. 'So you'd expand further, if this went well?'

'It would be crazy not to,' she says. 'New York's the obvious place for a second club, but LA would also be fun, and the opportunity for seasonal resort pop-ups is huge, too. It's all I think about, usually. Alchemy, that is. So it's good to get a break from it.' She smiles. 'Even if we're supposed to be here for work.'

'I'd rather you were here to play,' I tell her in my most predatory voice as I brush my thumb over her knuckles.

She gives a nervous little giggle. 'That works.'

'But it's going well, overall? Alchemy, I mean. It certainly seems to be.'

She cocks her head, considering the question. 'Yeah. It is. A competitor has opened up, and they're causing us a few headaches. Let's just say their customer acquisition tactics are aggressive.'

'Rapture?' I suggest.

Her jaw drops open. 'Seriously? They approached you?'

'As a founding member.'

'Un-fucking-believable,' she mutters. 'Did you check it out?'

'Nope. I know some of the guys behind it, and I don't like them at all. Slippery as fuck.'

'Unlike you?'

I grin. 'Too like me for my liking. No, they're dodgy. Plus, I found another club whose clientele is more up my street.' I entwine my fingers with hers. 'I'm not looking for anywhere else to play.'

We gaze goofily at each other for a moment before I return to the matter at hand. 'So, are they giving you grief?'

She grimaces. 'Nothing we can't handle. But they're pursuing our members—hard—and they've even tried to poach a couple of our members of staff. They approached our concierge, Natalie, this week, but she turned them down flat.'

'What are you going to do about it?' I ask point-blank.

'Not sure there's much we can do. We stand by our repu-tation, and word of mouth brings us decent business. We just have to hope we have the superior proposition, and that people who are looking for that kind of offering realise that. But it's definitely been distracting me when I should be focusing on this pop-up.'

I frown. That's far too passive. Frankly, it's naive. If someone gets up in my turf, I don't sit back and hope the best man wins.

I make sure he does.

By any means necessary.

But something tells me she doesn't require or desire my input, so I go for a joke.

'I'm disappointed. I thought I was the only thing distracting you.'

She gives me a beautiful smile, and all is right with the world. 'Believe me, you're extremely distracting.'

'Glad to hear it,' I say. 'But, of the two of us, I suspect you work a lot harder than I do. Married to the job?'

'Probably,' she admits.

'How old are you? Mid-thirties?' I guess.

'I'll be thirty-seven in October.'

'Ever been married?'

She shakes her head. 'Nope.'

'Do you want kids?'

She raises her eyebrows so they crest the top of her shades. 'God, no.'

I laugh. 'Fair enough.'

'I mean, I like them, but I've never felt the need to procreate.' She pauses, then shudders a little. 'No, definitely not. No offence,' she adds hurriedly.

'None taken,' I tell her. And it's good news, because she could definitely still have children if she wanted to, and that's the one thing I can't give her. Four kids are quite enough for anyone. I had the snip a few years ago, and it was the best thing I've ever done.

Nope, I can't give her kids.

But, God knows, I'll give her every single other thing her heart desires.

The realisation jolts me, because I've spent one night with her, for fuck's sake. I circle back to safer territory.

'So, what's the age gap between those two?'

'Who?' she asks. 'Zach and Maddy?'

'Yeah.'

She considers. 'Thirteen or fourteen years, I think?'

I smirk. 'Nice one. And your other friend. Rafe?'

'Same. All of us are the same age—we were at uni together—and Maddy and Belle, Rafe's girlfriend, were at school together.'

'That's a big age gap.'

'It's less than ours,' she points out as she sips her rosé. 'I'm thirty-six. You're, what, fifty-two? That's sixteen years.'

'Our gap isn't that big in percentage terms,' I retort.

'Theirs is a lot bigger. There's nothing wrong with our age gap.'

She sits back, still holding her glass, and surveys me. 'And what about the age gap between you and Athena?' she asks sweetly.

Oh, fuck.

I walked right into that one.

54

ANTON

'Athena's an employee,' I say matter-of-factly.

'That wasn't my question. And I've seen her suck your dick and hump your leg, so don't gaslight me.'

'Fine.' I reach desperately for my wine. 'She's twenty-four.'

She remains impassive behind her sunglasses.

'Don't even think about sex-shaming me, Gen. She's an adult, and she knows exactly what she's doing, and I pay her fucking well.'

'I wouldn't do that, and I don't doubt it.' She sips her drink. I don't know why, but her lack of reaction is pissing me off. Probably because it feels like a trap. There's no way she can have no opinion on the fact that I'm fucking my EA.

Can she?

'If you have something to say, you should say it,' I tell her.

'As long as you're treating her properly and looking after her well-being, it's none of my business.' She picks up her menu and starts to peruse it.

She is a cool fucking customer.

'Gen.'

She looks up at me.

'It should be your business,' I say.

I wish she'd take those bloody glasses off. I can't see her eyes at all, but something about the way she puts down her menu and places her hands flat on top of it strikes me as vulnerable. Like she's being very careful with her reactions.

'I've spent one night with you, Anton. I'm not under any illusions as to what this is.'

Right. That's quite enough of that crap. 'Take off your glasses,' I say, pulling my aviators off. 'I want to see you.'

She sighs, then removes her dark glasses slowly and sets them down on the table. When she raises her blue eyes to me, I see exactly why she didn't want to take her glasses off.

Those beautiful eyes are the windows to every last insecurity she has.

'Do you remember what I said to you in your office the other night?' I ask. 'Before I left?'

She nods once. 'Yeah.'

'And what did I say?'

She squares her shoulders defensively. 'That if you touched me, um, that would be... it. You wouldn't be with anyone else.'

I'm unfeasibly pleased that she committed my words to memory.

'Exactly,' I say, reaching across the table and smoothing my hand up the soft skin of her arm. 'Because I wouldn't *want* to be with anyone else.'

She doesn't say anything, just looks away from me and out to the golden hues of the setting sun. She tugs her lower lip between her teeth and chews.

'Sweetheart,' I say. 'It may have technically been only

one night, but this is a very deliberate decision on my part. Okay? I've wanted you from the second I laid eyes on you, and neither Athena nor any other women at the club or anywhere else hold an iota of interest for me. I really want to make sure you know that, because I wouldn't have got you here under false pretences. I told you you could trust me.'

'You also told me you liked "women, plural" in your interview,' she says, turning back to me. Her face is carefully expressionless. There's no blame in her voice. It's measured. Polite.

Too fucking polite.

I want her to fight for me.

'I'm sure you remember I also told you that I'd failed in all my relationships to find a woman I was sexually compatible with,' I say. I lean forward. '*This* is what I was talking about, and yeah, I thought I'd have to fuck God knows how many women to get the kind of satisfaction I need. But I knew—I fucking *knew* you'd be dynamite if you gave me a chance.'

She's staring at me, still chewing that lip, and I wish I could pull her onto my lap. Instead, I turn her hand palm up so I can stroke up over her pulse point, and I keep talking.

'That's why I'll be redistributing Athena when I get back.'

'No,' she says with an alarm I'm not expecting. 'You can't do that.'

'Yes I bloody can.'

'Anton. I'm not going to let another woman lose her job because of me,' she says. 'Even if I don't like the nature of your relationship.'

There it is. It *does* bother her. Thank fuck.

'It's a professional relationship,' I insist. 'I pay her almost as much as I pay Max, but don't tell him that. She's from an agency I founded a few years ago. The reason I pay her through the roof is because she's very good at both sides of her job, but she's also on a monthly rolling contract, and that's a key part of our agreement. She's only been with me four months, so it's no great hardship at my end to have her hand over to another EA and move on.'

I can tell she's agitated. 'Why can't she just stay and do her day job for a reduced rate?' she asks, and I'm in awe. Because it's not every day a woman you're involved with lobbies you on behalf of the employee you're fucking, and I love her for it. I love that she'd put aside her dislike of having me and Athena working closely together in favour of safeguarding my EA's job.

'She could,' I say, 'but I doubt she'd want to, because she can earn between five and ten times more fulfilling this particular combination of roles, which is what she's specifically trained for. And, more importantly, I don't want her around, even if I never give her a second glance, which I won't. Because if I'm involved with you, I don't want you to have a single second of doubt about what I'm getting up to at work. Ever.'

She gives me a sad smile. 'Well, thank you. But I don't think you should jump into anything. I'm a big girl—I can handle myself. And I feel uncomfortable having this conversation when I literally kissed you for the first time yesterday.'

We're back to this again. Jesus. 'Why?' I ask her, my tone more harsh than I intend. 'Because I'm freaking *you* out by talking about the future? Or because you're worried I'm backing myself into a corner and at some point *I'll* freak out and run for the hills?'

'The latter,' she says, so quietly I can barely hear it.

It should be reassuring to hear how concerned she is

about whether I'm committed to this. Gratifying, even. But really, it just hurts my heart.

As I look at the spectacular woman in front of me, the woman who owns the very club I joined on a mission to emancipate myself, the woman who represents every fantasy and desire and need I didn't know I have, I vow to myself to show her over and over that I'm committed to making a go of this.

'I want to know what you do with her,' she says, her voice still low.

I stare at her in horror, hoping I've misunderstood. 'I beg your pardon?'

'Tell me how you use her,' she says.

'No.' I shake my head. 'Absolutely not. Why the fuck would you want to know that?'

She licks her lips and fixes those eyes squarely on me. 'Because I'm jealous.'

Oh, Jesus. I knew it. I squeeze her wrist. 'I know you are, sweetheart. Which is why I think we should both put my little arrangement with her behind us. Okay?'

She pushes on. 'That's not what I mean. Yeah, of course I'm jealous you've been with her. But I mean I'm jealous that she got to be used like that by you, whenever you wanted. Because that's my ultimate fantasy.'

55

GEN

Anton looms over me, smiling with satisfaction.

He's still in his white polo shirt and aqua-coloured swim shorts, but he has me fully naked.

He also has me spreadeagled and tied to the railings on the prow of his beautiful boat. I'm lying on a smooth cream mattress that fills the entire prow, and Captain Kinky here has performed some kind of rope trickery on me that's impressive and arousing and alarming in equal measure.

My wrists and ankles are completely secured to the railings, and I'm strung up like a fucking starfish. Thanks to the white canopy over us, I'm shaded from the sun, but that hasn't stopped my captor from lovingly massaging suncream into every inch of my skin. Now he surveys his handiwork—and his captive—with pride.

'Happy with yourself?' I ask.

He grins, bending to run a hand up my thigh. 'Extremely.'

'And here I was thinking we'd enjoy a nice picnic and a gentle swim.'

'Time for all of that when I've got what I need from you,' he tells me.

'And what's that?' I ask, although I know. Because I now have clarity on several fronts.

Anton can drive a huge boat perfectly.

He can tie a rope like he's spent a decade in the navy.

And he won't be happy until he has full control over not only my body but every recess of my mind.

Especially the darkest ones.

My little allusion to my fantasies at dinner last night definitely poked the bear. I refused to give him more than a high-level summary of what it was about the idea of being his sexy, willing secretary that did it for me. Because, come on. I want him to see me as his equal. So when I have all these gross but delicious fantasies about serving him, I actually offend myself.

Plus, it would make him insufferable if he knew the full details.

So I've held off from providing any more colour, but I should have known he'd be relentless. Like a fucking dog trying to unearth a buried bone.

Unfortunately, it seems like he now has the upper hand.

'I want to know what your ultimate fantasy is,' he tells me now. 'We've come a long way, sweetheart, but you're still not letting me in.'

I twist my mouth as I gaze up at him. He's so beautiful. So arresting. So fucking huge and dominating and sexy. He's everything I could possibly want in a man, all wrapped up in one gorgeous package. And, for some reason, he seems as transfixed by me as I am by him.

And he's right. I'm still not letting him all the way in, because every survival instinct in my body is shouting at me to have some sense of fucking self-preservation.

'You take my breath away,' he whispers. His knuckles brush up and down my thigh. 'And I know you think it's all happening quickly, that I'm pushing you. But that's only because we're so fucking similar, sweetheart, underneath it all. And you know I'm greedy. I don't just want what you've already given me. I want that part of you that you seem to think you have to keep hidden beneath all those layers of decorum.'

My lips part at his words, because, impossibly, I fear and desire giving him that very part of me in equal measure.

'I want you to let me in,' he says. 'I've seen flashes of it, mostly at the hands of people who aren't me, which really fucking hurts. But I don't want you to feel like you need to hide any part of yourself. I want you to embrace it, because you already know that if you share it with me I'll lap it up. You know we have the same tastes, Gen.'

'I know,' I whisper, because I do. And I know how desperately Anton adores that wanton side of me, where I'm so crazed with desire that I'll let him tear me apart.

I also know that I've shown him flashes, but I haven't let him in properly.

His demeanour changes. 'Well, that was my little speech,' he says, shifting, 'but if you won't do this the easy way, we can do it the hard way.'

The way he looks down my spreadeagled body makes me shiver. 'Meaning?' I manage.

He grins. 'Meaning I'll touch you until I get you to that point where you're so fucking desperate for relief you'll do *anything* for an orgasm. Including telling me every darkest desire you have.'

I grin back. We both know I'm a foregone conclusion. We both know that the beautiful, predatory Anton Wolff will get everything he wants from me, and then some.

And we both know we'll have some fun along the way.

He kneels on the mattress and braces himself over me, and I'm flooded with a sensation that's somewhere between happiness and anticipation. It's the knowledge that this is a sure thing. That whatever paces Anton puts me through, however hard he works me, we both ardently want the same outcome.

And we'll get it.

I sigh and stretch as fully as I can in my restraints, which aren't too tight but don't give me much room to manoeuvre.

He lowers himself down onto his elbows and kisses my jaw. My neck. I wish so much that my hands were free to rake through his gorgeous thick hair.

'Tell me a story,' he whispers seductively. 'In your erotic dreamland, when you're touching yourself at night, who are you?' He kisses down my neck. 'Who do you fantasise about, and what do you let them do to you?'

I swallow. My imagination is a lush garden, but I don't love putting its fruits into words. I don't enjoy articulating them aloud. 'Usually variations on a theme,' I tell him. 'Or themes.'

'Mmm-hmm.' He moves down my body and takes a nipple in his mouth, rolling his tongue over it like it's a little sweet. 'What're the common themes?' he asks against my skin.

I consider how to summarise. 'Being outnumbered. Dominated. Used, mainly. Like I'm a plaything.'

'Very good.' He moves to my other nipple and bites it lightly. The sensation echoes right through my core. 'And what's the scene, usually?'

'I dunno.' It's hard to keep a clear head when Anton has my pussy spread open for him and his delicious, dangerous mouth on my nipple.

He stops. 'Try.'

I exhale in frustration. 'I'm usually... subservient. Like, they're more powerful than me. I'm a maid, or a bartender, or a server. Or a secretary.' I stop and screw up my face, squeezing my eyes shut. When I open them, he's reared up so he can stare down at me.

'That's nothing to be embarrassed about. You're a smart, successful woman. You bear a lot of responsibility. It's completely normal to want to hand all your power over—I'd go so far as to say it's the oldest dynamic in the book.'

'I know,' I say. 'I just feel... guilty. It's not very emancipated of me.'

'Fuck emancipation. If you want to be a fucking virgin who the Vikings kidnap and ravage, do it. You know this is normal. You don't need me to tell you.'

'You're right,' I admit. 'I just—it would be a lot easier to do this if I was drunk and in a darkened room, not out here in the middle of the day.'

He grins. 'You feel exposed, don't you?'

'Yep.' I pop the *p*, because that's an understatement.

'Good. Keep going.' He lowers himself back to my nipple, mouth hovering right there.

This man will be the death of me. 'Fine. Let's see.'

'You can do it,' he says. 'Tell me something really good, and I'll touch your cunt.'

56

ANTON

S he groans at that.

I'm a patient man when it counts. When I really want a certain outcome. But my best strategy here isn't patience but action. Because the more I work her up, the more she'll shed her inhibitions and move to the places she deems dark in her head. So I dip my head and play with one pretty pink nipple. It's no hardship, because Gen's tits are the most spectacular thing I've ever seen in my life, and I could suck them all day long.

It's also the right call, because she starts talking.

'Okay,' she says, 'let's say I'm a server at your offices. You're in a big boardroom, all glass table and chrome fixtures, and I come in to serve everyone coffee.'

I hum my appreciation. 'What are you wearing?' I ask her before licking her nipple hard and reaching over to pinch her other one.

'Heels. Maybe a white shirt and a black skirt.'

'And the shirt is buttoned, but it's pulling over your incredible tits,' I tell her, getting into this, 'and the skirt shows off your amazing arse. Go on.' I let my mouth roam over her skin. It's velvet-soft and I could kiss it forever.

'You're sitting at the head of the table, and your eyes are on me from the second I walk into the room,' she confesses. 'And your whole demeanour is so fucking entitled, and arrogant, and I know you want me. And I know you get everything you want, because my colleagues have warned me about you.'

My cock, which has been standing to attention since I stripped that sexy one-piece off her and tied her up, thickens further. 'And how does that make you feel?' I ask.

I want to see her, so I sit up on my knees and run my hands up and down her torso. I play with her nipples, I pet her beautiful breasts, and then I return to her stomach.

She moans, and looks me in the eyes, and says, 'It makes me feel scared. Super apprehensive. But also wet, because I know I'm not going to walk out of that room the same person. And I already know I'm going to let you do whatever you want to me.'

I clench my jaw, because this is a powerful fucking fantasy, and it, of course, feeds into everything I know about Gen so far, both from observation, and personal experience, and gut intuition.

It's also something I can absolutely make happen for her, but I won't suggest that right now. Because in this moment I'm providing a safe place for her to share the filthy fucking things she wants, and I want every last salacious crumb from her.

'Damn right you are,' I tell her. 'So what happens then?'

'You beckon me over, and I lean forward and fill your cup with the coffeepot. You're talking, and everyone's hanging on your every word. And you don't even stop what you're discussing, you just say *good girl* when I fill your cup, and you slide a hand up my inner thigh and brush my panties.'

I could die from the happiness of kneeling here and watching this incredible, naked, restrained woman narrate her darkest desires to me. It's no exaggeration to say that none of the women with whom I've had a serious relationship have ever come out with shit like this.

I could take over the narration from here. I could tell her every filthy, demeaning thing I'd do to her in that board meeting, but she needs to get there herself.

'Like this?' I ask, and I brush a featherlight fingertip between her legs, barely touching her wet cunt.

She sucks in a breath. 'God—yes.'

'What kind of panties are you wearing? Thong?'

'No—white cotton ones. Sensible work ones.'

'Wholesome,' I say. 'Because you're a good girl, and you wouldn't usually dream of doing this kind of thing.'

'Exactly.' She smiles at me, and I know in that instant that I have her trust. That she realises how fully on the same page we are. That I'll never knock back a single one of her desires, or kinks, or needs. That I'll be her biggest cheerleader and her greatest enabler. Her face is open, and I've never seen a more beautiful sight then my Gen, naked and trussed up and showing me her true self.

'What happens then?' I ask. I make my voice harsher. More dominant. I'm not her confidant, the lover she's been so intimate with these past couple of days. I'm a stranger, a predator who's about to demean her and unravel her in front of all these other strange men.

I'm a guy she doesn't know and yet can't look away from.

I can tell she feels the shift, because her smile disappears and in its place there's pleading. 'Then it all, um, gets pretty filthy.'

I press my hand down on her pubic bone, my thumb brushing the very bottom of her landing strip. We both know that a few millimetres south will have me finding that hooded clit that's already swollen and throbbing for me. 'How so?' I ask in the same tone.

She opens her legs even further so the ropes binding them slacken a little.

'You—um. You tell me you need a little entertainment and that I should help. You say surely I'm not shy about letting you play with me in front of everyone. I try to protest, but your voice is so commanding. I think I forget that I'm even allowed to say no. And I'm so turned on that I couldn't say no if I tried, because all I can think about is having you look at me and touch me. It's kind of shocking, but it's also so thrilling, and so arousing. Like the more stuff I think about letting you do to me, the more turned on I'll become.'

I slide my thumb down to her slick clit and hold it there. 'Because you're a greedy, filthy girl,' I say, 'and you want my hands and my mouth and my cock all fucking over you.'

'Yes,' she moans.

'Go on.'

Her eyes drift closed, and I don't mind, because she's getting deeper into her fantasy, and God knows I want her totally immersed.

'You sit there, and I can tell how much you want me, but you're also so cold. You order me to take off my shirt so everyone can see my bra, so I do. I unbutton it, and I take it off, and then you make me take off my bra, so I do, and you just say something like *very nice*, and then you go to the next slide on your PowerPoint presentation, but you reach up and you start playing with my nipple, even though you're still talking through your slide.

'And I'm just standing there, totally topless, and I'm

completely mortified, but the way you're treating me so dismissively has me practically coming there and then.'

'Fucking *yes*,' I groan, because this movie she's playing in our minds is the best porn I've ever seen. I release her clit and move both hands to her insane, plump tits, working them as I rub and pull and pinch her nipples. 'Am I doing this?'

'Yes,' she manages, arching off the mattress and into my touch.

'And how does it feel?'

'It feels like I want to die of shame and spiral into orgasm there and then. I want to sink into the floor, but I also want you to fuck me in front of everyone.'

'I will,' I promise. 'More.'

She squirms on the mattress. 'The other guys are kind of... conflicted. I suspect they've seen you do this before, but they're also getting more and more turned on. But you're such an arrogant dickhead that you just make them watch— you won't let anyone else touch me.'

'Quite fucking right,' I growl. 'And now I need to take off those little white panties and touch your cunt.' I glide my hands slowly, lightly down over her stomach to her hips and wait for her to catch up.

'You slide a hand up my skirt and shove my panties aside and you finger me roughly—like in a *this is mine* kind of way.'

Yes.

57

ANTON

I'd definitely do that. I'd want to shock her. Remind her who calls the shots. I drive two fingers inside her, careful not to touch her clit at all, and she jolts.

'Oh my God—just like that.'

'Yeah?' I twist my hand and crook them, and she sucks in a breath. 'Ow. Yes. And you just sit there and finger-fuck me under my skirt for a few minutes, and I'm still topless, and everyone's staring at my boobs.'

'Do you like them staring?' I ask through gritted teeth as I finger-fuck her with calculated thrusts. I watch with satisfaction as her entire body jolts each time I do it. As her face contorts.

'Yes. I'm just standing there and taking it, and my face is burning, and it feels so fucking good. I never, ever want you to stop.'

Her face is indeed flushed. Extraordinary. The human mind is stunning. My own mind is squarely and happily split between the glorious images playing in my mind and the spectacular sight right in front of me. 'I won't stop,' I say with a savage thrust.

'But then you want more. So you make me slide my panties off, and you just yank my skirt up around my waist and you get me on my back on the table, right there in front of you, and you scoot your chair back in and spread my legs, and you hand over the presentation to someone else and start eating me.

'And I'm just there, laid out on this table for you with my boobs hanging out, and you're so, so good at it, but you're still detached, you know? You haven't lost control at all. Like you do this the whole time and it's no big deal for you, even though you'll ruin me.'

I hate and I love that she's imagining this. And I hate and love that she's got herself in pretty much the same mental position that she was in when Max ate her out on my board-room table. I wonder if that's deliberate or subconscious. All I know is that, in this moment, I want to be that guy. That monster who's preyed upon some beautiful woman and fucking takes, takes, takes whatever he wants with no regard for anyone around him.

I reach over and untie the knots around her ankles, replacing them with my fingers and hauling her legs up and back so I can shimmy down onto my stomach and go to fucking town on her. I'm not sure how well I'll be able to emulate the detachment she describes from my porno alter ego, but I'll try.

I give her a long lick from front to back, my tongue slicing through swollen flesh and soaking arousal, and she cries out so loudly I worry she'll come there and then. 'Like this?' I ask her, jabbing my fingers back inside her.

She shudders, clenching around my fingers. 'Oh my God, yes.'

I start licking and talking. Licking and talking. Alternating my assault on her needy cunt with some filth of my own to help her along, to bring her fantasy even more to life.

Look at you spread out on the table for me.

Everyone can see your tits.

Everyone wants to touch you.

You like it, don't you?

You like my tongue on your clit while everyone watches?

You've interrupted my meeting with your greedy little cunt, and I'm going to make you pay.

I'm going to get you nice and wet, and then I'm going to bend you over and fuck you in front of all these men, and no one will be able to hear poor old Barry droning on about next year's projections because you'll moan the fucking place down as I rail the living daylights out of you.

Okay, maybe Barry was a step too far, because I actually make myself laugh. It feels like a good time to stop talking and to send her over the edge.

To send us both over the edge, because I'm rutting against this fucking mattress and I can't last another second without being balls-deep inside her.

I push up onto my knees to pull off my polo shirt and extricate a condom from my swim shorts before losing them, too. The moan she gave as I abandoned my licking turns to a hungry, filthy stare as she watches me sheath my length.

'What happens then?' I ask as I crawl over her and position my cock right at her entrance. She shimmies against me like she's trying to get me inside her, and I grin. 'I said *what happens then?*'

'You fuck me,' she breathes, staring up at me. She's a fucking sight for sore eyes, tits heaving, breath shallow, voice needy.

'On the table.' I push in, rough and fast like I know she needs it, and she groans.

'In front of everyone.'

'Yes.' She can barely speak. 'You fuck me so hard, and I just lie there with my legs open for you, because I want you to do whatever you want to me. *Whatever* you—I'd do anything.'

'Because...' I drag my cock almost all the way out and glare down at her. I'm braced on one hand, the other hand gripping her hip because I'm going to need it to stop her flying off the fucking boat.

'Because I need your dick so badly that nothing else matters,' she confesses.

Her admission is a red rag, and I fucking let her have it. I abandon all vestige of control with a volley of drives so fucking hard that I might actually pass out.

Below me is my favourite Gen.

The woman she keeps so carefully hidden beneath those pristine, glossy, irreproachable layers.

The woman who screams and cries and bucks, every last inhibition blown to smithereens as she harnesses her beautiful, incredible appetites and fucking *owns* them.

And when she falls apart in spectacular fashion, the sea blue and sparkling around her, I'm right there behind her.

58

GEN

Alchemy feels different when I walk back in on Monday morning.

I suspect it's that *I'm* different.

My time in France felt like far longer than four nights. How could it not? Four days and nights wrapped around Anton. Sleeping in his arms. Talking and kissing and fucking. Devouring each other. Seeing one of the most beautiful places in the world through his eyes. Letting myself be suspended from real life for a short time in a bubble of desire and hedonism.

How could I not feel like a different person after that?

The wrench I felt leaving his villa yesterday was agonising. But the atmosphere on the plane was lighthearted, especially because Max had stayed the weekend too and regaled us with hilarious tales of his rapacious French lover. Anton insisted on giving me a lift home.

And then he insisted on coming in.

And then he insisted on kissing me until I had to practically push him out the door to rescue his illegally parked driver.

And then he called me as I was getting into bed. It turns out he's highly accomplished at phone sex.

No surprise there.

He really is a dirty bastard.

So I haven't had much time to feel bereft. And he's given me no reason to believe that the end of our crazy, Mediterranean fuck-fest marks the end of everything for us.

On the contrary, as he lathered up my hair in his huge stone shower yesterday morning, he explicitly told me I wouldn't be getting rid of him.

I believed him.

So it's with a happy heart and a spring in my step that I arrive at work. What I'm not expecting, as I walk into our front meeting room, is for four people to take one look at me and burst out laughing.

I put my Birkin down and cross my arms. 'What?' I demand in my sternest voice.

'Holy shit,' Cal says, getting to his feet, 'I have never, ever seen an orgasm glow quite that good on anyone. They could see you from space.'

'Fuck off,' I tell him, but he wraps me and my crossed arms in a huge bear hug.

'You look fucking amazing,' he says into my ear.

'I assume Maddy blabbed?' I ask the room at large when he's released me.

'Sure did,' she singsongs cheerfully.

'Not that she needed to,' Zach adds. 'Your silence on Thursday and Friday spoke volumes. Usually you're all over us when you're away, nit-picking everything we're up to.'

'That's not true,' I say halfheartedly as I take my seat next to Rafe on the sofa. But I'm too happy to argue the point more aggressively.

'You look fab,' Rafe says. 'Clearly it was sunny over there.'

'Yeah, the weather was beautiful. We got a bit of sunbathing in.' *Between being tied up on boats and the rest of it.*

'Oooh!' Maddy shrieks. '*We*. You hear that? They're already a *we*.'

I roll my eyes. 'Grow up, for God's sake. Who's made me a coffee?'

'We didn't know if you'd make it in this morning,' Zach points out, 'or if you were too busy shagging.'

'Pot.' I glare at him and Maddy, who's practically sitting on his lap. 'And kettle.'

'Give the woman a break,' Cal says.

I turn to him. 'Thank you. I knew I liked you.'

'Seriously, though,' he says. 'Tell us everything. And I don't mean the venues. You had a good time with him, yeah?'

I let my head fall back against the sofa. 'I don't even know where to begin,' I say. 'It was the best long weekend of my life.'

I HAVEN'T HEARD from Anton yet this morning, which is quite understandable. After all, the guy has a global business empire to run and an EA to redistribute, at his insistence. Still, I'm feeling disgustingly needy and uncharacteristically co-dependent. It's only natural after such an intense few days together—we went from nought to sixty in the space of a single evening—but I still despise myself.

Sometime after twelve, as I'm sipping what I tell myself will be my last espresso of the day, the doorbell rings.

Maddy, like the good little girl scout she is, scampers off to answer it with Norm plodding behind her. She comes back through the double doors to our desk area, eyes wide and the biggest smirk on her face.

'Flower delivery for you, Gen,' she says.

I don't have time to ask her where the flowers are, because hot on her tail is none other than Anton, looking tanned, gorgeous, and uncharacteristically bashful. He stops in the doorway, his arms full of an enormous bouquet.

'Afternoon,' he says with a nod at the room in general.

'Hi!' I squeak in a voice so uncool that Cal actually sniggers as I jump up from my desk. I shoot him daggers and round my desk, stopping in front of Anton as the others sling casual greetings his way. Before anyone can do anything embarrassing, I usher him out into the front room and pretty much slam the double doors shut.

As soon as I do, he backs me up against them, looming over me and looking so tall and broad and hulking that I feel a little swoony. I look up at his handsome, bronzed face and I just fucking beam at him, because he's in my office, and he's brought me flowers, and I'm done trying to act cool around him.

'When Genevieve Carew gives me a smile like *that*,' he says softly, dumping the beautiful bouquet unceremoniously on a side table and closing the gap between us, 'it makes me think I must have done something right in my life.'

And then he's tugging me into his arms and kissing me, and I finally understand why smelling salts have their place, because I'm swooning so hard that if he lets me go, I may slide to the floor in a pathetic, love-sick pile.

But he doesn't let go.

He bands one arm more tightly around my waist and

clamps the other one around my neck in such a way that he drags his thumb and forefinger down the skin there, and I've never felt anything better. His mouth is firm on mine, his tongue warm, and I swear when he slides it into my mouth it makes me want his dick inside me.

I abandon myself to him. To our kiss. I've never been one of those dainty women men can sling over their shoulders or pick up with one arm. In fact, my mother has distinctly referred to me as 'a big girl' on more than one occasion. But he's so massive, and protective, and so fucking alpha that right now I feel positively waif-like.

'Last time I was here you kissed me on the cheek,' he whispers against my mouth when we finally break our kiss, 'and it was the first time I really felt like I had a chance with you.'

It's an oddly chaste, poignant, thing for someone as overtly sexual as him to share, and it may just finish me off. It's also too generous a gesture on his part for me to leave him hanging.

'I've never spent a second in your company without torturing myself over what it would be like to kiss you,' I confess, and I feel, rather than see, that sensual mouth curve into a grin.

'Glad to hear it.' He smacks my arse.

'What are you doing here?' I ask.

He pulls away and surveys me. 'Well, there's no one to fuck at work anymore, so I thought I'd come over.'

I smack him ineffectually on his formidable bicep.

'Ouch. Too soon?'

My only reply is a goofy smile.

'I missed you,' he says, 'and I wanted to see if you missed me, or if you'd moved on like the callous little ice queen you are.'

'I think we both know you melted her a few nights ago,' I admit.

'Yes, we do. And I wanted to deliver these in person.' He picks the bouquet up again and holds it out to me, clearing his throat. 'They felt more appropriate than camellias, given you're no longer pretending to be all proper and buttoned-up.'

They are a stunning hand-tied bunch of early season white peonies, blousy and luscious and imperfect and undone.

The man is a master of symbolism, and I'm so touched I can barely speak.

'They're perfect,' I tell him softly. 'Thank you.'

'You'll have to leave them here tonight,' he says, 'because I also wanted to ask you to dinner. I'd like to cook for you.'

59

ANTON

'Hades, *no*,' I tell my dog in the hallway as I prepare to open the front door. '*Sit.*'

I'm using my most commanding voice, the one that's had women scrambling to their knees for decades, but my dog is either too stupid to understand or just not fucking scared of me.

I shoot him the look that's brought multiple employees to tears, to no avail. With a huff, I open the door.

What a fucking sight. Gen on my doorstep, with damp hair and a sundress and, best of all, what looks like an overnight bag. The little beauty.

'Well, hel—' I begin, but before I can even finish saying hello, my stupid mutt has barrelled forward and is shoving his nose in her crotch.

'Hi, gorgeous boy!' she croons, dropping her bag on the step so she can squish his face. 'Aren't you a beauty!'

'Hades,' I say sternly. 'Come *here*.' No one else gets to put their face there. Especially not my fucking dog.

To his credit, he backs away from her mournfully before throwing himself down in the middle of the threshold and rolling onto his back, paws clawing at the air and scrotum on full display. Needy, much?

Gen laughs as she picks up her bag and steps around the dog. 'Hades? Please tell me you named him ironically.'

'Afraid not,' I say. 'He's not quite the Prince of Darkness I was hoping for. He's a doberman, for fuck's sake. He's supposed to be scary.'

'Sounds like the perfect analogy for you. Neither of you are quite as scary as you seem, are you?' she says, giving me a once-over, and I instantly forget about my dog.

'Not with you around,' I tell her, stepping towards her.

She runs an appraising hand down my upper arm. 'This domesticated thing looks good on you.'

By *domesticated*, I assume she means my rolled-up shirt-sleeves and the tea-towel slung over one shoulder. I shoot her a grin that aims for charming. 'Why thank you.'

I dip my head and take a moment to enjoy the pure, but not remotely simple, pleasure that is kissing her. I find her lips with mine and slide a hand around the back of her neck while tugging her against me with a hand on her gorgeous, shapely arse.

I don't stick my tongue down her throat, mainly to prove to myself that this woman hasn't obliterated every last vestige of my self-control, but I do linger over several gratifyingly slow slides of my lips against hers.

Until I hear—and feel—the irregular thud of two pairs of feet tearing down the top flight of stairs.

Fuck's sake. I reluctantly withdraw.

'What the hell is that?' Gen asks, her eyes wide.

'The Terrible Twins,' I tell her. 'Don't worry. They're on their way out.'

I can see from the wary expression on her face that she has *not* factored in meeting any of my kids quite yet, but I'm not particularly bothered. If I have my way, she and my kids (and probably ex-wives) will coincide at some point over the summer in Antibes, anyway.

And if I really have my way, down the line, she'll be their stepmother.

I turn and put my hands on my hips. 'Hey!' I yell in my deepest Warning Voice. 'Take it easy!'

They ignore me.

They always do.

They catapult themselves down the final flight of stairs so fast they'll probably break an ankle and most definitely leave friction burns on the woollen runner. I stand and watch in Unimpressed Dad mode as they slither to a halt at the bottom of the stairs in a pile of hair and limbs.

'Girls,' I say, 'this is my friend Gen.'

'Hi,' Annabel says. 'Dad, my Uber account's not working.'

'I disabled it. Say hello to Gen properly, please.'

'Nice to meet you, Gen,' Amie says. She's marginally the less feral of the two.

'You *what?*' Annabel shouts. 'Why'd do you do that?!'

'Because the last cab you took home was forty-five quid,' I tell her evenly. I will not rise.

I will not.

'It was peak pricing!' She's still shouting. No fucking volume switch.

Just like her mother.

'It was seven-thirty at night.'

'We could've got raped!'

'Again. It was seven-thirty at night. And you don't need it tonight. Clem's place is a ten-minute walk from here.'

She puts her hands on her hips, mirroring my stance,

and scowls at me, thrusting her lower lip out in a pout for good measure.

Again, just like her mother.

'My darlings,' I say, 'I suggest you both scarper quickly before I make you go and change those pathetic excuses for dresses.'

'It's called *fashion*,' Annabel says as she pushes past me in her mini dress. 'But you wouldn't know 'cause you're too *old*.'

'Got it,' I say mildly, holding my hands up in what I consider a remarkably good-natured gesture of defeat. 'Now piss off, loves of my life.'

Amie wraps her arms around my neck, and I lean in for a good hug. 'Night, Dad. Love you.'

'Love you so much, angel,' I say into her glossy hair. 'Annabel, get over here.'

She obeys sulkily, because she knows the rule. We never walk out on an argument without a hug and an *I love you*.

Life's too short.

I gather them up in a messy, uncomfortable group hug.

'Love you,' Annabel mutters.

'I love you,' I tell her. 'Now, get out of here.'

I shut the door behind them with a sigh and lean against it for a moment before making a beeline for Gen, who looks totally shellshocked.

'Sorry about that,' I tell her. 'Bit of a baptism of fire.' I wrap my arms around her, and she reciprocates.

'They're absolutely stunning,' she says. 'Are they identical?'

'They're not, but they're really fucking similar,' I say. 'Or they were until Annabel started wearing far too much eye makeup.'

She laughs against my chest. 'It's very odd and very sweet to see you in Dad mode.'

'It's very *emasculating*,' I correct her. 'No one in this fucking house is scared of me. Including my fucking dog.'

'Poor baby,' she says, smiling up at me. 'No wonder you're so aggressive in bed. I didn't realise all that alphahole behaviour was a desperate cry for help.'

'Alpha what?' I wonder aloud.

'Don't worry,' she says. 'You can remind me who's boss later.' And she stands on her tiptoes, pulling my head down to kiss her.

60

GEN

Anton was right.

That was a baptism of fire.

At least Hades likes me.

And if I have, at any point over the past few whirlwind days, wondered how Anton's kids might react to meeting me, clearly I needn't have worried. They're far too absorbed in their own lives, which is a relief, I suppose.

I follow him through the archway from his hallway and into a palatial living space. It's a kitchen and living area and garden room all in one, it seems, and it's beautiful. White. High-ceilinged. Light-filled.

The appliances are industrial level—stainless steel and impossibly shiny—and a massive slab of marble forms an island down the centre of the kitchen. Further back, low sofas and huge, modern art works give way to a wall of glass that leads out onto the garden. More critically, the whole place smells incredible, like being back in the South of France.

'Do they... live here?' I ask tentatively as I follow him in.

He laughs. 'No. They live in Highgate with their mum,

most of the time. But their sleepover is in Notting Hill, so they came to see their old man this evening before they went out.'

'I hate to be the one to tell you this, but there's no way they're going to a sleepover dressed like *that*.' They looked like they were ready for a night of clubbing. Microscopic dresses and flawless makeup that probably came straight off a TikTok tutorial, even if Annabel's smokey eye was on the aggressive side.

'Don't worry,' he says, doubling back and gathering me up in his arms again. 'They're going to an end-of-term party at a school friend's house—fully supervised, apparently— and *then* a sleepover.'

'Ahh,' I say, looping my arms around his neck. 'And what smells so good?'

'*Linguine alla vongole,*' he says with a wink. He gives me one perfect kiss and then backs away, grabbing his tea-towel off his shoulder.

'Oh wow,' I say. 'Heaven.' I draw closer to the enormous range for a peek. He has cherry tomatoes and garlic simmering in what smells like white wine, and it's so incredible my mouth instantly waters. I accept the glass of chilled white he pours me and wander around the vast space as he lovingly tends to the contents of his pan. My host, Hades, the least terrifying and most inappropriately named Doberman ever, pads sweetly at my side.

It's clear his place has been professionally put together with a probably limitless budget, but it's also strikingly clear to me that this is a *home* and not just a beautiful bachelor pad. There's no clutter—not down here—and each vase, each coffee table book, has been chosen for the beauty it adds to the overall vignette.

Even so, there are family photos everywhere, both on

the walls and in silver-framed clusters on console tables. I sip my wine as I take in this unexpected photographic history of the man who consumes me so much.

I've had this assumption, I realise, that Anton and I have both been living in splendid isolation. The Anton I met first was the guy with the corner office, the intimidating, ruthless conqueror of corporations by day and women by night.

I assumed he was cold.

Calculating.

But he's not. He's fire. He's a man with an enormous capacity for all parts of his life—work, sex *and* love—and he knows how to live fully. To feel. He has layers I can't even conceive of.

The photos are spellbinding. Not least because they speak of happy families. You wouldn't guess he had three divorces behind him. There's a continuity here, a message that every moment is to be celebrated, even when circumstances change.

Of all the images of Anton with his arms around the beautiful women of his past and their equally beautiful children, the one that hits me hardest is the photo of him and his twins. He's standing proudly, grinning at the camera. His hair is shorter, and it's clear from the hospital backdrop and the purple shadows under his eyes that he's shattered.

But in the crook of each arm lies a tiny baby girl, swaddled in pink with a little pink cap. They're so insanely small they make him look like the Incredible Hulk. And there's nothing in his smile but utter pride and joy.

I can't even imagine the life experiences he's had. I've never wanted kids, but there's no doubt that birth is the greatest miracle we can experience as humans. And, as I look at his exhausted, elated face in that moment of new fatherhood, I know I've just scratched the surface of what this man is capable of.

I bring it up over dinner. 'I like that you have photos of your exes everywhere. It must be nice for your kids.'

He shrugs. 'Life's a continuum. Just because I don't want to be married to my exes anymore, doesn't mean they didn't play an important part in my life. Two of them gave me my children. It's insane to think you draw a line under marriage and pretend it didn't happen, you know?'

'Yeah,' I say as I balance my linguine on a spoon and roll it around my fork. 'I suppose a lot of people let bitterness get in the way. Or pride.'

'That's just stupid and self-sabotaging,' he says. 'I love my exes. I love my kids. I have enough room in my heart for everyone. And all those memories are special. I like having the photos around. When things are shit at work, or I'm letting myself get stressed about a deal or something equally unimportant in the grand scheme of things, being surrounded by photos of my crazy, messy family reminds me I've achieved something worthwhile.'

61

ANTON

I love having Gen in my home. Obviously, France was incredible—it's my special place. But these four walls form the basis of my daily life. I feel closer to her here.

We've already made good headway on stripping each other bare. I've been an open book with her since the beginning; she just didn't understand what I was showing her.

She saw game-playing.

Gimmicks.

All I showed her was intent.

France was where she finally took me at my word, and this is the next step.

The reason it's so fucking good with Gen is that there's an edge and an intimacy. They're so complementary. The edge makes me crazy, and the intimacy makes me happy.

I've had intimacy with every woman I've had a serious relationship with. Obviously I have. But I haven't given myself over to them completely, because I know they don't get it. They don't share my predilections, and that's meant there's a side of me I've always had to tamp down in my relationships.

The second I saw Gen, the very *second* I laid eyes on her, I had her number. And one of the reasons I've been so intent on drawing that darker side out of her is because I know that the moment a person allows another human to see their whole self, that's when they start to see themselves as a fully rounded human whose every side deserves to be celebrated. Tended to.

I knew what she needed before she did.

Another reason is that I knew she was the person who could draw that out of me, too. She was the woman who I could unleash my own dark side on. Because I knew she could take it.

We've both been fragmenting ourselves. Keeping our true needs veiled while we show a version of ourselves to the world in different ways. In many ways I've been more transparent than she has, but I've still tried and failed to succeed in three marriages where I've subjugated my own needs.

That's decades of my life.

Gen's told me she's struggled too on lovely dates with charming men who leave her cold in bed. She and I have both found channels—Alchemy, Athena—to scratch our itches. But what could be more glorious, more fully human, than to find a mate who embraces and feeds and loves all our facets?

Nothing.

That's what.

That's the allure of being with her. I've spent the evening in my kitchen, enjoying a wonderful, thought-provoking, entertaining conversation that's filled my soul with joy.

And now, instead of taking her to bed and making polite, perfunctory love to her, I get to do whatever the fuck I like to her in the knowledge that not only can she take it, but she wants it.

She fucking craves it.

She needs me to tear her apart in that precise way, just as I need her to let me.

And *that* is what makes her different from any other woman I've let into my sanctuary.

'I'll be back in a sec,' I say, rising from my place on the sofa in our living area and kissing her on the cheek. She smiles up at me. She's beautiful. Golden. Relaxed. She has no clue she's about to be ambushed, but one thing I've learnt about my lovely Genevieve is that she adores her Anton Ambushes even more than she adores pretending to be outraged by them.

I run up to my room and stuff my pockets with the treats I'll need, all of which I've stocked up on especially for her.

She's lounging on the sofa when I get back, the picture of laid-back elegance, one arm still slung over the back of the sofa from where it rested while she was tousling my hair just now. She won't be laid back in a few minutes. She'll be screaming my name. Begging me for release.

I stand in front of her, and she looks up at me. I lick my lips. 'Safe word.'

'Camellia,' she says slowly. 'But...'

'Stand. And strip.'

Her eyebrows shoot up and her eyes widen. 'I beg your pardon?'

'You heard me.' I jerk my head in a *get up* motion. 'Do it.'

She looks around the room.

'No one's here,' I tell her. 'Just us. I've put Hades to bed. I'm running out of patience.'

There's no smile on my face, because that's all part of the game. The game where I tell her what the fuck to do and she does it because it's as much of a turn-on for her as it is for me.

I see the very instant she decides to play ball, because that gorgeous face of hers changes. It's so much more expressive since she's let me in. A flicker of understanding, of need, crosses it, and I think *good girl. Right decision.*

She stands slowly. Gracefully. Fully aware of my eyes watching her every move.

She licks her lips. 'Here?' she asks.

'Over by the island,' I say with studied dismissiveness.

Her only visible response is a little purse of her lips. She turns and leads the way over to the marble behemoth in the centre of my kitchen, and I admire the way her arse moves under the lightweight dress she's wearing.

Then she's turning to face me again, and I put my hands in my pockets as I watch the world's most beautiful woman reach behind and unzip herself.

Her dress falls softly to the floor, and fuck me, her body is lush. Tits full and heavy, begging for my hands to take their weight. Nipples standing to attention. We're both trying not to show our cards, and we're both doing a terrible job of it. I step forward and cup her tits reverently, my thumbs strumming over her nipples. But my eyes are on her face as she tugs her lower lip between her teeth.

'If you please me, I'll make you come so hard,' I whisper. 'Got it?'

She nods, and her breathy *yes* goes straight to my dick.

'Thong off,' I tell her, and she hooks her thumbs through it and pulls it down so she's standing completely naked in the middle of my dimly lit kitchen.

'I'm going to blindfold you.' I finger the silk tie in my pocket as I await any pushback from her.

'Okay,' she says, and looks me straight in the eye. Her

expression is one of relief. As if she finds solace in knowing that I'm always a step ahead of her in anticipating her needs. I tie the blue tie around her head and step back to admire my handiwork, my nostrils flaring at the sight of her.

She's not the sophisticated, assured businesswoman whose conversation I find so stimulating.

For the next hour or so, she's my whore, to do with as I please.

To use, and push, and delight in.

'You are everything,' I tell her. 'Now, get on your knees and suck it.'

62

GEN

Part of me wishes I could see Anton. Admire the angry flare of this crown I'm taking out of his trousers. Enjoy the sheer hulking size of his body from my position down here. Revel in the pleasure and anguish I'll draw across his gorgeous face as I suck him.

But a larger part of me is pleased he's blindfolded me. Is thrilled he's chosen to deny me my sight. To skew the power dynamic further in his favour.

Because, since the very first moment I laid eyes on Anton Wolff, I have craved being the focus of his raw sexual energy. I've craved having him unleash his insane power over me.

So I'll submit and endure and enjoy every second of finally being in that position. Where it's just me and him, and I'm his to do what he pleases with.

As I wrap my fingers around his painfully hard cock, he slides his fingers through my hair and says, 'Wait. Do you need a cushion?'

'I'm fine,' I say, though the kitchen floor is hard as fuck. Kneeling for Anton on a hard floor feels right. It feels more demeaning. But knowing he's concerned for my wellbeing has warmth spooling around my heart.

His crown is swollen and wet with salty precum. I lick through it and feel his thigh tense under my palm. I know how he'll be, standing there in the beige chinos he's wearing tonight, the couple of open buttons on his blue shirt showing off a tantalising V of soft, dark hair and his jaw working as he watches me.

I know how much this will do it for him—not just my going down on him, but my being naked and blindfolded, kneeling for him. I know how intensely he'll get off on this dynamic, and I want nothing more than to bring him to his knees too.

I take his hot, velvety crown in my mouth and lick it like an ice cream, and the harsh sound of him sucking in a breath through his teeth echoes through my core. I've gone down on him several times over the past few, crazy days, but more spontaneously, as part of whatever we're getting up to in bed, or on his floor, or by his pool...

This is the first time he's ordered me to get on my knees and suck, and I fucking love it.

I let myself sink into this dark, quiet world where there's nothing but the smell and taste and feel of him against my lips and tongue and teeth. The sounds of wet flesh on flesh, and grunting, aroused, barely controlled man, and my breaths. I find a rhythm, and I float right above my head and the trivialities that usually consume it, focusing instead on making him feel as good as possible. On using my mouth to service him.

He's so hard. So close. He has my face in a tight grip now, his hands over my ears so the sounds of my breath and my sucks echo, magnified, through my head as he holds me still and fucks his way in and out of my mouth. He's so fucking huge, and he's so desperate for release, that I'm gasping and gagging and scrambling, clawing at his thigh with my spare hand as I try to hold it together and tamp down my gag reflex as much as possible.

My eyes are watering behind my blindfold, my movements are sloppy and unfinessed, and I'm so turned on by being the outlet for Anton's animalistic needs that I can barely focus on the job at hand.

Right before I expect him to come in my mouth, he releases my head and pulls out, and there's the undeniable sound of him pumping his cock wetly before jets of his cum hit me over and over in warm ropes. My tits. My shoulders. My stomach. My jaw. And all the while, he's grunting out anguished curses.

'*Fuuuck*,' he groans. 'Oh my *fuck*. Jesus, look at you. Shit. Shit. So fucking—'

I barely have time to catch my breath when he's hauling me up under my armpits. I briefly register the pain in my poor knees before my arse hits cold marble. Then his mouth is on me, his tongue thrusting hungrily into my mouth as he groans out his appreciation while he takes a hand and smooths it over my skin, rubbing his cum into my boobs and over my hard nipples and down my stomach.

He's branding me in a way he hasn't been able to do yet, thanks to our condom usage.

He pushes his way between my legs and lowers me with a hand behind my head. The marble is cool and soothing against my skin.

'Knees up,' he urges me.

Jesus Christ. I'm laid out on his kitchen island for him like a feast, legs splayed, blindfold still on, and totally in his power.

When he speaks again, his voice is more measured.

More commanding. He's wrestled back his control. 'Remember in my office?' he asks.

I was just thinking the same thing. This is how Max had me. This is how Anton got to see me, that first time.

'Yes,' I reply.

'Now I've got you all to myself,' he says.

His tone is predatory rather than vulnerable. I should feel terrified. But there's something about the way he says it that tugs at my heartstrings.

'I only want you,' I tell him, arching my body on the marble. 'You can do whatever you want to me.'

It's true.

He can.

I feel shameless and empowered like this, because I know the effect I have on him. I'm also at his mercy, and the combination is so heady I may combust.

'God, sweetheart.'

He presses a palm down onto my pelvic bone, which is sticky and rapidly cooling. His other hand runs up my inner thigh, and I wish I could see him ranging over me. I wish I could see those dark eyes as they bore into every inch of my naked, available flesh. As they take in my pussy, laid bare just for him.

I'm glad we made each other suffer. I'm glad we both underwent the torture. Because I bet what went down in his office will make his victory all the sweeter now. He has me where he wants me, and I know he won't go easy on me.

I'm counting on it.

'This is what you wanted in your fantasy, too,' he tells me.

I can barely breathe. 'Yeah.'

'You are such a good girl. You know how it needs to be, and I'm going to make you lose your fucking mind.'

There's some jangling and the sound of something hitting the island next to me. I roll my shoulders and let my arms fall out to the side in surrender. 'I need you to touch me, Anton,' I tell him.

A buzzing noise starts up. 'Why?' he asks softly.

It's easier to be shameless when I can't see him and when I'm so turned on I might combust.

'Because I need you to make me come,' I gasp. 'You're the only one who can touch me like this.'

'Good,' he says, his voice strangled. I hear the spurt of something wet being squeezed, and I practically lift off the table when whatever vibrator he's turned on teases the puckered ring of flesh between my legs.

'Fuck,' I say involuntarily.

63

GEN

'Don't worry,' he says. 'It's very narrow—it's like a pen. It'll make everything else feel even better, okay? Just relax.'

'Okay,' I say shakily as he inserts it. He's right. It's tiny. But it's *there*, vibrating against walls I don't explore that much. It feels invasive and ticklish and uncomfortable, even if it's not painful.

'And this is just until I can fuck you,' he says, and another noise starts up.

Oh *shit*.

He fiddles around a little, and then a lubed-up vibrator —a far girthier one, this time—is breaching my pussy and sliding in. Holy crap. This is a lot. I claw ineffectually at the marble.

'Look at you,' he says reverently, and I pant out a kind of deranged laugh, because my entire lower half is vibrating, and it's so much. I daren't move in case something flies out or that little wand gets jammed inside my arse. But, at the same time, it feels amazing. Intense, but amazing.

'Touch your tits,' he tells me, and then his hands and

mouth are on me, thank God. He strokes my thighs, and kisses down my stomach and down my landing strip, and then, holy fuck, his mouth is on me. It's right on me, exactly where I need it, and he kisses and laps at my clit with that perfect, dextrous tongue of his.

I do as he says and reach for my nipples, rolling and pinching and squeezing them as Anton works me with rough strokes, making guttural, hungry, *carnal* noises of appreciation that only serve to stoke the flames inside me.

Because my body is on fire. The warmth that's coursing through my entire pelvis is almost too much, thanks to his tongue and my double vibrator situation. He's stimulating me everywhere. It's an assault on my senses, an onslaught the likes of which my nervous system barely knows how to handle.

But it's also threatening to give me the most complete, most well-rounded orgasm I've ever had, because nothing is lacking. Every erogenous part of my body is singing. And that singing becomes a fucking aria as he winds me higher and higher.

I explode in a tidal wave of sensation that's positively violent, and as my climax courses through me Anton holds my hips in a death grip and keeps on licking. Over and over and over like he won't be satisfied until he's wrung every last drop of pleasure from my body. I realise hazily that the death grip is because I'm practically bouncing off the island, crying out as my body convulses in its attempts to process this relentless deluge of pleasure.

When he's licked me through the last of it, when the storm in my body has begun to ebb away, leaving that ecstatic, stupid brain mush that only a seriously good orgasm can deliver, he turns off the devices and slides them gently out of me before helping me up to sitting. I'm lightheaded and floppy, and when he pulls the blindfold off me, all I see is him, smiling at me.

His smile is pride and adoration and wonder, and it's so broad those dimples of his have disappeared into his laughter lines again. I reach up and trace one side with shaky fingers.

'You're so fucking beautiful when you've just come,' he tells me. His voice is soft but there's an edge of need to it. 'I mean, even more beautiful than normal.'

I smile bashfully and manage to reach forward to tug his shirt up over his head. I need some serious skin on skin right now. Then he's reaching for a condom from the pile of treats he has on the island next to me and rolling it on as he simultaneously attempts to stagger out of his trousers and boxer briefs.

His skin is warm and tanned and beautiful. It's skin I could lose myself in. But I'll have to hold that thought, because he's tugging me right to the edge of the island and lining his crown up with my still-pulsing entrance as he wraps a strong arm around my back and uses his other hand to fist himself.

I glance down at the glorious sight of his angry cock disappearing inside my body, inch by inch, and then up at his face, so close to mine. Those eyes of his are dark and hooded and filled with need. The lines on his face are craggy. There's effort etched on every gorgeous feature. His hair's falling softly over his forehead, and I reach up to claw my fingers through it.

This island is the perfect height for him to fuck me, and this position is seriously intimate. I wrap my legs around his bare arse and tilt my head up so his lips can find mine. He begins to move, dragging his dick out slowly and thrusting in hard with a groan, the hand on my back sliding down to cup my bottom and hold me in place as he drives into me.

I swear, the noises this man makes when he's inside me are the hottest I've ever heard. They come from somewhere deep inside him; they're so primal that they rip my heart out and make my pussy flutter. It's only fair that he demands I harness every raw, animalistic instinct I have and let him have them, because when he fucks me, he lets me have everything he has to give.

He doesn't hold back.

It's right that he doesn't let me hold back, either.

So I don't.

I lean in, and I open my legs and my mouth wider, and I take and take. I take his thrusts, and his ravenous kisses, and I grab at his hair and scratch over the skin-covered muscles of his back and shoulders. I moan into his mouth as he rams his dick inside me, bottoming out in me again and again.

And when he lays me back down on the island so he can get in deeper, one hand digging into my waist and the other groping and grabbing at my breasts as I lie there spread out for him, I lie there, writhing and undulating with pleasure, and I marvel at the otherworldly experience that is Anton Wolff, out of control and fucking me into oblivion.

His need is catching.

His desire is contagious.

I thought he'd wrung every last drop of pleasure from my body, but, impossibly, the walls of my pussy fire up again. It's not just what he's doing with his magical dick.

It's the emotional overwhelm of letting him strip me bare like this. Of throwing my dignity and my poise to the wind and letting him ravage me like a fucking caveman while I lie there and take everything he has.

Most of all, it's the intimacy of holding his gaze, of

keeping my eyes on him as he ploughs into me, over and over, of watching as he comes apart at the same time I do, of seeing his jaw clench and his face contort and his mouth move as he lets rip a string of beautiful obscenities.

Because the blindfold was erotic as hell, but when we have eyes on each other, me and him?

That's when the alchemy happens.

64

ANTON

She's a fucking kitten when she's like this.

I hold her under the torrent of water in my ensuite shower. I have her wrapped up tightly in my arms. If I let her go, I think she might sink to the floor in a contented, woozy pile.

But there's no chance of my letting her go.

I can't stop kissing her. Can't stop myself from sucking on her lower lip, from teasing her tongue with mine under the spray. She's tucked into my body, her glorious tits cushiony against my abdomen and her face tilted up to mine, soft and starry-eyed.

I feel like the king of the world. Or at least:

'I finally feel like a man again,' I murmur against her lips, and she breaks our kiss to laugh. Her arms are looped around my neck, and she's playing with my hair.

'Oh, *that's* what that was about, was it? Your daughters and your dog gave you a hard time so you thought you'd fuck me senseless on your kitchen island?'

'Something like that,' I admit sheepishly. 'But mainly it

was that you allowing me to do whatever I like to you is the single most erotic thing there is in life.'

'Good comeback,' she says sleepily, and I bend my head and find her mouth again.

It's true.

I've said it before, and I'll say it again.

There are women who aren't interested in the kink of sexual power dynamics I like to practice. Case in point: my exes.

There are women who are naturally submissive and long for a man to take charge. They're lovely, but not exactly a challenge. Case in point: Athena.

And then there are women like Gen. Women who are strong and fierce and awe-inspiring. Women who could rule the world, if they wanted to. And who, when the lights go down, feel the strongest need to abdicate that power. To yield their mind and their body to a man who can take charge. Who can turn them inside out. Think for them.

See them.

That's the beauty of our dynamic. I need to dominate; she needs to submit. And when she grants me carte blanche to fucking tear her apart, she doesn't have to explain.

Because I already understand.

Because I already know and see and worship the darkest, neediest parts of her.

It's terrifyingly good between us. Terrifyingly right. It enthrals and amazes me how clearly our bodies and souls can communicate.

I adore her like this, when she's relaxed and pliant and trusting. When the creases have gone from her brow, when I've fucked every last vestige of stress about the Cannes popup and that fucking Rapture place out of her system.

Even if it's temporary.

When I turn off the shower, and kneel on the mat so I can dry every inch of her, when I squeeze out her hair with a towel and lead her through to my bedroom and lay her down on the bed, I don't need to ask her how she wants it this time.

I don't need to 'fuck anything out of her', because, for now, there are no demons left.

Instead, I sheath myself and I lower myself on top of her, testing her, consuming her, and I move inside her so slowly, so deeply, that our bodies feel like one.

And that, for me, is the rawest kind of sex I know.

65

ANTON

I have been summoned.

It was only a matter of time. It's been three weeks since I persuaded Gen to take a chance on me, and I haven't looked back. I even managed to drag her out to Antibes again this weekend for a quick 'n' dirty forty-eight hours.

We've been to Alchemy a few times, too, and I've fucking loved walking into that place, knowing I'll get the most beautiful woman in the club into a private room before the evening is up. Knowing those fantasies I've had about her since the moment she gave me that bloody tour will come true, and she'll submit to me.

To be honest, my fantasies fell short. Because the reality of what she and I get up to in those rooms after some light foreplay in The Playroom is so fucking incredible even I couldn't have imagined it.

Saying I'm falling is inadequate, because the truth is that I've fallen. I was falling from the moment we met, and I was a goner from the second she allowed me access to her body and her soul.

Our trysts at Alchemy mean a lot. And let me tell you, that place is well kitted out. But they fall short of our trysts at home, at my place or hers. Or our dates at neighbourhood Italian bistros. Because every single way she lets me get intimate with her has me falling further.

Harder.

I'm sure she's not perfect, but I've sure as hell yet to see a single flaw in her.

I knew we were similar animals, but each moment we spend together confirms that in my heart.

It was only a matter of time before her closest friends and protectors demanded an opportunity to shake me down. To investigate my true colours for themselves.

And I don't blame them in the slightest.

I'd do the same in their place.

The inquisition comes disguised as an invitation to a 'family barbecue' at Gen's colleague Zach's house one Wednesday night.

'They're all dying of curiosity,' she tells me. 'They want to see if you live up to the hype.'

'*The* hype or *your* hype?' I ask, because when you get to my position in the business world, most people have an opinion. An assumption.

'Both,' she says seductively.

And so I present myself on Zach's immaculate doorstep. His home is only a three or four minute stroll from mine, and it looks stunning. Gen wasn't kidding about those guys raking it in through their hedge fund.

Zach's girlfriend, Maddy answers the door with the black lab I've met a couple of times at Alchemy. She's wearing a very short dress and looks pleased as hell to see me. Gen may have let slip that Maddy's been a confidant of hers since we've started seeing each other, and that she's aggressively 'shipping' us. I have an idea of what that means, thanks to Amie and Annabel, and I'm grateful Maddy's in my corner.

Not sure Gen's male friends are, but I intend to show them tonight that I'm serious about her.

'They're out the back,' Maddy says now, twisting her mouth in delight. I hand her the bottle of champagne I brought and give the sweet dog a good rub before following her through what looks like a beautiful family home. I know from what Gen has told me that Zach lost his wife a couple of years back.

So fucking horrific.

I can't even imagine.

These days, 'barbecues' for me involve my chef cooking up all sorts of fancy marinaded joints and producing epic salads. It's been a long time since I stood in front of a grill with a pair of tongs. But it looks like that's exactly what Zach's doing. He's got an enormous Weber going, and whatever he's cooking under that hood smells incredible.

'I think you'll know everyone except Zach's girls,' Maddy says as we step outside. 'It's just us guys.'

Us guys is Gen, Callum, Rafe, his girlfriend Belle, Zach and Maddy, as far as I can see. There are a couple of little girls loitering by the bowl of crisps. But my eyes don't stray far from Gen, who's in a floaty floral sundress that I reckon I'll have on my bedroom floor in two seconds flat later.

She's chatting to Belle. Her face lights up when she sees me. I'm so fucking pleased that her poker face days are behind us. And I'm pretty happy when she makes an instant beeline for me, tilting her face up for my kiss.

I keep it PG. There are kids here, after all. But she looks and smells and tastes delicious, so I hope our audience appreciates my self-control. 'You look very beautiful,' I murmur against her lips before releasing her, and she smiles up at me in a way that's bashful and pleased and pretty fucking adorable.

The other guys greet me politely rather than effusively. They're a tough crowd. I get the best reception from Belle, who's been sweet each time I've met her at Alchemy, and from Zach's daughters. Forewarned by Gen that they were serious Swifties, I had Rix sort out a custom t-shirt for each of them printed with, respectively, *Stella's Version* and *Nancy's Version*. They're absolutely, and noisily, thrilled, and I'm reminded of little girls' ability to make you feel like utter shit or a fucking god, depending on the circumstances.

The others kick off the inquisition shortly after the girls' nanny has appeared to usher them inside and we're relaxing on Zach's terrace with a few magnums of Rock Angel on ice.

'So,' Callum says. 'Gen tells me you've been married three times.'

'Cal!' Gen exclaims, practically spitting out her rosé. 'Jesus Christ! You promised to play nicely, remember?'

I'm amused. I'd have tapped Zach or Rafe as her protector—Callum seems the most laid-back of the three—but it appears he's looking out for Gen, which I have no problem with. Besides, we all know why I'm here, and I'm in a jovial mood. It's a beautiful evening, and, through the fabric of her dress, Gen's thigh is warm and toned under my hand.

'It's all good,' I tell her. 'That's right, mate. Three ex-wives and four kids. My life is a circus.'

Rafe shudders. 'Brave man.'

'I'd say it's less telling that Anton has three ex-wives and far more telling that he's on very good terms with all of them,' Gen retorts. She must like me if she's fighting my battles on my behalf, surely?

I'm being disingenuous, obviously.

I know very well how much she likes me.

'Three wives, four kids, and a PA with benefits,' Callum muses aloud, and I almost spit out my drink, because this guy is not pulling any punches, and it's pretty funny.

Gen puts her drink down and looks ready to slap him. 'What the hell is the matter with you?' she hisses. 'I told you that in *confidence.*'

'Ex-wives,' I tell him. My smile says I'm amused, but my eyes are steely. 'And an *ex-EA*, as a matter of fact. I'm not interested in benefits with anyone other than Gen, these days.' I massage Gen's thigh. 'I can give you the number of the agency, if you want, but I'm sure a good-looking guy like you who owns his own sex club has no need to pay anyone for sex.'

Not that you could afford Seraph, anyway.

Callum's dark eyes are spitting fire, until his entire face breaks into a huge grin. 'Okay, okay. He's passed round one. Don't get your knickers in a twist, Gen. If he can't handle some uncomfortable questions, he's not worth your time.' He holds out his hand, and I release Gen's thigh so I can shake it a little too firmly.

I smile. He's got a nerve. 'You're a cheeky little fucker,' I tell him.

'Damn right, but I'm Gen's cheeky little fucker,' Callum tells me. 'And you're right, mate. Some of us don't have to pay for sex.'

I throw back my head and laugh. He's a piece of work. I know the type. Charming playboy. Joker. Never lets things get too serious.

'So you're the only one without an extremely beautiful, much younger girlfriend,' I muse aloud, just to fuck him off.

ELODIE HART

Everyone else around the table smirks. Maddy tosses her hair dramatically at my compliment.

'Don't want a girlfriend,' Callum protests. 'Like you said, I run a fucking sex club. I have no intention of settling down. No offence,' he mutters to his friends.

'Your loss, pal,' Rafe tells him. Belle's wearing a backless black jumpsuit that makes her look like she's just walked off a Bond movie set, and she's tucked cosily into the crook of his arm. Looks to me like monogamy is working just fine for him.

Just like it is for me.

GEN

'So you were all at uni together?' Anton asks as Zach takes a magnum and tops up everyone's glasses. It's a gorgeous evening out here, and the rosé is going down nicely. I'm not sure what the hell Cal thought he was playing at earlier, but he's being nicer now.

'Yep.' Rafe holds out his glass for Zach. 'The four of us lived together in our second and third years.'

I roll my eyes. The indiscretions will flow right alongside the wine; I can feel it.

'Really?' Anton purrs, his hand warm on my knee. His touch anchors me, as does the heat of his cotton-covered arm against my bare one. 'Interesting. How was that?'

'In a word, messy,' I say. 'They were pigs.'

'She's not wrong,' Zach observes. 'We were pretty revolting. That's why it was great living with a girl.'

'Yeah,' Rafe says. 'She was the only one who ever cleaned the bathroom, remember? Because it always bothered her long before it bothered us.'

I modify my earlier descriptor. '*Sexist* pigs.' I shudder.

'God, that bathroom was disgusting. It stank of damp, and they never washed their towels.'

The boys laugh while Belle twists in Rafe's arms and looks at him in absolute horror. My friends have come a long way in terms of being civilised human beings.

'There was a quid pro quo, though, to be fair,' Cal says. 'We spent a lot of time with wet sleeves from the amount of time you spent crying on our shoulders over boys. We even had to beat a few of them up for you.'

'Christ, you always went for the tossers,' Rafe groans, raking a hand through his hair and pulling Belle back against his side. 'It was like your twat radar was always on high alert. If there was a guy who was a giant fucking twat, you'd be all over him.'

'Some things never change, eh?' Anton asks me softly, and I smile and nudge him with my shoulder.

'You said it.'

'Why'd you go for the twats?' he asks. He sounds genuinely interested.

'Ugh, I don't know.' I take a defeated drink of my wine. I really don't like where this conversation is going.

'To be fair,' Zach says, 'it wasn't that she went for them. They went for her. I'd argue she had a twat-attractor rather than a twat-radar. And that was because she was so insanely beautiful—still is, obviously—so I think they saw her as some kind of trophy. Like, the guy who went home with Genevieve Carew got major kudos in the locker room or at lectures the next day. The nice guys stayed away because they assumed she was out of their league.'

'That's ridiculous,' I argue.

'I'd say it's pretty accurate,' Cal says.

'You thought I was a twat when you met me,' Anton

observes. It's not a question. 'Is that why you ran for the hills?'

'Maybe,' I muse. It's more than a maybe, but I'm not entirely comfortable with this spontaneous group psycho-analysis session. 'Once I got into the City, I got tough. No more dickheads. The whole environment was far too male centric, and I didn't want to be seen as a target or not respected for my abilities. So I may have over-corrected.'

'And the walls went up?' he guesses.

I shrug. 'Something like that.'

'Quite right,' Rafe says. 'You're amazing. You know we all adore you. It's right that guys should work their arses off to earn your trust. You were too trusting at uni—you got burnt too many times.'

'Plus they were all crap in bed,' I point out. 'Fucking rugby players. They never had to learn any skills when they were in a different girl's bed every night.'

'Oi,' Cal says, and I laugh, because all three of them played rugby.

'So that's why the guys are a little over-protective,' I tell Anton. 'They've had to put plenty of guys before you through their paces.'

He puts his arm tightly around me and finds my ear with his mouth. 'I'm very glad you made an exception to your *no more dickheads* rule for me,' he whispers.

A nton insisting I'm his girlfriend is one thing.
Anton insisting I accompany him as his date to the Serpentine Gallery's summer party is quite another.

This annual shindig is one of the highlights of the British social calendar. It's full of fashion, art and finance types with a healthy sprinkling of celebrities and the necessary journalists and photographers you'd expect. It doesn't surprise me to hear that Anton gets an invitation each year —the time I've spent at his house over the past couple of weeks tells me this guy likes his art and spends big.

He got into an impassioned discussion with Belle at Zach's barbecue on this very topic. She works at Liebermann's, the high-end gallery in Mayfair, and it turns out Anton knows her boss pretty well. He's also a patron of the Serpentine Gallery. Has been for years, apparently.

And so, I find myself on his arm celebrating the gallery's current installation—there's a new one every summer. I've dressed for the occasion in a pale pink one-shouldered gown, with my hair in loose curls.

Just the way he likes it.

I would have expected Anton to get plenty of attention at an event like this, but the sheer quantity of females who fawn over him, and their persistence, is pretty jaw-dropping. It's like I'm not here.

I know he's a bit of a social media hottie. I know from my TikTok stalking before he joined Alchemy that there's an abundance of Anton Wolff edits and that he has his own hashtag.

#Bigbadwolff, if you're wondering.

I don't blame any of his fans. He's the world's most gorgeous man, especially tonight in a custom tuxedo. There is no denying he's the full package. Not only is he a physical specimen to die for, with his height, and broad shoulders, and gorgeous looks, and athletic physique, but his bank balance will always be attractive to some people. As will his intelligence and business acumen.

Above all, though, the women who flock to say hi and introduce themselves and ask for selfies, whether they're fans or groupies or gold-diggers, are attracted to the same thing I am.

That Big fucking Dick Energy.

He exudes raw masculinity. Power. Entitlement—in the hottest possible way. Sexuality. Dominance. It's as much the essence of who Anton Wolff is as his brown eyes, and it's magnetic.

He keeps me close. Introduces me to everyone as *my girl-friend, Genevieve*. And only lets go of my hand when I have to play photographer to him and his groupies.

Their interruptions range from the polite—*I'm so sorry to bother you, Mr Wolff, but could I*—to the obnoxious—*Anton! Hi! We met at Silverstone, remember? Mwah!*

Yes. That's the sound of an unwanted air kiss.

An astonishingly beautiful, Mediterranean-looking woman sashays over and proceeds to completely zone me out.

'Anton,' she says, swatting him playfully on the arm. 'You promised me drinks weeks ago when I bumped into you at Nobu! *Where* have you been hiding?'

What happened to the sisterhood? I wonder idly. It's clear we're together. He has his fucking arm around me. But I suppose when it comes to men as gorgeous and as eligible as Mr Wolff here, there is no sisterhood. Because the prize is too dazzling.

The stakes are too high.

Anton smiles thinly in my peripheral vision. 'Hi, Raffaela. No can do, I'm afraid. I've been spending every free second I have with my girlfriend, Genevieve.'

He squeezes me more tightly, and I swear the woman shoots me a death stare before bidding Anton the hastiest farewell in history and flouncing off.

Not that I can blame her, or any of his other hangers-on. Because I'm smitten too. Tonight I'm a swooning fangirl. I'm everything I swore I wouldn't be when I first laid eyes on him. When he knocked the air right out of my lungs with the sheer power of his presence.

Gazing at him is one of my favourite things. Drinking him in. Letting my eyes wander over his gorgeous face. His huge body encased in tailored perfection. Seeing if I can make him smile, or laugh, so those dimples play peekaboo just for me.

Everyone wants a piece of him tonight. But I'm the one who gets to go home with him, and undress him, and let him fuck me senseless. And I simply don't know how I got so lucky.

It fucking terrifies me.

This is why I held out for so long with Anton. Not because I wasn't desperate for him—like everyone else in London, it seems—but because I knew how terrifying it would be to allow myself this level of intimacy without him potentially hurting me.

It's like standing on a precipice in a fucking gale as the treacherous sea rages far below me.

Exhilarating and petrifying in equal measure.

Even more petrifying is what I want to say to him. How easy it would be to whisper three little words that encompass the depth of my feelings for him.

Because this man is everything. He's already my whole world.

I stretch my neck and put my mouth to his ear during a lull in the lines of women flocking to him. But I don't say those words, because a girl has to have some means of self-preservation. Instead, I whisper something else I know will be music to his ears.

'I wish I was sucking you off right now,' I tell him, slipping a hand under the lapel of his jacket and enjoying the hard heat of his stomach muscles as they contract under my palm at my words. At his sharp intake of breath.

I pause to smile demurely at someone who waves at us —but more likely Anton—as she passes. 'I wish I could get your beautiful cock out right here and worship it. I wish you could shove me to my knees and fist all my hair up and fuck my mouth till I choked on your dick.'

'Jesus Christ, sweetheart,' he grits out. He turns his head so our lips are touching and slides his hand under my hair, getting a firm hold on my neck. 'You little fucking beauty. I'd pull your hair so hard and fuck that mouth till you were begging for mercy.'

'I know you would,' I whimper. It's not the warmest

night, but my entire body is flooding with heat. A pulse pounds between my legs as I imagine it. Anton looks a million dollars right now, but I'm the only one who gets to enjoy the animal concealed beneath all this finery and charm and civilised conversation, and I want him desperately.

I want to unleash my beast.

'I want this eye makeup all smeared,' he tells me. 'Lipstick all over my cock. I want you taking every inch of me, and doing everything I say, and then I'll fuck you so hard you won't know your own name.'

I claw at his stomach through his starched shirt. 'Do it,' I tell him. 'You can do whatever you want to me. You know you can. You know I trust you.'

He pulls back slightly and his hungry gaze flicks up from my mouth to my eyes.

Those words are his kryptonite.

God knows, the poor man waited long enough to hear them, so now I tell him as often as I can. I green-light him and his peculiar, amazing, beautiful appetites whenever I get the chance.

He licks his lips, and I think he's going to say something utterly filthy, but then he drags his thumb over my jaw. 'To have earned your trust, sweetheart, is all I could ever ask for,' he says. 'I'm serious.' His brown eyes are warm and dark and filled with emotion.

We stand there in the fading sunlight, surrounded by a throng of people, by the heady chords of soft jazz, as our faces tell each other things our voices aren't ready for yet. I want to burrow inside his jacket and wrap both arms around his waist and press my face to his chest for the rest of the evening.

Then he shifts. Stiffens. 'Fuck.' He mutters it under his breath.

'What?' I ask against his lips.

'It's those Rapture dicks,' he says.

68

ANTON

There are two absolute twats heading our way, sleazy grins on their faces. Jad Touma and Henrik Hansen. I know these guys. I know them far too fucking well, from the City and from sex parties and everything else in between.

We run in the same circles, unfortunately, though I could buy and sell them both a thousand times over. They like to think they have their grimy fingers in every fucking pie in London, of the business and female varieties.

They stop in front of us. 'Wolff,' one of them says. His dark hair is slicked back in a ponytail, and his beard is so well groomed I'm surprised he gets any work or fucking done. I shake his hand reluctantly. 'Touma.'

'Hello,' he says, turning his admittedly dazzling smile on Gen. 'How do you do? I'm Jad, and this is my mate, Henrik.'

I look on in amusement as my girlfriend turns her legendary *froideur* on these poor fuckers. I'm a far bigger fan of her ice-queen act when it's not aimed at me.

'Genevieve,' she says without inflection, shaking their

hands with her inimitable poise. I mentally remind myself never to play poker with this woman.

She'd annihilate me.

'Thought so,' Hansen says, running his eyes openly down her body. She's mesmerising tonight. She's the classiest, most impeccable, most stunning woman I've ever encountered, and I'm not surprised he's looking. But I'm the only man who'll get to ravish her tonight, who'll get to smash that pristine surface as she writhes on my cock, and these two jokers can hightail it back to their sleazy, gimmicky club.

'Big fan of what you've built at Alchemy,' Touma tells her.

Funny way of showing it, mate.

She arches an imperious eyebrow. 'Is that a fact? I heard your tastes ran a little more... *flashy* than what we offer.'

Fuck, I love this woman. And I love even more that I'm the only man on the planet she lets see the carnal, wanton, unrestrained side of her. I'm surprised her icy demeanour hasn't frozen these guys' pencil dicks off yet.

'It's important to cater for all tastes, isn't it?' Hansen offers. 'You two should swing by sometime and check it out.' He winks at Gen. 'You might surprise yourself with what floats your boat. You'd do well there.'

I take a step towards them. 'Gen and I have no interest in getting herpes from your little experiment, thank you.'

'C'mon, mate,' Touma says. 'You can do better than that. Anyway, we should get back to it. We've got a fucking avalanche of Alchemy members beating our door down. Right, Henrik?'

Henrik pretends to look embarrassed. 'Afraid so.'

'Fuck off, both of you,' I tell them. 'Right now, before I have you kicked out.'

'You wish,' Touma says.

'I don't have to wish,' I say through clenched teeth. I jerk my head towards the gallery. 'My name's on the fucking building. Now clear off.'

They smirk at Gen and saunter off, raising hands in salute as they go.

'What odious little turds,' Gen comments. Her voice is even, but her jaw is tense.

'Their behaviour tells you everything you need to know about the way they do business,' I say. 'They'll implode before the year is out. Watch.'

'Maybe.' She takes a sip of her champagne. 'But they're not wrong. We've been haemorrhaging members this week.'

I stare at her in horror. 'Seriously? What the fuck?'

'Yeah.' Her gaze is trained on their departing backs. 'I hope to God karma comes and bites them on the arse.'

69

ANTON

'I need you to handle something for me,' I tell Max first thing next morning. I'm relaxed and well-rested after earth-shattering sex with Gen when we got home from last night's party.

I did fuck her mouth.

I did fuck her cunt.

And I almost let slip how I felt about her, but I managed to hold it in.

I may have slept like a champ with her wrapped around me, but I'm on business turf now, and my inner pit-bull is unleashed.

'Name it,' Max says.

'It's for Gen. You know that Rapture club?'

He makes a face. 'Yeah.' Max got his membership to Alchemy last week, and I think he's practically sleeping there. He's fucking addicted.

'Touma and Hansen were at the Serpentine thing last night. Slimy fucks. They're poaching members from Alchemy. Gen said there's been an outflow. We need to shut them the fuck down.'

'Above board or back channel?' he asks without pausing to take a breath.

This is why he's my Chief of Staff.

He gets shit done.

No questions asked.

I consider. 'Try official routes first. See what Steph can find out. If there's nothing, we'll reconsider.'

Stephan is our forensic accountant, and he's the fucking Hercule Poirot of the audit world. If anything sketchy is going on, he'll find it.

Max nods. 'Consider it done.'

'It's time-sensitive,' I tell him. I want these little twats out of the way quickly. I want to crush them like ants under my shoe. We've got the Cannes launch in ten days, and Gen doesn't need anything derailing Alchemy's opportunities.

Because I know that pop-up will be a money-spinner.

I know it'll open a world of doors for her and her team.

So let's head off this problem at the bat, before they really get their claws into the market.

70

GEN

I rub my forehead with my thumbnail. I'm shattered. The amount of manpower Anton has allocated to the Cannes pop-up is immense, but there's no way I can stand back and let them try to work it all out for themselves, so I've been hands-on. We're all heading out there on Friday, which is in just three days' time.

I'm also dealing with some HR headaches, namely that our wizard of a concierge, Natalie, handed in her notice two days ago.

She's off to Rapture.

They made her another offer. One she couldn't refuse, dammit. They've got to be running this thing at a giant loss, given the amount of money they're pumping into it, but clearly they've got deep pockets. As do we, but we also have sound business sense, and just because another player in the market is behaving irrationally, it doesn't mean we have to.

Thank God for Anton. Yes, he's fucking me senseless every night, which is definitely not helping with my exhaustion levels. But we're in such a heavenly love-bubble that I'm flying high on endorphins.

Who needs sleep?

Not me.

Simply being in that man's orbit is heady. Being what feels like his sole focus is fucking crack. In that period when I was lusting after him, and yearning for him, and wishing I wasn't, there was no way I could have imagined how adoring he'd be. How attentive. Or even... how needy.

I had this fixed impression of him as cold. Calculating. Brutal. And he can be all those things. But with me he's kind, and loving. He's generous with his emotions. Open-hearted.

And yes, he's intense. Demanding. But in the most intoxicating way. I knew he would see right inside my soul, and rip my heart out, and require that I laid myself bare for him. But he does the same for me. He holds nothing back. He consumes me, and I've never been so seen.

I don't know how that man had my number from the moment he laid eyes on me. I can only surmise that we're soulmates, and soulmates know the secrets of each other's souls, even the ones we hide away in the dark so the world can't suspect them.

Anton suspected.

More than that, he *knew*. He saw a woman flawlessly kitted out in her business armour, and he knew exactly what I needed. Knew just what would sate my body and send my soul soaring.

We both need the same thing. For him to dominate me completely, and for me to submit completely. Trust completely.

Because when he ties me up and edges me until I'm begging and practically weeping, he sets us both free.

Rafe interrupts my glowy, loved-up train of thought. 'Fucking hell!' he shouts, pushing his chair back and standing up, his fist to his mouth. He stares intently at something on his phone screen.

'What?' Zach demands.

Rafe pulls his fist away. He's grinning broadly. 'You'll never guess what. Rapture's finished.'

I frown. 'What do you mean?'

'I mean those tossers have been closed down. They're getting done for money laundering.'

Money laundering? My mouth hangs open. 'Holy fuck,' I say gormlessly, because I'm utterly shocked. I thought they seemed dodgy, but money laundering's a whole different level. 'Who's telling you that?'

He brandishes his phone. 'Ed at Cerulean.'

'There's no way that won't impact their day jobs, too,' Zach observes.

He's right. Those two guys who founded Rapture—Jed and Henrik—are both partners at Barbican, which is one of the biggest macro hedge funds in London. Surely the regulator won't allow convicted money launderers to trade.

'Jesus,' I breathe as the implications sink in. These guys are ruined, surely.

And our biggest headache is dust. Just like that.

Cal whistles and rubs his hands together in glee. 'Fucking *nice*. Let's see how many members and employees come crawling back to us, eh?'

'I have to tell Anton,' I say gleefully, picking up my phone. 'He hates those pricks.'

I shoot off a triumphant text to him.

> Guess what? Rapture's been closed down.
> Money laundering!!! Can you believe it? xx

His reply comes straight back.

You're welcome 😊 xx

I stare at my phone in horror.

You're welcome?

You're fucking *welcome?*

The joy in my veins turns to cold dread. I'm instantly nauseous.

Anton did this.

Anton destroyed these guys, and their business, and their entire careers.

For me.

I push my chair back and grab my handbag.

71

ANTON

I unlock my phone again and eye the last two messages from Gen with vague amusement.

> What the actual fuck?

> I'm coming over

That was ten minutes ago, and my office is only a few streets away from Alchemy. I started to reply. Started to explain myself. And I knew it wouldn't wash. I'm better off pleading my case to her face to face.

I've already told Rix to bring her straight through when she turns up.

She arrives a few minutes later. I stand quickly, rounding my desk. Not only does she look sexy as fuck in a black sleeveless shift dress that hugs her body in all the right places, but a single glance tells me she's fucking furious.

And there's nothing more arousing than my ice queen spitting fire.

I'm not stupid enough to attempt to kiss her. If I got that

close she'd probably knee me in the balls. So I stand in front of her, my legs planted wide and my hands in my pockets.

It's my trademark *don't fuck with me* stance.

I know it'll piss her off and turn her on in equal measure. Just like I know exactly why she's here. And like I knew not to tell her anything before I put the plan in motion.

'Come to thank me in person, sweetheart?' I enquire.

She knows exactly what I mean, because her gaze shoots to my dick before returning to my face.

I smirk.

She scowls.

Oh, this'll be fun.

'What the fuck did you do to Rapture?' she hisses, dropping her enormous Birkin on the floor and stalking over to me, hands on her gorgeous hips.

'I had an associate of mine access their books and make a little phone call to the good people at His Majesty's Revenue and Customs,' I say smoothly. 'You're welcome.'

'Did he falsify their accounts?' she demands.

'What? Fuck, no. They're shady as fuck—he didn't need to falsify a bloody thing. It was all there in black and white. Money laundering and tax evasion.'

She looks decidedly unconvinced.

'Seriously, sweetheart. They were using crypto and art to move money. It didn't take a genius to work it out—my guy figured it out in an afternoon.'

'Did he hack their accounts?' she asks.

'The less you know the better,' is my pithy answer to that. And it's true.

She glares at me. 'How fucking dare you.'

What the actual fuck? 'Hang on a sec. I did you a favour. You had a problem, and I made it go away.' I pull my hands out of my pockets and snap my fingers. 'Boom. Done.'

'You overstepped.' She looks wildly around the room, like she can't believe we're having this conversation. 'You butted in to *my* business without asking me, or even telling me. It wasn't your place. It's completely unacceptable, and it's fucking patronising.'

'What?' My jaw hangs open in disbelief. I can't believe she's getting her knickers in a twist over this when she should be on her knees, thanking me with her mouth on my cock. Jesus Christ.

'Anton,' she says, like I'm a small, obtuse child. 'Alchemy is none of your business. Literally. The guys and I can handle it. And for you to get involved in somebody else's company like that and undermine them—it's staggeringly inappropriate. Can't you see that? You're not my puppet master. I'm a grown woman, and just because I haven't amassed the same insane wealth as you have, I'm still perfectly capable of doing my job and running my company. It's demeaning that you'd think I need you to ride in and rescue me—it's a total joke, in fact.'

'Now, look here,' I say. I'm fucking furious. 'This isn't about wealth, or me trying to patronise you. It's about being ruthless enough to get the job done. The inconvenient truth is that you wouldn't have had the balls to do anything about those dicks. You're far too much of a rules follower. You would have sat back and moaned about them and just fucking watched while they made off with a chunk of your clientele. *And* your employees.'

'That's not fair!' she protests. 'I would have focused on making Alchemy the best offering it can be for our members. Not on destroying another club just because they're the competition. And I certainly wouldn't have sunk as low as to back-channel and break the law to take them out.'

'I didn't break the law,' I lie. 'And stop being so fucking disingenuous. You've been worried about them since France. Can you honestly stand there and have a go at me for removing the entire problem for you?'

'Yes,' she says. 'I can. It's the principle of the matter. You don't seem to understand that what you've done is a huge violation of our boundaries. You've made me feel like a silly little girl who can't handle herself. You can't help yourself, can you? You're so controlling. I thought you liked me because I have some backbone, but you can't help wading in and getting involved when you had absolutely no justification in doing so.'

'I thought you liked me controlling you,' I say, my voice dangerously quiet. My words deliberate.

She steps right up to me so we're almost touching, and I gaze down at her.

'Let me be very clear,' she says. 'You get to control me in bed because I like it. *Because I let you.* Make no mistake about that. I will not let you control me outside the bedroom. You've made me feel small and weak and pathetic, and you've never made me feel like that before. So if you're trying to get your kicks by controlling me in my professional life, know this. I will *not* stand for it.'

We glare at each other, the air around us thick with tension. She's beautiful, and she's amazing, and she's so fucking wrong about my motivations I don't know where to start.

I wrap my fingers around her wrist and stroke her pulse point with my thumb. 'For fuck's sake,' I hiss. 'You've got it all backwards. I did it for you because I wanted to help you. *Because I love you.* And I'll always do whatever it takes for you. Even if it means getting my hands dirty in ways you'd rather not know about.'

She stares up at me in shock, the wind taken out of her sails. I know she wasn't expecting this kind of declaration yet, but it's the truth. And I'm willing to lay myself bare to clear up this little misapprehension of hers.

Then she pulls her wrist away from my grasp.

'How dare you use those words to manipulate me into rolling over?' she asks, those big blue eyes wet. 'And don't *touch* me.'

She steps back and stoops to pick up her bag. And then she's storming out of my office.

'Gen!' I bellow. 'Get back here!'

But she doesn't fucking do as I say.

72

GEN

I'm still so angry I can barely function. That little rendezvous with Anton yesterday reminded me of two of the qualities I dislike the most about him: his business morals are decidedly dodgy, and he always thinks he's right. He assumed that, just because he's okay with unethical—and illegal—practices, I'd be okay with them too. He judged me by his own standards.

Standards which can safely be summed up as the end always justifying the means.

I won't stand for it. And, far more importantly, I will not stand for him undermining me like that. If Mr High Handed thinks he can sweep in and manipulate and back-channel and meddle like that on my turf, he has another think coming.

His declaration of love is something I'm refusing to think about. What the hell kind of declaration was that? He practically threw the words in my face to make his point and shut me up. He's shamelessly manipulative.

I daren't consider, even for a second, that his feelings are real.

I daren't let myself hope that he sees a future for us. Because I can't possibly let myself entertain any thoughts on that front while we have an enormous pile of shit to wade through.

I cancelled our evening together last night and told him via text that I'm not interested in seeing him until he's ready to apologise. He has to work this out for himself. Heaven forbid a man like Anton should ever take counsel from another human. He has to be the one to see that he can't just ride roughshod over my business. Or my boundaries. The apology has to come from him, rather than my forcing one out of him, so I'm intent on leaving him to stew.

God knows, I can freeze people out with the best of them. If Anton's forgotten how it feels to have the full force of my disapproval, then he's about to be reminded pretty damn quickly.

Happily for my desire to stay strong and keep away from him, I'm holding an interview this afternoon with a prospective Alchemy member, and this particular diary event has my interest piqued for a couple of reasons.

One, she's a celebrity.

And two, she's requested that we chat not at Alchemy, but at a women-only members' club in Soho.

It's a request I'm happy to accommodate. Aida Russell is a respected BBC TV presenter and documentarian, an American who married a much older member of the British aristocracy and recently divorced him in spectacularly public fashion amidst rumours about his alleged but rampant infidelity. The tabloids have had a field day with these two.

Not that Aida has made a single comment about the divorce. She's remained tight-lipped as the tabloid war has waged around them, choosing to act with grace and dignity.

But that hasn't stopped the press speculation about the demise of one of the UK's favourite imports and the current Lord Russell.

The fact that Alchemy is her next move is fascinating to me, and it's certainly a welcome distraction from my spiralling thoughts about a certain overbearing billionaire I know.

We meet in a shady corner of her club's rooftop terrace. It's a chic space, the floor tiled in sea-green and white, with ivy and clematis and jasmine jostling for space on the walls. The women around us are well-heeled and jovial. I like its vibe a lot. I make a mental note to check out its membership. I spend far too much of my time with men—it would be healthy for me to have a space where I can come and think and work and socialise away from the men in my professional and personal life.

I smile to myself. Anton would be outraged not to be allowed past these walls.

I'll definitely apply.

Even in a place as discreet at this, Aida causes a bit of a stir when she arrives. She looks stunning, as always. She's impeccably dressed in a plain white t-shirt tucked into tailored khaki shorts that show off her killer, tanned legs. A scarlet lip, chunky gold necklace, sky-high nude suede heels and a huge quilted Chanel tote complete the look.

I'm pretty sure her lineage is Italian. She certainly looks like the lead in a Fellini movie, with her dark hair curled perfectly into a long bob and the huge, feline eyes she reveals when she tugs off her sunglasses. Her smile, when she bestows it on me, is face-splitting. She must be almost a decade older than me, but she's bloody gorgeous.

'Thanks for coming here,' she sighs as she collapses into

the wicker chair opposite me and crosses her long legs. 'It's still a fucking shit-show out there.'

'Paps?' I ask sympathetically.

'Yeah. Hordes of them.' She arches her back and raises her arms, raking her fingers unselfconsciously through her hair. 'They need to get a fucking life. Is it too early for wine?'

'Not at all,' I tell her. 'It's four o'clock.'

'Great. I'm gonna need wine for this conversation.'

Aida Russell has made a name for herself by being an intellectual powerhouse and a hard-hitting interviewer who is also not afraid to shoot her mouth off. She's articulate, and terrifyingly well-informed, and hilariously witty, the queen of the devastating one-line rejoinder that's put many a male politician in their place.

She is punchy as fuck, 'the thinking man's bit of skirt', as the British press has delightfully dubbed her. Men who weren't blessed by the thinking functionality are, inevitably, threatened and horrified by her.

Once our bottle of Sancerre has arrived and our server has poured us each a glass, she dives right in.

'So, I've had shitty marital sex for fifteen years, and I hear you're the gal to help me change that.'

I almost spit out my wine. I *really* like this woman. The press has definitely painted her ex-husband as a bit of a lothario, so her damning indictment of his sexual credentials pleases me enormously.

'Definitely,' I manage. 'You thinking of joining Alchemy?'

She sits back and assesses me, parting her lips and licking along the inside of her lower lip. It's a trademark gesture of hers, completely unconscious, and one that's made her a huge sex symbol in this country. It's also populated a million gifs.

If this woman has been having bad sex for a decade and a half, it's a fucking travesty.

'I mean, a total fuck-fest might be a little too much for me, right off the bat. No offence.'

'None taken. It's a lot. Especially if you've been in a long-term relationship.'

'Right? But'—she leans forward conspiratorially—'I hear you have a programme that can sort me out.'

I raise my eyebrows. *Interesting.* 'Unfurl?'

'*Yes.*' She jabs a fingertip at me. 'Exactly. Is it just for, you know, actual virgins, or will you take on people who are virgins when it comes to good sex too?'

I laugh. 'It fulfils all sorts of roles. And yeah, we can definitely accommodate anyone who wants to use it to broaden their horizons for whatever reasons.'

'I have a couple reasons,' she says slowly, those feline eyes narrowed as she watches me for my reaction. 'I wanna rediscover my sexuality. Like, properly. My marriage was a fucking disaster. Everyone has an opinion on me, thanks to the *Daily Mail* and their horrible little friends. So I'd like to experiment a little. But I need to feel safe while I'm doing it. And I *definitely* need someone who knows what they're doing.'

'Unfurl's completely bespoke,' I assure her. 'We have women come through the programme who are very inexperienced, or who've been traumatised. We also have women who want to shoot the lights out, so they can be with several guys, or women, or both, at the same time. It really is up to the individual and what you're looking to achieve.'

'Great sex,' she says immediately, and I laugh. 'But, yeah, I think one guy's enough for me right now. I'll settle for great sex with one guy.'

'You don't have to "settle" for anything,' I tell her. 'But I take your point. Baby steps. You can always rethink the programme as it goes.'

I walk her through some of her options, some of the ways we've structured Unfurl programmes for previous participants who may have backgrounds in common with Aida. She may not be a virgin, but I know there'll be no shortage of guys at Alchemy who'd tear off their own arm for a chance with this woman.

There's a vulnerability about her, a brittleness, that seeps through the bravado and the comedy. But I've been in the sex industry long enough to know that the woman right here can be a sexual powerhouse in the right hands.

We just need to find the right guy to bring her back to life. To give her back her confidence and help her own her appetites.

I'm musing on that front when she interrupts my train of thought.

'The other thing,' she says, 'is that I wanna film it.'

73

GEN

I blink. 'I beg your pardon?'

'I have this idea.' She spreads her hands wide. 'A documentary about me, a middle-aged woman coming out of a long marriage and finding myself again. Sexually. Bear with me. Much as I'd love to trash-talk John to every tabloid in the land, I won't do it because of the kids. He's still their father. Unfortunately.

'But what if I made a documentary about a woman who's dealing with a lot of shit, who's lacking confidence and finds it again because she decides to fucking own her sexuality? There's this expectation that men like John get divorced and sail off into the sunset with some hot blonde half their age. But if I did something like that, and I shared my experience, it would send the most amazing message to women out there. Newsflash: you're not damaged fucking goods. You have a future. You have value. Go fucking *own* it.'

I shut my eyes for a second and then give her my most sincere look. 'I absolutely love it. I love everything about it. I think it would be amazing for you, and extremely powerful for other women. But Alchemy's very discreet. Our entire

MO is discretion. So the mere concept of letting cameras inside is a huge red flag for me.'

'Please think about it,' she begs. 'I'm not talking about filming me having sex. Obviously. And we wouldn't need to do it inside the club, even. But please, please consider helping me out. Maybe it puts the spotlight on a whole new line of business for you guys, like you have this service where you matchmake members with men or women who need to have their confidence restored in a safe way, with rules and boundaries. It's a *good* thing.'

I take a sip of my wine and eye her, because, while I agree with what she's saying, I'm not remotely convinced about dragging the club into this. I don't think the guys would go for it, anyway. 'I'll consider it,' I tell her. 'You have my word.'

She salutes me with her glass. 'Thank you. I appreciate it. I think it could be fantastic. Obviously, the BBC would never go for it, but I feel like Channel 4 might? Or one of the streaming platforms.'

'That would be amazing,' I say. 'I'd love to see something like this told sensitively, and done in a way that's more reportage than reality TV, you know?'

'Exactly.' She shoots me a megawatt smile. 'Now, tell me everything about running a sex club. It's so cool. Do you avail of *all* the D?' She looks me up and down appraisingly. 'Because you're fucking gorgeous. I bet you do well for yourself. And you're not wearing a ring, so...'

I throw back my head and laugh heartily. 'I did avail, very much, until quite recently. I've been seeing someone.'

'How'd you guys meet?'

I pause. 'At the club.'

'Oooh!' She claps her hands. 'I love it. You dirty girl.'

'Yeah, well, he's in the doghouse at the moment,' I say drily.

'What'd he do? Tell me.'

I cock my head and survey her. 'He overstepped. He's a very strong character—used to getting what he wants.'

She rolls her eyes. 'Aren't they all?'

'Anyway. He forgot that I'm an actual grownup who's perfectly capable of making my own decisions, and he waded in and "rescued" a work situation that absolutely did not require rescuing. Without my permission.'

'Asshole.'

'Precisely.'

'So you're making him sweat?'

'Something like that,' I say. 'Not for the sake of it. But you know men. They need to work these things out for themselves.'

Once we've said our goodbyes and I'm hailing a cab back to Alchemy, I consider Aida's proposition. There's no way we'd ever agree to a documentary for the sake of publicity. Publicity like that could only be detrimental.

That said, if Cannes goes well and we want to expand internationally, putting our brand out there in a carefully controlled way could be positive for us. More importantly, I bought into her pitch. I believed in it, and I believe the world needs a documentary like that. What if the stars are aligning? Because investigative reporters and storytellers like Aida Russell don't fall into your lap every day.

Something she said as we parted stuck with me. I asked her, jokingly, who her ideal man would be.

'I mean, if you can hook me up with Theo James, that would be awesome,' she shot back immediately.

If we were to even consider doing this, we'd need to find someone perfect for Aida. Someone professional and considerate as well as gorgeous and sexy and fucking amazing in bed.

Someone we, and she, could trust to handle themselves perfectly.

Someone who'd love being on camera.

And someone with Theo James-level hotness.

Hmm.

I can't help but think this would be a job for Cal.

74

ANTON

I can't believe Gen's freezing me out like this. Can't believe she's played her old *don't touch me* card. She's being completely ridiculous, in my opinion. Not to mention disingenuous.

I feel like Henry II's knights must have done. The king famously mused to them about Thomas Becket, "Will no one rid me of this turbulent priest?" Off four of them trotted to Canterbury to appease their king and murder said "turbulent priest", after which Henry hastily distanced himself from the crime, claiming never to have issued any order.

I call bullshit. Then and now. My own little Henry, aka Gen, has been wringing her hands over those Rapture twats for weeks. She can't claim moral outrage now that I've taken action and done the dirty work for her.

Honestly. Stubborn fucking woman. There's nothing more irritating than ingratitude.

I used my clout to pull some strings.

For her.

I made this whole nightmare go away.

For her.

Call me naive, or even stupid, but I actually thought a business-focused grand gesture would be the way to her heart. She's a successful and super-smart businesswoman. She's not a gold-digger. She's not impressed by my bank balance or by the trappings of my wealth. She enjoys them, sure. But they're not the way to win her over.

I thought this would go further than hearts and flowers. I intended it to send a crystal clear message. To cut to the centre of what's important to her. It would show her that I see her. That I respect her. That I'm her biggest cheerleader and her most vicious pit-bull. That I'm squarely in her corner and I'll always have her back.

That she never needs to look over her shoulder from now on, because the moment something—*anything*—bothers her, I'll handle it.

I'll turn it to dust.

That I'm so fucking crazy about her that she's earned herself a besotted, and devastatingly effective, slave for life.

It seems, however, that I've managed to do the complete opposite. And, pissed off and bewildered though I am by her reaction, it's eminently clear that I need to make this right and do better if I'm to have a future with her.

Because she's my fucking future. I know that to be true. It may feel quick to her, but I've made my fortune from having impeccable judgement, crystal-clear self-awareness, and from having sufficient faith in those skillsets to strike with one-hundred-percent confidence.

If my declaration of love blindsided Gen, she should know I've made ten, eleven figure acquisitions before now on a shorter timeline.

When I find something I want, I *act*.

I lock it down. Make it mine.

I acquire. Assimilate.

But it seems I'm losing my touch.

Or, at least, I've underestimated the complexity of this consolidation with this spellbinding woman. I've operated on a set of fixed assumptions that have served me well in business but have fallen abysmally short in the most important merger of my life.

I mentioned I'm self-aware. One of the most important skills in business is knowing your strengths and weaknesses. Knowing what you can achieve on your own, and when it's better to build a strong team.

Knowing when to call in the cavalry.

'THANKS FOR SEEING ME,' I say to Zach, Callum and Rafe. They've agreed to my desperate plea that they meet up and help me extricate myself from this mess. If anyone can solve Gen-gate, surely it's her oldest and dearest friends? And if anyone can give it to me straight, I'm assuming it's them.

'Not a problem, mate,' Rafe says, lifting his tumbler of scotch in salutation. We've met up at a gentleman's club in Mayfair of which I'm a member. It's more old-school than I'd like, but at least there's no chance of running into Gen here. 'We told her we were off to a battle ropes session together.' He smirks. 'That got her off our tail pretty quickly.'

'Yeah,' Callum says, 'if she thought we were meeting you she'd go apeshit.'

I grimace. 'She's still pissed off?'

Their decisive nods are all the answers I need.

'Look.' I clear my throat. 'The first thing I should do is apologise if I overstepped on the Rapture front. I thought I was doing Gen a favour by getting rid of them. But it's your company too, and I'm sorry if I butted in where I shouldn't.'

They exchange a look. 'You've done us a favour, no question,' Zach tells me. 'I think we can all agree we would have appreciated you asking first, though. Or at least giving us a heads up.'

'That said,' Rafe interjects before I can say anything, 'if you'd told us you were going to have to play dirty to get it done, our morals might have got in the way. So maybe it's a good thing we were oblivious.' He shrugs.

I consider. 'That's fair. Look, I don't play dirty unless I have to. But if there are other fuckers out there who aren't playing fair, then I have zero qualms about doing what I need to do to see justice done. I didn't like the way they were doing business. There are codes, you know? Touma and Hansen have been burning bridges for a long time before Rapture—they've had it coming to them. So I'm not going to waste any sleep over their little venture going south.'

'Neither are we,' Callum says. 'But I see where Gen's coming from. And it's a lot more personal for her than it is for us, mate.'

I lean forward, resting my elbows on my spread thighs and steepling my fingers. 'Give it to me straight.'

They exchange another glance.

'What you've got to understand about Gen,' Callum says, 'is that on the surface of it, she's very strait-laced. Not just in business, but in life. She was head girl at her school, for fuck's sake. If that doesn't tell you everything you need to know, I don't know what does.

'She's from a wealthy, respectable family that puts way too much emphasis on optics. Her dad barely speaks to her now. Her mum tells everyone Gen runs a kind of Soho House-like club. She's in denial, basically. The idea of their precious golden girl running a sex club is so seedy they can't bear it. It's a massive bone of contention, because it makes the family look bad.'

I inhale sharply. 'I had no idea,' I say, raking my memory for what Gen's said about her family in the past. I know they live in Tunbridge Wells, but she hasn't volunteered anything particularly profound about them. Now I'm wondering why I haven't bothered to delve deeper so far.

'Yeah, well, her dad's an overbearing arsehole,' Rafe says. 'They were always so proud of her when we were at uni, because she was overachieving left, right and centre. When she got a place on the JP Morgan graduate scheme she said he was insufferable. Boasting to everyone he knew. But they're only proud when she's being what in their minds constitutes the quote-unquote perfect daughter. Now she's running Alchemy they don't want to know, basically.'

I purse my lips. My blood is boiling. How fucking dare they be so shallow, so conservative? Gen is a rare diamond, and they should damn well know it.

'That's despicable,' I say finally.

'No disagreement here,' Zach says. 'So you can see why we're so protective of her. You can also understand why she puts so much emphasis on keeping this very practised veneer of respectability. She's so sick of being judged, and her family's been of no fucking support, except for her sister, who's even more of a black sheep, but she's in Australia so she's not much help. Gen feels like she's let her family down, when they're obviously the ones who've let her down.'

'If her father's an overbearing arsehole, I have no idea what she's doing with me,' I muse aloud.

Callum sniggers. 'You and me both, mate.'

'Gen's an incredibly strong woman,' Zach points out, 'and she likes strong men. Anyone who can't stand up to her is a massive turn-off. I'm not remotely surprised she's fallen for you.'

My heart warms at his language, and I go to speak, but he's not finished.

'But she's also seriously independent,' he continues. 'She's had to take a huge stand against her family—a stand that doesn't come lightly—and dig her heels in so she can grow Alchemy with us. She's fought hard for this and made some tough choices. You can imagine how hard it is for a woman like Gen to embrace what being a sex club owner really means. It's like she's given into her dark side.'

'Just like you,' Rafe quips.

'Fuck off. I just came on board to run your books.'

'Until Maddy flashed her pretty little smile at you and dragged you down,' Callum teases.

'I'm pretty sure that's not all she flashed at him,' Rafe says.

'You're not wrong. I didn't stand a chance,' Zach says with a grin on his face. '*Anyway.* My point is that Alchemy's not just a business to Gen. It's a part of the identity she's chosen for herself, and she guards it fiercely. So when you wade in and ride roughshod over something so important to her, she's going to feel completely undermined. Like it's just another male in her life trying to tell her what's best for her.'

'*Fuck,*' I hiss, dragging my hands over my face.

He's fucking right.

They all are.

Alchemy is Gen's jurisdiction, not mine. It's something she's built for herself at a great personal cost, and I completely failed to appreciate that. My past relationships have taught me nothing about how to make a woman like Gen happy. Because they were all with beautiful, charming, loving women who were more than happy to be in my orbit, rather than being queens of their own.

To roll over and let me call the shots in life.

Just not in bed. Not as much as I needed to.

And now I've found myself this strong, ballsy woman who desperately needs me to control her in bed but goes fucking nuclear the first time I machinate on her behalf. And quite rightly, because I've completely misjudged her needs.

If that's not ironic, I don't know what is.

Her three friends and champions and cofounders are watching me.

'Okay,' I say. 'I have some serious humble pie to eat.'

They grin at me in unison.

75

GEN

I *knew it.*

I knew I shouldn't get involved with a man like Anton because the crash would hurt like nothing else. His very presence is so overwhelming that his absence is the worst form of cruelty.

I miss his size.

His warmth.

The sheer force of his personality.

And, most cruelly of all, I miss his touch. Its absence is once again by my own choice, but it's far, far worse this time.

Because when Anton Wolff spends every second of his time with you putting his hands on you, kissing you, holding you, you feel completely bereft without those gifts.

That's without even considering the orgasm gifts he loves so much to bestow on me.

We haven't spoken since I went to his office three days ago. I'm flying to France with the boys and their girlfriends at lunchtime, and we're staying at the Martinez in Cannes. I was supposed to be travelling on Anton's jet, and staying with him, obviously, but I bottled it the morning after I went to give him a piece of my mind. When no apology had been forthcoming overnight, I asked Rafe if I could join him and the others on the jet he's chartered for the occasion. He's taken care of everything.

'I'm glad I have you guys,' I tell them wearily from the front seat of the people-carrier that's taking us all to Biggin Hill airfield. 'This is going to be hideous—I need my people around me.'

Maddy leans forward from her seat behind mine and puts her hands on my shoulders. 'We've got you, babes. Okay?'

I pat her hand weakly. 'Thanks, hon.'

Maddy's been furious about the whole situation. She gets it—she gets what a gross betrayal Anton's interference in Alchemy's business has been for me. The boys have been quieter on the subject. I suspect they're conflicted between loyalty to me and relief that Anton has metaphorically burnt Rapture to the ground.

'Any word from him this morning?' Belle asks.

'Nothing,' I say sadly.

We've shared a few text messages. He's been in pretty regular contact, the past couple of days, most of the messages along a similar vein.

> I want to see you, but I understand you feel you need space.

> We should talk it out before France.

> I care for you very deeply, Gen. Everything I do is to make you happy.

And the last one, as I was getting into bed last night:

Sweet dreams, my love.

He kills me.

He fucking kills me, and I resent the fact that I have to stay strong. That I have to stand up for my principles and my self-respect, because I'm exhausted, and all I want to do is crawl into that man's bed with him and have him shatter me into a million pieces and put me back together again.

But I cannot.

Because until the words *I'm* and *sorry* cross his lips, I need to uphold my boundaries. If I cave this time, I'll be giving him tacit permission to walk all over me again and again.

It feels like the first night of puppy training. I have to be resolute, no matter how adorable he is. No matter how much he whines. I just hope I can teach this old dog some new tricks, because if he continues to be a stubborn arsehole, I simply don't know what I'll do. I'll feel compelled to give up the perfect man because he can't respect my wishes.

It's so ironic. I held him off for so long. I gave him such firm boundaries and he upheld them (even if he danced around them like only Anton can). He didn't touch me until I granted him permission.

So why the fuck can't he stay out of my business? He's won over my body, my heart, and my soul. I've given them freely to him. They're his.

But he can't have Alchemy.

We arrive at Biggin Hill and tumble out of the people carrier. The boys go to help our driver unload our bags from the back. It's no surprise to anyone that Belle, Maddy and I have about five times more luggage than the guys. We trail through the front doors into the main departures lounge

when Cal puts down his bag and stands in front of me, his
hands going to my upper arms.

'Darling,' he says, 'this is where we say goodbye to you.
We'll see you tomorrow night at the party.'

I blink. 'What the hell?'

Rafe steps up beside him, Zach coming to his other side.
'You're going with Anton,' Rafe says kindly, as if I'm a small
and confused child.

'No I'm fucking not,' I say. I let go of my suitcase handle
and put my hands on my hips.

'Yes you are,' Zach says. 'We've sorted it with him. I
promise you, he has a lot of things he wants to say to you
and you'll like them all. He gets it.'

'Yeah,' Cal chips in. 'We talked sense into him. He knows
he's done badly.'

I give the three of them my most withering glare. 'What
the *fuck*? You met up with him behind my back?'

Cal flinches. 'He begged us. He's a mess. He absolutely
adores you. I know I thought he was a bit of a twat at first,
but he has my blessing now. He really, really wants to make
this right. Honestly, we wouldn't let you walk into the lion's
den if we didn't think it was the right thing.'

'Jesus Christ,' I grit out. 'Just what I need. More men
patronising me and thinking they know what's best for me.'

I feel a bit faint. I don't—I'm not ready. I've been
obsessing about him and fuming at him and missing him so
fucking much this week, but the idea of him being here, of
being alone with him and having it all out with him, makes
me feel nauseous.

And I do *not* like my so-called friends colluding with
him behind my back. It makes me feel small, and foolish,
and vulnerable.

'It's not like that,' Zach insists. He's gone pale. 'Seriously,

Gen, we'd never presume to tell you what's best for you. We laid into him—I promise you. There were no concessions. But we also can't stand by and let you lose your shot at happiness. Life's too short, believe me.'

I narrow my eyes at him. That's a low shot, coming from the widower, and he knows it.

But he may also have a minuscule point.

'Did you know about this?' I ask Belle and Maddy, who are hovering. Their bashful smiles tell me everything I need to know.

'It's so romantic,' Maddy hisses. 'Zach just told me this morning 'cause he knew I'd never be able to keep it a secret. He really is sorry, apparently.' She jerks her head in the direction of the gates. 'Go on, babes. Go make up with your man.'

'I'm not happy about any of this,' I hiss as I grab the handle of my suitcase and swivel in the direction of check-in. I'm pissed off with Anton for going to them behind my back. I'm pissed off with them for rolling over.

But they're right on one count.

I really should have it out with him properly before we get to France.

76

GEN

Traitors.

Why does this feel like another Anton Ambush of epic proportions?

Because it is.

That's why.

I reluctantly leave my so-called friends and get myself checked in. And as I walk towards the gate, my heart stops.

There he is.

Oh my dear God.

If I thought for a second I could live without him I was plain delusional. He's so beautiful my heart physically hurts. He's in a lightweight blue shirt and chinos, dark hair raked back in a perfectly messed style, hands in his pockets and those big brown eyes fixed solely on me. In them I see reflected the pain and heartache I've suffered this week. However badly he's overstepped, the proof that he feels deeply for me is etched into every line on his gorgeous face.

'Hi,' he says softly.

I stop in front of him. 'Hi.' My voice sounds almost shy. I feel shy. I feel like a nervous teenager, my stomach a net of butterflies. The sense of betrayal I felt mere moments ago is dissipating, leaving a more complex emotion in its wake.

He gestures at my case. 'May I take it?'

'I've got it, thanks,' I say.

He holds out his hand. 'Can I at least hold your hand, then?'

I look up at him. I want to fling myself at him like a koala bear and never let go.

'I need a moment, okay?' I say gruffly, because God knows, if I hold his hand, I'll melt.

'Of course,' he says quickly. I don't miss the hurt in his eyes.

We cross the tarmac and he hands my suitcase off to one flight attendant as his usual one, the immaculate Carly, greets us at the bottom of the steps.

The cabin is as opulently relaxing as usual. Miles of cream leather and cream carpet and walnut panelling and the obligatory *W* monograms. There are platters of antipasti and fresh fruit laid out on the table next to a crystal vase bearing beautiful blue delphiniums, and a bottle of champagne is chilling in an ice bucket, a white folded napkin around its neck and two champagne flutes waiting beside it.

Anton ushers me into a forward-facing seat and takes the one next to me, effectively hemming me in.

'Why don't you give us the safety briefing now, Carly?' he suggests. 'Then you can retire. I can take care of the drinks —we don't want to be disturbed for the rest of the flight.' There's a faint tremor in his otherwise commanding voice.

My stomach jolts at the thought of being all alone with him for the duration of our journey. I don't know whether to feel terrified or exhilarated. I'm a bit of both, probably.

'Of course, sir,' Carly says with a bright smile. She delivers a speedy and efficient safety briefing and then bids us an enjoyable flight. 'Wheels up in five minutes,' she informs us before closing the partition door behind her.

As soon as she's out of sight, Anton twists his body so we're facing each other. His eyes sweep over my face.

'God, it's such a relief to see you,' he says on an exhale. 'I've missed you so much.'

I swallow. 'I know. Me too.'

'Champagne?' he says suddenly.

'Yes, please.' I'm definitely going to need a drink for this. I feel lightheaded just being this close to him. Being trapped here next to him. Being able to smell him, sense the heat coming off his huge body.

'Excellent.' He busies himself with opening the bottle, botching the tearing of the foil. Good Lord. He really is nervous.

He doesn't speak again until he's filled both our flutes and handed me mine. He holds his up and looks me intently in the eye. 'To me earning back the privilege of your trust,' he says quietly.

I have no words, so I clink my flute against his. I give him a little nod. It's a strong start, but I need to hear him articulate how he sees our situation. I need to see whether he gets where I'm coming from.

Anton looks down, finding my free hand and clasping it tightly before turning those brown eyes back on me.

I should pull my hand away.

I should.

But I don't want to, and I've missed the simple pleasure of having my hand engulfed in his warm, strong one. God, it's intense being the sole focus on his attention. And we're not even having sex.

'My darling,' he says, his thumb stroking the back of my hand. 'I cannot apologise enough for what I did. I went gangbusters into a situation that was solely your jurisdiction, and it was completely unacceptable. From the bottom of my heart, I'm sorry.'

'Thank you,' I murmur.

He takes a deep breath and keeps going. 'Your friends helped me understand it from your point of view, and now that I have that perspective I'm disgusted with myself.' He shakes his head. 'I made a unilateral decision about someone else's business and I just waltzed right in and threw my weight around. When I look at it like that, I can see why you were so fucking furious. And rightly so.'

'Exactly,' I say. 'I can't have you wading into my professional affairs, Anton. Not only is it *literally* none of your business, but you made me feel like you didn't think I was capable of handling it myself, which was probably the most hurtful part of it all. Especially after all the chat you gave me about finding me impressive. It made me wonder if it was all bullshit.'

He screws up his face like he's in pain. 'I know. I can see why it would look like that, and I can't bear it, because obviously I feel exactly the opposite about you. And I'm not here to try to make excuses, but if you'd let me, I'd like to make this point. It absolutely wasn't about control, or about undermining you or not having faith in you.

'It honestly came from a place of adoration and righteous anger on your behalf. Those guys were such pricks at the Serpentine, and I just saw red. I know how hard you work. I know how much Alchemy means to you, and there was no way I was letting those dickheads destroy what you built, so I went nuclear.'

I raise my eyebrows. 'No arguments here.' He looks so crestfallen that I add softly, 'I do get it. It's kind of romantic, when you put it like that, but you've got to understand I don't need a white knight. When you do stuff like that, it makes me feel weak rather than strong.'

He exhales, his nostrils flaring. 'I get it. I don't like it, because that's not how I feel, but if that's the effect it has on you, then that's absolutely not okay.'

'No, it's not,' I agree.

He looks down at our joined hands and loosens his grip so he can interlace our fingers. 'I'm at a loss here, because this is what I want you to know. I think you are an incredible woman in all areas of your life, including the business you run. Clearly, I'm an Alchemy fan.' He grins, and it's so adorable I can't help but give him a little smile in return. 'I promise you faithfully that I will never go behind your back again, and I'll never wade in where my involvement isn't wanted.'

I nod. 'Glad to hear it.'

'But. I want you to know that *if* you ever require a henchman, I'm a very effective one. Very dastardly.' He winks, then sighs. 'I'm trying to say you have me in your corner, sweetheart. Permanently. Not because you're weak or inadequate or you need me, but because every human deserves to have someone who'll always be on their team. I'll *always* be Team Gen. And woe betide anyone who tries to hurt you. Consider me your personal pit-bull.'

I smile. 'But I get to control the leash.'

'You always get to control the leash. Keep me in a fucking kennel if you want. But maybe just knowing you have me around will give you peace of mind.' He looks at me pleadingly, and I acquiesce.

'I can live with that,' I tell him.

'Yeah?'

'Yeah.'

'I have one more thing to say,' he says hesitantly, 'and another apology to make, come to think of it.'

I raise my eyebrows. 'Okay...'

'You quite rightly accused me, when I told you I loved you, of weaponising those words.'

I shift uncomfortably.

'And you were right. I was desperate to make you understand where I was coming from, but it doesn't change the fact that I threw those words at you. It was manipulative, and you deserved far better than that, and I'm sorry.'

'Wow.' I exhale. 'Okay. Good.'

His apologies, and his sincerity, have my head spinning. Contrite Anton is my new favourite version of him. He's saying all the right words, and I have to trust that he'll back them up with his actions—or lack of them, as the case may be.

I *want* to trust.

'How am I doing?' he asks, tilting his head to one side. Our faces are so close, and he has my head spinning with his words, and his gorgeous looks, and his fucking *scent*. Jesus, this guy messes with my brain chemistry.

I'm still clutching my flute. I set it down on the table and allow myself to touch his face. To run a fingertip down the laughter lines bracketing his mouth. The lines I love so much.

'You're doing adequately,' I tell him, and he grins, his dimple flashing under my fingertip.

'Yeah?'

'Yes,' I whisper, and I close the distance and kiss him on his beautiful, plush lips. He makes a strangled sound at the back of his throat before his other hand comes around my neck, his fingers raking through my hair. Then his lips are parting and his tongue is seeking access.

I open, and it thrusts inside my mouth like he can't bear to wait another second. He holds the base of my skull in a clamp as he kisses me, releasing my hand so his other hand can roam over my shoulder. Down my bare arm and around my back so he can tug me even more tightly against him. Relief hits me in a cascade.

His tongue invades my mouth. It's so thick and taut and muscular. Being thoroughly kissed by him is so intensely *sexual*. It's like nothing else. Already he's consuming me. He's short-circuiting my brain, and my entire body is keening for him. God, he's so hungry and insistent and delicious. *This* is the kind of control I'll give him all day long.

So I do. I put myself in his hands. We're so good together like this. We know our roles. We know instinctively what the other wants. If we can find this clarity, this amazing synergy, beyond the physical side of our relationship, then there's no limit to how incredible we can be together.

He pulls away a little. 'Do you trust me again?' he asks against my mouth, his voice husky with emotion. Desire.

'Mmm-hmm. Yep,' I manage.

'Say it.'

I claw my fingers through his hair, understanding that it's as important to him that I absolve him as it was to me that he apologised. 'I trust you. I mean, I trust you to try, and I trust you to listen and respect my wishes if you step out of line again.'

'Good.' He kisses my lips, and it's dreamy and gorgeous and otherworldly. 'Because I have something else to say.'

77

ANTON

'**I**'m saying this without any agenda,' I say, staring at this beautiful woman who's turned my life upside down and whom I nearly lost through my fucking egotistical actions. I relax my grip on her neck and allow my fingers to enjoy caressing the smooth skin of her neck. 'I'm fifty-two. Sweetheart—I don't think you understand how I feel about you.

'I've been married *three fucking times,* for Christ's sake, and *this*'—I break off and attempt to pull myself the fuck together—'is what I've been looking for the entire time. *This.* With you. And I've wasted half a fucking century without you. And I don't regret anything that gave me my kids, but I wish I'd met you sooner. I wish that so much.'

She widens her beautiful pale blue eyes. Eyes I lose myself in every time I look at her. I let my gaze roam over her face and trail the pad of my thumb across the plump perfection of her lower lip.

'Anton,' she whispers.

I plough on. I need to get this off my chest before I become a blubbering mess. 'What you and I have is so extraordinary,' I tell her. 'I can show you sides of myself that everyone else I've been close to has judged and rejected, and, amazingly, you accept them. You seem to actually like them. *And* you've trusted me enough to let me see your darker sides, too, and that's what makes it so fucking incredible between us.

'Because what we have is raw and authentic, and it feeds our souls. And I can't live without it, sweetheart. I love you so much. So much. It seems amazing to me that I ever thought anything else was love, because this is...' I trail off. I can barely articulate what I feel for Gen.

'You are the real deal,' I tell her. 'You're everything I've been looking for in a woman, my whole life, and I will do anything—*anything*—to make sure you never have cause to doubt me again. Do you understand?'

Her eyes are brimming with the prettiest tears, but she's smiling and nodding frantically. 'Yes. Yes.'

'And I love you. In case you missed that bit.'

She laughs, and it's beautiful. 'I didn't.'

'Good,' I say sternly, but I'm grinning like an idiot.

She cups my face in her hands. 'I love you too. I'm completely besotted with you.'

'You don't need to say it back,' I protest, raising a hand and trapping hers against my face.

'I know. But it's true. I knew before I even met you that you'd make me feel all sorts of things, and I was right. What you just said—what we have—it's like nothing I've ever known. That's why I was so fucking terrified about giving it a shot with you. And it's why I was so upset the other day. I felt like I'd met the guy for me but then he wasn't going to be healthy for me.'

I'm a mess of emotions. Relief, and awe, and ecstasy that

Genevieve Carew loves me, and disgust that I almost derailed everything.

'I promise you I'll be healthy for you. I will *only* be good for you,' I tell her. 'I'm so fucking happy you love me.'

Then I'm kissing her again, drowning in her, and fuck, I've missed this. My bed has been a cold and depressing place these past few days. I even put Hades' dog bed in my room which is a low I've never stooped to before.

She's pliant in my arms, her beautiful tits pressed up against me, her mouth hungry, her tongue entangling with mine.

I need her.

That reminds me.

'I got you something,' I tell her when I've found the strength to break away from our kiss. I reach into the bag on the floor beside me and present her with a flat Bulgari jewellery box.

'Oh my God,' she says, and the shock in her voice makes me smile.

'Don't pray to God until you've opened it,' I tell her wolfishly.

She licks her lips and opens the box. Her hand flies up to cover her mouth, but her gasp is still audible.

'Jesus Christ, Anton.'

'Do you like it?' I ask.

'I—I love it. It's absolutely stunning.' She stares down, rapt, at the contents of the box.

I bought her Bulgari's iconic Parentesi choker of platinum and diamonds. It reminds me of her. Strong. Sculptural. Understated. Sophisticated.

And very, very beautiful.

'You can wear it whenever you want, obviously,' I say, 'but I thought it might work for our boundaries. When you put it on for me, you're mine to do with as I like. You wear your collar of sorts, and I call the shots.'

She jerks her head upwards, and I swear her pupils are dilating before my eyes.

'You like that idea?' I say softly.

She smiles at me coquettishly. 'I do.'

'I'm committed to an equal partnership,' I tell her, 'but I want it crystal clear who calls the shots in our sex life.'

'You do,' she whispers.

'Right answer.' I pause. 'Would you like me to put it on you?'

'Very much,' she says. She hands me the box and raises her arms so she can hold her hair up off her neck. I take the choker out and admire her swanlike neck and the view down to where her tits are straining against that elegant sundress she's wearing.

This is what I need. This is what I've been craving like an addict. I will build her up and kneel at her feet and worship her in her professional life. But when it's just the two of us, I have this sick need to know she'll do whatever the fuck I say.

I lean forward and fasten the choker around her neck by feel alone, my gaze fixated by the sight of her looking up at me through thick eyelashes.

'There.' I drag a thumb along her delicate collarbone. 'It looks beautiful on you.'

'Does it?' She picks up her phone and presumably likes what she sees in her camera, because a pleased smile plays on her beautiful lips. 'God, Anton. It's stunning.'

'*You're* stunning,' I correct her, my thumb moving to the thick strap of her dress and sliding beneath it to stroke her skin there. 'But you know what would be even better?'

'What?' she asks, amused.

'Just the choker. Lose everything else.'

Her eyes flutter closed for a moment. 'Oh, God,' she whispers.

'Because I may have been out of line, sweetheart, but you withheld yourself from me. You wouldn't let me touch you.' I push the strap off her shoulder and bend my head so I can suck on the glossy skin there. 'And you know what that does to me.' Fuck, her skin is delicious. I bite her lightly there, and she shudders gratifyingly as she palms my chest. I drag my teeth over the skin. 'It makes me *crazy*. So you need to get on that sofa and lose the fucking dress.'

The visual floors me. Gen stripped bare for me, every sacred spot on her body mine to play with. To sample. To devour. Nothing on that flawless skin of hers except the choker that signifies my claim to her and any marks I should choose to leave with my hands and my teeth and my lips.

She hesitates and glances towards the closed door between us and the flight attendants.

'It's more than their jobs are worth to disturb us,' I promise her. 'Go on. Do it.'

78

ANTON

I stand and extend a hand so she can slide out of her seat. Across the aisle lies a sofa running the length of the cabin. There's a bedroom at the rear of the plane, but I don't want a bed.

I want the woman I love sprawled across the main cabin of my jet like a banquet for one.

She stands, the strap I nudged still hanging down her arm, her shoulder still slightly pink from where I sucked it.

'Undo me, then,' she says, her eyes bright with challenge. Anticipation.

'That I can do.' I take her by the upper arms and turn her around. A quick tug at her dress' zip has the entire thing sliding to the ground, leaving her in just a black lace thong.

She turns her head and smiles at me over her shoulder, and I'm speechless. That knowing smile. That creamy skin. The perfection of the globes of that arse.

'Turn around,' I say huskily.

She turns, kicking her dress away.

Fuck me, her tits. I grind my jaw. My mouth is watering, so desperate am I to get one of them in my mouth.

'So fucking beautiful,' I tell her. 'I'm going to come all over those tits. Now, lose the thong.'

'Yes, sir,' she says, the corners of her mouth lifting. She doesn't break eye contact as she hooks her thumbs into the lace and tugs it down. She loves this game as much as I do.

And then she's naked. Naked except for her heels and the choker. *My* choker. My mark of ownership.

'On the sofa,' I tell her. 'Legs spread. I want to see every bit of the pretty cunt you've been keeping from me.'

'Certainly,' she says, and saunters over to the sofa. I watch her cheeks move. We've reached a cruising altitude and the air is calm. Sunlight drenches the cabin and catches on her hair. The diamonds around her neck. It makes her luminous.

She's a celestial being that's all mine to defile.

There's something about being up here with her, away from the crowds and the noise and the various financial markets and the people wanting a piece of me.

We're suspended.

Untethered.

The air feels filled with possibility.

She takes her seat on the cream leather, reclining languidly, arms stretched out along the back of the sofa. She plants her heels on the floor and opens her legs wide for me.

Jesus fucking Christ.

She's every fantasy I have ever and could ever have—this stunning, classy, intelligent woman who has submitted to me, body and soul.

The ways I want to desecrate her.

I pick up my champagne flute and survey the delicious scene before me as I sip.

'So many options,' I muse. 'What do I want to do first?'

'You can do anything you want,' she murmurs, watching me. 'I trust you.'

And with those magic words, she spurs me into action.

I bend and tilt my flute, pouring a thin drizzle of Krug over her chest. The pale golden liquid hits her skin with a splash and drips over her tits. Down her stomach. It'll end up on her cunt, I hope.

The sight of it, wet and glistening on her skin, has me losing my glass and falling to my knees in front of her. I push her legs further apart and pull her in for a quick kiss before I feast on her beautiful body. I bend my head and I lick the champagne off her tits. I slurp at her skin. I suck on her nipples. I grab handfuls of flesh and revel in the exquisite pleasure of having Gen all to myself once again.

She arches into me as I suck on one taut, juicy nipple, her fingernails digging into my shoulders through my shirt. 'Oh my God,' she grits out. 'So good.'

'You're fucking delectable,' I growl. I squat down further and plant a hand on either knee, holding her wide open as my mouth hits that sweet, sweet cunt. Jesus Christ, my head is spinning and my cock is straining against my trousers. I need inside her so badly, but I've waited long enough for this moment, and I've come so close to losing her.

My cock can wait. This is about reminding Gen who she belongs to. Reminding her she'll never get the same kind of satisfaction from anyone else.

Not even close.

I wedge my shoulders between her thighs to hold them open for me and find her nipple with one hand. Then I ram two fingers hard inside her, and she cries out. She's tight, and wet, and warm, and I want to make my home here. I never want to leave. I give her a single lick, from my fingers to her clit, and look up at her. Fuck, she tastes sublime.

I feel positively murderous with desire.

I'm a wild animal whose prey has taunted him, evaded him, for too long, and now there'll be hell to pay.

'How does that feel?' I ask, crooking my fingers for good measure.

She jolts. 'Oh my God—amazing. It feels amazing. I need more.'

I arch my eyebrows. 'Because it's been a while?' I ask before touching my tongue to her clit for a split second.

'Y-yes.' She's already in that state I love so much, where she's so aroused the world around her has ceased to exist, and it's just her, me, and the release she's chasing.

'Not much fun being kept waiting, is it?' I enquire airily. I pull my fingers out and wait.

Her eyes narrow. She may be halfway to heaven, but she's just worked out my game. 'No.'

'Did you get yourself off this week?'

'Yes.'

I push my fingers back in, hard. 'Did it feel like this?'

'No. It was shit.'

'What did you think about?' I let my mouth hover right over her clit so she knows a good answer will get her rewarded.

'You. Always you.'

'Good.' I swirl my tongue around her swollen clit, and she shudders with happiness. 'How?'

'We pretended I was your assistant, and you bent me over your desk at work.'

I make a mental note to have that happen as soon as possible when we're back in London. 'That's my girl. Do you want to come?'

'Yes,' she moans. 'Please, baby.'

I withdraw my fingers from their slick sheath.

'You can come when you've earned it. You've made me wait long enough. Take my cock out and suck it.'

She pulls herself upright, and I can see in her face she's conflicted. She needs to come, but she wants my cock. I toe off my loafers and hastily unbutton my shirt as she makes quick work of my belt and chinos, pushing them down my legs before extricating my cock from my boxers and shoving them down too. Then I'm naked in front of her, and my poor, aching cock is in her hand, and she's gripping it tightly.

Fuck me. This is what I need.

I reach behind me and grab my flute. 'Here, sweetheart.' I hold it to her lips so she can take a mouthful, and then she's feeding my cock into her mouth as the cool liquid sluices around my crown and champagne bubbles pop against my flesh.

'Yes,' I hiss, and she looks up at me adoringly.

This.

My girlfriend, naked before me, her pink lips around my cock and looking like I've summoned the world's most high-class hooker to play on my jet in her Bulgari jewels and stiletto heels.

The sense of power rolls over me. The possibilities swirl in my brain and in my dick. She's mine to do what I like with.

Fuck knows, I'll fuck her six ways till Sunday before I land.

'Suck it,' I order, and she swallows the champagne, her mouth contracting around me. Then she's working me, one hand cupping my heavy balls as the other claws down my stomach. She swipes her tongue through the precum weeping from my slit. She teases the sensitive underside of my crown and then deep-throats me.

Holy fuck.

She sucks like a whore, too, and I love it. I slide my hands through her hair so I can clamp them on either side of her head and throw my head back as I guide my cock deeper and deeper. Every time I hit the back of her throat, I let out an involuntary sound that's somewhere between a growl and a bellow. She's just too good.

When I look back down at her, she's rubbing herself on the sofa.

'Sweetheart,' I say sternly. 'If you make yourself come, you won't get another one from me. Stop it.'

She rolls her eyes at me, and I smirk.

My Gen is back, in that version of her I love so much— wanton and desperate and greedy, her delicious mouth stuffed full of my cock. I cast my mind back to that first glimpse of her at Alchemy. So immaculate. So buttoned-up.

This is what I wanted.

This is what I saw, even then.

I let her do what she does so well—licking and sucking and mouth-fucking me—until I'm so close I can no longer trust myself not to blow. I release her head and pull out. Jesus. I'm so fucking hard. My balls are high and tight and ready to explode, and my shaft is slick from Gen's wet mouth.

'Turn around and bend over,' I order her in a ragged voice, and she does as I say, draping herself back against the sofa. I'm so lightheaded I can barely string a sentence together. I fully intended to shoot my load all over her tits, but this is no time for fun and games.

I need to be balls deep in her *now*.

We both need it.

She stands and brushes her lips against mine as I stare down at her in a kind of stupor. Then she's turning and hingeing forward at the waist, planting her legs wide and her palms firmly in a brace position either side of one of the small windows.

She'll fucking need to brace herself for what I have in mind.

I admire the staggering view of Gen bent over for me, holes on display, tits hanging heavily, her face turned to one side so I can admire her anguished profile as I run the tip of my dick up and down her slit.

'God,' I tell her. 'You're dripping for me, my darling. You are so *fucking* perfect.'

And with that, I line myself up and push in hard, thanking my lucky stars that we had the conversation around protection and got tested last week. Because I want nothing between us.

I want skin on skin.

Flesh on flesh.

I want it to be her and me and nothing else except for the otherworldly pleasure of being sheathed in her like this.

I bottom out, and she lets out one of those noises that tells me my little ice queen is way too close to care about being polite or appropriate right now.

She's lost.

As am I.

I knead the plump, perfect flesh of her arse with one hand as the other holds her hip tightly. As I bottom out in her, I practically black out at the overwhelming pleasure of it.

'This is how it's supposed to be, sweetheart,' I grit out, grinding my hips against her and marvelling at how beautifully she's gripping me.

'Yes,' she agrees. I suspect if I told her it was midnight, she'd agree too. I pull out as slowly as I can, every nerve ending in my dick singing as I drag my swollen flesh against hers.

'It'll be hard and fast,' I warn her. 'It has to. You've made me wait too fucking long.' I ram in savagely, frustration and blind need warring in me. 'Too. Fucking. Long.'

'Show me how angry you are,' she gasps. 'Fuck me like you're really fucking pissed off.'

Her words ignite something in me. Because my dick is really fucking angry that she's withheld herself from me this week when we could have been doing *this*. 'You've got it,' I tell her. Jesus, I'm close. I exhale hard through flared nostrils and I release her arse so I can grab a handful of that gorgeous hair.

I fist it in my hand.

And I fucking let rip.

I really let her have it as I piston my hips as hard and fast as I can. The world blurs around me, and I screw my eyes shut tightly as sensation builds and builds like a fucking tsunami. It's going to take me out any minute. I'm dimly aware of the rhythmic slaps of our flesh and sweet, sweet sound of Gen gasping and moaning as she gamely attempts to hold on for the ride.

I've never been this rough with her.

I've never needed to come inside her this badly.

Because this isn't just about release. It's about claiming her in the most primal, complete way I know how.

She comes first, bucking against me as the incredible muscles of her cunt clamp around my cock. She's chanting my name like it's the only thing anchoring her in sanity.

Like it's a mantra that will save her.

I pound her through her orgasm, and then I fucking detonate as she continues to go off around me. Every muscle in my body cramps as I go rigid and then shoot my entire fluid supply as deep as I can inside her. The pleasure goes on and on, pulsing through me like a current.

'Fuck!' I bellow. 'Fuck, fuck, *fuck*.'

I keep myself firmly inside her until I've emptied every last drop. I feel as though I've run a marathon. She's sagging as she comes down, so I lean forward and gather her up in my arms, gently tugging her upright so her back is against my chest, my dick still jerking inside her.

She's floppy and sated and flushed. I wrap my arms around her upper body, enjoying the softness of her tits against them, and find her mouth with mine.

We kiss tenderly. I swipe my tongue languorously through her mouth, then rest my forehead against her temple.

'I've never had this before,' I tell her. 'Not with anyone I care about. I hope you understand how unique this is.'

She puts a hand up to cup my face. 'I do. It's insane. I don't know how we got so lucky.'

'Not sure I'd call it lucky,' I mutter darkly. 'I've been waiting half a fucking century for you.'

79

EPILOGUE: GEN

CANNES, TWO YEARS LATER

The sunset over the Bay of Cannes is spectacular.

But not as spectacular as my husband.

Clad all in black, as is his tradition each year on Opening Night of Alchemy Côte d'Azur, tonight he's at his most sensual.

His most predatory.

I'm the only one who knows quite how warm and cuddly he is behind that facade. Well, my friends have a suspicion, too. Once again, he's hosting our entire gang for the opening weekend. Besides, they've had front-row seats to Anton's teddy-bear side for the past two years.

If his moonlit proposal six months in on his fairylight-dotted yacht in Mustique didn't give the game away, the way he's shown up for me, and worshipped me, and supported me every single day did.

This villa has proven such a perfect backdrop for our Mediterranean orgies the past two years that the owners have gladly leased it to us for the summer months for a third year running. It turns out they prefer avoiding this part of the world during peak season, anyway.

My filthy husband's filthy vision of seasonal pop-ups for the beautiful players of Europe has proven, like everything else he touches, to be pure gold. We opened pop-ups in Ibiza and Mykonos last summer, and last week we launched our most intense and adventurous project yet: an eight-week pop-up on an incredible superyacht moored at the Marina Grande in Capri.

The price of the yacht rental is eye-watering, as are the mooring fees, but it turns out there's no shortage of people willing to pay through the nose for a night onboard. Anton wants to duplicate it in Monaco next summer, because the yacht experience just hits differently.

We opened our permanent New York club with one hell of a party this past New Year's Eve. Alchemy New York will always be synonymous in my mind with my husband dousing himself with Krug until he was drenched as adoring fans—both male and female—mobbed him.

But, once midnight struck, there was only one person he had any interest in dragging off to a private room.

I understood from the moment Anton Wolff stepped into our offices that he was *more than*. And I knew, once I made peace with my feelings for him, that he would demand more of me than I could possibly imagine.

I was right.

This man feels *hard*. He fucks hard and plays hard, too. He loves fiercely. So fiercely. It turns out I never needed to worry that he'd ruin me and wreck me, because he has never once given me a second of doubt.

He's so all in it's not funny.

And all my sweet, incredible man demands is that I, in return, give him all of myself.

I've never met anyone with an appetite for life like his. He spends less time in the office these days and more time enjoying his homes. His family. His friends.

Enjoying *me*.

I'm still flat-out with Alchemy, despite the fact that we've hired people to take over many of the day-to-day operations in London so Anton and I can make better use of his French pad in the summer months and his Mustique one in the winter.

I know, I know.

Don't ask me how I got so lucky.

My working time is spent executing on the aggressive expansion plans we have for Alchemy. It's scary and heady in equal measure, but I have my favourite pit-bull by my side in all things business.

I keep him on a tight leash, mind you, but I'm always happy to let him off it when I need to play dirty but want to keep my own hands clean.

He's so well-trained.

Adoring to me and devastating to our enemies.

'WHAT'LL IT BE TONIGHT, Mrs Wolff?' Anton whispers in my ear in a decidedly vulpine tone that has goosebumps breaking out on my neck. 'Room or tent?'

There are two hundred and fifty people here tonight. It blows my mind. To handle the shortage of rooms, we've had beautiful free-standing tents erected all around the grounds where people can find some privacy. Not that privacy is a pre-requisite for the many people who'll end up fucking under the starry sky on the numerous mattresses dotted around the grass.

I was right about this format opening Alchemy up to a wider audience. Free spirits and party-goers have flocked here each summer, and many have ended up dabbling. Those who choose to abstain still dub it one of the most glamorous, most fantastical party spots of the summer season. It seems it's less intimidating to rock up at a glamorous al fresco party than it is to cross the forbidding threshold of a Mayfair townhouse.

I lean back against Anton, loving having his arms around me, strong fingers splayed over my stomach.

There is no one on this earth who can make me feel simultaneously as safe and as endangered as Anton can. I'm in the most skilled, loving, demanding hands, and he won't be satisfied until we've fucked each other senseless and wrung every drop of desire from each other's bodies and souls this evening.

I let my fingertips trail over his taut, hairy forearm. His black shirt fits him so well it's sinful, and he has the top few buttons open and the sleeves rolled up.

Just the way I like it.

'Hmm,' I muse. 'I still like the view the rooms gives us, if there's one going.'

I love it when we make love in the dark as people splash and party and fuck beyond the glass, illuminated in the lush gardens in every shade of the rainbow. I'm a private person. I allow my husband to unwrap my layers and blow away my inhibitions, but he's the only person who gets to see me like that.

Anton fucking loves that he's the only one who gets to unveil me.

He scoffs. 'For the woman who makes the magic happen? There's a room.' He inhales sharply against my skin and kisses down my neck. I tilt my head to give him more space. I'm so in love with this man it's actually ridiculous. The concept of a life without Anton is too bleak, too colourless, to even consider.

Every day, he pushes me and challenges me and calls me out when I'm holding back.

He demands everything.

He gives me nowhere to hide.

He sees me so clearly it's frankly terrifying.

But then again, he always has.

'Have you seen my sister?' I ask dreamily.

'She's fine,' he mutters against my skin. 'I saw her disappearing into one of the tents with the guys. She looked *very* happy.'

I laugh. Since Darcy came home about eighteen months ago she's managed to find extraordinary love with not one but two men. The relationship the three of them have is nothing short of spectacular.

Let's just say they've very much kept things in the Alchemy family, but that's another story for another time.

Because tonight is about pleasure. Decadence. Hedonism. It's about partying and fucking. It's about marvelling that we're in the business of providing people with some of the most memorable, transcendent experiences of their lives.

Tomorrow will be a recovery day around our pool for some of us. Definitely not for Maddy, who's heavily pregnant. This will be the last overseas trip she takes before her baby is born.

Rafe and Belle are taking it easy tonight, too. Their sweet little daughter, Elsie, is only two months old, and she's back at the house with their maternity nurse. They'll duck out of the party early so Belle can head home for the late feed.

I'm enjoying a couple of glasses of champagne, but I don't need booze to lose myself.

My husband will take care of that all by himself.

Which is to say that my money for most hungover tomorrow is, as usual, on Cal. If his beautiful wife doesn't have other plans for him, that is.

In case you think we're all very boring these days, I'd like to disclose that my husband is currently grinding his rock-hard dick against the cleft of my arse cheeks as he drags his bared teeth over my neck, and I am a Pavlovian dog where he's concerned. I drag his hand upwards so he can feel the effect he's having on my nipples, which are already tight and aching.

We fucked before our afternoon siesta 'to take the edge off', but my Big Bad Wolff wants more of his prey.

And who am I to deny him?

He gave me my very own Happily Ever After.

I'll damn well give him as many happy endings as I can.

THE END

Get Gen and Anton's romantic and spicy Bonus Epilogue here.
https://BookHip.com/THTTBJN

Preorder Cal and Aida's steamy HEA here.
https://mybook.to/untether_alchemy

Come join my FB reader group so we can fangirl over Anton together.
It's called Sara Madderson & Elodie Hart's Book Nerds, and it's a wonderful corner of the internet.
https://www.facebook.com/groups/3060624120889625

ACKNOWLEDGMENTS

Gen and Anton's story was a pleasure to write and a welcome break from having to delve into the draining topics of religious trauma (Unfurl) and bereavement (Undulate).

That said, writing it was *intense*.

Anton Wolff didn't just ruin Gen.

He ruined me, too. He pushed me and Gen way beyond our comfort zones, and we both loved every minute of it.

I'm so, so grateful to everyone who's helped to bring this book-baby into the world. I set myself an unhealthily tough deadline for this one, and I honestly wasn't sure on any given day whether I'd make it.

(Spoiler alert: I made it!)

Firstly, my FB reader group, my Nerds, who support me and cheer me on every day. Thank you for being there for me and being as compassionate in the face of the overwhelm I've shared with you these past few months as you are enthusiastic when I've shared salacious tidbits from Unveil.

You are my people, and I'm so grateful for you every single day. Thank you for making Nerds a safe place for me to hang out and be real.

A massive thank you to my gorgeous beta readers, Lyndsey Gallagher and Jennifer Brooks Brown. You ladies carried me through this book when I in hormonal hell and persuaded me that I was more than on the right track. Thank you for your kind words, and your incredibly fast reading, and your very astute feedback and suggestions. It wouldn't be the book it is without you.

Thank you, as always, to my amazing ARC team! I love our ARC team FB hangout... sending the book out and seeing the hilarity and disbelief ensue as you process my stories is so much fun for me. Thank you for supporting me and for having found time to read four of my books this year!

Thank you to YOU for taking a chance on me, for downloading and reading, for giving me your hard-earned cash and time. I'm so grateful to have such lovely, lovely readers.

Sara / Elodie xx

Printed in Great Britain
by Amazon